Diva

Jeanne Moon Farmer

Word Light Press

Diva *(Book Two of the Shadow Series)*
Jeanne Moon Farmer

ISBN: 978-1-938643-04-0

AUTHOR'S NOTE: The book, Diva, is a work of fiction. Names, characters, events and incidents are either the products of the author's imagination or used in a fictitious manner. Any resemblance to actual persons, living or dead, or actual events is purely coincidental.

WORDLIGHT
PRESS

Word Light Press
P O Box 94-8636
Maitland, Florida 32794-8636
theshadowbooks@gmail.com

Cover Design: Rik Feeney / Rik@PublishingSuccessOnline.com

Photograph: ©Bigstock | Sergey Nivens

Dedication

Dedicated with love to my three Durward's –

father, brother, son -

- because they always believed.

Prologue

The Miami Herald - July 16, 1980

"Brazil's Paolo DaSilva Dead at 52"

Miami Police say the body of Paolo DaSilva was discovered yesterday in Biscayne Bay by two fishermen. The cause of death is under investigation but foul play is not suspected. DaSilva was wearing swim trunks and sources believe he may have gone swimming in the Bay.

DaSilva, a well-known playboy and heir to the DaSilCo fortune, had been a guest at MarGrove, the Coconut Grove estate of pop star Margo. A spokesman for the family confirmed Margo and DaSilva were engaged and planned to be married next year.

DaSilva often traveled to the United States as a representative of the oil company founded by his grandfather, Eduardo DaSilva. The spokesperson also reported that members of DaSilva's family were en route to Miami to escort his body to Brazil. Plans are underway for a funeral to be held in Rio de Janeiro later in the week.

Police say one of Margo's twin daughters, 18 year-old Sunni Anderson, reported DaSilva missing two days ago. Anderson claimed DaSilva failed to attend breakfast or lunch and he could not be located during a search of the estate. Investigators say DaSilva had not been seen since the previous evening at dinner.

Calls to Margo's representatives have not been returned.

PART ONE

I heard a thousand blended notes,
While in the grove I sate reclined,
In that sweet mood when pleasant thoughts
Bring sad thoughts to the mind.

To her fair works did Nature link
The human soul that through me ran;
And much it grieved my heart to think
What man has made of man.

(from Lines Written in Early Spring)
by William Wordsworth

Chapter One

Brentwood Academy, March 1980
Alli

"I don't know what you want from me. I've already told everyone in the world that I'm sorry."

Alli Anderson rolled her eyes at the psychologist and tapped her fingernails on the table. It was an annoying sound, but she didn't care. It wasn't her idea to sit in the head-doctor's office twice a week for an hour. But that was her punishment for breaking curfew, getting caught with booze, and being in Gary Prescott's bed.

She remembered that Dr. Hastings, the headmaster of Brentwood Academy, had actually scowled when he doled out her punishment and she laughed to herself at his attempt to make her feel guilty. She didn't do guilt.

"Alli, we want you to try and find some answers for yourself. There has to be a reason why you continue this pattern of misconduct. You're an honor student and I would hate for you to jeopardize your senior year."

When he sighed with resignation, Alli knew she was in a winning position, as always. "You are confined to campus, you will be monitored for alcohol use, and I've asked Dr. Patrice Morgan, a local psychologist, to meet with you twice a week for the next three months. It's your choice, Alli. You can accept my decision and graduate, or I can call your mother and tell her that you are being expelled from school. What will it be?"

There was no way she was going to be expelled and have to deal with her parents. Yes, she was certain the headmaster's punishment would be easier to take than that.

And now, as she sat in a more comfortable chair designed to encourage her to spill her guts, she stared at the picture above Dr. Morgan's head and tried to zone out.

"Alli, I asked you a question. I don't believe you heard me." Dr. Morgan spoke in her 'be gentle with the patient' voice and Alli resented the woman even more for talking down to her.

Exhaling, she turned her attention back to the doctor in the hope the session would end soon. "I'm sorry, Dr. Morgan. I must have been daydreaming. What did you ask?"

"I was hoping you would tell me about your relationship with your family. I know your mother is Margo. But in our other sessions you rarely mentioned her or your father. And, I know you have a twin sister named Sunni. Today I'd like for you to think about the roles these people play in your life."

"Fine." Her petulance was deliberate and she hoped her voice reflected her disdain for the whole process. "I see my mother at least once a year. My father might manage to see me about once a month." She placed her finger to her chin and sighed for dramatic affect. "Does it count that my sister is my roommate and I see her every day?" She smiled slyly. "Remember the fairy tale? She's the good twin–I'm the evil one." Then she softened a little. "Sunni's my sometimes best friend." She turned to look out the window and quietly went on. "I trust her but she really gets on my nerves." Snapping her head around, she regained her composure. "Did I leave out anything?"

Dr. Morgan ignored her and went on with her questions. "Why is Sunni a sometimes friend?"

"My sister doesn't know how to have fun and it upsets her when I do. It's as simple as that. Sunni observes life–I live it."

Sitting back in her chair, she folded her arms and looked demurely at the doctor. “Can you tell that I really don’t want to talk about my family?”

“Let’s move on. I’ve read Dr. Hastings’ disciplinary report, Alli. Perhaps you would rather talk about why Dr. Hastings sent you to see me.”

“I’m here because I was having fun. Besides, I’m eighteen so it’s not a big deal. It was a little embarrassing to get caught.” Alli shrugged and began tapping her fingernails on the table again. “Do we have to go over this again? I got caught and I’m sorry. It’s over and I’ll be a good girl until I leave Brentwood in June.”

Sarcasm was one of her favorite tools when she was faced with a situation that made her uncomfortable, and Dr. Morgan was really making her uncomfortable.

“Unfortunately, Alli, it’s not over. You have to meet with me for the next three months. Why not relax and answer some of my questions?”

“I said I will. What do you want to know?” She slumped down in the chair, her arms crossed tightly across her chest, and wished the hour with Dr. Morgan was over instead of just getting started.

“Talk to me about your mother. What do you like about her?”

“She’s beautiful. She’s rich enough to give me the things I want. She has some great friends. She likes good booze and good drugs. What else can I tell you?”

“What else is there to tell?”

“Margo is a star, not a mother. Sunni and I have pretty much been on our own all our lives and I like it that way.”

“You feel like you have had to raise yourself? Is that what you mean?”

“We had a nanny until we were eight years old. That’s when we were sent away to school. Since then it’s been pretty much just me and my sister. It bothers Sunni, but I'm okay with it. If I want something, I call my parents' assistant, Lara Finley, and she sends me a check. My life is easy."

"Do you spend any time during the year with your family? I thought your parents were divorced."

"My parents divorced years ago. But Dad's still her business manager and agent. They work well together, but my mother doesn't like being tied down to just one man. That doesn't usually fit into the rules of marriage, does it?"

"Okay, but do you spend time with either of your parents? Do you go home for summer and holidays?"

"Let's see.... Last summer we spent a month at MarGrove, but Margo was in Paris."

"Excuse me, Alli. Is MarGrove your mother's house in Miami?"

"You mean her estate, Dr. Morgan. Margo doesn't live in houses." She waited for a reaction, but when none came, she went on. "We spent a month with Dad at his house in the Berkshires. And we traveled to Italy for two weeks with our grandmother. Christmas and New Year's we were with Dad. Part of the time we were skiing in Aspen and part of the time we were at his apartment in Miami because Margo was in Brazil. That's my quality time with family. Aren't you jealous, Dr. Morgan? I have an exciting life."

"I guess I need to know more about what you do every day before I can decide if I'm jealous." Dr. Morgan smiled. "Tell me more about your time at MarGrove when your mother is there."

"What does this have to do with anything? Why do you want me to talk about all of this? I've promised not to break any more of Brentwood's commandments and I'll be graduating in three months. So what's the point?"

"You sound angry, Alli. What's that about?"

"I'm not angry, Dr. Morgan. Anger would mean I'd have to give up all the things Margo's money buys and I'm not ready to do that."

She sat back down. "Margo's girls aren't allowed to be angry, Dr. Morgan. I've known that since I was just a few years old. Margo's girls play nice. Besides, if I was angry, it would mean I care--and I don't."

Sunni

"Alli, you're a slob. Can't you hang up some of these clothes? I hate having to walk over your underwear to get to my closet." Sunni picked up one of her sister's blouses and threw it across the room.

"I said I'd take care of it. You're such a neat freak." Alli laughed which made Sunni even madder. "Changing the subject from my lace undies, I saw a message that Dad called. What did he want?"

"Mom's tour has been extended and they won't be back in Miami until the middle of June. We can either join them for the last month of the tour or we can go on to MarGrove. He said if we want to go home, Mrs. Davis would open the house for us." Sunni paused for dramatic effect and then added, "He thinks Paolo might be at MarGrove in June." She watched for some reaction, knowing that bit of information would get her sister's attention.

"Hold on, Sunni. Are you saying Paolo will he be at our house even if Margo's not there?"

"Dad said Paolo and mom apparently made plans for him to join her at the house before she found out she would have the extended concert tour. Paolo has business in Miami that he can't change."

"Really? How delightful." Alli's face brightened. "Me and the Brazilian playboy home alone for a month." She winked at her sister who turned away in disgust. "That settles it, I'm going to MarGrove. How about you?"

"Alli, sometimes you sound just like Mom."

"Sunni, if I sounded like her, I'd shoot myself."

"Yeah, right. You and Mom are nothing alike." Sunni was sarcastic, but didn't want to start a war so she backed off. "Go with me to join the tour and forget this nonsense about Paolo. It's our chance to be a family, and who knows what it might do for your singing career."

"You're a dreamer. Do you actually think they'll give us the time of day if we join the tour?" She leaned over and picked up the tennis outfit she had left on the floor. "No, I'm going home. You do what you want. But you're setting yourself up. They won't even know you're there. As for my career, who needs them?"

"Who's the dreamer? Do you really think Paolo DaSilva will give you a second look? He's old enough to be your father, for heaven's sake." The remark about the career surprised her. "I thought you wanted to try your hand at the stage? Mom's name recognition could open some doors for you. Why wouldn't you use that?"

"Paolo is nothing to me and if I want a singing career, I'll do it my way. What's wrong with wanting to go home?" She hesitated and then asked, "Did Dad say if they were coming to graduation?"

"He apologized but Mom has a concert that weekend, so they won't be here." Sunni tried to make light of her own disappointment and didn't want to think of the embarrassment she would feel because her parents couldn't take time to attend their daughters' graduation.

"How typical," Alli shrugged. "Where are you going to pick up the tour?"

"Daddy's going to send a car for us. Well, for me, anyway. They'll be in Philadelphia the week after graduation and it's a short drive from Brentwood. You better call Lara to make plans to fly to Miami."

She sighed as she looked at the mess around her. "Oh, and Lara is sending a mover for our things on the Monday after graduation. She said to pack a few things to take with us and they'll put the rest of our stuff in storage until we leave for Sarah Lawrence in September."

Sunni loved her twin sister, even when she thought Alli was making bad choices. And, it was a very bad choice for her to go to Miami. Nothing good would come from Alli and Paolo in the same house with only the housekeeper as a chaperone. She'd seen the way Paolo looked at Alli when their mother wasn't around and she knew her sister would play right into his hands and his bed if given the chance.

She caught her reflection in the mirror and, like always, laughed when she saw Alli's face looking back at her. "For two people who look exactly alike, we sure do see things differently, don't we?"

"Wouldn't it be dull if I was just like you?" Alli taunted.

"Why do you think my life is so dull?" If her sister wanted a fight she'd give it to her. "Is it because I'm not sleeping with every guy that passes by? Or, maybe it's because I don't come in drunk and you don't have to hold my head while I'm throwing up all over the house? Or, maybe it's because I know where I'm going and you don't have a clue about your own life?" Sunni was on a roll and once she got started the words kept spewing out of her mouth. "You're a mess, Alli. And you can't even see it."

"You're so jealous of who I am, you can't stand it. All this coming from a goody two-shoes who's never had a date. How dare you criticize me!" Alli's voice rose to a fevered pitch. Then, she stopped and whispered seductively, "Sunni, if you'd ever been to bed with a man who knew what he was doing, you'd never criticize me again."

Sunni was resigned to losing every argument with her sister. It was their pattern. But, she retorted anyway, hands on her hips. "Are you kidding? I'm shocked that you don't have every disease known to the medical world. I happen to want a committed relationship or is that too hard for you to comprehend?" Sometimes she felt sorry for her sister and worried about her choices. "There's more to life than sex. I want someone in my life who loves me and I want a family. I've got plans to be a writer. I'm not going to be in Mom's shadow forever."

"You'll always be in Margo's shadow." Alli laughed. "Just like me. She got to the top before we even had a chance to know the top from the bottom. And how many men do you know who are faithful to one woman?"

"If there's one out there, I'll find him." The energy of the argument was cooling down and the tone changed from angry to wistful. "What about Sarah Lawrence? Aren't you excited about going to college? I can't wait to start English and writing classes at that level."

"Talk about dull. Listen to yourself." She became animated. "Sarah Lawrence means New York and New York means fun! I'll open doors for myself once I get to New York. I'll make it happen." Then defiantly she added, "I don't need Margo to have my own singing career."

Sunni gave up. It would be nice to have a month without worrying about Alli–where she was, who she was with, whether she'd had too much to drink. She was tired of covering for her sister's irresponsible behavior. What did she care if Paolo broke her sister's heart or if she failed out of college? Alli would bounce back just like she'd done so many times before. She had a voice that was probably better than their mother's and like their mother, Alli would simply move on to another man or make adjustments that changed her failures into successes.

Turning back to the mirror, Sunni sighed. Maybe if she changed the color or cut of her hair she would have a better chance of separating herself from her twin. Right now, they were identical, except Alli had a tiny birthmark above her right eye that Sunni didn't have. With make-up, no one could tell them apart. They were tall like their mother and had her coloring-chestnut hair, green eyes, olive skin–but they were not beautiful like Margo. Alli could be striking when she wanted to be, but Sunni wasn't adventurous when it came to clothes, make-up, and hair styles. Alli flaunted her mother's fame and wanted everyone to know she was Margo's daughter. Sunni never wanted to be in the spotlight and prayed no one would discover who she was.

"Alli, I'm sorry. I got carried away." Sunni always apologized. She hated when she and her twin argued. "I'm upset about being alone for graduation and I took it out on you. Not fair and I'm sorry."

"Me, too. Forget what I said. It was stupid."

Watching as Alli bent over to pick up some of the clothes on the floor, Sunni smiled. As much as she wanted things to be different, it felt like her sister was her only family.

Alli

"Alli, you can sit there silently for the entire hour if you wish. But if I report that to Dr. Hastings, he will probably rethink your situation. You're flirting with expulsion from school."

"Great. Let's hold expulsion over my head. Is that the way you play the game, Dr. Morgan?"

"I don't play games, Alli. Remember, I have nothing to lose. My only goal is helping you work through some of the issues that may be impacting how you make decisions. I get paid whether you cooperate or not. But I do have to report your progress to Dr. Hastings, and that's where you win or lose."

Alli looked at her fingernail polish and decided it was time for a manicure. As soon as she got out of the office she was going to call and make an appointment. She stifled a yawn and looked up at Dr. Morgan.

"Since you put it that way, ask me anything you want to know."

"I'd prefer that you talked about what's on your mind."

"Sex is on my mind, Dr. Morgan. Hot bodies entwined in passionate embraces. It's been on my mind for weeks. Dr.

Hastings's mandates are forcing me to live like a nun. So, all I think about is sex. Is that unusual, Dr. Morgan?"

"You tell me, Alli. If you think about sex often, then maybe it's not unusual for you."

"I don't think about sex, doctor. I have sex. I have a lot of sex. You might say it's my hobby, or it was until this past month."

"How long have you been sexually active, Alli?"

"Dr. Morgan, I hope this doesn't shock you..." Alli looked at the doctor to see how she was going to respond. "I've been having sex since I was fourteen."

"Do you want to tell me about that experience?"

To Alli's surprise, the psychologist's expression didn't change. She just sat and waited. Alli thought for a moment about that afternoon in California and smiled. With all that had happened since, it seemed like decades ago instead of just a few years. She had never talked about her experiences before, especially not with her prudish sister. This was going to be fun.

"Why not, Dr. Morgan? It was the last summer we lived in California. We had been invited to join Margo for a few weeks during our summer break and I was bored out of my mind. It was one of the times in Margo's life when she was trying on lots of men. No serious love affair, just hot bodies coming and going. And some of her dates came to stay for longer than one night."

Alli continued to look Dr. Morgan squarely in the eyes. "His name was John. I guess he came to stay overnight but he ended up staying for weeks. At first he didn't know I existed, but one afternoon I was alone at the pool and he asked me if he could sit with me. He was handsome and looked great in swim trunks, if you know what I mean?"

She smirked. "At fourteen, I was just beginning to enjoy my own body and I knew I looked pretty good in my bikini. Of course, I couldn't compete with Margo, but I was more developed than most girls my age and he noticed. We laughed and talked all afternoon."

Unconsciously, she rubbed her hands along the sides of her body. "I felt special and I liked it. At some point I jumped in the water to cool off and the top of my bikini came loose. I didn't bother to retie it because I liked the way he was looking at me."

Her mind wandered and she smiled as she remembered the look of admiration in John's eyes when she let her bikini top float across the water. He may have been the first to notice her body, but he certainly wasn't the last. Alli liked for men to look at her–whether she was clothed or nude–and she knew she could move her body in ways that attracted a man's attention.

She glanced at Dr. Morgan to see if there was a reaction. But the good doctor was quietly watching her and seemed to be listening intently. "I played around in the water for a few minutes just to see what he would do. I floated on my back, splashed water on my breasts, even spread my legs wide and did a scissor kick. But he didn't come in the water. All he did was watch my every move. When I got tired of playing by myself, I got out of the water and walked to the pool house. It worked. He followed." It was fun to remember. She felt her pulse race and her body react to the erotic nature of her story.

"I was eager for whatever was going to happen, even though I wasn't sure just what to expect. He closed the pool house door and pushed me up against the wall."

Enough, she decided. It probably wasn't in her best interest to let the good doctor know everything. She raised her head as though proclaiming victory. "When I left the pool house an hour later, I left my virginity behind. It was exhilarating–two minutes of pain, an hour of pleasure."

Dr. Morgan's expression remained unchanged. "What else do you want to tell me about that first experience, Alli?"

Alli smirked. "Do you want to know all the details?"

"I want to know how you felt, Alli. I want to know why that event was significant."

"It made me feel great. I discovered what my body was meant to do and I loved it. The feelings started at fourteen and they've never gone away. John taught me to enjoy pleasure with all of my body and how to give him pleasure in return. I couldn't have asked for a better teacher and the best part was having sex two or three times a day for the next two weeks. I don't know how he had energy for sex with my mother, but I didn't care. I enjoyed her boyfriend, at her house, and it was magnificent. I've been enjoying the men in Margo's life ever since."

"How do you think this relates to your mother, Alli? Are you getting even with her for all the hurt you feel because she wasn't there for you?"

Alli jumped up out of the chair with her hands balled into fists. "My sex life isn't about my mother and it's not about anger," she yelled at Dr. Morgan before she realized what she'd done.

Uncurling her hands, she ran her fingers through her hair. It was embarrassing to lose control. In a calmer tone, she completed her thoughts.

"It's about sex and how much I love what men can do with my body. And, Dr. Morgan, I adore older men. I had my first experience with an older man and I soon found out that boys my age are clumsy and boring. I like sex with a man who knows what he's doing." She smiled as she began to feel more in control.

"You've mentioned the word sex a lot, Alli. What about making love? Where does that fit in?"

"It doesn't. For now it's just about sex. Love has nothing to do with it. Does that answer all your questions?"

Chapter Two

On Tour, June 1980
Sunni

The luxurious motor coach rolled along the highway headed to Boston. Sunni glanced at her mother who was stretched out on one of the sofas reading and thought about the energy it took for her mother to be Margo.

Rehearsals, hours in make-up and hair styling, three hours on the concert stage, autographs, after-show parties. Sunni was exhausted just thinking about it and she was twenty-two years younger than her mother. Margo should look pale and drained, but instead she looked rested. Even with no makeup and her hair tied back in a loose pony tail, Margo was exotic and beautiful. Her natural beauty was the kind that Sunni could appreciate–soft features molded out of rare, warm-toned clay, not the hard, cold beauty of chiseled features created by a woman with a makeup brush. She watched her mother's shallow breathing and let her eyes follow the contour of her mother's long body. On stage, her costumes were designed to exaggerate and showcase her body as voluptuous and sexy, but in the tee-shirt and jeans that she wore today, Sunni was stunned by her mother's thinness and fragility. In the few minutes of quiet, when she and her mother were alone and she had time to actually see her, she wondered who her mother really was. It hurt her to acknowledge, even to herself, that she had no idea how to answer that--no idea of Margo's dreams, her hurts, even her likes or dislikes. This woman she loved with all her heart and whose love she craved more than anything, was as mysterious and alien as a stranger who passed on the street.

"Mother, may I get you something to drink?"

Sunni hated sounding so formal, but she didn't really feel comfortable talking to her mother and her words always came out stilted. "A cup of coffee or maybe some tea? I'm going to make myself a cup of tea and I'd gladly bring you one."

Sunni spoke softly but when her mother didn't respond, she wondered if she had only voiced the thought in her head. She got up slowly and started walking toward the kitchen at the front of the motor coach.

"You can bring me a cup of coffee with an added shot of Kahlua. That would be nice." Margo replied without taking her eyes away from the page she was reading.

Surprised, Sunni turned to look her mother in the face, "I thought you weren't drinking. Are you sure you want alcohol so early in the morning?" Her voice was beseeching and she tried to hide her disappointment.

"Darling, just bring me what I asked for and stop sounding like your grandmother. I'm fine, Sunni, and one shot of Kahlua doesn't mean I'm drinking again."

Sunni stood still for a moment longer and stared at her mother.

"Sunni, if you can't do this simple little thing, then call Sam. He'll do as I ask." Margo's voice had changed from soft to harsh and demanding, and Sunni knew that if she didn't comply her mother would soon be in a rage.

Would Sam, her mother's body guard, really go along with everything her mother wanted? If so, then she hated him for getting paid to enable her mother. And, at this moment, she was angry with her father because she wanted him to fix all of her mother's problems. Long ago she accepted that he wouldn't do anything to jeopardize their careers, and she knew enough about addictions to know her mother was the only one who could change things, but, the little girl in her wanted her daddy to make everything better.

It never changed. Every time she thought the pattern had been broken, she was forced to acknowledge one more time that her mother's addictions had not been conquered, even though she had spent weeks, and sometimes months, in rehab. Sunni tried to hold on to the hope that this time it was just alcohol; that her mother's small relapse didn't mean cocaine was once more part of her daily routine.

She wanted to cry, but what was the use?

*****

The next evening, sitting backstage waiting for her mother to go on stage, she saw him. He was tall, his brown hair was pulled back in a neat pony tail, and his large brown eyes were looking directly at her. She knew he played guitar in the band but she didn't know his name and had never been introduced. Feeling self-conscious, she tried to turn where she didn't have to look at him, but he started walking toward her and called her by name.

"Sunni," he hesitated. "That is your name isn't it? My name's Mark Sanders and I was wondering if you'd like some company?"

He had a pleasing voice, and as he got closer she saw how good looking he was. "Why not?" she responded. "But don't you have things to do to get ready for the show?"

"Everything's done. I'm just waiting for the warm-up act to finish. We've probably got ten minutes or so before your mother goes on." He pulled up a metal folding chair and sat down beside her. "Are you going to be with us to the end of the tour?"

"Yeah, unless I get so bored I can't stand it. Do you enjoy being on the road eight months out of the year?"

"I hate being on the road, but I love working. Your folks pay me well, so I've got no complaints. And, I love that I have three or four months of down-time every summer. It's not a bad life."

"How long have you been with the band?" She stammered over what she knew was a stupid question. But talking to guys wasn't easy for her.

"I started playing with the guys in 1975. I figure I can stick it out until your mom decides to retire. Like I said, working is good and I love playing guitar."

At that moment the applause became deafening and they knew the warm-up act had finished. Mark stood up, "Nice talking to you Sunni. See you around."

He walked away and joined the other members of the band at the stage entrance. He picked up his guitar and gave her a wave just as Margo approached.

Her mother looked breath-taking and Sunni was caught off-guard by the power of her presence. When Margo was ready to walk on the stage she became a magnet that drew everyone's attention and energy to herself. Like always, she wore red on stage. Tonight her one shouldered gown hugged her body and her signature three-inch heels accentuated her height. At 5'9" she towered over most women, but when she wore high heels she towered over most men. The shimmering red dress complimented her chestnut hair and olive skin and she seemed to glow. Yes, my mother is stunning.

A voice off-stage shouted to the crowd, "Ladies and gentlemen, the incomparable, the one and only, Margo."

*****

"Your mom blew everybody away last night. I think it was one of the best shows we've had on this tour. What did you think?"

She heard his voice before she could see him. Looking up from her book, sun glasses hid his eyes and she couldn't tell if he was teasing. For almost an hour she had been sitting alone beside the hotel pool and decided it would be nice to have some company. So, forgetting her shyness, she encouraged the conversation.

"I don't have much to compare it to, but it seemed like the fans were more than satisfied. Does she always have that much energy?" Sunni hated to admit to Mark that she had only seen her mother in concert three or four times. "I don't know how she does it night after night."

"It's the adrenaline." Mark's voice was hard and the expression on his face matched his voice. Sunni wondered what his look was all about but didn't ask. If Mark had issues with her mother it was none of her business. "It takes a lot to produce the kind of energy she needs on stage. It takes a lot."

She put aside the book she was reading and gave him a tentative smile.

"Is this your first time on tour? I don't remember seeing you before." He grinned and took the lounge chair facing her.

"Yes, first tour and summer vacation," Sunni answered shyly. "You know, family bonding and all that."

"How come we've never met?"

"My sister and I are Margo's best kept secret. We've been away at school forever. After we graduated last week, I postponed going to MarGrove so I could see firsthand what it's like to be on the road."

There was no comment, so she asked, "Where are you from, Mark?"

"Wait a minute, you mean there's two of you?" He looked surprised.

"I have a twin sister. She's already at MarGrove."

"Unbelievable. I've been in your mom's band for five years and I never knew you existed. Boy, did I have my head in the sand."

Sunni tried not to be hurt by Mark's admission that he didn't know his boss had two daughters. Hadn't she known all her life that Margo did everything possible to keep the twins out of her life? "I'm just trying to protect you. You have no idea what your life would be like if everyone knew you were my daughter." No matter how many times she heard her mother make those statements, they still hurt.

"Oh, sorry," Mark said quickly. "You asked me a question and I didn't answer. I'm from Miami; born and raised there. That's where I go when we're not on tour."

"You're a native? That's rare. Almost everyone I meet in Miami is from somewhere else. Do you have family in Miami?"

"Yeah. My mom and dad live in south Miami and I have an apartment on the beach side."

"Wife, kids, girlfriend? Is there someone waiting for you beach side?"

"My girlfriend, her name is Jocelyn, lives with her dad and step-mom in the Grove." He gave Sunni a pensive look, "Something about you reminds me of her."

Was that a pick-up line or was he being serious? If Alli was here she'd know how to handle this, but all Sunni could do was follow her instincts. "I hope whatever that is, it's a good thing."

Smiling, he pushed his sunglasses to the top of his head. "Have you had lunch, Sunni? We could go over to the pool bar. I think they have sandwiches and salads."

"I'm starving, but are you sure you don't have something else to do?" Feeling bolder, she jumped to accept his invitation.

"You're mom doesn't own all my time. I'm off the clock for a few hours." He laughed. "Come on and let's see what we can find to eat."

Sunni packed her things and slipped a cover-up over her bikini. She had enjoyed working on her tan, but decided lunch with Mark sounded better than spending time alone by the pool.

He grabbed her tote bag and walked in front of her to the poolside cafe. She liked watching him walk and could tell he worked out or did something to keep himself in good shape. He was taller than her 5'8, which was often a challenge with the boys she knew. The sunlight on his long ponytail made his hair look more golden than brown and even this early in the summer his skin looked tan.

Usually she was tongue-tied around boys, but he was making it easier for her to talk to him. Except none of that mattered now that she knew he had a girlfriend.

They chose a table in the shade and ordered lunch. "What's the most important thing I should know about Sunni Anderson?" Mark leaned across the table and looked directly at her. "By the way, did you know you have beautiful eyes?"

"Oh, brother. Aren't you the charmer?" Sunni laughed to cover up her nervousness. She couldn't remember anyone complimenting her like that before. Even though she and Alli were identical, it was Alli who always got the compliments. Her sister's vibrant personality attracted the attention. "Maybe you should know I'm going to Sarah Lawrence in the fall. I want to be a writer or editor."

"That's interesting, but I want to know something about you right now."

"Okay." She thought about how she should respond and finally said, "You should know that right now I'm really hungry."

"Ah, the mysterious daughter of Margo doesn't like to talk about herself. So what would you like to talk about?"

"Let's see." She closed her eyes and pretended to be deep in thought. "I'll ask you a question and then you can ask me one. You'll see by my answers that I'm not mysterious at all." She paused a minute. "How old are you and what's your last name? If you told me, I forgot."

"I'm Mark Sanders and I'm twenty-five. Do you have a boyfriend?"

"No, no boyfriend. Tell me about your girlfriend."

"Jocelyn is my best friend. She's pretty, not beautiful like you, but very pretty. The two of you have the same coloring, but her hair is shorter than yours. She graduated last year from Barry College and has two jobs. She works part time for the Miami Herald as a copy writer and part time for a guy who writes detective stories. He's retired from the FBI and is using material from his job to write some great books. Jocelyn helps him with editing and research."

"Her job sounds fascinating. Any wedding plans in the future?"

"There are a few complications, but we keep trying to move beyond them. Maybe someday, but right now we're both happy with the way things are."

Not wanting to pry, she asked, "What are you going to do all summer?"

"Sleep in, get reacquainted with the people I love, go see my Aunt Roseanna in California, and did I mention sleep? I never get enough sleep when we're on tour."

"I'm surprised you're up before dinner time. Every other person on tour sleeps until late afternoon."

He didn't respond at first. "I don't party like they do, Sunni. Sorry, but the hard stuff and drugs are not my thing. I flirted with it several years ago when I was going through a rough spot, but it didn't take me long to realize it's not for me. I usually go back to my room, take a long, hot shower, then wind down with a cold beer and some good, easy jazz. I'm asleep by two, up by ten, and I don't have a hangover."

"Maybe I shouldn't ask," she hesitated. "Is my mother back on all that stuff? I thought she was clean, but the other day she asked me to put a shot of Kahlua in her coffee."

"And, maybe I shouldn't answer."

The look on his face told her that her suspicions were true.

*****

Alli had been right. Her parents rarely acknowledged that she was on the tour and her dream of spending some quality time was just that, a dream. During the first week, the only time she saw her mother was on the bus as they traveled from city to city. After Philadelphia, they had gone to Boston. Then they spent one night in

Providence, Rhode Island. Now they would be in Baltimore, Maryland for two days. Twice her mother had joined her in the lounge of the motor coach, but conversation between them had been sparse. Mostly Margo kept to herself.

It was the same way with her dad, but she didn't even have time with him when they traveled. As soon as one show was finished, he flew on ahead to take care of the details in the next city. He had taken her to dinner one night, but that was the extent of their time together.

Mark was always polite, but he had not sought her out again after that one afternoon in Boston. She was lonely. So lonely that she even missed Alli. Maybe she should tell her dad she wanted to go on to MarGrove.

"How did you like Boston, Sunni?" her mother asked when she came into the lounge. "I'm sure you found a few museums and galleries to keep you busy."

"As a matter of fact, I did. Boston is a great place--so much history, so much to see. I even took a tour of Harvard."

"That's nice. I'm glad you can entertain yourself. Why don't you have Lara book a couple of tours for you while we're in Baltimore. There's a lot of history there, too. Then we have several days in DC, before we go on to Charlotte. Talk to Lara. Tell her what you'd like to see and she'll make it happen." Margo walked to the kitchen area, poured herself a glass of wine, and returned to her bedroom.

*****

Baltimore was not fun. It rained from the moment they arrived and sightseeing in the rain was not her idea of a good time. Lara Finley, her mom's assistant, had suggested she wait until they got to DC to go on any more excursions. Out of boredom, she headed to the hotel gift shop.

"Hey, Sunni. Are you enjoying this messy weather?"

She turned at the sound of Mark's voice.

"You'd be surprised what you can learn sitting in a hotel lobby." She laughed. "I'd hoped to take at least one tour while we're here, but the thought of going out in this storm isn't appealing."

"Would you like some company? We could go over to the cafe."

"Why don't you just come to my room? It's a nice suite with a living room where we can visit." Sunni surprised herself by asking him to come to her room, but she figured since he had a girlfriend, she didn't have to worry about what people would think.

"Great. Give me the number and I'll see you in a few minutes. I've got to pick up a few things in the gift shop."

She looked down at the sweats she had on and decided she needed to wear something a little more presentable if she was going to entertain Mark in her room. Rushing to her room, she grabbed a bright green silk top and jeans out of the suitcase. If she hurried, she might even have time to brush her hair and put on some lipstick.

When he knocked on the door, she took one last glance in the mirror. Her reflection told her she had made a good choice. The green silk was a nice color for her and the drape of the neckline gave her a soft feminine look. The jeans were snug enough to show off her figure, but not tight enough to make her uncomfortable.

"I'm glad you have some free time, Mark. Come in and have a seat." Sunni waited to see where he would sit and then chose the chair across from him. "I thought you had a rehearsal this afternoon."

"It's not 'till five, so I have a couple of hours to kill. What're you reading?"

"Don't laugh 'cause I'm not reading anything academic. I picked up *Rage of Angels* by Sidney Sheldon in the gift shop last night. So far it's holding my interest. Do you like to read?"

"I don't have too many chances to pick up a book on tour. But I get a lot of reading done when we're home for the summer."

Sunni decided this might be an opportunity to find out some things about her parents. It was risky but she took the chance. "Mark, what's it like being in my mom's band? I can't begin to imagine what that life must be like."

"It's good. The music is great and I've had a chance to see just about everything in this country, parts of Europe, and South America."

He wasn't responding to what she wanted to know, so she continued. "But what's it like? What's she like?"

"Uh, Sunni, you're asking me questions about your mother. That's not fair."

"I want you to be honest with me, Mark. Your life–my mom's life–is so foreign to me. I was hoping you could give me some clue that would help me understand her better."

At first he looked uncomfortable. Then he sighed and said, "This is a hard life, especially for your mom. She is hounded where ever she goes; she's expected to be beautiful all the time; and she's supposed to be gracious with thousands of people who think she should have time for only them. Fans can be very demanding. The hours are crazy and life on the road is hard. But, I love music and so does your mother."

"Can you have a real life and do what you do?"

"You mean like a family? I don't think I'd want to do it. It wouldn't be fair to a wife or kids. But your mom has a family so it must work for her."

"Maybe. Is that why you and your girlfriend haven't gotten married?"

"That's part of it. Jocelyn wouldn't want to be on the road. But there are other reasons."

He looked at Sunni for a long time. Then he shrugged, as if he'd come to a decision. "We're first cousins, but we didn't know it until we had already started our relationship. My aunt gave Jocelyn up at birth and nobody knew who her real mother was. Then things kind of exploded in her life and that's when we found out that my Aunt Rosanna is Jocelyn's mother. You can imagine the family's reaction. It was too hot for me to handle, so I jumped at the chance to go on the road with your mom. I was hoping time away would give everyone a chance to calm down."

"That's incredible. What are the odds of that happening?" Sunni tried to imagine what it must have felt like to discover that about someone you were dating and serious about. "That was five years ago, right? Everyone must be dealing with it if the two of you are still in a relationship."

"I wish that was true. My folks love her, but will never approve of us marrying. Her dad and step-mom are a little more understanding, but my Aunt Rosanna still cries when she thinks about us. It's a soap opera whenever I'm home. It's like there's this giant shadow hanging over every family get-together."

"You must really love her. But aren't there laws against first cousins marrying?"

"Not in Florida. There isn't a law against it in our state, but most other states wouldn't allow it. In our case, it's more about the church and having children. We're all Catholic." Mark shrugged. "But what about you? Any serious love interests in your life?"

"I haven't had time for relationships. You know, with school and everything. You can imagine what it'd be like if some guy found out that I'm Margo's daughter."

The afternoon went on with more small talk. Mark told funny stories about being on the road and Sunni shared a few things about life in boarding school.

"Wow. Time's gotten away from me. I've got to go or I'll be late for rehearsal. Will you be at the show tonight?"

"I wouldn't miss it. I'll see you there."

*****

Three weeks later, the tour was wrapping up in New Orleans. For Sunni, the month had flown by and her feelings for Mark Sanders were growing stronger. This tour had been one of the happiest times of her life, even though she hadn't spent any quality time with either of her parents.

Her time had been spent with Mark. Whenever they had a chance, they were together-working out at hotel gyms, grabbing a bite of lunch or dinner, seeing the sights in cities like Washington DC, Charlotte, Charleston, Atlanta, and Birmingham. And, now they were in New Orleans and she was in love--with the city and with him.

"I've got the evening free. Would you like to go with me to the jazz clubs? I know some great places to go in this city."

Mark's voice gave her a thrill even though she knew she was playing with her own heartbreak. Lately all she wanted to do was talk to him, spend time with him, dream about him. She had never had a serious boyfriend so how could she so suddenly want to give her heart to someone who loved someone else? I must be crazy!

"I can't think of anything I'd rather do. What's the plan?" She didn't hesitate to accept the invitation and wanted to dance across the hotel lobby in anticipation. While they'd spent time together during the days, this was the first night the band had been free since she joined the tour and her heart beat faster to think he wanted to spend it with her. Then she stumbled. Maybe this was a group thing; maybe the other guys in the band were going with them. "Where are we meeting the other guys?" She asked trying to keep a sound of disappointment out of her voice.

"It's just us. The guys have other plans. Meet me back here at eight and we'll start out on Bourbon Street. Then there are some out-of-the-way places I want to take you. You're going to love it."

*****

The night air was humid and stagnant. It was hot. Not Miami hot, where there was always a breeze off the ocean, but New Orleans hot–heavy and still. By the time they got to the fourth club, Sunni's blouse was wet and the hair at the back of her neck was sticking to her. But she didn't care. She was having fun. The club atmosphere, the crowds, and the music gave her energy. Each band seemed to be better than the one before and the jazz music was tapping into her emotions. She was captivated by the sultry tones and moods created by the sounds of the saxophones, the bass, and the drums. The spontaneity and vitality of the jam sessions enlivened her and she didn't want the evening to end. At midnight she should have been tired, but she wanted more.

"I'm having so much fun, Mark. This is great. Thank you for one of the best evenings I've ever had." Mark had found them a small table at the back of the club, but she still had to shout to be heard over the music and voices all around her. Cigarette smoke was heavy; people were pushed up against one another; and the dance floor was so crowded it looked like a sea of bobbing heads. Everywhere she turned couples were swaying and moving together in a rhythmic ritual of intimacy that Sunni could not resist.

"Could we dance just one number, Mark?"

Making her way to the dance floor, she hoped he would follow. She had only taken a few steps when he reached for her and pulled her to him. He held her close and slowly led her into the crowd of moving bodies. Sunni was in a trance as she responded to the music and the pressure of Mark's body against hers. Was it moments or hours that they danced? Was it his touch or the music that held her spell bound? She turned her head to look at him and his lips found hers--hungrily she welcomed the sensations his lips created.

"Let's get out of here," he whispered as he pulled away from her. "I need some fresh air."

They walked the two blocks to the hotel hand in hand, but strangely silent. She was confused by the quick mood change and wondered if what she had experienced with him was real or something she had wished for. As they approached the lights of the lobby, Mark stopped. "Sunni, I don't know what to say. I'm not sorry I kissed you, but I shouldn't have done it."

"Oh, Mark, I wanted you to kiss me. Please don't be sorry. Please don't tell me it was wrong."

"Kissing you wasn't wrong. It's just bad timing. I wanted to kiss you. I wanted to keep holding you. In five years, you're the only girl I've kissed besides Jocelyn. You're the only girl I've wanted to kiss. But, I've made promises, Sunni, and it's not fair to you. I'm sorry." The look on his face and the sadness in his eyes made her want to cry.

"I understand," she dropped his hand and turned quickly toward the elevator. She didn't want him to see her tears–she wanted to get as far away from his sad eyes as she could.

*****

At five o'clock that morning she was awakened by a knock on her door. She had cried until she had no more tears and knew she had only been asleep for a short time. The knock continued until she finally crawled out of bed and went to the door.

"Who's there?"

"Sunni, please open the door. It's Mark. I need to talk to you."

"Go away, Mark. Please just go away."

"Not until I've said what I came to say. Please let me in."

She unlocked the door and opened it. "What is it? What else could you possibly have to say?" She knew she looked like a freak--eyes puffy, hair messy, juvenile nightshirt.

He walked in the room and sat down. "I couldn't sleep. I need to talk to you until I've worked all this craziness out of my head."

"There's no craziness. You've got a girl that you're in love with and the mood of the evening just got to you. It's as easy as that. I've had my cry and I'm fine. There's nothing more to talk about."

"You've got it all figured out, don't you? You're in control of all the parts–yours and mine." He stood up and started walking toward her. "The problem is, you're wrong. Yes, there is a very special person in my life. No, I've never cheated on her. Yes, you've changed all the rules and I handled it badly. Over the past few weeks, we've become friends and I thought I could deal with that, but I can't. I'm falling for you and it's scaring me to death."

By the time he had finished talking he was standing in front of her. He didn't try to touch her. He just stood and looked at her. His eyes didn't look sad anymore; they seemed to be begging her to understand. He opened his arms and drew her to him. His embrace did not contain passion, it was an embrace of tenderness and honesty. "Sunni, tell me you'll give me time to figure this out. Tell me you have feelings for me or tell me to leave."

There was sweetness to the way he was holding her and his voice was deep with emotion. "Oh, Mark. Please don't leave. Hold me and tell me everything is going to be all right." She laid her head on his shoulder and locked herself into his embrace.

They stood that way until he pulled away and lifted her face in his hands. "I don't know if it's okay, Sunni. I just know you're changing things in my life. I want to be with you. I think about you when I'm not with you. And, I'm going home in a week to the one other person in the world I've ever felt this way about."

"Kiss me, Mark. Pretend for a little while longer that I'm the only one you feel that way about."

Next week was going to hurt, but right now all she could think about was the way this man made her feel. "Kiss me like we're the only people in the world."

Chapter Three

Miami, June 1980
Alli

After being excited and anxious to get to MarGrove, Alli was disappointed to find herself alone in the house with only Mrs. Davis, the housekeeper, for company. Restless and bored, she regretted her decision. She expected Paolo DaSilva to be at the house when she arrived, but she'd been in Miami for three days and there was no sign of him. She hesitantly asked Mrs. Davis when he was expected to arrive, but so far, he hadn't contacted anyone at the house about his plans. Perhaps coming to MarGrove had been a mistake.

When she called Sunni yesterday, her sister seemed to be having the time of her life on tour. She decided she'd give it a few more days and if he wasn't here by Wednesday, she was going to fly to Baltimore to join the tour.

Her olive complexion was already deepening in the warm Florida sunshine and she had bought a white swimsuit to accent it. She knew the skimpy pieces of fabric barely covered the parts they were designed to cover which made her more alluring and provocative than if she were nude. She had wanted to save it for Paolo's arrival, but today, something was needed to lift her spirits, so she slipped it on and wandered out to the pool.

Mrs. Davis was setting the lunch table for two when Alli walked out on the patio. "Who are you expecting for lunch? I thought I was the only one here."

"Mr. DaSilva arrived about an hour ago and he asked me to serve lunch for the two of you on the patio. He's taking a shower and will join you in about thirty minutes."

Alli could feel Mrs. Davis's eyes giving her the once over, but she didn't care.

"You ought to put on a cover-up for lunch, Alli. That suit shows more of you than it should. Especially when we have a guest in the house."

"Mrs. Dee, I think you're jealous of what you see." The last thing she needed was another lecture on her behavior.

Alli laughed and walked to the other side of the pool area. Sitting down on one of the lounge chairs, she waited for Mrs. Davis to go back in the house, then began to put oil on her body. The guest room window was on the second floor directly above the pool and she willed Paolo to stand there and watch her.

Slowly, sensuously she began to stroke her body, moving her hands seductively up and down her arms and then her legs. This is fun! Glancing again at the upstairs window, she saw his face and knew he was enjoying the show. Her hands moved across her stomach and midriff like she'd seen an actress do in a movie her father would have never allowed her to watch. Slowly, remembering the scene clearly, she lifted the top of her bikini. As she began to massage the oil across her breasts she decided to prolong her own pleasure. As long as he was watching there was no reason to hurry, and it felt good. Her hands continued to move around and over each breast, lifting them as though she was offering them to him. Then she slowly pulled her top back in place, stretched her long legs the length of the lounge, and waited.

"Bonita baixa menina, I think you forgot a spot and you surely do not want to burn. Let me help you." She opened her eyes to see Paolo smiling down at her. "I have missed you little one. Come, let's enjoy the lunch Mrs. Davis has prepared so we can have our siesta."

"I thought you'd never get here. I'm so hungry for you I don't think I can sit here and eat lunch without putting my hands all over you. You're cruel, Paolo."

"Beautiful one, be patient a little while longer. We don't want to give Mrs. Davis any reason to talk, now do we?"

"Do you know how long it's been since I've seen you? A few stolen hours last January. Paolo, you're playing games."

"Alli, you know the rules. We've been over this before. I'm going to marry your mother, you're going to find some nice young man to settle down with, and in the meantime we are going to have fun when we can. That's all this is, Alli. We're about having fun together. That's what we both want, little one. Now, eat your lunch and pretend that I'm an old, bald, fat uncle that you're being forced to entertain."

"And, what will I get in return for this little charade?" She smiled demurely across the table.

"Ah, Alli, you know what is waiting for us upstairs. Eat your lunch, take a swim, and come to my room in an hour."

Paolo

Paolo laughed when he thought of the beautiful young woman who brought him so much pleasure. She was always so eager and willing. When she was sixteen she had been enchanting, now, at eighteen, she was delicious. The first time he laid eyes on her, he knew he would seduce her, but to his surprise, she had seduced him. He and Margo had been vacationing in St. Maarten when Margo asked him to join her at MarGrove. She had nonchalantly mentioned that her twin daughters were at the house for the summer, but had quickly added they would not be in his way. He'd been unprepared for Alli. Her exotic beauty rivaled Margo's and her young body was waiting to be explored.

Two days after they arrived in Miami, Margo had been called to New York for a meeting and his business in Miami had kept him from going with her. He would have two days to see if Alli's seductive looks and come-ons were for real.

He and Margo had a quasi-drug-induced sexual routine that they embraced, sometimes several times a day. But when he thought about Alli he wondered what it would be like to experience pleasurable sex without the cocaine? He wondered what it would take to entice the daughter to his bed.

Several hours after Margo left for New York he got his answer. Alli was in his room performing her own teasing little dance. As he watched, he recognized her raw desire and understood that she was not an amateur. The girl knew what she wanted and she knew how to get it. For two days, and every time they could find a way to be together for the rest of the summer, Alli was there. She was insatiable. He had no need for drugs, as Alli became his new addiction.

After that summer, he had flown to Pennsylvania once a month for two years to meet her for weekends and, now, it had worked out for them to have the entire month of June without interruption or interference. Margo's tour had been extended, Alli's father would be with Margo, and amazingly, the sister had chosen to tour with her parents instead of coming to MarGrove with Alli.

He would enjoy the month and then he would tell her their affair was over. As much as he delighted in Alli and her passion, he knew Margo was becoming suspicious. She had confronted him about another woman and made it clear his affair had to end. He knew she didn't suspect the other woman was her daughter. His goal was Margo and he didn't want anything to spoil their wedding plans. Yes, he would have to end this thing with Alli. But first, he would enjoy the next few weeks and whatever she had to offer him.

Alli

Like a cat, she silently slipped down the hall and opened the door to the guest room. The curtains were drawn, the room was aglow with candlelight, and tango music played softly. As soon as she could see him in the shadow of the room she dropped her robe and began to move to the mesmerizing sound of the music.

Each tantalizing movement was calculated to increase sexual tension as she stretched and twisted her body to the throbbing cadence. His hungry eyes burned her flesh and his rapid breathing enticed her to open her body even more seductively. Her only thought was his naked flesh moving with hers.

The music began its crescendo as he undressed and motioned for her to come to him. He wrapped her legs around his waist and gently pushed her down on the bed. As he melded their bodies together, the strength of her desire was unleashed. The dance she had been craving for months, finally began.

Chapter Four

Margo

Staring at the face in the mirror, she started to laugh. Who the hell are you and what did you do with Margaret Alison Maxwell?

At forty-one years old, she was famous beyond her wildest dreams, and wealthy. But this morning, like every morning for the past twenty-five years, she had no idea who she really was. The eyes that stared back at her didn't reflect the heart and soul of anybody she recognized. Every day, no matter where she was, mobs of people shouted the name they called her–Margo. But they didn't know her any more than she knew herself.

At sixteen she had walked into a club on Miami Beach and told the owner, "I'm a singer and I'm going to be a star." He had laughed, "Yeah, you and half the other kids in Miami." And then she started to sing. He offered her a job on Friday and Saturday nights and when she told him her name, he had simply called her Margo.

When she was Margaret Alison Maxwell, she knew who she was–a young girl with a good voice who was pretty enough to turn heads. She had grown up in a loving, working class family in Miami Springs where she and her brothers laughed a lot, teased each other, and, as far as she knew, they didn't have issues with their identity.

They loved her. No, they loved Margaret. They didn't know who Margo was because she had never invited them into Margo's world. She didn't know her brothers, their wives or their children. Hell, I don't even know my own children.

The weight of her depression held her in the chair and she struggled to let go of unwanted thoughts. She didn't want to remember how she got here. Remembering hurt.

*****

Long ago, she walked off the small stage and heard him ask her to join him at his table. She was used to men coming on to her and she brushed him off with a polite comment about management not allowing her to mingle with the patrons. But, he insisted it was business and he would get permission from Tony Mandor, the club owner, if he had to.

"Okay, what kind of business are you talking about?" She remembered how cynical she had sounded and how his eyes crinkled up when he began laughing at her.

"Margo, I can assure you this is strictly music business. Please sit down and give me a chance to explain."

He was tall, good looking, and very smooth. "My name is Michael Anderson and I'm a talent agent in search of a talent. You're what I'm looking for and I know I can make you a star."

"Thanks, but no thanks. It was nice meeting you, Mr. Anderson." She stood up and turned to walk away.

"I've never been more serious in my life, Margo. I want to represent you and I have contacts that will open doors for you–like a recording contract and a concert venue. But I guess you're content to stay in this third-rate club."

When she heard him say recording contract, she turned around. "Okay, what's in it for you, Mr. Anderson?"

"Standard agent cut, Margo. This is business." He smiled and motioned for her to sit back down. "I've been watching you for several months and I think you're ready to move on."

It sounded like Hollywood fiction when she thought about it, but that's how it all began. Within a week she had packed her bags and followed him to New York. Michael made good on his word–she made a demo recording that he promoted and he got her a gig in one of the biggest clubs in New York. For two years she was on a whirlwind tour that launched her as a star. By the time she was twenty, she had three gold albums, two platinum singles, and a performance schedule that included some of the best venues in the country. She had her own band, stylist, publicist, and fan clubs in every major city. The amount of money she made was outrageous and it was decided that she needed Michael to manage her income and expenses as well as represent her.

She had been on tour four years when she landed a three-month contract at a major club in Las Vegas. She would headline five nights a week. “You’ve made it to the big time, Margo. This is what we’ve been working for. Let me take you to dinner to celebrate.”

How simple it had been to change the nature of their relationship from “strictly business” to something personal. After an evening of good food and too much wine, she invited him to her room and to her bed. The week her contract ended in Vegas, they were married in a small chapel near the hotel. Her stylist was her maid of honor and the bass player was Michael’s best man. They had a week before she had to be in Los Angeles for a series of concerts, so they honeymooned in Lake Tahoe.

Margo was happy. Michael became her world–agent, business manager, best friend, lover, and husband. He had molded her career, he had created Margo, and now he was unleashing her passion and potential as a woman. In all aspects of her life, she relinquished control. She curled up like a kitten and let Michael take care of her. And, for a few months it worked.

“Michael, I need to have a bank account of my own. There are times I need money and you’re not around. It’s embarrassing.”

“What do you need to buy? Just tell me and I’ll take care of it.”

“That’s not the point, Michael. I want an account of my own. That’s not unreasonable.”

“Wait ‘till we’re off tour and I’ll take care of it.”

Several months later, she asked again and was shocked, then enraged, when he said, "I've thought about it and it's best to leave things the way they are."

"Excuse me. I don't believe I heard what you just said." Her anger jumped out in front of her and really surprised her. She never lost her temper.

"Why are you yelling, Margo? It's your money and all you have to do is ask when you need something." His calm manner infuriated her even more.

"You're so right! It is my money and I'd like a bigger say in how I can spend it." She stood up, crossed her arms in front of her and glared at him with fury. "Am I making myself clear?"

"Calm down. Do you want everyone in this hotel to hear you?"

"Do you think I care? Right now, I don't care who hears me. You have no right to treat me this way." She shouted even louder.

He turned and started for the door, "When I come back you better be over this!"

"How dare you walk away! Come back here and tell me why I'm being treated like a two-year-old!" She demanded, but Michael had already closed the door behind him.

She walked over to the bar that was set up in the room and picked up a bottle of vodka. She poured herself drink after drink after drink until she couldn't feel the anger any more.

When she woke up on the floor of the room, she was sick and vowed she would never drink that much again. Instead she was going to file for divorce.

For the next week, the sickness continued. Michael apologized and promised he would do as she wished, and Margo dropped the idea of the divorce. When the sickness continued for another week, she knew she was pregnant. It was the worst possible thing that could have happened. They had decided not to have children–she wanted her career and so did he. There was no room for children in the type of life they had chosen. Margo blamed Michael and Michael blamed Margo.

"There is no way you're going to have this baby. How could you let this happen?" Michael's voice was hard and cold and the lines on his face deepened with every word.

"Are you crazy! There is no way I'm going to get rid of this child. I don't want this baby any more than you do, but I'm not even going to think about what you're suggesting." She stormed out of the room and slammed the door.

The argument continued for the next several weeks. Her sickness continued and so did the concert tour. Margo felt like she was in hell.

"Do you know how many appearances we're going to have to cancel because of your carelessness? Do you know how much having this baby is going to cost us?"

Michael lashed out at her every chance he got, but she stood her ground. I will control this part of my life. He can't take this away from me.

As it happened, they only had to cancel two concerts on the tour. Margo watched her weight; gowns were made that concealed as much of the pregnancy as possible, and Michael did everything to squash any rumors that surfaced. He told the press that Margo was exhausted and the doctor had ordered rest. She would be back on stage as soon as the doctor released her.

During the sixth month of the pregnancy, the doctor told her there were two heartbeats. She was going to have twins. I need a drink. Of course she knew she couldn't have a drink until she had delivered, but all she could think about was the oblivion that came with a bottle of vodka. When she recovered from the shock of this news, she told Michael they had to find a house and a nanny. There was no way she was going to have children on tour with her and there was no way she was going to lose a minute of sleep because of them.

The last month she was on stage, she sang from behind the piano. And, she was living the lie they were telling–she was exhausted. After her last performance, she flew to Los Angeles where Michael had found a house surrounded by ten acres of land. She fell into bed and slept for two days. She hated the way her body looked, so she avoided mirrors. And, she hated that life. The peace and quiet made her restless, staying in one place made her edgy, and doing nothing every day frazzled what was left of her emotions. She had to find a way out or she would go mad.

She interviewed nannies, contracted with a physical trainer who would begin the week after the birth to help her get back in shape, and began practicing new songs with the band three days a week. She was determined to leave the house as soon as possible. And–she would leave it looking like Margo.

Her twin daughters were born in a private clinic after twenty hours of labor. When the nurse brought the babies to her, there was no bonding. She held them long enough to know they were real and then turned over their care to their nanny, Mrs. Brice. As far as Margo was concerned, her duty had ended. She had a tubal ligation to make sure there would be no more accidents.

She was surprised that Michael had the opposite reaction. He was fascinated by everything the babies did and she watched as he drew closer and closer to his daughters. When she showed no interest, he decided to name them Alli and Sunni after her middle name.

“Look, Margo, aren’t they beautiful? You hold one and I’ll hold the other.”

“Not interested, Michael. Babies are not my thing.”

“Ah, sweetheart, these are no ordinary babies. These are our babies.”

“Leave me alone, Michael. You and the nanny are doing a great job.”

She didn’t have time to waste on lullabies. She was getting ready to go back to work.

*****

Returning to the stage was the best therapy for Margo. She worked hard to get her body back in shape and knew she looked great when her stylist was astonished that her pre-pregnancy gowns did not have to be altered.

Once a month, no matter where they were, Michael flew to Los Angeles to spend several days with his daughters. Margo was elated. This gave her time without him and she felt a freedom she hadn't experienced since she left Miami with him years before. She laughed when she realized the twins had delivered her from Michael's suffocating control. Her pregnancy had been worthwhile after all.

She had been back on the road for six months when she met Roger Baker. He had sent flowers back stage before the show with a note inviting her to a dinner party at the Hilton after her performance. The note said he would send a car for her.

This is a joke. Like all the other invitations she received, she tossed it in the trash. Michael was in California with the twins, but he always made arrangements for a car to pick her up after the show and for her stage manager to get her safely to her hotel.

She was walking out of the theater when a man approached her. He was tall, his hair was grayed at the temples, his eyes were dark and piercing. He was distinguished and, from outward appearances, very wealthy.

"Margo, I'm Roger Baker and I've been looking forward to this evening for a long time. I've invited several friends to join us for dinner and drinks. Just an hour or so of your time and then I'll have my driver return you to your hotel."

"I appreciate your invitation Mr. Baker. But I have plans for this evening." She smiled, grabbed the stage manager's arm, and continued walking to the exit where her car was waiting.

"I know you don't know me and my invitation was very forward. But I promise you a wonderful evening with some delightful people.

If you would feel more secure with your own driver, just ask him to follow me." Roger was handsome and charming and persuasive. "I've reserved a private room, so you won't be hounded by fans or reporters."

The stage manager stepped between Margo and the intruder, but the man continued to talk around him.

"Dinner and drinks--that's it? In a public place with you and your friends?" Margo sounded skeptical.

She had never had to deal with unwanted invitations before. Michael always took care of getting her to the car undisturbed and he handled the situations without causing problems with her fans. But tonight Michael was gone, she was feeling restless, and Roger Baker was a very attractive man. "I'll have my car follow yours." She walked away before she could change her mind.

Michael had been the only man in her life. He had sheltered her from everything but her work. They had no friends. They didn't entertain and, other than the band members, no outsiders had ever been invited to their home. Tonight she had glimpsed something she wanted more of–adoration when she wasn't in the spotlight.

*****

After her evening with Roger, a new and more worldly side of Margo emerged. Her needs and desires intensified. Whenever Michael was in California, Roger or some other man filled her bed. She drank more and had begun to experiment with drugs. She searched for the next high. In the past, the adrenalin high of being on stage had been all she knew and all she wanted. Then she discovered there was more.

For three years she managed to live a double life. For weeks at a time she was Margo–singer and wife–but for three or four days every month she became a woman addicted to sex, recreational drugs and alcohol. Her life had a pattern and the guys in the band covered for her, both on stage and with Michael.

Then it all exploded and she had her first meltdown. Michael was in California with the girls and she was doing a series of concerts in New Orleans as part of Jazz Fest. This event was almost as popular as Mardi Gras and the city was alive with people. Concerts were everywhere, street music gave the city a carnival atmosphere, and she didn't want to be alone.

She accepted an offer from one of her admirers and invited him to her suite. She asked him to pour her a scotch on the rocks while she changed into something more comfortable. Within minutes she was out of her red evening gown and into a soft, silky caftan. She walked out of the bedroom and he handed her the drink. As she took a sip he led her to the coffee table where he had set up a line of cocaine. "This is good stuff, Margo. Care to join me?"

She tossed back the scotch and sat down next to him on the couch. It only took a minute for the coke to send her swirling into a place of incredible energy and desire. They made love, drank, and every hour or so did another line of coke. Margo lost count of the number of times the pattern was repeated.

*****

At five o'clock in the afternoon the phone in her room began to ring. Why is it so far away?

She knew it was ringing, but she couldn't sit up to answer it, and then there was blackness.

*****

When Margo failed to show up for rehearsal and didn't answer her phone, the guys in the band started to sweat. At seven o'clock that evening, Ed Tanner, the bass player, said he was going back to the hotel to find her. They had a show at nine o'clock and no star.

The 'Do Not Disturb' sign was on the door, but Ed ignored it and began knocking. He called her name several times, but there was no response. Panic gripped him as he realized something was wrong. He ran down to the front desk and asked to speak privately with the manager. No matter what was going on, he had to be discrete. Michael would be furious if the media got wind of this.

"I'm Ed Tanner and I'm in Margo's band. I need a favor and I need it to be confidential."

When Ed finished explaining that Margo had not shown up for the rehearsal and wasn't answering her phone, the manager agreed to open the door to her suite.

They were shocked at what they found. The living room was strewn with liquor bottles and the evidence of coke was on the coffee table. The heavy drapes were still drawn in the bedroom and when they turned on the light, Margo was lying nude on the floor. Ed grabbed the blanket off the bed and quickly covered her body, while the hotel manager tried to rouse her.

"Oh, God, please don't let her be dead." The manager called her name and shook her but there was no response.

*****

The concert was called off using the excuse that Margo had food poisoning and all ticket holders were given a refund. Ed called Michael in California and listened to him rant for ten minutes before finally asking how Margo was doing.

"Michael, I don't know. I came back to the theater to take care of things for the show and I'm just now headed to the hospital. I'll call you when I know something."

As soon as Ed walked into the hospital, the doctor began to grill him. "Do you know what she was taking? How much does she drink? What drugs does she take?"

"All I know is she went out with some guy and that's the last time I saw her. I know she drinks and I've heard she experiments with some of the recreational drugs. There was evidence of coke on the coffee table in her hotel room. I've called her husband in California, and he'll be here as soon as he can get a flight." Ed looked at the doctor ruefully. "Don't be surprised when he says she never drinks more than a glass of wine and would never do drugs. When he's in California, she sort of goes wild." Ed frowned and hoped the young doctor understood how complicated it was going to become when Michael arrived.

"Does she have a concert set for tomorrow? If so, you better cancel that one, too. She's not going anywhere."

"Oh, dear God," he whispered. "Are you telling me she's not going to be all right?"

"I'm telling you she'll be lucky to leave this hospital."

Michael

When Michael arrived the next morning, the hospital parking lot was filled with reporters who surrounded his car before the driver realized what was happening. But Michael was prepared.

"Good morning. I don't have any news for you at this time. But I promise as soon as I've talked to the doctors and seen my wife, I'll let you know. Please let me through. I've just flown in from California and I need to see my wife. Apparently food poisoning and exhaustion got the best of her last night. A little rest and she'll be back on stage."

The doctor was waiting for him in the lobby and directed him to a conference room. "I'm Dr. Jarvis and I'm not going to pull any punches with you, Mr. Anderson. Your wife is in critical condition, but she made it through the crucial first twelve hours. I'm waiting for the reports, but the evidence points to alcohol and cocaine in large quantities." The doctor stopped talking and looked at Michael. "Does your wife have an addiction?"

Almost before the doctor could finish his question, Michael responded, "No. Absolutely not! I've never seen her drink more than a few glasses of wine and she doesn't use drugs. They tell me a man was involved. All I know is something dangerous and suspicious happened to my wife and I intend to find out what's going on. When can I see her?"

"I'll take you to her room. Please follow me and we can avoid all those reporters. I assure you, the leak did not come from this hospital. We have done everything possible to protect your wife's identity and privacy."

The last time Michael had visited his wife in a hospital was when the twins were born. Even though he had been upset about her pregnancy and didn't want to be tied down with children, that day turned out to be one of the happiest of his life. He had not been prepared for the emotion of seeing his daughters; of holding them and recognizing that they were part of him. He had changed.

But sadly, Margo had not. He couldn't wait to get home to Alli and Sunni–he talked for hours with their nanny, Mrs. Brice, about their care. He never tired of hearing her tell him about their accomplishments. But, today was not a happy day. Something was terribly wrong with his wife and he knew, once he heard the facts of how this had happened, he would no longer be able to pretend that their marriage was secure.

He followed the doctor into the room and gasped. Margo looked like a corpse except he could see the sheet move as she took a breath. She was attached to an IV bag and several machines and she had an oxygen mask over her mouth and nose. When the door closed behind him, the gentle whine of machines scared him.

"My god, you didn't tell me it was this bad. Is she dying?"

"Mr. Anderson, I told you she was critical. We were able to rouse her within thirty minutes when she was first brought into the ER so I'm confident she has gotten past the crisis point. But she is still a very sick woman. We've run tests and will know more when we have all the results. She is breathing on her own and responds to stimuli. We have determined that she didn't have a heart attack, but, unfortunately, there has been some damage to her vocal chords. That's about all I can tell you at this time."

Michael walked over to the bed and took Margo's hand in his. "Her hand is so cold. Is there some way to warm her?" His voice trembled as he tried to grasp the seriousness of her situation.

"She is warming up. Her temperature is almost back to normal. It was very low when she was first admitted. Why don't you sit with her awhile? Perhaps you can hold her hands and talk with her. Your voice may be a stimulus. I'll be back after I check on her test results."

The doctor left the room and Michael wept. Tears rolled down his cheeks and he struggled to regain his composure. "Why, Margo? Why did this happen to you? Why did this happen to us? You know I love you." The silence overwhelmed him as he sat on the edge of the hospital bed and watched the face of his sleeping wife.

He sat in stunned silence. What was happening to his world? His head was pounding and he raised his hands to cover his eyes until the pain went away. How could he have been so stupid, so trusting, so naive?

Margo belonged to him–hadn't he made her a star? He had protected her from all the dangers that went along with celebrity. And then it dawned on him–he had given up control of Margo because of the twins. He had been trying so hard to be a part of his daughters' lives that he had let Margo slip away from him.

Anger boiled up and he threw his coffee cup across the room. The cup didn't break, but hot coffee splattered the wall and the floor. He tried to separate his pain from his anger. The fact that Margo had betrayed him hurt like hell. He had cut ties with his other clients when he took on the job of promoting her, so all his assets were tied up in her talent and ability to produce. Professionally, there was no way he could leave her without having to start over. As far as he was concerned, his wife was damaged goods. But how was he going to stop loving her?

He walked down the corridor and out of the hospital where the reporters were waiting. "Margo is not well and the doctors have advised us to cancel the remainder of the tour. She has contracted a viral infection that has impacted her vocal cords. She'll be moved to California at the end of the week where she'll continue treatments. As soon as she is well enough, she'll be back on the stage where she belongs. I'll keep you posted. Thanks."

He cancelled the tour, went back to California to make arrangements for Margo to enter a treatment facility, and never went back to the hospital.

Margo

The treatment center sat high on a cliff overlooking the Pacific Ocean. She had been there for over a month. At first she was too sick to care, but then she wanted out. She was tired of the routine–talking about her feelings, trying to uncover the mystery of her supposed addiction. I'm not an addict and all of this is a waste of my time. Every day that she spent in this place was like being in a luxurious jail and she resented Michael for putting her there. She had talked to him on the phone twice since she got here, but she hadn't seen him since before she was hospitalized. It wasn't like him to abandon her and she wondered what he had been told. Whatever he thought he knew didn't matter, because she had decided to ask for a divorce. That was the one good thing that had come out of all the counseling sessions. She knew she had to leave her marriage. She just didn't know how she was going to leave Michael.

*****

Michael was seated in the doctor's office when Margo walked in and took the chair beside him. "Hi, Michael, thanks for coming," she whispered. "It means a lot that you're here."

She knew he heard her but he didn't respond or look at her. This is not going to be a good meeting.

Dr. Marconi sat across from them and Margo knew he would not try to interfere with the awkward reunion. "Dr. Marconi, can we get this over with? It's apparent that Michael doesn't want to be here and I can't carry this off by myself."

"Michael, do you have any questions or comments that you would like to share with Margo?" Dr. Marconi asked quietly.

"I'm here to listen to what she has to say. Right now I can't think of a thing I'd like to say to her that wouldn't create a greater chasm between us."

"All right, Margo, you've heard what Michael wants. Are you ready to tell your story?"

"Michael, I'm sorry you're disappointed in me. You had the girls and I was so alone. I needed something to fill the hours while you were away and it got out of hand. I never meant to hurt you."

She could feel the tension increase across her shoulders and her hands began to sweat. "Please believe me. I gave you control when I was eighteen years old and I didn't understand at the time what that would mean. I knew you were going to do what was best for Margo, but I forgot there is more to me than the woman who stands on a stage and sings." She was aware that Michael hadn't looked at her. He was stone-faced and staring straight ahead. She tried to take a deep breath to calm her nerves, but her throat felt like it was closed.

She looked at Dr. Marconi for encouragement and began again. "I know you don't want to hear all the details, but part of my treatment is to be able to say to you that I cheated on you, I drank heavily when you were away, and I experimented with drugs. The man I was with in New Orleans was just one of many, but he was not like the others. He wanted to hurt me. It's a sordid story and I'm not proud of what I've done." Michael still hadn't looked at her and she had to get his attention. "I'd like the chance to show you I've learned my lesson."

Michael slowly turned and looked in her direction. She saw the hurt in his eyes and almost broke down. When he finally spoke, his voice was steely and cold. "I have filed for divorce, Margo. You abandoned our daughters before they were even born and now you have betrayed me. Our marriage is broken and can't be fixed." He didn't take his eyes off of her. "I will stay on as your agent and manager," he continued, "but I will be taking on additional clients. I can no longer afford to work exclusively with you. You have shown me that you are not dependable and can no longer be trusted."

How dare you, Michael! I'm the reason you're a success. "You're not serious." Her voice rose to a shout. "You can't do this."

"I can do this Margo. You have committed adultery which gives me grounds for divorce. I've worked out the terms of our agreement to include joint custody of the girls and the expectation that you will try to be a bigger part of their lives. You may keep the house in LA. I've already taken an apartment near there so I can see the girls as often as possible. There is a more than generous monetary settlement and in the future I will take 40% of your net earnings as my salary. I will be cordial in all of our work-related dealings, but I will no longer be available to assist you with any matters that are not connected to your career or our children."

He sounded like he was reading a script and that hurt even more. She didn't want to cry and she didn't want to get hysterical, but she was close to both. She looked at Dr. Marconi for help, but the doctor remained silent.

"There is no way we can just work together, Michael. I can't believe you are suggesting this impossible situation. We can get in counseling together and find a way to work through this. I know we can."

This was all her fault–she had wanted her freedom. The irony was, she had wanted a divorce, but now that he was giving it to her, she was more afraid than she had ever been in her life. She felt her body start to crumble in the chair. She was too tired to fight. "I need time to think, Michael."

"Margo, that's a luxury you don't have. The papers will be served the minute you walk out of this facility. There are no second chances in this world, Margo. Try to remember that in the future."

Michael stood up. "I have another appointment this afternoon, Dr. Marconi. Please keep me informed of Margo's progress so I'll know what kind of recording and concert schedule to plan."

Hurt was written all over his face when he turned to look at her. "You're looking well, Margo. I hope that means you will be ready to go back to work soon. Surely you have figured out that we are losing a great deal of money while you are in here trying to recover from your indiscretions." He walked to the door and didn't look back.

Margo began to sob. "Now what do I do, Dr. Marconi? What do I do?"

Dr. Marconi's voice was soft but firm. "That's easy, Margo. Now you begin to grow up."

Michael

He had moved out of the house, but remained in close contact with Mrs. Brice. He tried to arrange his schedule so he could visit with the twins at least three times each week. His girls were eight years old and he was having more fun with them than he could have ever imagined. They made him laugh, they trusted him, they liked to spend time with him, and they loved him. He brought them expensive gifts. And they were always pleased when he created adventures for them. Don't they know how hard I'm trying to make up for the absence of their mother? He knew Mrs. Brice cared for them as though they were her own daughters, but it was not the same as having Margo in their lives.

Alli and Sunni rarely talked to him about their mother. He had noticed, on the chance occasions when Margo was home, that the twins tried their best to stay out of her way. Alli acted as though Margo didn't exist, but he had seen the look of longing in Sunni's eyes whenever she thought her mother was going to be in LA for a few days. And he had seen the disappointment when Margo brushed off Sunni's attempts to gain her attention.

He had given up hope that Margo would change and he tried to protect his girls from her indifference. He made a conscious choice to get them through the divorce without further damaging their ideas about their mother. His thoughts about Margo were his business, not Alli's or Sunni's.

When he put the word out that he was looking for new talent, he was surprised at the opportunities that came his way. He had met with two bands, three singers, and one rock group in the months that Margo had been in rehab, and had decided to sign contracts with the rock group and two of the singers. Promoting Margo was still his priority, but she would no longer be his sole interest. Margo was his money-maker; representing her would let him continue the lifestyle he had grown to enjoy. But his new clients had potential that might allow him to cut his ties to Margo completely at some point in the future.

No, that wasn't true. He couldn't let go of her and he knew it–she was his addiction. He would bide his time, he would listen, he would be patient. When the time was right, she would come back to him.

Margo

"Michael, they're discharging me next week. Would you please come and drive me home?"

"Sorry, Margo, I'll be in New York. One of my new clients is opening in an off-Broadway show and I wouldn't think of missing it."

"Did you say a new client? You didn't waste any time did you?" She couldn't believe what she was hearing.

He had told her he was looking for new clients, but she had dismissed it as his anger talking. Jealousy gnawed at her, but before she could respond, he continued.

"Margo, perhaps you can call for a car? No wait, I've got a better idea. I've hired a bodyguard for you. He's a former Navy SEAL and

I know he can handle the rift-raft you seem to want in your life. His name is Sam Baxter. He's a friend from back home and I trust him. Give him a call at 310-895-6262."

"You've done what? The last thing I want is a bodyguard, especially someone who's a friend of yours. As usual you didn't consult me about this."

"That's right, I didn't. I won't be traveling with you as much, so you need someone to run interference for you. I would think, after the way you botched things up in New Orleans, you'd be grateful."

"Damn you, Michael. You still think you can control me, don't you?"

"Margo, give Sam a call. I'll let him know to be expecting you. The girls will be glad to see you."

The phone went dead and she fumed. Michael always threw the girls in her face. She had talked with Dr. Marconi about her lack of maternal instinct and he had tried to uncover some deep meaning that she knew didn't exist. Why couldn't everyone just accept that she didn't like to be around children? If Michael thought he was going to keep her in line with a bodyguard, he was mistaken.

On top of everything else, now she had to deal with another intrusion in her life named Sam Baxter. Seething, she slammed down the phone knowing she wasn't going to win the battle. Michael was making sure she knew he was still in control. As she dialed Sam's number, she tried to imagine how this man was going to impact who she could see and what she could do.

Curtly, she said, "Hello, I'm calling for Sam Baxter. This is Margo and I need to be picked up next Thursday."

*****

When she was told her car had arrived, she walked out the door of the rehab center and vowed she would never return. Six weeks had seemed like an eternity and all she wanted to do was leave. She looked up at the man standing by the car and was surprised.

Sam Baxter was medium height, medium build–not imposing at all like she thought he would be. His mustache was graying, like his hair, and he had the bluest eyes she had ever seen. She had been expecting a brute of a man, but instead she was looking at a school teacher or an accountant. Navy SEAL or whatever, this guy will be easy to dodge. She smiled.

"Hello, Margo. Let's go home."

That was all he said as he opened the door of the Lincoln Town Car and motioned for her to get in. He walked around to the driver's side, started the car and began the two hour drive to Los Angeles. For the first fifteen minutes, there was silence. She couldn't decide how to start a conversation and it drove her crazy.

"Okay, Sam, you must know that I'm not happy about our situation. But, if we're going to be inseparable, why don't you tell me what I can expect from you?"

"I'm not your jailer, if that's what you're thinking. I work for you and, even though I've known Michael most of my life, I don't report to him. I'm not here to tell you what to do, I'm here to keep you as safe as possible."

"You're kidding me, right? I can't imagine that Michael doesn't want a detailed report of my activities every week."

"That's not part of the deal. Look, you're a big star and people want a piece of you–whether it's an autograph or something more. I'll do my best to make sure there is always security in place and you can feel safe."

The rest of the drive home was eerily quiet as Margo tried to figure out if Sam Baxter was telling her the truth. Could he be for real?

*****

After a week at home, Margo had two things on her mind–getting back to work and sending the girls to boarding school. Michael had called to discuss the new tour schedule and to make arrangements for her next recording session. He wanted a new album out by the end of the year, followed by an extensive promotional tour. Making a new album would require her to be in LA for the next four or five months and the girls were already getting on her nerves. Boarding school was the only solution.

Without Michael around to handle the details, she realized she needed a personal assistant. She met and hired Lara Finley. Lara was in her mid-thirties, had worked in the business for more than ten years and seemed to know her way around. She was attractive in a non-threatening way, dressed like an executive, and understood the demands of the job. Margo, who usually didn't feel comfortable with other women, liked Lara's efficiency and professional manner. The first task she assigned her was to find an excellent school for the girls, get them enrolled, and make arrangements for them to move.

The arrangements were made and Mrs. Brice was told her services were no longer required even though the woman cried and begged Margo not to separate her from the girls.

"Mrs. Anderson, your girls need me. Please don't do this."

"I'm sorry, Mrs. Brice. The arrangements have been made and the girls will leave the end of the month. You will receive a generous severance package and letters of reference. I know you will have no trouble finding another position." Margo couldn't look at the hurt and disappointment on the woman's face, so she walked out of the room.

Telling the girls was more difficult than Margo had expected. "Darlings, I have some wonderful news. You've just been accepted to one of the most prestigious schools in the northeast. Isn't that exciting?"

"But we live in California. We already have a school," Alli protested while Sunni stared at their mother in shock.

With trembling lips, Sunni pleaded with her mother, "I don't want to leave Mrs. Brice."

"Girls, this will be a wonderful adventure for you. I know you're going to love it and Mrs. Brice can't care for you anymore. So, I don't have a choice."

When she told Michael, he exploded.

"What are you thinking? We have joint custody. Why wasn't I included in this decision? I'm going to court to get full custody."

"Stop, Michael. I did this out of concern for all of us. You're on the road most of the time and I'll be on the road again soon. Since you're spending so much time in New York, it's just more reasonable for the girls to be in Pennsylvania. You'll be able to spend more time with them."

"This isn't the end of this, Margo. Your decisions will come back to bite you."

*****

The band had been working with her on several new ideas for the album and as she settled back into the music, her life began to feel more normal. Music and performing framed her persona and she vowed not to stray from them again. It was hard for her to admit that Michael had kept her focused and she began to feel the void his absence created. What would happen to her career if she got off track again? Her fans would forgive her once, but she knew how fickle they were. If she wasn't producing, they would find someone else to adore.

She worked hard for three months and felt confident about the album. Michael had worked with the production staff and the band, but had little contact with her. He had spoken with her several times on the phone about the ideas she and the band were working on for lighting, sets, costumes, and choreography. The back-up singers and dancers were hired. Rehearsals had gone as well as expected and Margo felt good about the show. Michael had hired a strong opening group that everyone agreed would get the crowd warmed up for her. He had been in constant contact with their stage manager and had come to LA for the last week of rehearsals, but his interaction with her had been formal and business related.

"Michael, tomorrow is the first show of the tour. You'll be here, won't you?" She had taken a chance and called him at his apartment.

"No, Margo. You're on your own. All the arrangements are made, so there is no need for me to be in Chicago."

"But you've always been with me to open a tour. As my agent, you should be here." She could feel insecurity seeping into her voice. How could he do this to her? All of her past thoughts of being smothered by him seemed to evaporate as she realized how profoundly her past actions were impacting her life. She wasn't well enough yet to go it on her own and the urge to find a vodka bottle became stronger.

"Michael," she whispered, "Don't do this to me."

*****

It was two hours until show time and she was pacing. She hadn't been on stage for almost a year. Michael wasn't there, and doubts about the new album gnawed at her.

What if I'm not ready to go back on stage?

When Michael had been by her side, she had never doubted her ability to mesmerize an audience. But now.... She knew Sam Baxter would make sure she didn't have access to alcohol or drugs, she knew he was somewhere near her dressing room door, and she knew he would protect her from the outside world. But there was no one to protect her from herself. That had always been Michael's job.

The room filled with people and her world got busy–makeup, hair styling, costumes–and as Margo became visible in the mirror, the doubts and fears began to fall away.

"Honey, this new hair style is the best we've tried. Don't you agree?" The stylist had convinced her to let her hair grow longer and had curled it to make it look fuller. "You look sexy! And, with the new costumes, your fans are going to go wild when they see you."

Her first outfit was stunning. The red halter dress was shimmering and shiny, with lines that accentuated every curve of her body. At the knees it flared out around her feet to make it easier to walk and when she moved from behind the dressing screen, the appreciative looks of her crew renewed her confidence.

By the time the stage manager knocked on her door, she had recreated who she was and what she had to do. Walking out of her dressing room, she had no doubt that she was Margo, the star. As she neared the stage entrance, her heart beat quickened when she saw Michael standing in the wings. The thread between them had not been broken. She smiled.

Michael

The divorce had forced Michael to make changes professionally and personally, but his obsession with Margo continued to draw him back to her. As his anger slowly cooled, he realized he could never completely remove her from his life.

He'd promised himself he wouldn't attend her opening concert when she returned to the stage, but he couldn't stay away. He rationalized that he had to protect his investment in her–it had nothing to do with the fact that he still loved her. So little by little, his involvement began to go beyond the professional. As her agent and business manager, he communicated with her; as a parent, he discussed the children with her; as a man, he wanted her.

During the first tour, he began showing up for every opening. He usually stood in the wings with Sam Baxter to make sure that she saw him. He didn't approach her or go to her dressing room, and he didn't stay in that city beyond opening night. By the fourth opening night, he knew she had regained her confidence. He didn't pump Sam for information but he talked with several of the band members who assured him Margo had not returned to her dangerous habits. She was doing well on her own and he really didn't need to follow her from city to city. But he couldn't stay away.

One night half way through the tour, he left the wings during the middle of the show and walked to her dressing room. When he opened the door, her presence was everywhere. He felt her energy. He smelled all the fragrances that were so familiar to him. He touched her things and it was like touching her. All of his senses responded and he knew he had to wait for her, to be with her, even if it was only for a moment.

When she walked in the room she was startled to find him there. "What are you doing here?"

"I'm here for you." His voice betrayed his desire and he walked over and took her in his arms. "I want you."

She broke away from his embrace and locked the dressing room door. Without a word she took off her costume and walked back into his waiting arms. "It took you long enough, Michael."

There was new passion and hunger in their love making. Two bodies that knew each other so well suddenly felt like they were coming together for the first time. This wasn't about love, it was about desire and lust and anger and years of memories. It was about letting go of pain and releasing tension, but it was not about forgiveness.

When their bodies fell away from each other, there were no words. But there were looks that passed between them--looks of permission and promise. They were not finished with each other and the looks captured that recognition.

Michael dressed and quietly left the room, knowing there would be other opening nights and other rooms. Margo still belonged to him.

*****

Jumping up from the chair, she turned away from the face in the mirror. Enough of this nonsense. No more memories. I can't change the way it is. She walked over to the counter and poured herself a glass of wine to help clear her head of the thoughts that dragged her down.

Then she opened the bottle of pills and decided to take three of them. She had a show to do in two hours and she had to be alive and energetic. She had to be Margo.

Chapter Five

Sam

Sam Baxter didn't care whether he looked the part of the typical bodyguard–all muscles and few brains. His body wasn't brawny and his manner wasn't aggressive. But he did his job well and that was all that mattered.

Trained as a Navy SEAL, he had used his skills and stamina to make a living after leaving the Navy when he was 42 years old. He had agreed to take the bodyguard job as a favor to his boyhood friend, Michael Anderson, and in some ways he had looked forward to the changes it would bring to his life. He was paid well to protect Margo from the crowds, the hangers on, and herself. He got to travel, meet interesting people, and live well. He was able to provide his ex-wife with generous alimony and send his son to one of the best universities in California. Most of the time his job was easy. Besides, he liked Margo.

When he took the job, he knew there would be men in Margo's life, but he didn't know there would be so many.

"Margo, let's talk about how you want me to handle all these guys that try to get back stage? I don't want to interfere with your life, but I've got to be able to protect you."

"Oh, Sam, just shoo them all away!" She'd laughed at the serious expression on his face. "Let's make a deal! I'm not interested in having my dressing room over run with testosterone. But every now and then, if someone catches my eye, I might want to have dinner and an evening out. You keep the crowds away and I'll always let you know who I'm with and where I'm going."

"I can keep the crowds away, but I'm not sure how I can protect you if I'm not around. You let me know what restaurant and I'll be there, somewhere in the shadows. And, if you want more than dinner, always go back to our hotel. That way I can make sure you are always safe."

"You're either serious or crazy. I just don't know which one." She wasn't happy with the part about going back to the hotel so Sam 'could watch over her.'

"I'm very serious. It's most of the world that's crazy. My job is to keep you safe and that's what I intend to do. That's my deal, Margo. If we can't agree, then you'll have to find someone else for the job. What happens between you and the men you see is your business as long as they don't step over any lines. Then it becomes my business."

"You have certainly made your position clear." She snapped. "There's a part of me that wants to tell you to get out, but I'll go along with your over protectiveness until you get in my way. Then I'll reassess our situation."

Their deal had worked well for several years. He knew that frequently she and Michael still slept together, he had kept the lotharios as far away as possible, and he had watched the men around Margo very carefully. He had done background checks, talked with cab drivers, made inquiries of other people he knew in the business, and he had never let her be far enough away that he couldn't get to her if she ran into a problem.

He checked her dressing room, hotel room, and travel coach for alcohol and drugs. He knew the occasional nights when she had a glass of wine with dinner.

Their partnership was in its second year the first time she gave him the slip and from then on a pattern developed of back-sliding, rehab centers and doctors warning her about her voice.

"You keep breaking the deal, Margo. I'll let Michael know I'm leaving." He was fighting hard to stay calm, but his insides were churning. "Good luck."

"Wait, you can't leave!" she shouted after him as he walked toward the door. "I'm still on tour–you can't leave me now."

"No reason for me to stay. You think you can take care of yourself, so do it. I don't need to hang around and watch you kill your career and yourself along with it."

"Sam, please. No more, I promise. Please don't walk out on me."

She had looked awful before she started pleading with him, but then, with mascara running down her face and her hair in tangles, she looked vulnerable and child-like. Sam stared at her and wondered if he could stay. Like a fool, he had started caring about her, and knew he was the thing that stood between her and total destruction.

"Damn you, Margo," he said as he sat back down.

*****

Three months later, on the last night of the tour, Margo disappeared for two days. Sam had no choice but to call Michael.

The second morning Margo walked into the lobby of the hotel as though she had just been out for a stroll. Michael and Sam were waiting for her. Michael walked up beside her, grabbed her arm and began to steer her toward the elevator. Without missing a step or changing his expression he said through gritted teeth, "Where the hell have you been?"

"Who wants to know?"

"Don't play cute, Margo."

Sam followed them to Margo's suite but stayed in the background as Michael continued. "Sam and I were about to call in the police. What a headline that would be. I can see it now, 'Margo is at it Again!"

"Why are you here Michael? I thought Sam reported to me, not you."

"You've been gone long enough that he could report you missing. Sam did the right thing to call me."

"Where is he by the way?" Apparently she didn't see him standing near the door.

"You should count yourself lucky that he isn't on his way back to California." Michael's voice was getting louder as his anger increased. "The guy's been up two nights trying to find you."

"I was with a friend."

"Margo, one more of these little indiscretions, and you'll be back in rehab."

"Is that a threat, Michael?"

"No, Margo. It's a promise. You're messing with my income and if you think I'm not serious, try this again."

"I had a few drinks. What's the big deal?"

"The big deal is I don't believe you! Sex, alcohol, drugs–your addictions are taking over again. If you don't care about anything else, you better start caring about your voice. You're ruining it, Margo. And, without a voice, what have you got?"

Michael turned to Sam, "She's all yours. I've got to get out of here before I do something I'll regret."

Chapter Six

Margo

When Margo's new album went platinum, Michael capitalized on the success by scheduling a grand tour that included international venues like Rio De Janeiro, Brazil and Cape Town, South Africa. She knew it would exhaust her, but the idea of taking her music to new and exotic places was thrilling and she looked forward to the challenge.

Although she was concerned about the language barriers, she breathed a sigh of relief when the crowds in Brazil responded to her with shouts for more. The adrenalin flowed as she performed encore, after encore. Leaving the stage for the final time, she felt alive and wired. It would take her hours to unwind. As she reached her dressing room she caught a glimpse of Sam talking to an attractive man and smiled to herself as she wondered if there was the possibility of a new adventure. She stepped into the shadows of the hallway and listened.

"How is it possible that I had never heard of Margo until this evening? She is breath-taking and I must meet her," she heard the man say to Sam. Her interest was heightened.

"Senhor, I would appreciate it if you would deliver this note to the lovely Margo. I'll wait here for her answer," the man continued in Portuguese-accented English.

"I'll see what I can do when she comes off stage. But I don't guarantee an answer." Sam was used to running interference for

Margo and making sure her fans were kept at a distance. "By the way, how did you get back here to her dressing room?"

"I own the theater." Paolo smiled.

She waited until the men had left the hallway before she continued to her dressing room.

*****

"Margo, I have a note for you. The guy says he owns the theater." Sam handed Margo the note. "He's outside waiting for an answer."

Dear Senhora Margo, I would be honored if you would allow me to take you to dinner this evening. I am a devoted fan. Yours, Paolo DaSilva.

"Ask him to come in, Sam. The least I can do is thank him for the hospitality we've been shown."

Margo had changed out of her costume and was dressed in slacks and a silk sweater. She had removed her stage makeup and was trying her best to relax after being so keyed up on stage. This guy would have to be a monster for me to say no. She knew better than to let on to Sam that Paolo DaSilva interested her. She picked up a magazine and started flipping through the pages.

"Ah, the lovely Margo. It is a pleasure to meet you. My name is Paolo DaSilva. I want to welcome you to Brazil."

He was handsome. Tall, muscular, with ebony hair, and eyes the shade of the deepest, darkest night. She was mesmerized as she watched those dark eyes travel the length of her body. As he brought his gaze back to her face, she knew he liked what he saw and a connection was made between them. She held her breath as he walked toward her, lifted her hand and kissed it. Her body responded with sensations that usually required more foreplay. The man was electric and she flushed with excitement.

"Muito obrigado, senhor. You have a beautiful country and a beautiful theater. Won't you have a seat?"

"But I have come to take you to dinner. I know a wonderful place where you will not be hounded by fans and reporters."

"Perhaps another time. I'm exhausted and plan to return to my hotel." As much as she wanted to explore this man further, she knew better than to eagerly accept his invitation.

"Certainly you must be tired. My apologies for not anticipating how strenuous the performance would be for you. I will join you at your hotel and order dinner served there."

Margo laughed. "Don't you think you're being a bit presumptive? How do you know I don't have other plans?"

"Cancel them, Margo. I promise you an evening of charming conversation and laughter."

His magnetic smile could not be ignored and his eyes continued to draw her to him. All she wanted was to spend time with him. It was a bewitching moment.

"You know my bodyguard will be outside the door the entire time." Sam had kept her out of trouble for four years and she knew he would protect her tonight. All she had to do was allow his protection.

She picked up a card from the table and hastily wrote on it. "Here is my hotel and room number. I'll see you in thirty minutes."

As her car made its way back to the hotel, she leaned forward and spoke to Sam. "Mr. DaSilva will be joining me for dinner in the suite. I don't think you need to stand guard. The man seems harmless."

"Margo, be careful. This guy is very smooth."

"Sam, you're like a mother hen. Don't worry. If I need you, I'll call."

*****

When she opened the door to her suite, the maitre'd and several waiters were already setting the table with linens, fine china, silver and crystal. Candles were casting a warm glow over the room and soft music was playing. "My goodness! Does Senhor DaSilva own the hotel, too?" she asked.

"Oh, no, senhora. He called and made the arrangements and we are always eager to please him. I hope you will find everything to your liking. He has ordered a wonderful meal and some of our best wines. He has thought of everything." The maitre'd and his crew slipped out the door and closed it behind them.

Before she had time to look around there was a tap on the door and she almost ran to open it. She was eager for the evening to begin.

Paolo delivered on his promise. The conversation was engaging and they laughed. She was more relaxed than she had been in a very long time. At first she declined the wine, but before the evening was over, she had enjoyed several glasses. I can handle a few glasses of wine.

It was two in the morning when Paolo looked at his watch and stood to leave. "This has been a wonderful evening. You are delightful. Would you join me for dinner after your next concert?"

"I would love to, Paolo." His name rolled off her lips and she loved the sound.

"And, please tell Mr. Baxter that I have my own guards, so he can have the evening off." He closed the door softly behind him.

Margo was intoxicated with the man and the wine. She hadn't had a drink since her indiscretion the year before when Michael had threatened her with rehab. But, tonight she thought she could handle a glass or two of wine. I won't do this again. I feel like I'm drunk. She sank down on the bed and fell into a deep sleep.

*****

The next week was like a dream. Three nights in a row, she went from the concert stage to Paolo's home. But, on her last night in Brazil, she arrived at his house in a pensive mood. She was sad that she would be leaving the next day and she was frustrated that he had not tried to take her to bed. Is there something wrong with him or with me?

She had made up her mind to intensify her seductive charm and had chosen to wear a white gown that flattered her olive complexion and hugged her body sensuously. As she walked in the living room of his grand house, she had every intention of finding her way to his bedroom.

"You look lovely tonight, Margo. No, you look more beautiful than I've ever seen you." He took her hand and gently pulled her toward the French doors. "Come with me to the terrace. There is a soft breeze and a brilliant moon. It is the perfect evening for you to see the lights of my favorite city in the world."

The view from his terrace was magnificent. The lights of the city, the rolling sounds of the ocean waves, and the smell of bougainvillea and jasmine created a sense of paradise. The breeze lifted her hair and she felt a chill. Paolo quickly removed his jacket and placed it across her shoulders. At his touch, she turned her body into his and looked him directly in the eyes. "It would be a shame to let this beautiful night go to waste."

He took her hand and led her up the stairs. "Margo, you have me under your spell. I've tried to resist, but I want you more than I've ever wanted anyone."

As she slipped her dress over her head, he knelt in front of her. "You're body is more beautiful than I imagined. Tonight I will make love to you as though you are a goddess."

And, he did.

*****

Paolo convinced Margo to begin looking for a house in Miami. He often had business in the city and they decided it would be a convenient place for them to meet. At first she was reluctant to think about returning to her hometown, but the more she thought about it, the better she liked the idea.

She and Paolo made several visits to Miami to look at property but nothing they looked at seemed quite right. Finally, she enlisted the help of her mother who worked with a realtor and after six months of searching, sent her a listing in Coconut Grove that seemed ideal. The estate was located on Biscayne Bay and was gated. The main house had six bedrooms, plus servants' quarters, and 8,000 square feet of living space. The grounds included a tropical garden, a pool with pool house, and a two bedroom guest house. She called it MarGrove.

A housekeeper and gardener were hired, Sam was moved into the guest house, and a designer began to completely redo the interior. Margo called Michael to tell him she was selling the house in California and the girls would be spending at least one month of their summer vacation at MarGrove every year.

Once she moved into the estate, she remembered why she had loved growing up in Miami. It was a city of flavors, fragrances, and fever-pitched energy. Music was at the heart and soul of every neighborhood and the city pulsated to the distinct sounds of the myriad cultures. Also, it was the city of the family she had sorely neglected for more than sixteen years. Her father had passed away three years before, but her mother still lived in the house where Margo had grown up. Her brothers were scattered across the globe so she tried to talk her mother into selling the Miami Springs house and moving into a condo in the Grove.

"I don't have any friends in the Grove, Margaret. I'll be lonely down there." Her mother still called her by her given name and Margo knew she would never change.

"No, you won't. You'll be within walking distance of the girls and I'll be there every chance I get. This is a good move for you and I've found you a fabulous condo. It's on the ninth floor of a high-rise that overlooks Biscayne Bay. Meet me there this afternoon and you can decide if it's something you like."

As soon as her mother saw the place, the decision to move was made.

*****

Margo and Paolo met at the house often even when she was on tour and she invited him to spent time there when she and the band were on hiatus. As the music industry became a bigger presence in Miami, she began recording at a studio located near Coconut Grove which allowed her to spend all of her off-time in Miami.

As her life became more Miami centered, Michael made the decision to purchase a large penthouse apartment in one of the high rise buildings on Brickell Avenue. He explained to Margo that it would be more convenient for the girls if they didn't have to move around so much in the summer. They could spend a month with her at MarGrove and then move three miles down the road to spend time at his place. He had made a commitment years before to live as close to the twins as possible and had purchased a house in the Berkshires so he could be closer to their school. The penthouse in Miami was the next obvious move for him.

PART TWO

The world's light shines, shine as it will,
The world will love its darkness still.
I doubt though when the world's in hell,
It will not love its darkness half so well.
~ Richard Crashaw

Chapter Seven

Miami, July 1980
Paolo

"Alli, call an ambulance," Paolo screamed down the hall. "Something's wrong with your mother. I think she may have taken too many pills. We need help! Call 911 and then get Sam up here in a hurry!" As he rushed back to Margo's side, he heard Alli speaking to the 911 dispatcher.

"Hello, I'm at 5454 S. Margrove Lane. I think my mother has overdosed on something. We need an ambulance! I don't think she's responsive. No, I haven't seen her. Her boyfriend just yelled for me to get an ambulance. You've got to hurry!"

"Alli, go open the gate." Paolo knew he was shouting but the panic he felt was getting the best of him.

"Oh, God! I forgot," she called over her shoulder as she started down the stairs.

He tried to stay calm while he waited for her to push the call button for Sam and punch in the code to open the front gate.

Checking for Margo's pulse, he prayed the ambulance would get there quickly. This wasn't a death he wanted on his conscience.

For once, Paolo was glad that Sam lived on the estate. As much as he hated the man, he knew Sam would know what to do. When he heard voices coming from downstairs he ran to the landing and called Sam's name.

“I’m here, Paolo, what’s going on?” Sam sounded out of breath.

“Margo’s in trouble. I think she’s dying.”

Alli flippantly threw her arms in the air. “One more drama in the diva’s life!”she said to Sam’s back as he rushed for the stairs.

“Damn, Paolo. Get dressed and get out of this room before the EMTs get here. Do you want this all over the Miami Herald tomorrow?” Sam growled at Paolo as fury turned to concern. “How did she get the stuff this time?”

Paolo scrambled for an answer. One that would satisfy Sam without sending him over the edge. He knew Sam looked the other way when it came to Margo’s indulgences, but Sam never blinked if he thought he had to protect her from someone who might cause her harm.

Agony blended with sarcasm as they realized the gravity of the situation. “That’s a stupid question isn’t it? I should have asked you how much you gave her this time.”

“You’ve got it all wrong, Sam.” Paolo spoke quickly as he walked to the dressing area that separated the guest room from Margo’s bedroom. “She did this on her own. I had nothing to do with it.”

Kneeling over the inanimate body of his boss, Sam turned his full attention to her. “Margo! Margo!” He touched her face and then shook her shoulders. “Listen to me. Hang in there, help is on the way. Come on, Margo. Wake up. Don’t give in to this! Wake up.”

Paolo had finished putting on a shirt and slacks when he heard one of the EMTs talking to Sam. “How long has she been this way? Do you know what she took?”

“I was just called to the house myself. There’s the guy that might have answers for you.” Sam pointed toward Paolo and turned to leave the room. “Do you guys think she’s gonna be okay?”

“It all depends. She looks pretty out of it. We’ll start an IV and transport her right now. No more time to wait. Her blood pressure is dropping rapidly." The EMT looked at Sam with concern. "Meet us at the hospital and you can talk to the doctors."

Sam stopped abruptly and walked back in the room. "Wait, guys. Do you know who she is? We don't want everyone in the world to know about this."

"We know she's Margo. But right now our only concern is saving her life. We're taking her to Mercy Hospital. I'll call ahead and let them know we're bringing her in and we need privacy. That's the best I can do."

The EMT was all business and Paolo tried to stand well clear of where they were working. He wanted Sam to handle this and hoped the EMTs had forgotten he was in the room.

Watching as the EMTs wheeled the gurney down the hall toward the staircase, Paolo decided he needed to fix himself a drink.

He was out in the hallway when Sam walked up behind him and nearly shouted, "You made this mess! Damn you for keeping her so strung out."

Sam hit his fist against the wall and Paolo witnessed a side of the man he had never seen before. "Stay out of my way, Paolo. I don't want you to give me one more reason to get rid of you permanently." As the menace in Sam's words penetrated, Paolo stared at the melon-sized hole in the drywall and wondered what else Sam was capable of doing.

Sam was getting his emotions under control when Paolo caught a glimpse of Alli standing in the hall. There was a look of astonishment on her face. "We're okay, Alli. Sam's not going to do anything stupid."

"I'm fine, Alli." Sam's voice shook, but he looked calmer. "Go find Mrs. Davis and let her know what's happening and I'll call your dad. Where's Sunni?"

Alli shook her head as though to clear the picture she had of Sam's angry outburst. "She's not here. Are you sure you're all right?"

"Yeah, I'm fine and I'm sorry you had to see that little display. Our main worry is your mother. Go find Mrs. Davis."

He turned his back on her, picked up the phone, and dialed the number he knew by heart.

"Michael, it's Sam. We've got a problem. I just put Margo in an ambulance and she's on her way to Mercy Hospital. I'll meet you there in fifteen minutes."

He hung up the receiver and looked up at Paolo. "What's the story this time? We've got to be able to tell the doctors something and you're the one with the answers."

Paolo backed away to make sure he wasn't in range of Sam's fist. He knew better than to tangle with a former Navy SEAL. "I think she took pills. I found this empty bottle on the floor by the bed. That's all I know."

"There's more to this story and you know it. One way or another I'll find out what it is."

"Are you threatening me, Sam?" Paolo's voice was soft but sinister. He couldn't go one on one with the man, but he had ways to make sure that Sam paid for his threats.

"She was happy, Paolo. People who are happy don't take an overdose of pills!"

"One never knows what's really going on with Margo. Isn't that right Sam?"

"Get that pill bottle. You're coming with me to the hospital. The doctors and Michael will have a lot of questions and you better come up with some good answers."

The heat from Sam's rage was unmistakable and it unnerved Paolo. He handed Sam the pill bottle and headed down the stairs. He didn't want to tempt the man to kill him right there in the hall.

*****

Paolo knew why Margo took the pills, but it was not a story he was going to share with anyone. He had thought Margo was asleep earlier in the evening when he left her room to meet Alli in the pool house. Ohhh meu deus! I will never forget the look on Margo's face when she opened the door to the pool house and saw me enjoying her daughter.

He had planned to end the affair with Alli tonight, but she had been so enchanting, he didn't see how one more hour of pleasure would hurt anyone. He would enjoy himself and then tell Alli that it was over. Margo was home for the rest of the summer and he would no longer have need for Alli. But Margo foiled his plans by following him to the pool house. It was bad enough that Margo caught him having sex with another woman, but when she saw it was her daughter, she threw herself at both of them and began fighting and clawing like a mad woman.

"You little slut!" she'd screamed over and over again as she tried to get to Alli. He had shielded her as best he could while trying to defend himself from Margo's wrath.

"Stop now, Margo! Get hold of yourself." He grabbed her arms and pushed her away from them. Gasping for breath, he held her against the wall to prevent her from lashing out again.

"Alli, get out of here. Lock yourself in your room and don't come out until your mother has calmed down."

"Get out of my house, you little tramp! And take your lover with you. I never want to see either of you again. Never, do you hear me? Never!" Margo pulled away from him and ran back to the house.

"How could you do this to me? I hate you, Paolo," she sobbed as she ran from them. He heard the doors slamming as she went and then saw the lights come on in her room.

He pulled Alli up from the floor and threw her clothes at her. "Go to your father's until I can calm your mother down." As he spoke, he wondered how Alli could look so calm when their world had just unraveled.

Picking up the clothes he had thrown, she didn't put them on. Nothing about her conveyed worry or concern.

"No. I don't want my dad asking questions." Her look was defiant and seductive at the same time. "I'll stay here tonight and think of some reason to go to my grandmother's in the morning." Her voice grew soft and kitten-like. "I think we have some unfinished business, don't you?"

Smiling, she triumphantly moved across the room to where he was standing. The moon shining through the skylight of the pool house spotlighted her young, naked body and he watched her begin a slow, seductive dance. My beautiful little nymph--how could one so young have so much power? Reaching out, he roughly pulled her to him as desire overcame him. He would deal with Margo later.

Several hours passed before he and Alli walked back in the house. Just as he had allowed Alli to seduce him, he knew he held the same power over Margo. All she needed was a little time to calm down and a few minutes with a line of good coke. He knew he could make her forget why she had been so angry.

After he made sure that Alli was locked in her own room, he tried to open the door to Margo's bedroom. "Meu Deus! Margo, open this door." He knocked on the locked door several times, but there wasn't an answer.

His room adjoined hers through the dressing room and if she had not locked that door also he would be able to make amends. He hurried to his room and was relieved when the adjoining door was wide open. Glancing at his desk, he saw more evidence of Margo's violent anger. His files were torn and scattered around the room and she had ransacked everything around the desk. He clenched his fist and cursed the air. But, he had more important things to worry about than the mess in the room. Composing himself, he walked into Margo's room and glanced at the bed where she was sleeping. It surprised him that she looked so peaceful and he was hesitant to disturb the tranquility. Taking a step closer to the bed, his thoughts shattered when he realized with a jolt that she wasn't peaceful at all.

"Alli, call an ambulance," he'd screamed down the hall.

*****

Paolo sat on one side of the ER waiting room watching the interaction between Michael and his daughter. He hadn't witnessed this family dynamic before and was curious to see how she responded to her father. Alli was very quiet. In this setting, she seemed like any other teenager concerned about the well-being of her mother. She was holding her father's hand and assuring him that Margo would be all right. My god, what have I been doing? She is a child!

He had been so caught up in the sexual energy that always seemed to surround Alli that he had not allowed himself to think of or deal with the reality of her age. And now, Margo knew the truth. If she survives, what will she do? Will I go to jail because of Alli? He found it hard to breath and began to sweat. The noise in his head was deafening. I've got to get out of here! He stood and started to walk toward the exit.

"Wait a minute! I want to talk to you," Michael called.

Paolo stopped and waited for Michael to catch up with him, but he didn't want to talk to Michael. All he wanted to do was get out of the hospital. "What do you want?"

"What happened to her? I know you know what this is all about. Margo may die because of you and I want to know what you did to her!" Michael's voice was low, but Paolo sensed an edge of rage in every word.

"Who do you think you are?" Paolo's stance was arrogant and he almost snarled. "I did nothing. I wasn't even with her when this happened. Get out of my way, Michael." Paolo turned away, but Michael grabbed his arm.

"If she dies, I'll kill you!" Michael's face was red and his features were distorted. His words were barely a whisper, but his eyes let Paolo know that the threat was real.

"Daddy, no!" Paolo looked over Michael's shoulder into Alli's horrified face. He pulled away from Michael's grasp and hurried down the hospital corridor.

As he reached the exit doors, Sunni and a young man he recognized as a member of Margo's band rushed toward him.

"Paolo, what happened? Is mother all right?" Sunni pleaded. "Why are you leaving?"

*****

He was in his car driving away from the hospital before he realized that he had not answered Sunni. It didn't matter. His mind was on getting away–from the hospital, from the situation with Margo, and from Alli. He would fly to Brazil as soon as he could get a flight out of Miami.

He parked his car in front of the house and used his key to go in through one of the side doors. The house was too quiet and every small sound he made seemed magnified. The tap of his footsteps across the marble foyer drummed in his ears and he had never before noticed that the stairs creaked. He felt watched as he made his way toward the guest room and he chided himself for feeling paranoid.

Locking the bedroom door behind him, he turned on the light and noticed the telegram on the floor. Most likely Mrs. Davis had slipped it under the door while he was at the hospital. Opening the envelope he read the short message from his grandfather. He picked up a book that was lying on the nightstand and hurled it across the room. This has to be a mistake. Tomas wouldn't betray my trust. He reached for the telephone.

"Tomas, it's Paolo." He fought to regain his composure and spoke each word slowly and distinctly. "We need a flight out of Miami tonight." He waited for Tomas to respond. "Several things have come up and grandfather needs for us to come home. Call me at this number when everything is arranged." He had to get off the phone while he could still control his anger. "I'll pick you up on the way to the airport."

Tomas Labato, his cousin and business partner, always stayed at the Mayfair Hotel in Coconut Grove when they were in town. "Don't question me Tomas. We need to go to Rio tonight. We have business at home." He tried hard to disguise his rage. "Grandfather sent a telegram. Apparently it's urgent and he wants to see both of us."

He hung up the phone before he gave anything else away. It would be very dangerous for him to let Tomas know their grandfather had discovered a discrepancy in some accounts and suspected Tomas of stealing from the business.

He was packing his suitcases when the phone rang. Even though he had a private line in the house and knew no one else would pick up the phone, he rushed to answer it. "What do you mean?" He shouted. "We need to leave tonight." He felt the tension building as he waited for Tomas to explain. "If that's the best you can do, I'll pick you up at eight o'clock in the morning."

Slamming down the phone's receiver, he began pacing the room. They had missed the last flight out and wouldn't be able to leave until the morning. He wanted to laugh at the predicament he was in–if he stayed in Miami he would have to face Margo and Alli, and if he went home he would have to face his grandfather. Which one is the more formidable foe? he agonized.

The wet bar looked inviting and he mixed himself a scotch and water, heavy on the scotch. He downed the fiery liquid, but it didn't relieve the tension or take away his anxious edge. So he poured another–straight up this time. He needed to calm down, but he kept pacing from one side of the room to the other, stepping over all the torn and crumbled paper. He wished he could call Mrs. Davis to come and clean the room, but he didn't feel like explaining what had caused the mess. The room was large and luxurious–Margo had thought of everything when she had it decorated for him. One side of the room was set up as an office/living area with a large mahogany desk, sofa, and matching chair. It included a wet bar, television, and stereo system. On the other side was a king-sized bed, armoire, and reading area. As he looked around, he knew he would miss coming here.

After his fourth drink, he opened the French doors to the balcony and stood in the doorway. Even though it was one o'clock in the morning, the moon was still high enough in the sky to illuminate the bay. The breeze blowing in from the Atlantic tousled his hair and cooled his face. It was the kind of night that made Miami famous, but he had things to do so he could leave it behind.

Pulling a sheet of writing paper from the desk, he hastily wrote Alli a note. *Alli, My Little One, Your mother will forgive you, but she will never forgive me. So sad that this is our ending - you are my joy and I will miss you. Paolo.* He sealed the envelope and decided that he would slip it under Alli's door before morning. He was jittery and his nerves were shot. It was hours before he would meet Tomas but he knew he couldn't sleep. He had heard Alli and Sunni return from the hospital, but it had been hours since he had heard anyone moving in the house. There were no lights on in the guest house and he decided Sam was either asleep or still at the hospital. Perhaps a swim would make me feel calmer. He walked down the stairs carrying the half empty scotch bottle with him.

He walked through the house cautiously, listening for the sound of voices or any other indication that someone else might be awake. When he reached the pool house door, he thought he heard footsteps and froze. His breathing slowed. All his senses were heightened--someone is watching me. A feeling of someone's presence loomed just beyond his vision and a knot of fear formed in his gut. Waiting, barely breathing, he listened. His mind and body jumped to high alert even though he couldn't see or hear anything unusual. The prickling energy of the unknown made him shiver.

Inside the pool house, he opened the cabinet, grabbed some swim trunks, and changed out of his slacks and polo shirt. The cool night air was refreshing and he almost opted to just sit in one of the lounge chairs beside the pool, but he knew a vigorous swim would help him get rid of all his tension and nervous energy. He walked out to the end of the diving board and dove into the water. Yes, this is what I need. And he began to swim lap after lap, pounding the water with his hands and kicking furiously.

The pace was frantic and he kept it up for a few minutes before he leaned on the side of the pool to catch his breath. There was nothing out of order; still he felt it. His eyes darted to every corner of the patio and his ears strained to hear any sound of movement or breathing. The moonlight was so bright he could see almost every corner of the yard and the wall that surrounded the back of the house. The gate leading to the boathouse was closed, so he assumed it was locked. As he treaded water in the eerie shadows created by the moon, his skin began to tingle and he felt someone behind him. He shook his head and decided the alcohol was making him paranoid. Silently he swam across to the other edge of the pool and listened to the night sounds–crickets chirping, waves lapping against the sea wall, wind rustling the trees. There was nothing unusual but he couldn't shake the uneasy feeling of being watched. He looked for a slight movement or a shape that shouldn't be there. Then he felt rather than heard someone whisper his name. "Who's there?" he called. He waited for an answer. This is crazy! I need to clear my head. He let go of the side of the pool and began to swim vigorously.

Without warning, the weight of someone's body was painfully crushing his back. He was being forced to the bottom of the pool and no matter how he tried, he couldn't free himself from the heaviness that was holding him down.

Oh meu Deus, I can't breathe! I can't move my arms or legs. What's happening to me? He struggled against the weight–fought to rise to the surface. He needed air, not the water that was filling his mouth and lungs.

Then, there was only the blackness and the silence.

Chapter Eight

Alli

Sunni flew into the emergency room waiting area, almost knocked Paolo down, and immediately began asking a million questions.

Alli looked at her in disgust. "Sunni, you're making a scene. Sit down, for crying out loud, and give Dad a chance to tell you what's going on."

Alli's voice had stopped Sunni in mid-sentence and she dutifully took the seat next to her father.

"All we know is your mother combined alcohol and pills and is in serious trouble. They haven't told us much, but I'm sure we'll know something soon." Michael's voice was soothing and Alli saw a calming change come over her sister as she listened to him.

"Mark, what are you doing here? Has the news already gotten to the band?" Michael seemed startled to see the young man.

"No, I don't think so, Michael. Sunni and I had gone to dinner and when I dropped her off at the house, Mrs. Davis told us that Margo had been rushed to the hospital, so I drove Sunni here."

"I don't want any publicity on this, Mark. If anyone recognizes you, they'll start asking questions. Perhaps it would be better if you left." Michael's tone was matter-of-fact and left no doubt that he didn't want Mark there. "Oh, thanks for bringing Sunni to the hospital. I'll call you tomorrow with any news."

Alli saw a look of astonishment cross Mark's face. She knew as well as he did that Michael had dismissed him. She continued to watch him as he quickly recovered. Without another word, he walked over and placed his hand on her sister's shoulder. "Sunni, call me if you need anything. I'll try to see you tomorrow."

After she watched Mark walk to the door, she leaned over to her sister. "Who in the world is that? I can't believe you're dating someone and haven't said a word to me!"

"He plays guitar for Mom, Alli. And we're not dating. He's just a friend."

"I don't want you seeing the guys in the band, Sunni. Mark's too old for you and his life style is too chaotic. Stay away from him."

Alli smiled as her father jumped to interfere in Sunni's life.

Michael touched his daughter's arm. "I'm serious, Sunni."

Sunni bolted out of the chair and turned to look at her father. "Wait a minute, Daddy. Are you telling me I can't see him again?" Hands on hips, her posture and tone registered surprise at her father's demand.

Alli was astonished that Sunni was standing up for herself. This guy must be something special for Sunni to talk back.

"Yes, that's what I'm saying. You don't know what you're getting into." Michael continued.

"You're wrong about him." Sunni's voice did not waver as she looked her father in the eyes. "I can't believe you would tell me not to see him again. I think that's my choice to make, not yours."

Alli was enjoying the exchange between her father and sister. Sunni, the dutiful daughter, was actually standing her ground. She smiled to think what would happen if her father knew about the men in her life, particularly Paolo DaSilva.

"Dad, go easy on her. She's never dated anyone before and this guy might actually be good for her." Alli's voice was playful, but her mind had already jumped to the possibility of seeing Mark again. He might be fun to have around.

*****

It was after midnight when the doctor came to talk with them about Margo. He talked in medical terms about her condition and what the repercussions of the suicide attempt might be to her physical health.

"She will have to stay in the hospital for at least another day or two. Physically, we can provide short-term crisis care. But she needs a long-term addiction program and emotional health care. I have scheduled a psychological evaluation for later this morning."

"Wait a minute. Are you saying she tried to commit suicide? This isn't an accidental drug overdose?" Michael stood up and faced the physician. "I'm having a hard time accepting that."

"Mr. Anderson, I assure you I wouldn't make a statement like this if I wasn't positive. Mrs. Anderson is very weak and disoriented, but we have discussed the precipitating factors. This was not an accident."

Michael's head fell forward and he closed his eyes. "She seemed so happy. The tour went well, her new album is a success, and she was looking forward to a relaxing summer. This doesn't add up."

He turned to his daughters, "Do you know something I don't know? Did she and Paolo have an argument?"

Alli looked at her sister and shrugged. So Sunni replied, "When I left the house to have dinner with Mark, everything was okay. I met her in the hall and she seemed really pleased that Mark was taking me to dinner. She was smiling and joking with me about him. She didn't seem depressed or worried about anything." Sunni looked bewildered. Her voice broke and tears rolled down her cheeks. "She was happy, Daddy. She looked so happy."

"Alli, do you know of anything?"

Eyes wide, she let out a dramatic sigh. "I don't have a clue, Dad. You know how Margo is. One minute she's on Mt. Everest, the next she's in Death Valley." Alli looked flushed. "Why are you looking at me like that? Death Valley's a place. Did you think I was referring to her condition?" she asked her father.

"I didn't know I was looking at you in a particular way," Michael said slowly. "All I did was ask you a question."

But Alli knew differently. Her father's eyes were piercing and they were accusing her. There is no way he knows anything! She turned back to the magazine she was reading to escape his look.

"Girls, I'll stay here, but I think you should go back to the house. You need some sleep. There's nothing you can do for your mother tonight. Alli, do you have your car here or do I need to call for a car?"

"I've got the car. Sunni can ride with me. We'll be fine." Alli was relieved that her father wanted her to leave the hospital. He was making her very anxious.

*****

"Okay, Sunni. Tell me about this Mark." As soon as Alli got in the car, she began quizzing her sister. "How long has this been going on?"

"Nothing is going on. Mark plays in Mom's band and I met him while I was on the tour. He lives here in Miami."

"He asked you to dinner, Sunni. Don't tell me there's nothing going on!"

"He's got a girlfriend." She didn't want to talk to her sister about Mark. "Now, you answer a few questions."

"Like what?"

"Did Mom find out about you and Paolo? That's the only thing I can think of that would cause her to do something this drastic."

Alli nearly choked. It must be the twin thing, she thought. We really can read each other's minds sometimes. "You're way off base. There's nothing between me and Paolo. So, like you said, give it up and leave me alone."

"If it wasn't something you did, then what was it?"

"Ask her. She's the one who knows."

*****

It was three in the morning and Alli was restless. She tossed and turned and couldn't sleep. Her mind was playing the scene in the pool house over and over–the look of betrayal on her mother's face; the look of shocked embarrassment on Paolo's. She had felt so detached while she was in the pool house, like she was watching a movie instead of her own life. Until this moment, it had all been a game and she hadn't given any thought to how her actions would impact anyone else.

She jumped out of bed in an attempt to leave her thoughts behind, but she couldn't shake a sense of dread. Oh, my God. What if she dies and it's all my fault? No, that's not true. She's a very unstable woman. I didn't hand her the pills.

Alli wasn't accustomed to accepting responsibility for her actions or for considering whether she might hurt someone else. But, tonight she had seen the pain on her mother's face and she couldn't erase it from her thoughts. She pulled back the curtain and looked across the yard to the bay. The water was still and calm and, like the siren's song, beckoned to her. Nothing good will come from these thoughts. I need to get out of here.

The water was waiting for her and if she could get there, it would help her forget. Changing into shorts and a t-shirt, she quietly left the house. She walked in a trance across the lawn to the dock, but her reverie was broken when she saw that the Ski Nautique was already in the water. Who would have forgotten to take the boat out of the water? Oh, well. Easier for me.

She entered the boat house and turned the light on so she could see the key that was hanging on the wall, but it wasn't there. She walked back down the dock and climbed aboard the boat. When she reached the pilot's seat and reached toward the ignition, the key was there. Who would be stupid enough to leave the key in the ignition? Sam will have to look into this. She would have preferred to take the larger Sun Ray, but the ski boat was in the water and ready to go.

Alli was in her element on the water. Backing the boat out of the slip, she headed east toward Key Biscayne. For hours she moved across the water trying to tame the demons that were doing battle in her mind. She'd always loved the bay and the feel of the wind in her face as the boat sped through the rippling waves. The running lights on the boat helped her see the channel markers and she was experienced enough to know that if she went outside the channel she could ground the boat in the shallow waters.

Off the eastern end of Key Biscayne she slowed the boat and came to a stop. Her mind was calmer now, but she still couldn't wrap her thoughts around the possibility that Margo might die. She didn't know what she was going to say to her mother if she recovered and she was afraid that her mother's demand that she leave the house was real. She didn't know what her future relationship with Paolo would look like. And, she couldn't imagine what her father's and Sunni's reactions would be when they learned the truth. She sat quietly in the boat, lost in her thoughts. She gazed at the Miami skyline as it became more visible in the first light of morning and she listened to the water lapping against the side of the boat. Scanning the area for boat lights, she saw that several early morning fishermen already had their lines in the water hoping for a catch. She was calmer, but she didn't want to go back to the house. She didn't want to go back to the drama and chaos that she had created.

Suddenly a bright light illuminated the boat and she covered her eyes. She heard the sound of an approaching boat and wondered why it seemed to be easing closer to her. "Ahoy. It's the Coast Guard patrol. Is everything okay? Are you all right?" The man's voice was loud and clear as he shouted to her through some kind of bullhorn.

"Yes sir. Everything's fine. I couldn't sleep so I thought a spin around the bay might do me some good."

"Do you live around here? Are you familiar with these waters? It can be treacherous if you don't stay in the channel."

"I live in the Grove and I've been taking a boat out on this bay for years. Really, I'm fine. In fact, I was thinking it's about time to head back to our dock. The sun will be up soon. Thanks for checking on me."

She started the engine and turned the boat toward home. Great! All I need is the Coast Guard escorting me home and waking up everyone in the house. When she looked behind her, the Coast Guard boat was headed around the other end of Key Biscayne.

*****

Back in her room, she stretched out across the bed and slept for several hours before she became aware of Sunni shaking her shoulders.

"Get up, sleepy head. We've got to go to the hospital to see Mom." Sunni's voice woke her from a deep sleep and her body felt heavy and sluggish.

"Go away. I need to sleep." Alli muttered as she rolled over and pulled the pillow over her head.

"Come on, Alli. It's nine o'clock and I know Daddy is expecting us to be there." Sunni was insistent. "Mrs. Dee has breakfast ready. I'll meet you in the kitchen in ten minutes."

Sometimes Alli detested her sister. Sunni was always the one concerned with appearances and getting her brownie points.

"I'm not going. Leave me alone!"

Sunni pulled the pillow away and looked down into Alli's face. "Get out of this bed right now or I'll have Sam come up here and carry you downstairs."

"You're such a pain, Sunni. It's not going to matter whether I get to the hospital at nine or at noon. What can I do to help her come back from her stupor? You go--be the good little girl. Hold her hand and tell her what a great mother she's been." Alli's agitation was showing. "I didn't sleep last night and I'm exhausted. Get out of here and don't threaten me with Sam."

She listened as Sunni stomped out of the room and slammed the door behind her. Her last thought before she fell back to sleep was pity. Poor Sunni. She keeps pretending we have a normal mother who loves us.

Sunni

Sunni marveled that she could be giddy and happy in one minute and overwhelmed with fear and concern the next. Last evening had started with romantic promise and ended in the ER at Mercy Hospital. Even though she was concerned, she had been assured that her mother wouldn't die.

Breathing easier, she knew she could eat the wonderful breakfast Mrs. Davis had prepared. The omelet was fluffy and filled with things she liked–ham, cheese, mushrooms, tomatoes.

"Mrs. Dee, thanks for remembering that I don't like peppers or onions." Sunni smiled at the woman who was more like a mother than a housekeeper, and continued eating.

Mrs. Davis, or Mrs. Dee as she had always called her, was a tall, blonde woman in her late fifties with an easy smile. She was the girls' nurturer, teacher, comforter, and substitute mother, and Sunni loved her. She thought the woman was attractive and wondered why she had never remarried after her husband died of cancer fifteen years ago.

"By the way, have you seen Paolo this morning?"

"No, Sunni. I was beginning to wonder where he is. You know he's always the first one in the kitchen every morning. He loves to make the coffee before I get here." Mrs. Davis smiled. "I don't think he likes my coffee. You know," she changed her stance and her accent as she tried to mimic Paolo, "it's not Brazilian enough, Doña Davis."

Sunni laughed at Mrs. Davis and her imitation of Paolo. "Maybe he went to the hospital early."

"If he did, he didn't drive his car. It's still in the driveway," Mrs. Davis replied.

"That's strange. Have you seen Sam this morning?"

"He came in about an hour ago and said he was going over to the hospital. I haven't seen him since." Mrs. Davis walked over to the table with a platter of fruit. "Honey, is your sister coming down for breakfast? If she isn't, I'd like to get to my other chores."

"I don't think so. Go on and do what you need to do. I'll finish up and put my dishes in the dishwasher. Then I'm heading for the hospital."

"I'll have lunch ready for you at one o'clock. Why don't you ask your father and Sam to come for lunch? Has anyone thought to call Miss Finley? She'll need to know that your mother is in the hospital."

"You're right. I'll ask Dad if he called her."

Sunni jumped when the phone rang, but was pleased when Mrs. Davis handed her the receiver. "It's Mr. Sanders calling."

"Good morning, Mark. You're calling early." She blushed at the sound of his voice, the feel of his name on her lips. "No, we haven't had a call this morning. But I plan to go to the hospital as soon as I finish breakfast." She paused for a minute and listened. "Yes, I'll call you when I know something."

She hung up the phone and thought of Mark as she finished her eggs. Their dinner had been so romantic. He had taken her to a small Italian restaurant in Coconut Grove–red checked table cloths, candles, roaming violinists, and good food. They had laughed and talked for hours about everything from music to future plans to silly stuff like the difference in the beach sand in California and Florida.

She remembered his eyes and his smile; the way he turned his head when he looked at her; his hand on her back as they walked from the car to the restaurant; and the way he kissed her when they pulled up in front of the house. It was not the kiss of a friend–it was the kiss of someone who wanted more and all of her senses were alive to his touch. She didn't want to leave the car. Then the mood was shattered when Mrs. Davis called from the front door and told them Margo was in the hospital.

She shook her head and tried not to think of Mark. When the dishes were in the dishwasher, she walked out the side door to the garage and got in her car. At this hour on a Saturday morning, she wouldn't have much traffic. She and her sister had been given new cars for graduation–she had asked for a shiny black Pontiac Firebird. But Alli had chosen a silver Mercedes convertible. So like Alli to try and outdo me, but my Firebird will be more practical for Sarah Lawrence and the winters in New York.

Her dad was already sitting in the waiting room when she arrived on the third floor of the hospital. He was reading the paper and drinking a cup of coffee, and Sunni thought he looked exhausted. "Hi, Daddy. You don't look like you got much sleep last night. Did you even go home?" She sat down beside her dad and patted him on the knee.

"Hi, sweetheart. Yeah, I got a few hours. How 'bout you?" Michael smiled at her. "Where's your sister?"

"She had trouble sleeping so she'll be here later. Any news about Mom?"

"She's doing as well as expected. They let me see her a couple of hours ago. She was groggy, but she opened her eyes several times while I was there. The doctor is concerned because there was cocaine in her system on top of the alcohol and sleeping pills."

"Thank you for not sugar coating things for me, Daddy." She'd always been able to talk to her father more openly than Alli could. "It makes me sad. I was sure she was doing better." Sunni put her chin in her hands and felt the hopelessness of one who loves an addict. "I saw her take a few drinks of wine on the tour, but I never saw her with drugs."

"I think something happened yesterday to trigger her reaction. She's been messed up before, Sunni, but she's never tried to kill herself." Michael looked disheartened and Sunni felt compassion for him. Even though her parents were divorced, she always sensed that a strong connection remained between them.

"Where are they going to take her for rehab?"

"I was thinking we'd take her back to MarGrove in a few days. We'd have to bring in some full time nurses and a good psychiatrist to help with whatever drove her to suicide. Your mother hates the rehab centers so much that I think she'll get better faster if she's at home."

Sunni didn't agree with her dad, but it was not her decision. She stood up and started to walk away. "I'm going to the pay phone. I told Mark I'd call him as soon as I knew something. He's really worried about her. By the way, did you call Lara?"

"Yeah, I called her this morning. She'll be here sometime this afternoon. But, Sunni, there's no need to share all of this information with Mark. Just tell him she's doing better. I'll call the band and crew when I know more. They're all on vacation and I don't want to worry them until I know what's really going on." A look of curiosity came over his face. "Honey, I'm sorry about last night. I didn't know you and Mark were friends. What's that all about?"

"You're right. We're friends. He was fun to talk to while I was on your tour. There's nothing more."

"It's not a good idea for you to date one of the guys in the band. They can be pretty wild sometime. They're older than you and most of them are married."

"Mark's not wild, Daddy. He's not like that at all. Besides, he already has a girlfriend."

She walked down the hall to the row of phone booths and dialed Mark's number. After a few rings, a woman answered the phone.

"I'm sorry, I think I have the wrong number. I was calling Mark Sanders."

She listened as the voice on the other end of the line told her she had the right number and then asked who she was. When Sunni identified herself, the young woman's tone of voice changed. Sunni's gripped the phone tightly as Jocelyn McDeal introduced herself and asked if her mother was doing better. What is she doing at his apartment so early this morning? It was one thing to know about Jocelyn and quite another to hear her voice. Without another word she placed the phone back on the hook and walked away.

*****

The morning dragged on and on. She had been allowed to see her mother for a few minutes, but Margo did not wake up or respond to anything Sunni said. It had been a shock to see her hooked up to so many things–IVs, monitors and something that looked like a restraint. When she questioned her dad about the restraints, he told her that earlier in the morning, Margo had tried to rip out the IV and they had taken measures to make sure she didn't succeed. To Sunni's eyes the whole scene was out of a horror movie–dim lights, sounds of machines, eerie shadows, and the paleness of her mother's skin.

Silently, Sunni wept and wondered what disappointments and feelings had the power to reduce her vibrant mother to the frail, sad woman lying in the hospital bed. "I love you, Momma," she whispered. "Why can't you love me?" Suddenly she felt her father's arms around her and heard him telling her that everything was going to be all right. "Daddy, I wish I understood her. I wish I knew why I'm not part of her life."

"Sunni, your mother was so young when you were born. Her career was just beginning to soar and she didn't know how to be both a star and a mother. I'm sorry it's been this way for you and Alli. If your mother would let you get close to her, I think you would really like her." He smiled and lifted her chin so he could see her face. "In the meantime, you've got me. You know I love you, don't you?"

"I've always known that." She pulled out of his arms and found a tissue to dry her eyes. "Sometimes it just gets to me."

"I know, sweetheart. It gets to me, too."

"By the way, Mrs. Dee is making lunch for all of us. You will come back to the house, won't you?"

Michael hesitated. "I don't think so, but thank Mrs. Davis for me."

"Why not? I bet she's probably fixed something special."

"I don't think I want to see Paolo right now. You understand, don't you? You go on. I think I'll go back to my place and take a little nap. I'll check on your mom again later."

When she got back to the house, Sam greeted her in the driveway. "Is your mom any better this afternoon? She didn't look too good when I left the hospital a few hours ago."

"She's still hooked up to all those machines. Dad said he wants to bring her back to MarGrove in a few days, but I'm betting they send her to rehab again."

"You're probably right, Sunni. I'll call your dad later for the details." Sam started to walk toward the house. But he turned. "Sunni, did you happen to see Paolo at the hospital?"

"No, I think he must have slept in or something. He didn't come down for his coffee or breakfast while I was here. Why?"

"It's probably nothing. But nobody has seen him today and Tomas is concerned. He's in the kitchen with Mrs. Davis."

Sunni and Sam joined Alli and Tomas at the table. The conversation focused on Margo's condition and Paolo's absence.

"Did you talk to him last night?" Sam inquired, looking at Tomas.

"He called me around eleven o'clock last night. I think he had just come from the hospital. We had business this morning and he was supposed to pick me up at the hotel at eight. But he never showed. I tried calling him, but when he didn't answer, I came over here."

"Alli, when did you last see him?" Sam continued his questions.

"I saw him out at the pool house around eight-thirty last night. Then all hell broke loose in the house and I didn't see him after he left the hospital." Alli didn't take her eyes off Sam and she was frowning.

"How about you, Sunni?"

"Last night at the hospital. I thought I'd see him at breakfast, but he didn't come to the kitchen before I left to go see Mom."

"Okay, we need to see if we can find some clue about where he might be. Tomas, you go with Mrs. Davis to check his room. Alli, you take the rest of the house, especially your mother's room. Sunni, you go out to the pool house. And, I'll check his car and the boat house."

Chapter Nine

Margo

"Where am I? Somebody help me." Margo's words were garbled, her mouth was dry, and her head hurt.

She tried to open her eyes wider, but all she could see in the dim light was the ceiling and white walls. She was alone and nothing looked familiar. Fear took over her thoughts and she wanted to run. But when she tried to move there was a heavy weight on her chest and her arms and legs were lifeless.

"Oh, God, somebody help me!" she tried to shout but all she heard was a whisper. Oh, God, no! What's happened to my voice?"

She panicked–her body broke into a sweat even though she felt chilled. Her heart began to race, she couldn't breathe, and she heard herself screaming, "Get out of my sight. I never want to see either one of you again!"

When the nurse rushed into the room, Margo was gasping for breath and struggling against the restraints on her arms.

"Mrs. Anderson, it's okay. You're okay. Listen to me, please. You're okay." The nurse's hand was on her shoulder and she was speaking softly. "Mrs. Anderson! Lie still and listen to me."

Margo felt a cool cloth on her forehead and heard a voice crooning to her, "You're fine. Calm down. That's good, take another deep breath. I've replaced your oxygen, so it should be easier for you to breathe. That's better. You're doing fine."

"Mother," she whispered. "Mom, help me." She shook her head and opened her eyes. "You're not my mother! Who are you?"

"Mrs. Anderson!" The voice jolted Margo and she took another breath. "My name is Donna and I'm here to help you. Take a breath. Good, that's good. Your mother will be able to visit later, but right now I need for you to lie still and try to calm down."

Margo felt her body begin to relax, but she fought to keep her eyes open. She didn't want to go back to the darkness, but she was slipping and she couldn't stop.

The nurse turned to Michael. "She's okay. I gave her something to calm her down and she'll probably be drowsy for several hours. Why don't you try talking to her? I think she needs to hear a familiar voice."

"How long will she be like this? She keeps slipping in and out, and she seems so afraid." Michael looked at his ex-wife with concern. "I've never seen her thrashing around like that. It's almost like her body is trying to exorcise a demon."

"She's coming back from a dark place. It will take some time for her to be fully with us, Mr. Anderson. But she's doing fine." The nurse smiled warmly and touched his arm. "Talk to her for a few minutes, then why don't you go home and get some rest. It may be hours before she really wakes up." The nurse started out of the room. "We have her monitored. We won't let her get in trouble." She smiled and pulled the door almost closed behind her.

Michael moved over to the bed and looked down at the troubled face of the woman he loved. "Why did you do this, Margo? What made you do this to yourself? I need some answers." He whispered these questions then continued in a regular tone of voice.

"Sweetheart. I've been working on your next tour and I think you're going to love it. Do you want me to tell you about it?" He was rambling, but the nurse had told him to talk to her. "If you don't want to hear about the tour, let's talk about what we're going to do for the summer. What if we took the girls and went to the islands for a month? We could rent a house on the beach in Eleuthera and it would be like old times, Margo–you, me, Sunni and Alli. Wouldn't that be fun?"

Her eyes opened wide, color rose in her cheeks and she seemed to gasp for air. "Never see Alli again," she whispered. "Never." As quickly as her eyes opened, they closed and her breathing stilled.

"What are you talking about, Margo? You're not making sense. Tell me what you mean." There was no reply.

*****

"Mrs. Anderson, it's time to wake up. Come on, open your eyes." The doctor was issuing a command and she was trying to do what he asked. It was so hard to focus and all she wanted was to sleep. "That's right, open your eyes and look at me."

The man looking down at her was tall, grey haired and thin. She had never seen him before and she wondered if she had been out with him before she got so sleepy. But he had on a white coat and a stethoscope hung around his neck.

"Who are you?" She tried to talk but her throat hurt and her mouth was dry. She wet her lips and tried again, "Who are you?"

"Hello, Mrs. Anderson. I'm glad you decided to wake up and join us in this life for a little longer."

"What are you talking about?" All she could do was whisper.

"How are you feeling? You look so much better today." He was checking his chart as he talked. "Do you remember why you're here?"

"Where am I?" Again, her voice was a whisper. But she wasn't trying to whisper and it scared her. "What's wrong with my voice?"

"You're at Mercy Hospital. Do you know where that is?"

"It's near my house in Coconut Grove. But why am I here?" She tried to project her voice, but there was no strength behind her words. "What's wrong with my voice?"

"Apparently you took a few too many pills and had way too much to drink. Not a good combination for you or your voice. It is most likely a temporary side effect." He pulled a chair up to the bed and motioned for the attending nurse to move from view and stand closer to the door. "Mrs. Anderson, I need you to answer some questions. By the way, I'm Dr. Gentry. They called me when you were brought to the emergency room."

"What are you trying to tell me, Dr. Gentry? Did I have an accident or something?"

The pain across her forehead was making it hard for her to think and the loss of her voice made everything else irrelevant. Who would she be without her voice? A sob welled up in her throat. "I can't remember." She placed her hands over her eyes. "Please let me go back to sleep. Please go away."

"I know this isn't easy so we can save the talk for later, but right now I need you to get up out of the bed. The nurse and I will help you." He put his hand under her head and began to slowly lift it off the pillow.

She groaned and gagged as the dizziness and nausea overcame her. "Please, no. I can't do this."

"We'll take it slow. We won't rush you. But I need you to sit on the side of the bed." He stopped talking as he and the nurse worked to help her sit up and swing her legs off the bed.

"Don't let go of me," she begged and tears began to roll down her cheeks. "I think I'm going to be sick."

"We won't let go of you. I promise." His smile was caring and his voice was soothing. "You're doing great. Just a little more and you'll be sitting up."

The nurse was on one side of her and the doctor on the other. Their hands were keeping her steady and as she felt their strength, she relaxed somewhat.

"Ah, that's good. I can feel the tension leaving your body. Relaxing will make this so much easier. You don't have to sit here for long." With his free hand, he picked up the chart and began to look down at it. "Mrs. Anderson, where do you live?"

"Miami," she whispered, then added, "at MarGrove."

"When's your birthday? And do you have children?"

"Stupid questions." She was getting agitated and no matter how hard she tried, all she could do was whisper. "I need to lie back down."

"After we talk for a few minutes, you can go back to sleep. Please answer my questions."

Margo resented the intrusion of this doctor but she realized that he wouldn't leave her alone until he got what he came for. She looked around the room and didn't recognize one thing. It was all too confusing, but the longer she sat on the edge of the bed, the more focused she became. The feeling of weakness and lethargy was very strong but she didn't feel as queasy.

"My birthday is August 29th. I have twin girls. That's it for today." She lay back down and closed her eyes. She heard the doctor speak a few words to the nurse but she couldn't make out what he was saying. In a few minutes she heard a door close and knew they had left her room.

There was something she needed to remember. She stared up at the ceiling and wondered why nothing came to her mind. She knew it was important, but she didn't have the energy to recall whatever it was. Perhaps if she rested and came back to it later it would be easier to remember.

She closed her eyes and tried to get settled in the bed. But her mind was foggy and her body felt so heavy. She had so many questions, but no answers. If only Michael was here, he would know what it is. That was the solution–she would have to remember to ask Michael. A smile crossed her lips as she drifted off to sleep.

*****

"Mr. Anderson, I don't think this would be a good time to give Mrs. Anderson that kind of news. Are you sure the man is missing? He knows how ill she is, doesn't he? Her emotional state is too fragile for this information and she doesn't need any more high drama. It's too unsettling." The doctor paused. "You do remember that we are dealing with a woman who just tried to kill herself?"

"Dr. Gentry, you don't have to remind me of Margo's situation. If she hears about this from anyone but me, she'll be devastated. I can assure you, I have her best interests in mind," Michael said in an arrogant tone of voice.

"Mr. Anderson, you will have to take my lead on this. Her condition is fragile. So fragile that she will need long-term assistance if she is to fully recover. To further complicate her precarious emotional state, her heart and liver have been significantly impacted by her lifestyle choices. She needs psychiatric and medical attention. Her body can no longer tolerate the alcohol and drug abuse." His voice was low but uncompromising.

"I hope my message is understood. If my patient continues to abuse her body, she will die. I don't think you grasp just how serious the situation is."

"She had a few drinks and took too many pills by mistake. This was an accident, Dr. Gentry. Margo simply had an accident."

"The tests say otherwise, Mr. Anderson. That's why I'm recommending rest and long-term rehabilitation for my patient. There is an excellent facility in Boca Raton that treats dual disorders. It is very discrete and her privacy will be protected. Since you have her power of attorney and are advising her, you need to have this conversation with her as soon as possible. An immediate intervention needs to take place."

"Are you serious? Do you know who she is? In two months she will be starting a seven month tour that includes Europe and South America. Long-term rehab is out of the question."

"Perhaps you didn't understand what I was saying, Mr. Anderson. So let me be very clear. She just survived a suicide attempt, and we are grateful for that, but her major organs have been damaged by her long-term consumption of alcohol and drugs. If this behavior continues, you probably won't have to schedule any more tours. Margo is on a self-destructive path and it is killing her. Added to that, I don't know the extent of damage that has been done to her vocal chords, but there has been some. We need to run some tests."

"Are you saying a few months of rehab and she'll be okay?"

"No, Mr. Anderson. I'm saying that she needs at least a year, maybe more. And, that depends on test results."

Michael's eyes widened. "That's impossible. She can't take that much time off."

"I'm sorry to hear you say that. I'm sure that once you've thought about it you'll change your mind. Since we don't seem to have anything else to discuss, I have another patient to see."

"Wait. Let's talk this through some more. Maybe we can reach some kind of compromise."

"In life and death situations, Mr. Anderson, there are no compromises." Dr. Gentry's voice was icy.

"Oh, my God." Michael dropped his head and closed his eyes. "You're serious."

*****

Margo was sitting up in a chair by the window when Michael and the doctor entered her room. She glanced at them and then turned away. Looking out the window at blue sky and the shimmering bay was much more enticing than being grilled by the doctor, and possibly Michael. She was tired of the questions, tired of feeling so weak, and tired of the hospital.

"Go away," she whispered before they had a chance to speak. "Please leave me alone."

"It's good to see you out of bed, Mrs. Anderson. I hope that means you're feeling better." Dr. Gentry pulled over a chair so he was sitting beside her.

"Margo, I'm glad to see that you're ready to rejoin the human race." Michael stood behind her chair and placed his hand on her shoulder. "You had us worried."

"Okay, why am I being double teamed? What's going on?" Her voice was still raspy and her head hurt. Whatever they had to say was going to be unpleasant and she didn't want to deal with it or them.

"I'm sorry you think we're ganging up on you, Margo. But, there are a few things the doctor needs to talk with you about and I'm here to help you any way I can."

She continued to look out the window and tried to pretend the two men weren't there. Nothing mattered to her except the sailboat she had been watching. It looked so inviting and peaceful as it moved gracefully across the water. The fluid lines of the boat fit against the horizon so easily, like they belonged to each other. There was no chaos or confusion; one wasn't fighting the other. Not like me, she thought, I'm always fighting against the horizon. Why does my life always feel like chaos and confusion? She dropped her head and closed her eyes and longed for peace.

She heard the doctor and Michael talking and wondered if they were talking to her. Their voices were muffled and far away, like a bad connection on the telephone. Maybe if she kept her eyes closed, they would go away.

"Mrs. Anderson, in light of all that I've just told you, I'm recommending that you be moved to the Twin Palms facility in Boca Raton where you can receive the care and rest that you need."

The only word she heard was 'rest.' It was the only word that made sense to her. She lifted her head and whispered, "Good."

Dr. Gentry looked at Michael. "I was prepared for some resistance and her compliance surprises me. Mr. Anderson, I think she can be moved by the end of the week. Shall I request the social worker to make the arrangements with Twin Palms? It's a lovely facility, with luxurious accommodations and an expert staff. It's one of the few that deals directly with dual disorders. I can assure you she will be well cared for there."

"Please don't mention who she is to the people at the facility. It would be very damaging if word of this got out to the press. As soon as you've made the arrangements, our staff will begin working with the facility. They'll make sure that everything will be ready for Margo when she is discharged from the hospital," promised Michael.

"Good. I'll send her records to Twin Palms. I'm asking Dr. Sarsyn, an excellent psychiatrist, to oversee her case and I'll contact Dr. Mellon, an otolaryngologist at Jackson Memorial Hospital once she is well enough for the tests and treatment to begin on her vocal chords. He may refer her to New York University Hospital at a later date because the damage is so extensive." The tone of his voice grew warmer. "Good luck, Mr. Anderson. I hope the next phase of recovery is successful for her."

Dr. Gentry shook Michael's hand. "I'm a big fan. It would be a shame if she could never sing again."

Chapter Ten

Sunni

"Miss Anderson, I'm Sgt. Jackson from the Miami Police Department. I'm responding to your missing person call. Can you answer a few questions for me?" Sunni had been watching for the police to arrive and as soon as she saw the squad car drive up to the gate, she had gone outside to wait.

At first, Sam had been upset with her for involving the police and he had instructed her not to talk to them unless he was with her. "Please come in, Sgt. Jackson. There are others here who need to be included in our conversation. If you'll take a seat in the living room, I'll ask them to join us."

Within minutes, using the in-house telephone system, she had called Sam, Alli and Mrs. Davis to the living room. Then she called the hotel and asked Tomas Labato to come back to the house. She thought about calling her dad, but decided that he didn't need to be involved yet. She was still convinced that Paolo would walk in the door with a good excuse for worrying them.

"Sergeant, this is my sister Alli, Sam Baxter, head of my mother's security team, and Mrs. Davis, our housekeeper. Mr. Labato will be joining us in a moment. He's Mr. DaSilva's cousin and business partner."

Sam stepped forward and extended his hand. "Sgt. Jackson, I know you understand the necessity of keeping this as quiet as possible. Not only for Margo's sake, but for Mr. DaSilva's as well. His family holds an influential position in Brazil and we don't want this to become an international incident. I'm sure there's an explanation for Mr. DaSilva's disappearance, but, for the record, we felt it best to advise MPD of the situation." Sam's tone of voice was casual and his face was impassive. But Sunni saw his eyes dart in her direction as he was talking and knew that he was still displeased with her.

"Yes, sir. I understand." the sergeant's weathered features gave nothing away. "I just have a few questions."

"For the record, here's what we know." Sam began giving information before the sergeant started asking questions. "We had an early dinner yesterday and Mr. DaSilva ate with us, but he didn't come downstairs for breakfast or lunch today. All of his belongings are still in the house and his car is in the driveway. When we became concerned, we did a thorough search of the house and grounds. We became alarmed when his clothes and wallet were found in the pool house. I have questioned everyone in the house and no one remembers seeing Mr. DaSilva go for a swim. His cousin, Mr. Labato, received a phone call from him about eleven last evening, but hasn't heard from him since. They were supposed to meet at eight o'clock this morning."

The sergeant glanced at his pad. "Our records show that an ambulance was dispatched to this address at 7:05 last night. Does that have any bearing on this disappearance?"

"No, it doesn't. Mrs. Anderson was taken to the hospital after she became ill. Mr. DaSilva was here at that time and was at the hospital until after nine o'clock, when I assume he returned to this house."

Sunni knew Sam was trying to work around any discussion of Margo and the reason she was taken to the hospital. "I'll be glad to show you Mr. DaSilva's room and the pool house. I left everything as it was, but now my fingerprints are on the door knobs."

When the entry gate buzzed, Mrs. Davis excused herself to go to the door. The officer nodded and continued his questions.

"Mr. Baxter, do you live in this house, also?"

"No, I live on the grounds in the guest house. Why?"

"No reason. I was just trying to get a handle on who belongs where. Sunni and Alli Anderson live here with their mother, Margo. The housekeeper, Mrs. Davis, lives in the house, also. You live in the guest house and Mr. Labato is staying at the Mayfair Hotel in the Grove. Is that correct?"

"Yes, officer, I'm staying at the Mayfair Hotel and I can assure you that my family is most anxious about my cousin's disappearance." Tomas offered the information as he walked into the room.

"Thank you, Mr. Labato. Hopefully all of this is a misunderstanding and your cousin will return soon."

The sergeant looked down at his notes and began flipping the pages back and forth. "I guess that covers everybody but Mr. Anderson. What about him?" He raised his eyes and looked at Sam.

"Mr. and Mrs. Anderson are divorced and he lives in a high-rise on Brickell Avenue. To my knowledge he has no information about Mr. DaSilva's disappearance." Sam hesitated a minute before he offered, "The last time I heard from Mr. Anderson, he was still at the hospital."

"Technically, Mr. DaSilva has been away from the house for less than 24-hours so I can't file a missing person report. But I will be doing a preliminary investigation since there are so many suspicious circumstances. I'd like see Mr. DaSilva's room and the pool house. I'm asking the rest of you to remain on the property in case I have additional questions. Mr. Baxter, will you show me around?"

*****

After Sam and the police officer left, the room was very quiet. Sunni stared at her sister and tried to guess what was going on in her mind. Alli had been quiet since their mother had been taken to the hospital and she was defensive when Sunni tried to ask her a few questions. Sunni didn't want to read too much into her sister's behavior, but she knew Alli well enough to know that something was going on that she wasn't talking about.

Mrs. Davis broke the silence when she stood up and started walking to the kitchen. "I don't know if anyone will be hungry for dinner, but I better start fixing something. Tomas, will you be joining us this evening?" Mrs. Davis stopped in front of the chair where Tomas sat and didn't wait for the girls to invite the young man to dinner.

"Oh, yes, Tomas. Please stay for dinner." Embarrassed that Mrs. Davis had to remind her of her manners, Sunni looked at Tomas and smiled. "We usually eat around seven o'clock in the family dining room that's just off the kitchen."

His reply was so slow in coming, Sunni wondered if he'd understood her. After a moment, he said in very clear English, "Thank you. I would like that very much. This has been an exhausting day and I would enjoy the company."

"We have an hour before dinner. You're welcome to stay here or sit out by the pool. I'm going upstairs. Call one of us if you need something or go see Mrs. Davis in the kitchen." She glanced at her sister and wondered why she was just sitting there like she was in a coma.

"Alli, are you all right?"

At the sound of her name, Alli stood up and walked out of the room. "Wait, Alli. I'll walk with you." When she caught up with her sister and was sure they couldn't be over heard by Tomas, she grabbed Alli's arm and stopped her.

"What is wrong with you?" she whispered between clenched teeth.

"Let go of me, Sunni. And stop over reacting." Alli shook herself free from Sunni's hand and walked out to the patio.

"You're acting so weird. Tell me what's going on. I don't need you going off the deep end, too. Don't you think we've had enough drama today?" Sunni was persistent and followed her sister to the patio table. "I'm going to sit here until you tell me."

Alli's gaze was icy and so was her voice. "You can sit here all you want. I don't have anything to say to you or anyone else." She stretched out in the lounge chair and closed her eyes.

"That's fine with me. I was just trying to help." Sunni shook her head and decided to leave her sister alone.

*****

"Tomas, would you like something to drink? I can get you a cool glass of tea from the kitchen." Sunni had walked back in the living room where Tomas was sitting quietly reading the paper. She thought he was handsome in an understated way–not flashy like his cousin. And he was soft spoken. But there was something in his eyes that made her uneasy. Maybe she was imagining it, but he always looked like he knew something no one else knew. The few times she had been around him, she felt ill-at-ease and made sure she was not alone with him.

"No, thank you. I can't tell you apart from your sister." Tomas put down the paper and smiled at her. "Can you give me some information about what happened here last night? Where is your mother?"

"Didn't Paolo tell you? I thought you said he called you last night."

"He did. But it was a business call. We didn't discuss your mother."

"She's in the hospital." Sunni wasn't sure how much more she should tell him. "I'm surprised that Paolo didn't mention it to you." Why wouldn't Paolo tell his cousin?

"I'm sorry. Is Margo ill? Did she have an accident?"

"Mother wasn't feeling well. But she's going to be all right." Sunni didn't want to seem rude, but something told her to be cautious. "If you don't need anything right now, I think I'll take a walk." She turned and started for the door.

"Weren't you with Paolo last night?" The tone of Tomas's voice was suggestive and it startled her.

"What? Do you mean at the hospital? Actually, he was leaving just as I arrived."

"That's not what I mean and you know it." His smile was more of a smirk despite his soft tone.

"Excuse me, but I don't know what you're talking about. I saw Paolo last night at the hospital. Before that I was at dinner with a friend." She took a few steps away from him, but he reached out and grabbed her arm.

"I'm sure you know what I mean."

His voice was low and seductive, and Sunni felt threatened. She shivered as he continued. "Perhaps you would join me for dinner at the hotel this evening? Paolo has told me so many interesting things about you. I'm sure we could have a great time together."

She pulled out of his grasp and dashed from the room without responding. Her heart pounded so hard she had trouble catching a breath.

What a creep! He has some nerve. After she was out the front door, she sat down on the steps and put her head in her hands. Like a bolt of lightning, a new thought hit her and Alli's strange behavior began to make sense.

Dear, God! Tomas thinks I'm Alli! She's really having an affair with Paolo. How could I have been so naive? Hot tears welled up and streamed down her cheeks. Everything fell into place and her chest tightened until she was gasping for air. Mother must know. Alli, how could you? How could you do this?

She jumped to her feet and headed out the gate at a half-run-half-walk. She didn't have on her running shoes, but she wanted to run as fast and as hard as she could. She wanted to run until she couldn't see MarGrove or her sister.

God, why was I born into this mess? I can't stand it anymore. Either they're crazy or I am, and right now I don't know which is which. Tears continued to fall unheeded and her fists were clenched as her feet hit the pavement with such force that she felt the pounding all through her body.

Alli and mom are the twins, and I'm the family freak! I'm eighteen. I can leave Miami. I can be on my own. Daddy will give me the money for my own apartment. I know he will. Thoughts were racing in her head and she kept running faster and faster until her toes hit an uneven spot in the pavement. She was on her knees and elbows before she could catch herself.

Damn, that hurt! When she looked up, she realized she had run to the middle of Coconut Grove and she was surrounded by people who were trying to help her.

"Are you hurt?" a woman's voice asked.

"Here, give me your hand and I'll help you stand up," said an old man in a tan golf-shirt.

"Oh, my, your knee is bleeding. I'll go in the cafe and get some ice. Maybe they'll have a bandage," another woman offered.

Voices came from everywhere and she thought she might die of embarrassment before she got to her feet.

"Thank you. I'm fine, really. If you'll help me up, I'll be okay." When the man helped her to her feet she realized her knee was really scraped as blood trickled down her leg.

"I think you should sit here for a minute and let them bring some ice. You don't want to walk until that bleeding stops. The lady will be back in a minute." The man's voice was kind and she almost started to cry again.

"You're right. I appreciate your help." She sat down on the curb and began to brush the dirt and gravel off her legs and arms. Her elbows were scratched and one of her knees was cut badly enough to require some attention. Within a few minutes the lady had returned with a plastic bag of ice, napkins, and several band-aids.

"Sweetie, you must have been trying to crack this old sidewalk." The woman laughed as she wiped away the blood and applied the ice. "You need to sit here until we can get this bleeding stopped."

"Thanks for your help. But, please don't let me keep you. You don't need to stay." Sunni smiled at the people who were standing around her. "I promise I won't leave until my knee stops bleeding. I know you all have better things to do than sit here with me."

In a matter of minutes, everyone had left to go about their business and she slowly recovered her composure. The ice and the bandages helped and she thought she could manage to get back to the house.

As she stood up, she looked across the street and saw Mark Sanders walking toward her. Oh, great. I don't need this, too. She pushed strands of damp hair off her face and dropped the ice and paper towels in a near-by trash can.

"Looks like you just took a nasty fall. Are you okay?" He smiled and reached for her hand. "Hey, come join us for lunch and then I'll take you home."

"Hi, Mark. I'm fine. I'll walk home but thanks anyway." Feeling hot, dirty and just plain awful--too awful for Mark to see--all she wanted to do was get away.

"Oh, no you don't. Come on, at least have a cola or glass of tea." He pulled her across the street to an outside table at a small cafe. "Sunni, I'd like you to meet Jocelyn McDeal and her boss, Lawrence Fitz."

Sunni couldn't believe it was her fate to meet Mark's girlfriend when she looked so awful and felt so miserable. She looked across at the pretty young woman with dark brown eyes and a beautiful smile and her heart sank. No wonder Mark loves her.

"Hi, Sunni. Sit down and let us order you a soda or something. That cut on your knee looks really painful." Jocelyn's voice was caring.

"Young lady, I took a tumble like that in front of President Ford and lived to tell about it. Don't look so embarrassed." Mr. Fitz tapped her on the hand and laughed. "You're among friends. Mark has told us about your mother and we're all pulling for her quick recovery."

"Thank you. She's still critical, but she made it through the night. The doctor told us that's a good sign." Sunni liked the elderly gentleman and felt his concern was sincere. But she was uncomfortable intruding on their lunch and wished she could leave.

"We were just talking about some research I'm doing for my new book. I'm fascinated with the whole Mafia and Columbian drug cartel connection to Miami. Especially La Emperatriz de cocaina, and I'd like to include something about her in the book." He continued.

The waitress placed a large soft drink in front of her. When she took a swallow she realized how thirsty she was and drank half a glass before she put it down on the table. "I really need to get back to the house. My leg is okay and it's just a short walk. Jocelyn, Mr. Fitz, it was nice meeting you. Thanks for the drink." She stood up to leave. "I'll tell my mom you all asked about her."

"Wait, Sunni. My car's right there. I can drive you and be back here before they bring my sandwich." Mark jumped up and headed for his car.

"I'll drive her home and be right back," he called over his shoulder.

*****

"Why did you insist on driving me home? I could have walked with no problem," Sunni snapped.

"Sunni, don't be mad at me, please. You shouldn't be walking on that leg right now. And, I needed to talk to you."

"About what?"

"I know you were upset when you called my apartment this morning. Jocelyn's been out of town all week and I had just picked her up at the airport."

"You don't owe me an explanation. She's your girlfriend for crying out loud." Sunni was trying to hold it together. The last hour had been so emotionally charged she didn't know how much more she could take before she exploded.

"I wanted you to understand, okay?"

"Just let me out at the gate, please. Things are crazy for me right now. In fact, I'm thinking about asking my dad to let me leave for New York early. As soon as I know my mom is doing better, I'm going to leave, if I can."

"You're kidding, right?"

"I need to leave for more reasons than I can begin to explain. Thanks for the ride, Mark. Take care of yourself."

As soon as the car stopped she jumped out and headed for the gate. By the time she had opened the gate and walked through, she heard his car drive away.

*****

When Sunni walked into the hospital waiting room, her father looked up from the book he was reading.

"Hi, Sunni. Have a seat. They'll probably let us go in to see your mom in about an hour. She's resting."

"Hi, Daddy. How long have you been here?"

"I went home this morning and took a shower. When Sam called me about Paolo's disappearing act, I just came back here. I wasn't going to sleep anyway." Michael gave his daughter the once over. "What happened to you? You look like you were in a fight and lost. That's a sizable bandage on your knee."

"It's nothing. I fell. But I'm okay– it looks worse than it is."

"Were you running? What happened?"

"I was power running and not paying attention. I tripped over an uneven place in the sidewalk in downtown Grove. More embarrassing than anything else."

"Well. I'm glad you're okay. I don't think I could handle both you and your mother in this place." He sighed.

"You're funny, Daddy. How is she, really?"

"Sweetheart, your mom is going to be fine but it might take a long time. By the way, where's your sister? I thought she'd be here this afternoon."

"I guess she's in her room. I haven't seen her since this morning. Not since that policeman was at the house about Paolo. Daddy, do you think he's in trouble?"

"There's a logical explanation Sunni, and when he finally decides to show himself, he'll probably be very embarrassed that he caused all this fuss."

"You're right." She paused and then launched into her plea, "Daddy, I know the lease on the apartment at Sarah Lawrence doesn't begin until mid-September, but I was wondering if you would consider leasing another place now just for me. I need to get away and I've decided that I would like to try living on my own."

"Whoa, slow down. What are you talking about? The plans for college are all set. Why the big hurry to leave Miami?" There was surprise in Michael's voice. "Did you and your sister have a fight?"

"It's nothing like that. It's..." Sunni didn't have words to tell her father the real reasons. "Daddy, Alli and I need to learn to be on our own. You know, we need some space from each other."

"I can understand that, Sunni. But you've never mentioned anything like this before. What's going on?"

"I enjoyed being on my own when I was with you on tour and I'd like to have my own apartment. Is it all right with you if I ask Lara to check on another apartment in the same building? All I need is a studio or one bedroom." She didn't want to whine, but she felt desperate about making the split. She knew she couldn't live with Alli any longer.

"If that's what you want, give Lara a call. Tell her we discussed it. If there's something available, it's yours. But don't be too disappointed if she can't find anything. It will be tough this close to the start of school."

Before Sunni could thank him, the nurse was in the waiting room doorway.

"Mr. Anderson, you and your daughter may visit Mrs. Anderson for fifteen minutes She's awake, but she may not be very talkative."

"Come on, Sunni. Let's go say hello to your mom."

On the way down the hall, Sunni asked her dad, "Has Mom been able to tell you why she did this?"

"Your mom is barely functional right now. There will be plenty of time for her to explore her reasons. And, to be honest with you, we'll probably never know why. I doubt she'd ever tell us."

Chapter Eleven

Mark

"I really like your boss. The guy's had more than his share of adventures and he really knows how to tell a story. I guess he's got you working with him on a new Agent Joe Fielding book?" Mark was trying to fill the silence that was hanging between him and Jocelyn.

On the ride to her house she hadn't said a word, and as he settled on her sofa, he could sense that they were about to have a serious conversation. "Is the new book about the mafia? Mr. Fitz's stories about gambling and drugs in Miami Beach are exciting. Who is this lady drug empress that he mentioned?"

"What's going on between you and Sunni?" Jocelyn asked softly.

"What are you talking about, Jocey?"

Jocelyn was standing in the doorway to the kitchen and he knew from her stance that she wasn't happy.

"Oh, come on Mark. There is obviously something going on. I saw the way she looked at you and all of a sudden her name is popping up in our conversations. Do you think I'm naive?"

"We're just friends, Jocey. And, believe it or not, she needs a friend." His special name for Jocelyn was Jocey, and most of the time she softened when he called her that. But it wasn't working. She was more than a little angry.

"That's fine. But there's more between the two of you than you're telling me, and you know it."

He needed to choose his words carefully. He didn't want to hurt her, but sooner or later he needed to tell her what was happening.

"Maybe there is. I don't know." He had lowered his voice to a near whisper. "I'm really confused right now." He walked over and took her hand. "I love you, Jocey. I've loved you for a very long time. The last month we were on tour, Sunni was there and she was really all alone. Her folks don't seem to know she exists, so I tried to let her know she had a friend. And all of a sudden, I find myself questioning my feelings about her. I'm sorry. Nothing has happened between Sunni and me. I promise."

"And, you want me to believe you? When were you planning on telling me about this little confusion of yours? Answer me that!" She pulled her hand out of his and threw herself down in the big easy chair across from the couch. "Well?"

"Calm down, for crying out loud. You're getting worked up before we even know what any of this means."

"I know what it means and I'm sorry you don't!" Jocelyn blurted out the words as she glared at him.

"I don't want to hurt you. But you started this discussion before I've even had a chance to think about any of it." He stood up and began to pace the room. After a minute he turned to her.

"Our life is so crazy. I've asked you to marry me and you keep putting me off. Our folks keep throwing road blocks in our way and you keep letting them. How do you think that makes me feel?" The frustration of years seemed to spill out of him and he let it flow. "What are you waiting for, Jocelyn? Our situation is never going to change unless we do something to change it."

"That's a low blow, Mark. I can't help that we're cousins! I can't help that the Church will never accept our marriage! I can't change the way our mothers feel about our relationship! I've been trying to do that for years and it hasn't worked," she yelled at him.

He backed away from the sound of her voice. "You're right. We can't change it, but we can change the way we lead our lives."

"Your answer to everything is to run away. That's what you've been doing for the last few years. Running away! You joined the band so you wouldn't have to deal with it. You left me here to pick up the pieces and try to live through everyone's disapproval by myself. Do you have any idea what that's been like? No, of course you don't! You've been living it up as a hot-shot guitar player for the one and only Margo!" She stood up and faced him. "Well, why don't you ask me what it's been like? Why don't you take some of the heat that I've been taking? Better yet, why don't you do what you do best; run away and leave me alone!" She ran to the bedroom and slammed the door.

"You know you don't mean that!" His anger defused the minute she slammed the door, and all he wanted to do was take her in his arms. He slowly opened the bedroom door.

"Jocey, please don't send me away." She had thrown herself face down on the bed and he could hear her muffled crying. "Please talk to me."

He sat down on the edge of the bed and tried to take her in his arms. "I can't stand to hear you cry." He whispered as he cradled her.

"I...I need to cry." It sounded to him like she was choking. "Go away."

He took his arms from around her and stood up. "Are you telling me to leave?"

"Go away." She said the few words between sobs and turned away from him.

*****

"Mom, Jocelyn's really upset. I don't think it'd be a good idea to invite her to dinner tonight." Mark didn't want to go into the details with his mother. "We had a disagreement, but we'll get through it. I'll call you tomorrow."

An evening with his folks was the last thing he needed right now. He knew his mother wouldn't leave it alone until she knew what was going on. She had a way of pulling information out of him even when he didn't want to talk about it. Sometimes he wished he had a brother or sister so his parent's attention wouldn't always be focused solely on him.

He had hurt Jocelyn and Sunni, and he couldn't figure out how to handle the mess he had created. All afternoon he had beat himself up and it hadn't helped anything. He decided a walk on the beach would do him good. Maybe the salty air and sunshine would make a difference. He grabbed his baseball cap and sunglasses, put on flip flops, and headed out the door.

He loved the fact that his apartment was only two blocks from the beach. Even though it wasn't the greatest building, he'd chosen it because it was the closest to the ocean that he could afford. One bedroom and bath, a living room with a small kitchenette, and a balcony with a view–it was more than enough for him. From his fifth floor balcony, in the evening he could look across the bay at the lights of Miami and in the morning he could look out his front window and glimpse the sun rising over the Atlantic Ocean. He had found the place the summer after his first tour with the band and had decided to stay there until he and Jocelyn were married. Of course, he hadn't planned on still being there five years later. He made good money with Margo's band and didn't have that many expenses, so he could move if he wanted to. But his goal was to buy a house–a nice place that he would share with a wife and family.

When he first met Jocelyn, she was volunteering at the little theater in the neighborhood where they lived. She was a year younger than he was but he had noticed her right away. She had amazing brown eyes–the kind that seem to look through to your soul–and long brown hair that he thought looked like silk. But she didn't know he was alive. They both went to parochial schools but not the same one. He went to the boys' school and she went to the girls' school. But on the first day of his sophomore year at Barry College he volunteered to help the freshmen get oriented and he couldn't believe his luck when he saw her at the registration table.

They dated, fell in love, and then the world fell in around them. It was an almost unbelievable story when he thought about it, but it was their truth. Jocelyn's mother, his aunt Rosanna, had given her up when she was born, and the odds of them meeting were probably close to one in a million. He shook his head when he thought about how the pieces of their lives had come together.

Jocelyn's father, Carter McDeal, had been accused of kidnapping her when no evidence could be found to substantiate her birth. He was arrested and Jocelyn had been made the ward of Miss Moss, one of her teachers. Mark always thought of Miss Moss as the wicked witch and he got angry every time he remembered that the woman had been in love with Jocelyn and had wanted a relationship with her. But, that was a story for another day. If it was possible, he would never think about Miss Moss again.

On the day of Mr. McDeal's trial, his Aunt Rosanna came forward and confessed that she had left Jocelyn on the McDeal's front porch. It was the best day and the worst day for his family. It had changed everything about the world as he knew it. His aunt had believed she was doing the right thing when she decided that Mr. McDeal and his mother, Gracie, would be great parents for the child she had to give up.

Of all the girls in the world, why did Jocelyn have to be his aunt's child? The state of Florida allowed first cousins to marry, but the families were Catholic and the church would never give them consent. His aunt and mother would be devastated if he and Jocelyn went against the church. He had told them he was willing to leave the church, but over the years Jocelyn struggled with that option. She kept saying, "Let's give them more time, Mark. They'll see how much we love each other."

Mr. McDeal and his new wife, Sharon, were more understanding and had encouraged him to take it slow, but to follow his heart. He had waited too long and now his heart was being pulled in two directions–Jocelyn and Sunni.

He walked and walked. Although the beach was crowded, he hadn't paid attention to anyone or anything until he suddenly realized he was tired. When he looked around he was surprised that he was miles north of where he had started. He knew he should rest before he started back and he looked around for an empty bench. He loved the beach in Miami. There were tall palm trees growing everywhere, and instead of white sand, ground shells covered the shore line.

Across the road were old apartment buildings and new high-rise condos, but everywhere the profusion of tropical flowers kept the place from looking like a concrete fortress. He loved the architectural mix of the old hotels and the glass and steel of the new high rises that were being built so fast that the skyline changed every few weeks. But, more than anything, he loved the diverse cultures and people who were moving to Miami by the thousands. Cubans, Columbians, other Caribbean islanders, Jews, Italians, and so many more that it was a rarity to find a native like himself. He listened to the strains of Latin music that drifted from a store across the street and wished he had his guitar.

Taking off his cap, he leaned back and let the music take him with it. Each beat moved him farther and farther away from his troubles. Music was his muse and a source of healing. Margo would like this beat. I think I can use this as part of an opening for the new tour. As much as he loved playing the guitar, he loved writing and arranging music even more.

Thoughts of Margo jolted him back to the present. Margo, larger than life Margo, was in the hospital because she had tried to end her life. Why? Margo was a woman who had everything. Why would she choose death over life and how was this going to impact the band? He groaned. There was too much on his plate right now–if he continued to think about it he would be overwhelmed. He stood up and headed back down the beach to his apartment.

*****

He heard the phone ringing as he put the key in his front door and smiled when he thought it might be Jocelyn. But when he picked up the phone he was surprised to hear Sunni's voice. "Hi, Sunni. Is everything all right?" His surprise got bigger when the caller was Alli telling him she was calling to update him on Margo.

"Are things worse?"

There was a moment of silence and Mark was about to say good-bye and hang up when Alli began talking again.

"You're calling to ask me to take you to some of the clubs on the beach? And what Paolo thing are you talking about?"

"Uh, no. Sunni didn't mention that he's missing. The guy's probably upset about your mother and just needed some time."

"Sorry, Alli. I wish I could, but I'm meeting my girlfriend for dinner in a few minutes. Say hi to your sister for me."

Mark hung up the phone and shook his head. He had enough woman trouble in his life. He didn't need to add Alli to the list.

Chapter Twelve

Miami, July 16, 1980

Sunni was up early, sitting in the kitchen with a cup of coffee and the morning paper, when a man's voice came over the intercom. "This is Detective Todd Madison, Miami-Dade Police. Please open the gate. I need to speak to the family about Paolo DaSilva."

Walking over to the speaker, she feared she was about to hear bad news. "Good morning. The gate will open in a few seconds. Mrs. Davis, our housekeeper, will meet you at the front door."

"Mrs. Dee," she called down the hall as she ran to her room, "the police are here again. I'm still in my PJs. Can you get the door? I'll buzz Sam and ask him to come over to the house."

She hurried up to her room and changed into shorts and a T-shirt. She decided to find out what was happening before waking Alli.

By the time she walked into the living room, Sam was there talking to Detective Madison. The looks on the faces of the two men caused her to cringe. The detective had not come with good news.

"Good morning. Would either of you like a cup of coffee?"

"Thanks, Sunni. Mrs. Davis is bringing us a tray. Come on and sit down. The detective has some news for us." Sam motioned for her to sit on the sofa next to him and introduced her to the detective.

"Miss Anderson, I'm afraid I don't have good news this morning. I was just explaining to Mr. Baxter that Mr. DaSilva has been found."

"That sounds like good news to me." Sunni looked quizzical.

"At six this morning we got a call from Dinner Key Marina. They told us that two fisherman had been out trolling last night and found

Mr. DaSilva's body in the bay somewhere off Key Biscayne. They recovered the body and brought it back to the marina. I'm sorry, but your mother's friend apparently drowned while swimming."

He paused and waited for some reaction. When there wasn't one, he went on. "Mr. Labato was called and he has positively identified the body."

"That's unbelievable." Sunni turned to Sam for support. She knew she should feel something, but she hadn't liked the man and didn't know how to react. "How will Mom take this news? She's so fragile right now." She stood and walked toward the phone. "I've got to call my dad."

"Wait a few minutes before you make that call. I need to ask you and Mr. Baxter some questions. And, then, I'll need to talk to your dad, your sister, and Mrs. Davis."

"Detective Madison, can you give me some of the particulars? Where did the fishermen say they found the body?" Sam asked.

"I don't have the complete report, Mr. Baxter. But from what I know, the men told the investigators they put their boat in at the Dinner Key Marina about four-thirty this morning and they planned to troll along the southern side of Key Biscayne. One of them had to go to work at nine, so they were only going to be out for a few hours. About six o'clock, they were coming up on the marshy area at the tip of the island when they thought they saw something floating in the water.

"They eased the boat over and saw it was a body. At first, they panicked, but then decided the only thing to do was to net the body and take it to the marina. They tied up at the dock just as the marina store was opening and one of them ran in there for help. We were called and someone was on the scene within a few minutes. Mr. DaSilva was wearing swim trunks and there was no obvious trauma to the body. That's all I know."

The detective flipped through his note pad and looked back at Sam. "Mr. Baxter, you said the last time you saw Mr. DaSilva was the night Mrs. Anderson was taken to the hospital. I believe that was three days ago, correct?"

"Yes, he left the hospital somewhere around nine o'clock, and I didn't see him again."

"What would you say his state of mind was when you last saw him?"

"He was concerned about Margo and he seemed very anxious around us–that would be me, Mr. Anderson, and the girls."

"Did he give you any indication where he was going when he left the hospital?"

"No. I assumed he was returning to the house. But, I didn't ask."

"You're Mrs. Anderson's body guard. Right?"

"I'm her personal body guard and head of security for her band and production company."

"Do you live here year round, Mr. Baxter?"

"Of course not. We're on the road nine or ten months out of every year. This is where I live when we're not touring."

"But you also have a California residence? Isn't that correct?"

"My name is still on the house in California where my ex-wife lives, if that's what you're talking about. I haven't lived there in more than ten years." Sam stopped and looked at the detective. "What does that have to do with Mr. DaSilva?"

"Nothing. I was just checking out my facts. You know how it goes."

"I know how it goes when there's been a crime. I don't know how it goes when there's been an accidental drowning."

"There's no crime. I'm just checking my facts." The officer turned away from Sam to address Sunni. "Now, Miss Anderson, tell me again when you last saw Mr. DaSilva."

"I was at dinner with a friend and when I came home, Mrs. Dee, sorry, that's Mrs. Davis, told me mother had been taken to the hospital. As I was walking into the ER, Paolo almost knocked me down as he was leaving. That's the last time I saw him."

"How did he seem to you?"

"He was in a hurry, that's for sure. And, he was upset. He didn't say a word to me even though he almost knocked me down. I thought that was strange, but I was too worried about my mother to give him another thought."

"Miss Anderson, were Mr. DaSilva and your mother getting married soon?"

"I don't know. She hadn't told us anything about that."

"Who is us?"

"Oh, sorry. I was referring to my sister, Alli."

"Where is your sister, by the way?"

"I think she's still asleep. Do you want me to go wake her?"

"I don't think that's necessary. I'll talk to her later. But, I would like to talk to Mrs. Davis. Are there other people in the house that I should talk to?"

"We have a groundskeeper, but he's only here two days a week. We have a woman who helps Mrs. Davis with the cleaning, but she doesn't live here. She comes to the house Monday through Friday." Sunni looked at Sam and shrugged her shoulders.

"Madison, I don't think anyone here has any more information than we've already given you. I'm assuming an autopsy will be performed, correct? If you have questions later, we'll be available." Sam put his arm around Sunni's shoulder.

"Right now, we have to decide how we're going to break this news to Mrs. Anderson and how we're going to handle the reporters. Do you think in the future you could use unmarked cars if you have to come back to the house?"

"You're right, Mr. Baxter. I'll be in touch." Detective Madison walked toward the front door, then turned around. "According to Mr. Labato, Mr. DaSilva's family should be arriving tomorrow."

*****

After the police officer left the grounds, Sam called Michael. "Sorry to bother you so early, but I've got some news you need to know." He hesitated. "Michael, Paolo is dead."

There was a long silence before Michael finally asked for the details.

"He was found in the bay. Apparently he drowned," Sam answered. "Margo has got to be told and I'm sure we're going to have reporters all over the place before the day is over. Do you want me here or at the hospital?"

He listened as Michael talked through some options, then added, "I know we'll need security at both places. But for right now, I don't think the press knows where she is. Any chance we can get her moved to the facility in Boca Raton today?" He nodded his head as Michael talked.

"Michael, the house is secure from the street and the bay side, but anyone can get on the dock. Yes, the boat house is locked and I don't see how anyone can get over the wall to the back yard, but I'll double check everything. I'll meet you at the hospital in an hour."

He started to hang up the phone, but Michael continued to talk, so he listened.

"Yeah, sure. I'll tell them. Yeah, I'll ask Sunni to do that."

When he hung up the phone he turned to Sunni. "Your dad is worried about the reporters. I'll talk to Mrs. Davis about what to say to anyone who calls the house. I'm going to check the grounds, then I'm headed for the hospital. Your dad wants you to talk to Alli and then call the guys in the band. Our statement is, 'We're deeply sorry about his unfortunate accident and our prayers are with his family.' After that, it's 'No Comment.' Can you handle Alli and the band?"

"I'll try." She took a deep breath. "I can handle it. I kept thinking he was going to walk in the door any second and apologize for worrying us." She sat down on the sofa and stared at the floor. "I feel bad for my mom." She looked up at Sam, "You know, I never liked him, but this is awful." She didn't dare share how much she hated the man, but at least she could express her dislike to Sam.

"Sunni, I didn't like him either. But he was your mother's friend and we all tolerated him. I don't think any of us were ever unkind to him, so don't get your feelings tangled up. Yes, we're sorry the man is dead, but we didn't do anything to cause it."

"As usual, you're right, Sam." She smiled at him in appreciation. "I'll go wake up Alli and then make those phone calls. I don't know how Alli is going to take this news. She has been a pain to live with for the last three days."

"Do you want me to talk to her?"

"No, you have other things to do. I'll be okay. But, thanks again."

*****

She quietly opened her sister's bedroom door and crawled on the bed next to her. "Alli, wake up. I need to talk to you. Alli." She gently shook her sister's shoulders. "It's really important."

Alli grabbed the pillow and pulled it over her head. "Leave me alone."

"I can't do that. You've got to listen to me."

"What's so important that it can't wait?" Alli grumbled as she pulled her head from beneath the pillow. Then she threw the pillow off the bed and turned to glare at her sister. "Okay, you've got my attention. What is it?"

"A detective from the Miami police was just here and I'm afraid he brought some bad news. Alli, Paolo drowned." She waited to see her sister's reaction. When there was none, she continued. "They found his body this morning off Key Biscayne."

Still there was no reaction from Alli. She continued to stare at Sunni without saying a word.

“Sis, are you okay? I know you had feelings for him and this has to be hard.”

Alli turned away and pulled the covers up. “Go away, Sunni. Just go away,” she whispered and then closed her eyes.

“Don’t shut me out, Alli. Please talk to me.”

She was concerned by her sister’s reaction. She had expected fireworks and drama, but instead there was an awful nothingness.

“I’m tired, Sunni. There’s nothing to talk about.”

Chapter Thirteen

Tomas

He hung up the phone and stretched out on the bed at the hotel. That was one of the hardest phone calls he had ever made. His Aunt Inez was so distraught she couldn't talk, then his grandfather was so angry he had slammed the phone down before Tomas had finished talking.

What a horrible day! The police had awakened him around seven o'clock in the morning with the news that Paolo's body had been found. They'd asked him to go to the medical examiner's office to identify the body and ever since, he'd felt sick to his stomach.

But the hardest part had been calling the family in Brazil. Paolo was the adored one–the heir apparent–the favored grandson. And, his death was so unexpected. At least, it was unexpected by the family members he had called.

Tomas had not been totally shocked and his gut told him it wasn't an accident. The only question that remained was how long it would be before somebody figured out that Tomas was supposed to be the dead man.

*****

He and Paolo had been in Las Vegas for one of Margo's shows when he was first invited to join the high stakes poker game taking place in the penthouse of the hotel. He had been sitting at the hotel bar after the show when a beautiful woman sat down beside him and asked if he was Tomas Labato.

She had been sent to deliver the invitation and had made it seem that much more enticing. Her sultry eyes and sexy body were full of promise and he was more than willing to follow wherever she led him. He had the money and he was flattered. He had known that the games existed but had never thought about joining one. Gambling was not his thing. Yes, he made bets on the soccer matches, and when he and Paolo were in Vegas he took his chances in the casinos. But he had an aversion to losing and never stayed long enough to lose more than a few hundred dollars. Tonight's invitation was different and he was naive enough to think he could play for several rounds and then ask the young lady to join him for a different kind of recreation.

The penthouse was all glass and elegance, and the lights of Vegas were evident everywhere he looked. The main room contained five tables and the men at four of them were already in the midst of their games. He was seated at the fifth table with three older, very distinguished gentlemen who were eager to begin playing. There were no greetings when he sat down and there was no small talk going on in the room. The room was about business, not recreation. The liquor and drugs were free flowing and each woman he looked at was more beautiful than the next. Every man in the room was attended by one of the scantily clad females who sat in chairs behind them at the tables. The women sat quietly and waited until they were commanded to bring another drink or more food or another line of coke. Or until one of the men wanted to touch or be touched. Then they moved forward until their breasts were available to be squeezed or they were close enough for a hand to disappear under the edge of their dress.

At first, Tomas was mildly amused. But as he became part of this new world, he forgot that he had no idea of the rules. He played his cards, made outlandish bets, and took advantage of the girl that had apparently been assigned to him. Time passed quickly–he felt the effects of the alcohol and drugs–he was sexually aroused, and he was ahead by $20,000 when the game broke up. Each of the men left with the woman who had been sitting behind his chair and Tomas followed suit.

The woman was a plaything extraordinaire but she came at a high price. He couldn't remember all the details of the hours they spent together, but he could remember how she made him feel and how insatiable he had been that night. When he closed his eyes he could still see her incredible body and feel the ways that she used it to bring him pleasure. Only later did he realize that most of what happened was the effect of the drugs.

Around noon, when he had showered and dressed in casual slacks and shirt, she made sure he returned to the penthouse that night. He remembered wondering where she would go when she left his room, but he hadn't bothered to ask. All he wanted was an assurance that he could have more of her.

He and Paolo were due to leave Vegas the next day, so he had time for one more night in the penthouse. After Margo's show, he sat in the bar and waited. Within twenty minutes, the woman was at his side beckoning him to the exclusive elevator that wasn't available to anyone without a key.

The penthouse was the same, the men the same and the scene played out like a well written script. Except he was losing. He was losing big.

By the end of the evening he had dropped almost $50,000, but at the time he didn't care. He was playing cards for what was coming next. And, she didn't disappoint. He told her he didn't know when he would be in Vegas again but in conversation he had mentioned that he was in Miami often. That morning when she left his room, she also left a number for him to call in Miami the next time he was there.

The pattern was repeated every time he and Paolo were in Miami on business. The rooms changed, the women changed, but the intent did not. Cards, booze, drugs and incredible sex–until he started to lose more than he won.

When he was in the red, he was forced to get very creative in covering his debts and it had worked until recently. As a last resort, he had used shares in his grandfather's oil business to cover some of his losses. He thought he had reworked the books well enough, but last week his grandfather must have become suspicious because Tomas no longer had access to his portfolio and the bank had blocked his checking account.

Those events had happened the same day he received two phone calls: One from Paolo telling him they had been called home by their grandfather; the other from a mobster named Dario who told him to expect a visit.

Now his cousin, the family's favorite son, was dead and his grandfather would be in Miami tomorrow.

Chapter Fourteen

Margo

"Good morning, Margo, you're wide awake today. You must be feeling better," Michael said with a bright smile.

"Michael, I feel like hell and I look even worse, so stop with the BS." Her voice was still raspy and her throat was sore. She had worried for three days about her voice, but the doctor kept telling her to give it time. She wondered if the doctor knew that everything depended on her voice.

"Ah, it really is you! I thought for a minute I had the wrong room. Honestly, Margo, coming to visit you is like visiting a bear with a sore tooth."

"Why are you here, Michael? To make me feel worse? Is that it? Cause if that's it, please turn around and go home."

"No, I need for us to be serious. I didn't mean to come in the door and get into an argument with you. I'm sorry."

"Serious always means trouble. I don't need any trouble today. "

He sat on the edge of the hospital bed and smiled at her as he gently pushed a strand of her hair back away from her face. When his hand accidentally touched hers, he quickly pulled away, "Are you cold? Your hands are icy."

"They tell me my blood pressure is still very low." Why did Michael always like to drag things out? She wasn't in the mood to be sociable. "Michael, it hurts to talk. Please. Why are you here?"

"I have some bad news about Paolo."

"What? Did he go back to Brazil without saying good bye?"

"No, Margo." He was holding both of her hands and looking at her so intently that she almost laughed. "Paolo is dead."

Margo felt like he had slapped her and she jerked her hands away. "What are you talking about?" When she tried to sit up, she felt light headed, "Oh, Michael, I feel sick."

"Lie back down, Margo. Do you need for me to call the nurse?"

"I don't want to hear any more. I don't want to know anything else about Paolo."

"I know this isn't easy, but you've got to listen to me." He handed her the cup that was sitting on the nightstand and lifted her head and helped her take a sip. "I'm trying to tell you that Paolo drowned in the bay and they found his body this morning. I'm sorry."

She turned her face to the wall. "He drowned?" she whispered. "I don't believe it. I don't believe you're telling me the truth." She wanted to cry but the tears wouldn't come. There was some reason why she didn't feel sad, but she couldn't remember what it was. "Who found him? Do you know?"

"Some fishermen found his body off Key Biscayne around six o'clock this morning. They called Tomas to identify him."

He held her hand for a few more minutes, waiting for her response. "Hey, are you okay?"

"I don't know how I am anymore, Michael. Maybe it's all the pills they keep pushing down my throat. I just don't feel anything right now."

"Margo, you can't stay here. You've got to be moved today. There are reporters everywhere looking for you. So far, we've been able to keep you low-key. But I know with this news, somebody is going to start digging and they'll find you."

She stared out the window. "Why does the sun shine on sad days? Have you ever wondered about that?" She was numb and her whispers seemed to echo across the room. She wanted to separate herself from reality and go to a place where she could rest.

"Margo, look at me. I've arranged for a helicopter to fly you to Boca today. That's the best way to keep you out of the limelight."

"I don't have a choice, do I, Michael?" There was resignation and defeat in her voice. "I just need to sleep. Tell them to let me sleep."

*****

Twin Palms in Boca Raton was not like any of the other rehab centers. From the street it looked like any other south Florida high-rise condo building–twelve stories of amber glass and balconies, and on either side of the front lobby doors, two large royal palm trees stood sentinel. But other condo buildings didn't have a helicopter pad on the roof top, an ambulance parked in the underground parking lot, security guards at the front and back entrance, and a medical facility on the third floor.

Her tenth-floor suite had a large balcony where she could see the ocean in the distance, but she was too far away to hear the crashing of waves against the shore or the excited call of the sea gulls on morning fishing excursions.

She had been told there was an Olympic sized pool on the first floor and a green house on the fifth floor terrace, but she was still too weak to go exploring. A nurse was supposed to wheel her down the halls twice each day, but the thought of that exhausted her energy.

*****

There were no exterior grounds, no serene gardens where she could sit and reflect, no places for her to get away and not be reminded that she had failed. Fate had played a cruel joke on her. She was alive and Paolo was dead. No matter how hard she tried, she couldn't make sense of the madness. She remembered she was angry with him but she couldn't remember why. Perhaps she should be glad she couldn't remember, she just didn't want to feel guilty about his death.

On her second day at Twin Palms, there was a gentle tap on her door and a tall, exotic-looking woman, dressed in a bright orange and yellow caftan entered the room. She wore a matching turban and large gold hoop earrings. She smiled as she introduced herself to Margo.

"Good morning, friend. I'm Lulu Sarsyn and I'm here to welcome you to Twin Palms." She held out her hand. "I'll only stay for a few minutes today. But in the future we will be spending a lot of time with each other. How are you?"

"Who are you and why would I want to spend time with you?" Margo hissed.

Lulu laughed her bigger-than-life laugh, "Oh, Mrs. Anderson, my dear, I'm your new doctor. And, from everything I've read in your file, we have much work to do." She walked closer to where Margo was seated and sat down across from her. "It's all right if I call you Margo, isn't it? And you are to call me Lulu. My dear, I can assure you, we're going to be too busy to worry about the formalities."

"You've got to be kidding." Margo rolled her eyes and sighed in resignation.

"Honey, you'll get used to me. I've got credentials and diplomas hanging all over my office walls. I know what I'm doing, but that doesn't mean I have to wear a business suit and go to the beauty salon every day. You're surprised and that's okay."

Lulu Sarsyn stood up and took a small bow. "Margo, I'm on my own stage and I enjoy being my own person. I think we'll work well together." She checked her chart. "You're on my schedule twice a day. I'll see you at ten o'clock each morning and three each afternoon. And, tomorrow, honey, we get down to some serious business."

Lulu swept out of the room like an African queen dismissing her subject. Margo's mouth dropped open and it took her a few minutes to recover. Then she started to laugh. She had seen counselors and psychiatrists for years, but she had never encountered anyone like Dr. Lulu Sarsyn.

Chapter Fifteen

Sam

Tomas had called earlier in the day to complain that the autopsy wasn't completed and his family was anxious to leave Miami and take Paolo's body with them.

"The family has been here three days and nothing is happening. How long should it take for the medical examiner to do his job?"

"I don't have any control over this investigation. The medical examiner can take as long as he wants and there isn't a thing we can do to rush him. Why don't you suggest that the family return to Brazil and you'll wait here until Paolo's body is released?" Sam had suggested.

Tomas seemed to be coming unraveled and it was getting on Sam's nerves. All Sam wanted was for the DaSilva family to quietly leave for Brazil before there was a backlash of negative publicity for Margo.

He was relieved that Michael had arranged for her to move from Mercy Hospital before the reporters found out that Paolo was dead. Now that she was safely in Boca, it would be easier to keep the paparazzi away from her.

*****

Sitting on the couch in Lara Finley's apartment, Sam knew he could vent if he needed to. It was the thing he loved most about the incredible woman who had come into his life like a gentle breeze. She always knew when he needed her to just listen and not offer any advice.

For the past three days he had been vigilant about Sunni, Alli and Mrs. Davis because there was a hoard of reporters camped outside the gate at MarGrove. He wasn't worried about Michael–he knew the man could take care of himself.

But, the girls and the housekeeper had no experience in dealing with press hounds. He had to hand it to Margo and Michael for the job they had done protecting their girls from the public. Although he knew the girls didn't like boarding school, Brentwood Academy had given them a chance to have some kind of normal life. That is, he thought sourly, if you could call a private, exclusive boarding school 'normal'.

He hoped the current chapter in Margo's life would be closed for good in the near future and he could forget about Paolo and Tomas. He was sorry Paolo was dead, but he had never trusted him or his attachment to Margo. And the way Paolo looked at the girls disgusted him.

"You know I tried to discourage Margo from agreeing to let Alli be alone in the house with Paolo. But she was oblivious to his wandering eyes and her daughter's magnetic sexuality." He knew Lara agreed with him, so he continued. "Alli is every inch her mother's daughter-- beautiful, great body and sex appeal that could melt any man's resolve."

"Not every man." Lara smiled at him.

He gave her a sly smile. "I know Alli has been sexually active for years." As part of his job, he received a quarterly report from Dr. Hastings at Brentwood that had kept him apprised of the girls' activities. "But every time I tried to talk with Margo and Michael about her promiscuity and drinking, they told me I was over reacting. 'She's just testing her wings,' Margo had said. 'She's a normal teenager,' Michael assured me. But, Alli worries me, Lara, and I'll be damned if I know what to do about it."

"You know I've tried to talk to them about both the girls. Michael will at least listen to me, but Margo brushes me off. They have no idea who those girls are or what they need."

She sighed. "Alli is so strong-willed it's scary, and Sunni gets lost in the shadows." Curling up next to him, she wanted to forget about all the trouble at MarGrove. "If you're not comfortable leaving, we can always postpone our vacation."

"Absolutely not. Our plans are made and we both need a break." Sam was looking forward to a month away from the stress of his job. He had arranged with some of his security crew to cover for him at MarGrove and his worries about Margo had diminished now that she was in rehab.

"Next week we're going to Key West for a few days of relaxation and fishing before I head to California."

His son, David, had finished his residency in general surgery at UCLA and had asked for help to move to Michigan where he was going to do a fellowship in trauma surgery.

"After I've helped David move, I'll fly back here and the two of us are spending a romantic week in Costa Rica. So get your bags packed." He kissed the top of her head as she snuggled against him. "We need time away, Miss Finley. MarGrove can survive without us for a few days."

Lara Finley, Margo's personal assistant, had been a constant in his life all the years that he had worked for Margo. When he first met Lara, he thought she was attractive but he had kept his distance since she was a co-worker.

Two years ago she had decided to move to Miami and had asked for his help in finding an apartment. They had spent two weeks of their off-time looking for a place for her, and had discovered each other on a totally different level.

He had always seen her as efficient and boring. She took care of Margo and didn't seem to have a life of her own. But over the two weeks they spent apartment hunting, he experienced her humor, her intelligence, and her warmth. They found her a large two-bedroom condo five blocks from MarGrove. It was on the fourth floor of the building and faced the bay. The day she moved in, he had stayed the night.

He had told Michael that he was seeing Lara, but at the time they weren't ready for anyone else to know about their relationship. Now two years had passed and he was planning to ask her to marry him while they were on vacation.

*****

The next day he was sitting in the kitchen talking to the housekeeper when the gate buzzer sounded. "I'll get it. You keep working on my chocolate cake."

"Your chocolate cake is it? We'll see about that, Sam." Mrs. Davis laughed and continued to swirl frosting around the three layer German Chocolate cake that she knew was Sam's favorite. "That's probably those awful reporters trying to get us to tell them where Mrs. Anderson is hiding out. I'd like to give them a piece of my mind."

"Mrs. Davis, if those reporters knew they were dealing with you, they'd run for the hills."

Sam chuckled, but knew it was true. He had a soft spot for the woman who reminded him of a younger version of his mother, and he knew if it came down to a battle of words, Mrs. Davis would probably win.

"I'll be right back."

A few minutes later he walked back into the kitchen with Detective Madison. "Mrs. Davis, the detective has some news for us. Do you know where the girls are?"

"Good morning, detective. You're out early." She waved her frosting knife at the police officer and chuckled when some of the icing flew toward the young man. "I think Sunni is in her room and I saw Alli out by the pool. Do you want me to get them?"

"Thanks, Mrs. Davis. I think the detective wants to talk to all of us." He nodded at her and then waited until she left the kitchen. "What's this about?"

"The medical examiner has just confirmed that DaSilva's death wasn't an accident."

"What are you talking about? The man drowned in the bay."

"Yes, he drowned, but not in the bay. The water in his lungs was chlorinated. I'm afraid the man was murdered." Detective Madison was stone-faced and his words were very emphatic.

"Now we've got ourselves a mess. Has his family been told?"

"I'm on my way to the hotel to tell them. I came here first because I know you and Mr. Anderson are going to need some time to handle this with the press. The department will release a statement this afternoon."

"Give me till five o'clock. I'm going to need some extra security here once the media has been told and I've got to make sure Margo hears this from us, not the Miami Herald." Sam ran his fingers through his hair and sat down at the kitchen table. "Any suspects?"

"I've got a lot of investigating to do before I can answer that one. You know everyone here will have to be questioned–including Mrs. Anderson."

"Leave Margo out of this. There's no way she's involved. She was in the hospital, for crying out loud!" Sam's voice had risen and he leaned across the table to look squarely in the eyes of the detective. "She's off limits, Madison."

"Nobody is off limits in a murder investigation and you know it. When I need to talk to her, you're going to have to make sure she's available."

"I'm not trying to make your job harder, but you may have to get a subpoena for that to happen. I'll talk to Michael, but I know what his answer is going to be." Sam stood up and walked around the table.

"Look, Madison. You've got to give us some time. You go tell his family and I'll call Michael and take care of telling everyone here."

"That's well and good, but this house is probably a crime scene and in an hour or so it's going to be crawling with our people."

"Just give me till five o'clock."

"I'll try my best." Detective Madison stood up to leave. "When I come back I want to talk to everyone: you, Mr. Anderson, the girls, Mrs. Davis, the gardener, and even the guy who cleans the pool. I'll work with you and Mr. Anderson on how to go about talking to Mrs. Anderson."

Mrs. Davis and Sunni walked into the kitchen just as the detective was leaving. "What's going on, detective?" Sunni looked to Sam for an answer.

"I was just leaving. Mr. Baxter will answer your questions and I'll be back later. I can see myself out, Mrs. Davis." He walked past them and headed for the front door.

"Well, I declare. That man doesn't light anywhere for long, does he?" Mrs. Davis shook her head and walked back to the table where the partially frosted cake was waiting for her. "He's in some kind of snit."

"You both need to sit down." Sam would normally respond when Mrs. Davis made her sarcastic comments, but today he had too much on his mind to notice. "Where's Alli?"

"She'll be here in a minute." Mrs. Davis was getting agitated. "Sam, just tell us and get this over with. I've got things to do."

"I'll go get her if this is important, Sam." Sunni knew Mrs. Davis didn't like waiting when she had dinner to finish.

"I'm here. What's all the fuss?" Alli walked in the room and flung open the refrigerator door. "It's hot out there. I need something cold."

"I've got some news and then we need to get your dad over here as soon as possible. Detective Madison just got the medical examiner's report and it's been determined that Paolo was murdered."

There was a gasp from Sunni. Mrs. Davis stopped working and sat down at the table. And Alli let the glass slip from her grasp and shatter on the floor.

"There's got to be some mistake." Sunni shook her head. "This just keeps getting worse!"

"How in the world did that happen? The man went for a swim, for heaven's sake." Mrs. Davis said as she rushed over to Alli to clean up the spill.

"Alli, where are you going? Come sit down, we've got to talk." Sam followed her as she headed for the door. "I know you're upset, but we've got to talk."

"Leave me alone." Alli tossed the words over her shoulder as she continued to walk out the door.

"Please let her go, Sam. She hasn't been in a very good mood these past few days. I'll talk to her later. Can you tell us what you know?" There was no emotion in Sunni's voice, but she was tapping her fingers on the table and Sam knew she was upset. He was going to have to soften his approach with both of the girls.

"I don't know much right now. Apparently the water in Paolo's lungs was pool water, not bay water. Somehow the man was drowned in a pool and then his body was put in the bay. The police aren't saying it was our pool. But they've declared the estate a possible crime scene which means they'll be here later to start their investigation. Detective Madison was on his way to tell Paolo's family and he's giving us until five o'clock this evening before he releases a statement to the press."

He turned to Mrs. Davis. "Looks like we're going to have lots of company. We'll do our best to cooperate with them, but don't say anything until you've talked to me first." She nodded at him but kept her eyes on her cake.

Sunni frowned. "Somebody's going to have to tell Mom. She's not well enough to handle this kind of news."

"I'm going to ask your dad to come over. It's his call, Sunni. When he gets here, we all need to sit down and make some decisions." He patted her on the shoulder. "While I'm talking to your dad, you go talk to your sister. Try to get her to understand she's got to cooperate." Sam walked over to the far corner of the room where the phone was located.

"This is terrible. I can't believe it." Sunni groaned.

"Honey, there's something you need to know," Mrs. Davis whispered, then stopped. "Oh, never mind. Go see about your sister."

As Sunni started out of the room she heard Mrs. Davis whisper, "Alli has got to stop acting like she's the center of this tragedy."

"What do you mean, Mrs. Dee? Alli's just upset about Mom."

"Sunni, what's going on with your sister doesn't have anything to do with your mother. Just try to talk some sense into her. That detective is probably going to have a ton of questions and it sure will be easier for all of us if Alli cooperates." Mrs. Davis dismissed Sunni by turning back to her cake.

"Okay, Mrs. Davis. What do you know that I don't?" Sam was off the phone and had heard most of the exchange between Sunni and the housekeeper. "I don't need any surprises."

"Sam, let's just say that Alli and Mr. DaSilva had more than a passing interest in each other."

"For god's sake, are you telling me she was sleeping with him?"

"I'm not telling you anything. But use your imagination, Sam. I had a gigolo and an over-sexed teenager in this house without a chaperone for over a month. Let's just say JR Ewing and Dallas has nothing on MarGrove."

"I tried to convince Margo that letting Alli come here alone was a bad idea." Sam's face turned red and he slammed his fist into his hand. "Mrs. Davis, we're going to have to handle this information with great care. I'm not asking you to lie, but please don't answer any questions about this unless I'm in the room."

"There's something else you need to know about, Sam." Mrs. Davis reached into her pocket and handed him an envelope. "I think you need to read this and then destroy it."

Reading the note was painful and he wondered how he and his security team had let this slip. He had never ordered security for the girls directly, but he did have them checked on periodically. He should have followed his gut feeling about DaSilva and Alli. He looked at the note again to make sure he hadn't imagined the words: Alli, My Little One, Your mother will forgive you, but she will never forgive me. So sad that this is our ending - you are my joy and I will miss you. Paolo.

"Where and when did you find this?"

"It was on Mr. DaSilva's desk the morning he disappeared. I was straightening up a big mess in his room when I saw Alli's name. Something told me to get rid of that letter." The creases in her brow deepened. "I know it's not my business. But I didn't think it was a good idea to have it lying around."

His gut was tied up so tight he had to force himself to take a breath. "What kind of mess are you talking about?"

"His room looked like a hurricane had blown through it. There were papers and files thrown all over the place. His desk was the biggest mess I'd ever seen." She looked concerned. "He was always so neat. That's what worried me and then when I found this note I knew something crazy was going on. But, I never once thought it was murder."

"Mrs. Davis, keep this between us for the time being. I'll put this letter in a safe place." He tucked the envelope in his pocket.

"Detective Madison is going to have a field day once he starts his investigation. God help every single one of us."

*****

Within thirty minutes, Michael arrived at the house and Sunni had persuaded Alli that she needed to join them so she would know how Sam and their dad planned to deal with the questions and the investigation.

The group sat around the kitchen table to wait for Sam to initiate the conversation. Even Michael was unusually quiet as Sam began to outline what he thought needed to be done prior to the evening press conference.

"I'm surprised that we haven't heard from the DaSilva's or Tomas. Maybe it's a bit too soon, but I know they are going to be all over us with questions and accusations once the shock wears off." Sam was perched on the kitchen island looking at the people sitting around the table. "I've got to have some idea of every scenario and an alibi for each of you."

"Are you crazy?" Alli jumped up from her chair. She pointed her finger and shouted at Sam. "Do you think one of us murdered Paolo?"

"Calm down, Alli." Michael stood up and spoke sternly to his daughter. "Sam is just trying to help us understand how the police will approach us. They'll question all of us and we need to be ready. Sit back down and listen."

"Alli, I'm not suggesting anything," Sam said evenly. "I just don't want any of you to say something that can be misconstrued because you're not prepared." He slid off the counter and walked over to her chair. "We've all got to be prepared. Do you understand what I'm saying?"

"This is all so scary, Sam. Do you think any of us is in danger?" Sunni spoke before Alli had a chance to answer Sam.

"I can't imagine that whoever killed Paolo is after any of you. But, I have ordered extra security for the estate and for each of you. Michael, you and the girls will have someone with you from this afternoon until the investigation is finished."

Sam opened the notebook beside him on the counter and handed Michael a sheet of paper. "Here are the names of the men that will be assigned to each of you. You'll meet them this afternoon."

"You really think all of this extra security is necessary?" Michael asked.

"I was hired to protect Margo. And, under the circumstances, protecting all of you is in her best interest. We don't know why this man was killed or where. And until we do, we need to be vigilant."

"You know what you're doing, so I'll shut up and let you tell us what to do." Michael sat down and leaned back in the chair, but his square jaw remained tight.

"Here's the plan. Michael, do you want me to go with you to talk to Margo? I don't think we want her to find out about this from an outside source. Then you need to talk to her doctor and alert the facility that we will have extra security on site. This is non-negotiable until we have some answers."

Michael nodded his head, "I think you better come with me and I don't think we need to arrive by car. I'll order the helicopter for one o'clock this afternoon. Is that okay?"

"Good idea." He turned to Mrs. Davis.

"I'm sorry that you have to be part of this, but you do. I'm changing all the locks and security codes and I'll go over that with you later. I want you to check in with me every evening before you go to bed and I'll be here every morning when you come down to the kitchen to start breakfast. For right now, I don't think it will be necessary for you to vary your routine. But if I change my mind on that, we can work something out."

"Sounds like much ado about nothing, but I'll do whatever you say, Sam. I guess we're going to be feeding an army for the next few days with all these extra people. When you've got a minute I'll need a head count and some direction about who's eating here, who's staying here, and who belongs to whom. Lordy, this is getting complicated."

Sam looked sympathetic, "It may seem that way at first, but we'll help you out as much as possible."

He turned to the girls. "Sunni and Alli, you're going to be confined to the house until further notice. I don't want you out where the reporters can spot you and I don't want you answering questions from anybody unless I'm with you. Understood?"

Sunni nodded her head in agreement, but Alli threw back her head and laughed. "You're loving this, aren't you Sam? Everybody is under your thumb and we don't smile unless you pull the strings. If you think I'm going to do this for more than a day or two, you better think again."

"Enough, Alli!" Michael slammed his hand down on the table. "You will do exactly as you're told. This isn't a game. Paolo was murdered and we have no idea whether one of us is next." His face turned red. "Don't even think about giving us a hard time. Am I making myself clear?"

"Well, if you put it that way, Daddy, I guess I'd better be on my best behavior." Alli flipped the words at her father and slid down in the chair.

"Someday you're going to thank Sam for all he does to keep you safe, Alli."

Ignoring the sulking Alli, Sam continued, "The police will release a statement to the press this afternoon at five o'clock and I expect this place to be crawling with reporters within minutes of the announcement. The gates will only be opened for official police business until I give you further notice."

Sam looked at each of them and waited until they nodded that they understood. "Detective Madison will be back here later to question each of us and I've already told him that I will be present for all those sessions. If I think you're giving an answer that will lead to more digging, I'll interrupt you. If that happens, you remain quiet until I've worked around the issue. Again, do you understand?"

Sam didn't want to sound like a dictator, but he knew all about interrogation and the purpose of an investigator's questions. "Michael, have I forgotten anything?"

Michael shook his head, so Sam went on. "Mrs. Davis, what did you do after the ambulance left with Margo?"

"Let me think." She hesitated. "Oh, yes. That's the night I watch Magnum PI, so as soon as I finished in the kitchen and changed the sheets on Mrs. Anderson's bed, I went to my room. I don't think I came out of my room after that."

"Did you hear anything strange in the house?"

"From where my room is on the third floor, I can't hear much of what's going on in the house. I don't think I even knew when the girls came home from the hospital. No, wait a minute. I was still downstairs when Sunni came home from her date and when I told her about her mother, she and that nice young man left to go over to Mercy. Then, I went upstairs to my room." Mrs. Davis looked thoughtfully at Sam. "That's it."

"Alli, how about you? You drove your car to the hospital, right? And, then you and Sunni came home together?" Alli nodded. "Did you see Paolo after you got home? Did you hear anything out of the ordinary?"

"When Sunni and I got home, no one was up. The house was quiet and it was late, probably close to midnight. I went straight to my room."

"You didn't leave your room after you got home?"

"I just told you I didn't."

Sam sensed her defensiveness and knew there was more to her story, but he wasn't going to press.

"Sunni, what did you do?"

"Like Alli said, it was late and I was exhausted. I went right to bed. I know I didn't hear anything until the next morning." She stopped for a minute and gave Sam a quizzical look. "Do you think the police are going to ask us these kinds of questions? Surely they won't think we had anything to do with this!"

"Sunni, they will ask you these questions and more. I need you to anticipate what's coming so it won't fluster you." That seemed to satisfy her so he turned to Michael.

"Okay, Michael. What about you?"

"I left the hospital about four o'clock in the morning and went back to my place. I took a shower and slept until about eight. Then I went back to the hospital."

"Can someone verify that?"

"Good grief, Sam. How do I know? Maybe somebody at the hospital knows when I left and when I came back. The doorman at my building might be able to remember. I'll have to ask."

"That's a good idea, Michael. Talk to them as soon as you can. You're going to need an alibi."

Michael rolled his eyes. "Why me?"

"You know, ex-husband and all that jealousy theory. Check with anyone who might be able to verify your story."

Sam looked at the clock over the stove and decided to cut the meeting short so he could get everything accomplished before five o'clock. "Michael, call for the helicopter and I'll see you around noon. We can talk more on our way to the airport. Girls, stock up on some good books. You'll probably get a lot of reading done in the next few days. Mrs. Davis, I'd like to meet with you in thirty minutes to go over plans for feeding and housing our new security crew.

*****

Margo was sitting by the window looking out at the ocean when they arrived. Her long chestnut hair was pulled back in a ponytail and she was dressed in jeans and a t-shirt. Sam thought she looked beautiful, even if she was pale and had dark circles under her eyes.

He was amazed by the sense of tranquility that filled the room; the Margo he was used to was not a peaceful or tranquil person. She thrived on drama and adrenalin. But today she seemed subdued and at peace. He hated to bring her news that would disturb that.

“This is my lucky day. Both of you at the same time must mean trouble in paradise.” She yawned, but didn’t turn around to face them.

“You look like you’re feeling better. Are you resting well?” Michael was cautious with his words and Sam knew that he was trying to keep things as tranquil as possible.

“Michael’s right, “ Sam joined in. “It looks like this is a good day. They must be treating you like a queen here. What a view!” he said as he stood by her side.

“Cut the crap. What’s going on?” Margo still hadn’t turned to face them. She continued to stare at the ocean and sky. “There’s coffee on the table. Help yourself.”

“Margo, Sam and I need to talk to you. May we join you at the window or would you rather we all sit at the table?”

“Pull up some chairs, Michael. I’m comfortable where I am.” She turned slightly and nodded at him.

After they had moved two chairs closer to the window and sat down, there was no way she could continue to ignore them. “What’s so important that it takes both of you?”

They looked at each other and Sam let Michael answer her. "There's no easy way for us to tell you this. But we wanted you to know before it hits the papers." He cleared his throat before going on. "The medical examiner has finished the autopsy and the findings indicate that Paolo was murdered."

Margo began to laugh. The kind of laugh that begins in the gut and shakes the entire body. She doubled over in her chair and continued to laugh.

Michael jumped up and put his arms around her. "Margo, are you all right? What in the world is so funny?" He turned his head toward Sam for support. "Margo, get hold of yourself."

As the laughter subsided, she straightened and threw off Michael's arms. "That's the funniest thing I've heard in a long time. What a cruel joke." Her face was red and she had trouble catching her breath.

"You know we're not joking with you. The autopsy showed that he had pool water in his lungs, not bay water. Apparently he was drowned in a pool and then taken to the bay. It's murder, Margo. And, we don't know if he was the only intended target. Do you understand what I'm saying?" Sam waited for Margo to look at him. "We don't know if someone is also after you."

"You think someone may want to kill me?" She started to laugh again. "That's absurd."

"What kind of medicine are you taking? This is serious, Margo. Listen to Sam." Michael's voice reflected his impatience.

"We don't have any answers, but we're not taking any chances. We've ordered a tight net of security for MarGrove. Michael and the girls will have someone with them at all times and there will be additional security for you and this facility."

"Sam has taken care of everything. It's already in place. Except, this afternoon, you will meet a young woman who will be moving into this suite with you. What's her name, Sam?"

Jumping up from the chair, Margo stood defiantly. "Oh, no you don't. I'm not having someone watching my every move! I'm already in a jail house, now you're telling me I have to have a jailer, too."

"It's not like that and you know it. So stop with the drama." Michael's impatience had turned to anger. "It will just be until we know more about what's going on. We don't know if you're safe or not."

Sam walked over and knelt down in front of Margo's chair. "You may be a target and we want to make sure no one can get to you." He waited for it to sink in. "I've assigned a woman named Claire McGuire to stay with you. She's competent and friendly. I think you'll like her."

"I don't seem to have a choice. Again." She sighed and sat back down. "I don't want to talk to you any more. Go away and give me some time to digest everything." She stared out the window and tried to forget they were in the room. "By the way, when does my jailer arrive?"

"Claire will be here in a few hours. We're lucky that you're in a two-bedroom suite. I'll have someone get the second bedroom ready for her." Sam stood up. "And, Margo, this is non-negotiable until we learn more from the police."

"Not so fast! Didn't you hear me? She's not moving into this suite. Find her a room on this floor and give her an alert button." She grabbed the arms of the chair and glared at Sam. "Nothing doing. Do you hear me?"

"Calm down. I'll see what I can arrange." Sam had hoped that just once she would make it easy for him. "I'm not making any promises, but I'll try."

That seemed to satisfy her and he watched as she released her grip on the chair. "Let's go, Michael. We've got a lot to do."

"You should talk to my daughter." Margo growled.

She dismissed them by turning back to look out the window.

*****

"Why would she want you to talk to her daughter? Which daughter?" Michael asked.

"I'm not sure I know either. Whatever it is I want us to discover it and not the police. Every one of us is probably on Detective Madison's list as a suspect. If I were in his shoes, I'd be looking carefully at all of us. There are too many unanswered questions."

Michael sighed. "You know Sam, some days it just doesn't pay to get out of bed."

Chapter Sixteen

Alli

When Michael and Sam pulled through the gate at MarGrove, they were astounded at the activity. Everywhere they looked there were cars, crime unit trucks, and investigators.

"This place looks like a circus." Michael jumped out of the car before Sam could stop him and headed for the front door where Detective Madison was conferring with several men.

"What's going on here?"

"Mr. Anderson, we're just doing our job. I appreciate that Sam's men and Mrs. Davis have been so cooperative. I don't know how much longer it will take, but we've got to cover the house and the grounds."

The detective turned to answer a question from one of his investigators and then waved to Sam. "There were two reporters at the gate when we arrived. I threatened to arrest them for trespassing." He laughed. "Seriously, I told them to come back at five o'clock for the press conference and they left. But, I'm sure word is already on the street that we're here."

"Welcome to our world, Madison. Just wait until five. There will be hundreds of reporters lined up like vultures."

"I'm going to need a room in the house where I can talk to everyone individually. I'd rather do it that way than have you all come down to headquarters. Can it be arranged?"

Sam walked up on the porch and nodded to Michael. "I'll make sure that you have the privacy you need. Michael, I think the library would be the best place. Do you agree?"

"If it has to be, then I guess that's a good choice." Michael pushed past the men on the porch and entered the house. "By the way, Madison, when is all of this going to begin?"

"Within the hour." He looked at his notebook. "I'll begin with you. Then I'd like to see Sunni, her date, the gardener, Mrs. Davis, then Alli. I'll end with Sam."

Michael scowled at the detective before he closed the door. Then Madison turned to Sam. "I'm sorry he's upset, but this is the way it's going to be." He looked back at the notebook. "Do you know who Sunni was out with? Can you get him over here?"

"Sure. His name is Mark Sanders. He plays guitar in Margo's band and lives over near South Beach. I'll go call and ask him to come over. In what, an hour or so?"

"Better make it two hours. I have to finish up something out here, then I'll be in to talk to Mr. Anderson."

Thirty minutes later Sam called everyone, including Mark Sanders into the kitchen. Sunni wouldn't even look at Mark and hoped this meeting was over quickly.

"I want you to write out a timeline of what you remember from the night Paolo disappeared. Make sure you include everything from about four o'clock on. Where you were, who you were with, who can back it up if needed. We've probably got an hour before they start questioning us."

"Why do you want us to do this? Isn't this like over-kill, Sam?" Alli challenged him from where she was slumped in the chair with her arms folded defiantly. "You're making more of this than is necessary."

"Alli, just do what he asked you to. He's trying to make sure that the detective leaves here satisfied that none of us should be on his suspect list." Michael's tone reflected annoyance. He stared at his daughter for a few seconds and shook his head. "For some reason you aren't taking any of this seriously."

"Do you know why they want me here, Sam? I don't think I have anything to tell them that will be helpful." Mark sat at the far end of the table from Sunni and Alli, and everyone in the room was aware that Sunni had not spoken to him when he appeared in the kitchen.

"I think he will try to corroborate timelines. He probably needs to compare your timeline against everyone else's."

He looked from Mark to the solemn faces of the other's seated at the table. "Now everyone, to help you out a bit, the ambulance was dispatched at 7:05 PM and the EMT's clocked their arrival here at 7:12. They clocked their arrival at Mercy Hospital at 7:37. That should get you started."

He began to make his own notes, then looked around the room. "Write down everything you can recall. Even if you don't think it's important."

*****

Alli watched as Sam read her timeline. "You were in your room until Paolo yelled for you to call the EMT's? I thought you told me earlier you had been out by the pool that afternoon."

"No, you must have misunderstood. I was in my room all afternoon." Sam stared at her but she didn't blink. "This feels like an inquisition. And it's not fair. Paolo's dead and Margo is locked away in rehab somewhere, and you think I'm lying."

He ignored her outburst. "What did you do after you came back from the hospital?"

"I've told you this before, Sam. I went to bed."

She knew Sam was fishing and she wasn't going to give him an inch. She flinched as Sunni's foot connected with her shinbone.

"Are you finished with me, Sam? If so, I'd like to go watch some television." She shrugged and stood up from the table.

"Okay for now, but Detective Madison will be calling you to the library in the next hour or so." Sam shook his head as she walked out of the room. "I hope she doesn't act like that when she's being questioned."

Mrs. Davis leaned over and whispered to Sam, "You know she's not telling you the truth, don't you?" He gave her a slight nod and went on talking to the others.

*****.

Everything went well with the questioning until half way through the session with Alli. "I have some information that's in conflict with what you're telling me, Miss Anderson. Are you sure this is the correct timeline for you?"

"Yes, I'm sure. There's no conflict." Alli flashed a seductive smile at Madison and leaned back in her chair. She refused to look at Sam.

"Miss Anderson, let's go over this again. Now, where were you around two o'clock in the morning?"

"I was asleep."

Madison got up out of his chair and walked across the library to the large window that faced the bay and the boat house. "Do you like to take the boat out? It's a good sized boat for someone your size to handle."

"I can handle the boat, and yes, I take it out often." She didn't flinch.

"Did you take it out that morning around two o'clock?" He turned from the window and walked back to where she was sitting. "Did you go for a ride that night after you came back from the hospital?"

"I've told you before. I was sleeping."

"Miss Anderson, what would you say if I told you that I have two witnesses who will testify that you were in the boat that morning? That you were seen sitting in the boat off Dinner Key around two-thirty that morning? That you were also seen in the boat off the end of Key Biscayne at approximately the same location where Mr.

DaSilva's body was found?" He stood directly in front of her and his body seemed to dwarf her as she sat in the chair.

She stood up and faced him. "I would have to say that your witnesses are mistaken. Sam, why is he saying all this?"

"Alli, did you take the boat out that night? Maybe you wanted to unwind from all the craziness of your mother being taken to the hospital. Right?" Sam's voice was almost pleading with her.

"I know you couldn't lift DaSilva's body and move it from the pool to the boat. But, someone could have helped you. You drive the boat, someone else does the dirty work! Who was it, Miss Anderson? Your dad, Sam, Tomas? Which one of the men did you entice to help you after DaSilva broke it off with you?" Madison was relentless. He fired his questions at her like bullets. "Or maybe it was the new guy? What's his name? Oh, yeah, Mark Sanders. Was he in on this little drama?"

Her face ashen, Alli looked like she was going to faint. "No, I don't know what you're talking about. Sam, tell him I had nothing to do with Paolo DaSilva."

Sam turned to Madison. "You're crossing boundaries here, man. Are you charging her with anything or are you fishing?"

Madison didn't look at Sam, but kept his focus on Alli. "You know you have plenty to tell me. Why not make it easy for all of us?"

"Alli, sit down and don't say another word. Madison, no more questions until she has an attorney!" Sam's anger spilled out all over the room. "You've gone too far and you know it."

"Then you'd better get her an attorney." Madison sat down in the chair across from Alli. "You better consider the truth, Miss Anderson. My witnesses are very reliable."

"Go on to your room, Alli," said Sam. "I have to answer a few questions for the detective and then I'll be up to see you."

He watched as she quickly made her exit. When she was out of sight, he spun around to face the detective.

"You think she's capable of doing this? Madison, she's a kid!" The more he talked, the angrier he became. "For crying out loud, she's a kid."

"And, yes, I think she could have done this, but she had help. I have two witnesses–a fisherman who saw her near the Dinner Key Marina and a Coast Guard officer who saw the boat anchored off Key Biscayne and actually talked to her. They can positively identify her."

He waited for a reaction from Sam, but when there wasn't one, he continued. "Her finger prints are all over that boat, all over the pool house. The water sample analysis says the guy drowned in the pool in this yard. And, if that's not enough, I have someone who will testify that DaSilva was fooling around with her and had told her he was breaking it off."

"Slow down. When have you had time to gather all of this information? You just got the damn report this morning."

"I've had days to begin looking for reasons. And, this angle seems to be panning out. Now I need you to answer my questions." He picked up his pencil and wrote something in his notebook.

"Sam, how long have you worked for this family?"

*****

Sam was stunned. He sat in the library for a time after the detective left. It wouldn't take much more for the police to turn the case over to the district attorney, and when the DA got an earful, he would surely go to the Grand Jury for an indictment.

His thoughts were broken when Michael walked into the room. "How do you think it went with the police?"

"Not good, Michael. Not good at all. Have a seat 'cause you're not going to like what I've got to say." He motioned for Michael to take the seat across from him. "In fact, I should probably get you a drink before we talk."

"Just tell me for crying out loud. I don't need a drink."

"I'm playing my instincts, Michael. But the police are convinced that Alli is involved. They know Paolo died in this pool and they have two witnesses that will testify that she was out on the bay the morning Paolo was murdered. She was in the ski boat, and unfortunately, she even talked to a Coast Guard officer on patrol near Key Biscayne."

"Unbelievable. What was she doing out in a boat in the middle of the night? And, what motive could she possibly have? She hardly knew the guy." He walked to the bar. "You're right. I need a drink."

"They think she had an accomplice. They know there is no way that she could manage to get Paolo's body out of a pool and into the bay. They're fishing, that's all."

He waited until Michael was seated with his drink. "The kicker is, she denied it. She flat out lied and told him she had not been out in the boat that night. He didn't try to trap her, but he will. And, we'd better be ready."

"The girl doesn't have good sense sometimes. Why would she lie?"

"That's the million dollar question. It's time to call the lawyers. Nobody in this house should say another word without counsel present. It's out of my league now."

"My God, Sam, it just keeps going from bad to worse."

"And, I haven't told you the worst of it, Michael. Madison says he's got a witness who will testify that Alli and DaSilva were having an affair and he had told her he was breaking it off."

Michael slumped in the chair and closed his eyes. "I don't believe it. The man is trying to build a case and he doesn't have anything to go on. There is no way my daughter was involved with that man."

"Truth or not, we've got to plan for the worst, Michael."

Chapter Seventeen

Randall, Martinez, and Cannon, Attorneys at Law

Looking across the room at her husband, Elena Martinez was puzzled as she listened to Eric's side of the short phone conversation. He kept rolling his eyes, tapping his pencil, and nodding. She couldn't tell if he was planning a golf game with a friend or talking to a prospective client.

She leaned forward as he hung up the phone. "Well? What was that all about? We don't usually take client calls at home."

"You'll never guess who our next client is. I can hardly believe it myself." He walked over to the sofa and sat down beside her. "That was Michael Anderson and he wants to talk with us about possibly representing his daughter on a murder-one charge."

"Okay, but who's Michael Anderson? And, why should I be impressed?"

"He just happens to be the ex-husband of Margo." Eric Randall smiled from ear to ear. "Do you realize the kind of attention a trial like this is going to generate?"

"Margo, the singer? I didn't know she had a daughter. Come on, what's the scoop?" Elena's interest was piqued and she wanted to know all the details. "Come on, tell me how they got our name."

She was impatient, and he was prolonging his answers and enjoying her discomfort. "You are so nosy, my love. It's like you're reading one of those gossip rags." He started tickling her and pulling her to him.

"And, you're so full of yourself," she said as she pushed him away. "If we've been approached to defend a celebrity's daughter on a murder-one charge, it's going to take our whole team. I'm trying to be professional here."

Her voice rose higher as she squirmed away from him and worked to regain her composure. "Stop tickling me," she giggled, "and tell me what's going on."

"I've got other ideas, but if you insist." Eric straightened up and moved away from his disheveled wife.

"Like I said, that call was from Margo's ex-husband, who is still her business manager and agent. Remember last week, we read about Paolo DaSilva drowning in the Bay? Well, the autopsy report shows otherwise and Michael Anderson thinks they're trying to pin the murder on one of his twin daughters."

"This could get very interesting. Why the daughter?"

"The guy had water from Margo's pool in his lungs, the daughter was seen in a boat in the area where the body was found, and she lied to the police. Not a whole lot to go on, but he feels his daughter is going to need counsel."

"Why us? There are bigger defense names in Miami than us. How did he get our number?"

"We're good and you know it, Elena," Eric kidded. "All kidding aside, do you remember the McDeal case? You know, that bus driver who was accused of kidnapping his daughter? Seems someone connected to that case recommended you. Then Anderson's attorney in New York checked out our firm and agreed that he should call us to set up an appointment. If his guy Anderson thinks we can handle it, we'll get hired."

"The McDeal case? That was one of my first big cases when I was with the Public Defender." Elena stood up and walked across the room to check on their son who was playing in his room. "The circles of our lives. You just never know when one thing is going to lead to another." Satisfied that Jason was still interested in building with his Legos, she turned back to Eric. "When do we meet this daughter? By the way, what's her name?"

"Don't know that yet. But we meet her at Margo's estate in the Grove tomorrow morning at eleven." He walked over and picked up the phone. "I think Jeff should be there, too. If this goes forward, all three of us should be involved."

"You're right. Randall, Martinez and Cannon may have just hit the big-time."

*****

The iron gate and wall that surrounded the estate were not very distinctive, but once she started up the small circular drive-way, Elena could see that MarGrove was impressive. The main house was an imposing Mediterranean villa surrounded by tropical foliage that framed it against the blue of the bay. The beige stucco was highlighted by the black grill work on the lower floor windows and several upper floor balconies. Even though the house was eye-catching, the design did not detract from the view. The architect had masterfully designed the house to take every advantage of the small peninsula where it was located. Scanning the grounds, she assumed the smaller building on the right side of the circle was a guest house and smiled when she thought it was probably close in size to the house where she and Eric lived.

Pulling in behind Eric's car, she hoped she wasn't late. Today was not one of her usual office days so she'd had to arrange to take Jason to a sitter. Traffic on Dixie Highway was snarled because of an accident and it had taken her longer to drive than she thought it would. Stepping out of the car, she was greeted at the front door by a woman she assumed to be the housekeeper.

"Good morning, Ms. Martinez. I hope there was no trouble finding the house. The others were beginning to be concerned." Mrs. Davis smiled as she pointed the way to the living room.

"No trouble finding the house. There was an accident on the highway." Elena looked at the people sitting in the living room, but spoke directly to her husband. "Sorry I'm late."

"We're just glad you're okay. Everyone was beginning to worry." A tall, attractive man extended his hand to her. "I'm Michael Anderson. Please take a seat."

When Elena was seated, she was introduced to the others in the room. Alli and Sunni Anderson were identical twins, but their demeanor and dress told her they had very different personalities. Alli sat indifferently in a chair by the window, dressed in a pool cover-up. Her long chestnut hair was tied loosely and she was barefoot. Sunni, on the other hand, was dressed in slacks and a tailored shirt, her hair piled neatly on top of her head. And, she wore sandals. Alli scowled when she was introduced; Sunni smiled. Seated on either side of Sunni was her father and the head of Margo's security, Sam Baxter. Eric, and their law partner, Jeff Cannon, were seated across the room. The person noticeably absent was Margo.

"We were just beginning a discussion of the events that prompted our call," Michael resumed without emotion. "Paolo DaSilva was a guest in this house until his death ten days ago. He and my ex-wife, Margo, had an on-going relationship, so he was a frequent visitor. His home is in Rio de Janeiro, where his family owns DaSilCo Oil." Michael turned to an easel and chart board that were next to him. "We've developed a timeline of the events as we know them. Sam and I thought this would be the best way to help all of us keep things consistent. We've gotten input from my daughters, Mrs. Davis, the housekeeper, Tomas Labato, Mr. DaSilva's cousin, the gardener, and ourselves."

Eric interrupted. "Why wasn't Margo included in this? Isn't she a factor?"

"Margo was hospitalized the evening of July thirteenth and has not returned home. She has no knowledge of the events that took place at the house after that. DaSilva was reported missing on the fourteenth and his body was discovered in the bay on the fifteenth.

"At first, it was presumed that he went for a swim in the bay and drowned, but the autopsy report released yesterday confirms that he was murdered. The medical examiner found chlorinated water in his lungs, not salt water. It is strange that there was no evidence of trauma to the body. The evidence suggests that he didn't struggle against his attacker." Michael took a breath and continued. "The police have interviewed all of us, but they seem fixated on my daughter, Alli, who apparently was seen in a boat on the bay in the early morning hours of July fourteenth. That's why we called you."

Elena didn't take her eyes off Alli. The girl seemed detached from everything going on in the room and her behavior could be one of the reasons the police suspected her. "Mr. Anderson, have the police given you any indication why they suspect your daughter? It is apparent to me that this crime required strength that I don't think she possesses. From what I've heard so far, the police are presuming that Alli somehow drowned Mr. DaSilva in the pool, carried his body to the boat, and then lifted him over the side of the boat into the bay. That scenario doesn't make sense when I'm looking at a girl who probably doesn't weight a hundred pounds."

"Our sentiments exactly. We think the police are questioning her because they need a suspect. To make it plausible, they think she had an accomplice." Sam responded.

"What's the motive? Jealousy, scorn, drugs? I don't get the connection." Eric addressed his question to Sam but kept his eyes on Alli. The girl continued to look out the window as though she were not even part of the discussion.

"Neither do we, Mr. Randall. But, we thought it best to have a lawyer present from now on if someone in the household is going to be questioned."

"Do you know if the police have questioned anyone else? I'm thinking of the cousin. You said he was in town at the time, correct?"

"They asked him some questions before he flew back to Brazil for the funeral. But I don't know how extensively he was questioned."

Sam looked at the attorney as he spoke. "The issue here seems to be that Alli lied to the police about being out in the boat."

The back and forth conversation continued for a few minutes before Alli stood up. Without looking at anyone, she yawned, "I need to work on my tan. Please excuse me." She flipped the hem of her cover-up and headed out the French doors to the pool.

"Dear God! How can I get her to understand this is serious?" Michael ran his fingers through his hair and groaned.

Elena stood up and followed Alli out of the room. "I think I need to have a chat with her. Innocent or guilty, if she carries this attitude into a police inquiry, it won't look good."

*****

Recognizing the fear lurking behind Alli's blasé attitude, Elena knew their conversation was going to be tricky–but she had to try.

"Miss Anderson, if I'm going to represent you, I think we should get to know each other. Just knowing my name isn't going to build trust between us, is it?" Sitting down in one of the lounge chairs across from the girl, she laughed. "The men just want to talk facts and that does get boring, doesn't it?"

"I don't mean to be rude. But I could care less about any of this. I had nothing to do with whatever happened to Paolo DaSilva and I've told the police that. They can question me all they want, but the story will never change." Alli pulled off her sunglasses and squinted her eyes at Elena. "You're wasting your time."

"Have you ever been through a police investigation?" She watched as Alli shook her head. "Then you probably don't want to go through this without counsel. I've seen police tactics before and their strategies have one goal. They will keep at you until you say something they can use. It's not pretty, but I can help you if you'll let me." She couldn't read the girl's expression, but she knew she could wait her out.

"Whatever makes you happy." Alli's slapped her sunglasses on and adjusted the straps of her swimsuit. "As long as I can work on my tan."

"Let's start at the beginning. Why don't you tell me why you were out in the boat that night and why you lied to the police about it?"

"Very smart, Ms. Martinez. Assume from the start that the client is lying." Alli's attempt at sarcasm sounded hollow.

"If there are people who can identify you, then I don't have to assume anything, young lady. Do you want help, or not?"

"Look, my mother had just been taken to the hospital and I was upset." Alli waited for a reaction.

"I'm sorry to hear that. Is she doing better now?"

"One more drama in the life of Margo. My mother always lands on her feet."

"Back to the boat. What happened?" Elena knew the girl was trying to take the focus off the main issue.

"I couldn't sleep, so I figured a ride around the bay would help. That's all there is to it. The policeman caught me off-guard. I wasn't thinking straight when I told him I hadn't been out in the boat."

"That almost sounds believable. Now, why don't you tell me about your relationship with Mr. DaSilva?" Elena watched a shadow fall across the young girl's face but Alli quickly recovered.

"There was no relationship between me and Mr. DaSilva. What are you driving at?"

"He was your mother's financé, so I thought perhaps you could tell me a little about your interaction with him. I assumed that he was around here a lot." Elena wondered if she had hit a nerve and wanted to keep the girl talking.

"He and mother did their thing. I did mine. I barely knew the man."

"I see. Then you probably had no objections to his relationship with your mother. Is that right?"

"You're assuming we're a family. That's a joke. Margo has her life and I have mine and the two don't intersect very often." Alli rolled over on her stomach and closed her eyes.

"Was Mr. DaSilva an attractive man? I don't recall seeing a picture of him."

"He was nice looking for an old guy. I didn't pay too much attention."

"How long had he been seeing your mother? Months, years?"

"He's been around a couple of years. I don't remember how long." Alli lifted her head and smiled sweetly at Elena. "You see, Ms. Martinez, I don't have anything to contribute."

"Miss Anderson, you would be surprised at the information I've gathered in this brief conversation. And, I can assure you that everything I've picked up will not be lost on the police either." Elena wanted to scare the girl into understanding the precariousness of her situation. "We have more to talk about, but I'll let you get back to your tan for now."

*****

"That girl is something else."

Back at home, Elena put her feet up on the coffee table and sipped a glass of wine. "I don't know what her involvement is with this murder, but there is more to her story than is in this file."

Tossing the folder aside, Eric gave his wife a puzzled look. "What are you going on, Elena? You spent ten minutes with the girl. That's hardly enough time to make a judgment call."

"You should have talked to her. Then you'd know why my gut is telling me to 'walk softly' with Miss Alli Anderson." Elena couldn't find the words to describe her hunch, but she knew the girl was hiding something. "Did you learn anything new from the father or the body guard? And, where in the world is Margo in all of this? I heard them say she was hospitalized, but do you know why?"

"Margo is in some kind of a rehab center in Boca Raton. Seems she tried to kill herself the night all of this happened." Eric shook his head. "It always surprises me when celebrities who have everything in the world try to kill themselves. What a waste."

"No motive for the attempted suicide and no motive for the murder. It'll be interesting to see what the police are working with and what they know. What information do we have on Paolo DaSilva?"

"Right now, not much." Eric replied. "I've asked Jeff to do some background work on the guy and his family. From what I read in the paper, he's an international playboy who every now and then worked for the family oil business. Prominent family in Brazil, runs with a jet set crowd, and he had money to burn." Looking back at the file, Eric smiled. "And from all the pictures that have appeared in the tabloids, the guy always had some starlet or singer hanging on his arm."

"What about the other twin? Do we know anything about her?"

"Elena, call John Avery. We need our investigator to start making some inquiries. Tell him to get us as much as he can on Paolo DaSilva, Alli and Sunni Anderson, Michael Anderson, and Sam Baxter." Eric was making notes in the file. "And, lest I forget. We need the real scoop on Margo. She has to figure in this some way."

"You don't really think she's involved, do you?" Elena thought her husband was stretching what they knew about the case if he wanted to include the singer in their investigation.

"Don't underestimate anything. The lady tried to kill herself just hours before this murder supposedly took place. She's got to know something." He closed the file and leaned back. "Tell John she's in a facility in Boca, so he's not going to be able to get to her directly. But, he's good, Elena. He'll find out all he can and we'll see a clue in it somewhere."

*****

Elena spoke with John Avery and gave him as much information as she could. "John, I know you're going to have to muddle through all the media hype about Margo. But see what you can discover about her relationship with DaSilva. Apparently they were planning to get married. Finding out about the girls will be a bit more difficult. The parents did an a-plus job of keeping them under wraps. I've followed Margo's career for years and I didn't know she had children."

"You've given me names and that's good for now. Let me see what I can find out and get back to you. Any time frame on this one?"

"We're just starting to go over the information. We don't know yet whether anyone I've mentioned is going to be charged. Sam Baxter, the head of Margo's security team, seems to think the police are looking hard at Alli. She lied to them about where she was the morning of the murder."

"Okay. I'll start right away and get back to you by Friday."

*****

Later that day, John called Elena and told her he would need a travel budget. "I'm going to have to take a trip to Pennsylvania, and maybe even to Brazil."

He laughed when he heard her gasp. "Hey, the dead guy lived in Brazil. But I'll put that trip off unless I run into a dead-end."

Chapter Eighteen

Margo

Lulu Sarsyn walked into Margo's suite and took a seat near the window. "Good morning, girlfriend. You ready to start spilling your guts?" she called to Margo who was getting dressed in the bedroom.

"You are crass. Don't you believe in knocking? And what about professionalism?" Margo snarled. It was too early in the morning for her to have to deal with a clown who called herself a psychiatrist.

"Margo, we've got a few weeks to deal with years of garbage and we don't have time for small talk. I am being very professional, so trot yourself over here and take this chair across from me. We've got some talking to do."

Reluctantly, Margo walked over to the living room chair. "What do you think you're going to discover that a thousand others haven't?"

"Honey, I'm still trying to discover who I am. I don't need to know who you are. My job is to help you discover what you need to know to get yourself out of the mess you're in right now. So, let's begin with the day you decided life wasn't worth living any more."

"I don't remember that day." Margo looked sullen and her shoulders drooped. "What else do you want to know about?"

"Until you can talk about that day, there isn't any place for us to go. That day rules your future, Margo. You won't be able to move forward unless you can unravel the puzzle pieces that came together the moment you took all those pills. We humans are masters at covering over the layers of hurt, we're really good at using our sense of self-preservation, and we're even better at finding behaviors to help us mask our feelings. Some of us can do it for a lifetime and others can do it until a catalyst occurs that overrides all the mechanisms they use to justify getting up every day. You need to make friends with that catalyst and the mechanisms you use so you can let them go."

"You're crazy! What do you think you know about me?" Margo jumped out of her chair and moved closer to Lulu. "Don't kid yourself, lady. I know myself very well. I don't need for you to fix me. Do you understand?" Shouting at Lulu, she whirled around and opened the door of her suite. "Leave. I want them to assign someone else."

Lulu didn't blink. She continued to sit in the chair and Margo continued to hold the door open for her to leave. Seconds passed before Margo walked over to the phone. "Who do I need to call to get you out of here?"

"Margo, you're stuck with me. Now why don't you stop resisting and come talk to me? Sooner or later, you're going to want to leave this place, and that won't happen without my signature on your discharge papers."

Slamming the phone down, Margo held her head high and walked regally back to the chair by the window. "You are a bitch." Her raspy voice made the exclamation sound almost comical.

"That's a good place to start. A little anger never hurt anyone. Now tell me about that day, Margo. Even if all we talk about today is the surface stuff, we've got to begin."

"I live in a beautiful house by the bay. It's surrounded by a tropical garden that gives me a great deal of pleasure. You know, I'm a Miami girl. There's something about the salty air, the ocean breeze, and the plants that grow in south Florida that make it feel so different. Usually it feels like paradise. Don't you agree, Lulu?" Her sarcastic tone and the phony smile she pasted on her face were meant to irritate.

"Keep going, Margo. I'll listen to your Chamber of Commerce speech, if that's what you want. Eventually you'll want to talk about something significant."

Margo sighed and gave in. Maybe if she talked to this persistent and annoying woman, she would go away and leave her alone. "Paolo DaSilva was the man in my life. We'd been in relationship for a number of years and had decided we were ready to settle down together. We'd had enough of single life." She didn't want to talk about Paolo but she couldn't remember why. "He was visiting me at my house."

"You and Paolo were planning a wedding, right?"

"I was planning a wedding. He was going to show up and say I do."

Lulu laughed. "Sounds like every man I know. Keep going."

A cloud of sadness fell across Margo's face and she closed her eyes. "Go away, Lulu. Just go away. I don't remember anything else and my throat hurts too much to talk to you or anyone else."

"I know this isn't easy, Margo. But once you can verbalize whatever it is, it will lose its power over you." Lulu started to go on but was interrupted by the apartment door opening. "And, who are you?"

"Excuse me. I was told the session would only last an hour. I'm Claire McGuire and I'm on security assignment here."

"Yes, of course. They told me downstairs that you were here." Lulu stood up. "Ms. McGuire, I'm Dr. Sarsyn and I'm going to need privacy with Mrs. Anderson each day."

"Do I ever get a say in any of this?" Margo whined, but the women ignored her.

"Dr. Sarsyn, it's been an hour, so I was just checking." Claire McGuire was letting the doctor know she knew how to do her job.

"I appreciate that, but in the future, I'll let you know when the session ends."

"Good grief," exclaimed Margo. "The jailer and the inquisitor vying for time with me. I am truly blessed."

Chapter Nineteen

Randall, Martinez and Cannon

John Avery walked into the office and asked to see Elena and Eric. They were not going to believe what he had uncovered about young Alli Anderson.

"Come in, John. Eric and I are anxious to know what you've been able to find out. I'll let him know you're here."

Elena picked up the phone and asked her husband to join them in her office. "He'll be here in a few minutes. Can you tell me if you've found anything substantial?"

"Elena, you've got a tiger by the tail with this family. It's like a bad soap opera!" John Avery took out his notepad and prepared to begin listing his findings just as Eric walked in and took a seat.

"John, tell us what you found out in Pennsylvania." Eric crossed his legs and settled back in the chair.

"Okay, I'll start with Pennsylvania and the twins. Apparently Margo sent them to boarding school when they were eight years old and sort of forgot about them. Rarely visited the school, saw them for a week or two in the summer, and left parenting up to their father, Michael Anderson. Margo and Michael divorced around the time the girls were sent to the school in Pennsylvania. Michael bought a house in the Berkshires so he could be close to the kids when he and Margo weren't on tour. He visited at least once a month all the years they were at school. The girls graduated in May. At that point, Alli came home to MarGrove and Sunni joined her parents on tour. Oh, did I forget to mention, Michael is Margo's manager and they have remained close even after the divorce. Both on a business and a personal level." He looked at the attorneys and smiled. "If you catch my drift?"

"Even after she became engaged to DaSilva?" inquired Eric.

"Seems that way. But, let me start with Sunni. She's a good kid who did well in school. She'll start at Sarah Lawrence in September and wants to be a writer, editor or something like that. She's quiet, no demerits, has a few girl friends from school, and from a conversation I had recently with the housekeeper, Sunni has developed an interest in Mark Sanders. He plays guitar in Margo's band and has had an on-going relationship with Jocelyn McDeal for years." He turned to look at Elena.

"Oh, dear God. You mean those two are still in a relationship? I thought when he left Miami that would break them up." Elena shook her head.

"What are the two of you talking about?"

"Eric, they're the kids I told you about years ago when I was handling the McDeal kidnapping trial. Unlucky kids who fell in love and then discovered they're first cousins."

"Good grief. How'd he get paired up with the Anderson girl?"

"Sunni joined her parents on tour when she finished school in May and that's where she met Mark. I think he's the one that mentioned you to the family. Now he and Sunni are friends. That's about all I can find out about her. But, hold on. This story is about to really get good."

Elena and Eric laughed at John Avery's dramatics. He loved his job and really got excited when he found something he knew would interest them. "Go on John. You've got our undivided attention." Elena leaned forward and rested her arms on the desk.

"Let me tell you about Alli. These twins seem to be polar opposites. Alli was in trouble almost since she entered boarding school. The headmaster had to keep a tight rein on her and she still found ways to get herself in hot water. For years, she had issues with alcohol and men. I'm not talking about boys from neighboring schools. I'm talking about men. Several months before she graduated she got caught in a faculty member's apartment. She'd had too much to drink and his roommate caught them in bed. Her punishment for that indiscretion was confinement to campus and she had to see a psychologist twice a week until graduation."

"Did her parents know about this?"

"Apparently they got a covered-up version. She agreed to the headmaster's terms if he wouldn't give all the details to her father. But, that's just a small part of her story."

"You mean there's more?"

"The young lady has a great voice and got herself a gig at a local club near the school when she was fifteen. She sang every weekend until she was confined to campus. The club owner said she brought in a good crowd. Here's a kicker. The guy was shocked to find out she was Margo's daughter. The kid didn't use her mother's name to get the job. But the story gets even more interesting." John shuffled through some papers and pulled out a picture that he handed to Eric. "Do you recognize the people in the picture?"

"It's Alli and Paolo DaSilva. Where was this taken?" He handed the picture to Elena.

"It was on a bulletin board at the club where she sang. When I asked the bartender about it he told me the guy was there at least once a month and they were 'lovey dovey.' I asked him if he knew the man's name, but he didn't. Just said for the past few years, the guy came to the club and Alli always left with him when she finished her last set."

Elena was stunned. "Do you think they were having an affair? This is crazy. She's got to be thirty years his junior and if this was going on for years, she was way underage."

"After I got this info, I began checking around town. The guy had an apartment near the club that he had been renting for the past two years. He came in town once or twice a month and stayed the weekend. When I showed the landlord the picture of the two of them, he said the girl was there every weekend that DaSilva was in town."

"That's wild." Eric turned to Elena, "Do you see an ugly little picture developing here? This has got to be a big part of the scenario that took place the day Margo tried to commit suicide and DaSilva was killed." He turned back to the investigator. "Do you think anyone at the house knew about this? Her father, her sister?"

"From the facial expressions I got from the housekeeper, she knows something. I don't think anyone else does. I don't know what Alli told her sister about her weekends with DaSilva, but I'd bet she didn't tell her the truth, if anything at all. She apparently forged a letter from her mother to the school giving her permission to spend weekends at the home of a family friend and that allowed her to go off campus"

"What do you think our chances are that the cops don't know this stuff?" Eric asked John.

"Right now, we're way ahead of them. But when they start digging, they will see this as an even stronger case against the teenager. You know, a love triangle gone very, very wrong. The only problem I can see is the issue of Alli being able to get DaSilva's body from the pool to the boat and then from the boat to the bay. If she did this, she didn't do it alone."

"You think she had an accomplice?" Eric looked puzzled. "That doesn't make sense."

"I don't think she did it. And, you're right, it just doesn't add up. But there are others who might have wanted to do away with DaSilva for taking advantage of a young girl."

"Are you thinking her father did this?" Elena shook her head. "I don't think I go with that theory. But, it's certainly possible."

"How about the bodyguard, Sam Baxter? Did either of you know the man is a former Navy SEAL?" John handed Eric a report that contained information he had found on Sam.

"Are you serious? A SEAL would know how to take care of a sleaze bag like DaSilva in an instant. But, he'd be too smart to get caught. No, this had to be somebody who didn't stop long enough to figure out there'd be an autopsy. You know I'm not your everyday crime sleuth, but even I'd be smart enough to know that pool water and bay water are not the same."

"I love it when there are pieces to a puzzle that don't seem to make sense. The fun of being a defense attorney is moving the pieces around until the picture becomes clear."

"John, you've done a great job. What's next?" asked Elena.

"I'm leaving tonight to fly to Rio. There's got to be something in Brazil that will help us. This guy was a mover and shaker. I don't know how Margo got mixed up with him in the first place, but we haven't scratched the surface on him, yet. I figure I'll be gone about three days."

"Call us if you need anything and we'll see you when you get home."

Chapter Twenty

Detective Madison

"I'm running into walls all over the place with the DaSilva murder."

Todd Madison tried not to sound like a quitter, but he hadn't turned up anything new in several days that would help with his case. "I know the girl didn't do it by herself, but there's got to be some link between her and the murder." He looked at his supervisor and shrugged. "A couple of my informants on the beach have mentioned DaSilva and Labato's names, so there might be a drug connection. Maybe one of them was supplying the girl with drugs."

"Go over all your notes again. You'll see something you missed the first time."

"I know the logical choices here would be Michael Anderson or Sam Baxter, but I can't find a hole in either of their stories."

"There has got to be a reason that girl was out in a boat in the middle of the bay at four o'clock in the morning. She knows something, even if she didn't do it. Put some pressure on her and she'll crack. She's a kid, not a hard-nosed killer."

"Whatever you say, but you don't know her. She's a tough one." Resignation was in his voice when he replied. He knew it was going to take more than pressure for him to crack Alli Anderson.

*****

"Mrs. Davis, I'd like to see Alli. Would you ask her to come down to the living room?"

The housekeeper frowned. “Detective Madison, you know her father told me not to let her talk to you unless her attorney is present. You’ll get me fired.”

“May I use the phone to call her attorney? I need to talk to the girl today.”

He made the call to the attorney’s office. “It’ll take the lawyer about thirty minutes to get here. Do you mind if I keep you company in the kitchen until she arrives?”

“All right, but I don’t have any answers for you. So, don’t start asking me questions,” she said sternly.

He followed her into the kitchen and gladly accepted a piece of her apple pie and a cup of coffee. “How long have you worked for the family, Mrs. Davis?”

“Long enough not to answer your question. Young man, I told you not to ask me anything.” Mrs. Davis was warming up to the serious detective. He was always polite, even when others in the house were rude to him. But, she knew Sam had his reasons for telling her to be cautious about what she said.

“Right. I’ll just overwhelm you with praise. This is a great piece of pie. Do you bake every day or do I need to time my visits to certain days when you have something good to offer?”

“You keep asking questions, don’t you? But I’ll tell you that I usually have something good coming from the oven every day. You act nice and stop trying to get me to tell you something that’ll get me in trouble and I’ll make sure to save you something.” Mrs. Davis smiled, but she was shrewd enough to know he would try to trick her if she wasn’t careful. After all, he had a job to do–just like she did.

“That’s a deal. I won’t ask you anything else. But if you knew something that would keep Alli out of trouble, you’d tell me wouldn’t you?”

"You are questioning yourself out of your next piece of pie, young man. So be quiet and eat."

The door to the kitchen swung open and a hot, sweaty Sunni ran over to grab a glass of water. So far she hadn't seen the detective, but after she had gulped down half a glass she turned to Mrs. Davis. "I ran three miles in this heat. I'm nuts!"

"Sunni, dear, we have a guest." She pointed behind Sunni toward the man sitting at the kitchen counter. "Why don't you sit down and keep the detective company while you're cooling off?"

"How embarrassing! I'm sorry, Detective Madison, I didn't see you. Please excuse how awful I look." Sunni tried to cover her disheveled appearance with a laugh. "I decided that the sun wasn't really as hot as the temperature showed. Boy, was I wrong." She carried her glass over to the counter and sat down. "What are you doing here?"

"I came to see your sister. But I have to wait until her attorney gets here. Mrs. Davis has threatened me, so I'm afraid to ask you any questions." Madison looked at the pretty young girl sitting across from him and smiled. He hadn't been around the twins much, but he did know there was a world of difference between them. "Do you run every day?"

Before Sunni could answer, Mrs. Davis held up the wooden spoon she had in her hand. "That was a question. I told you not to ask any more questions."

Sunni laughed and Madison shook his head. "You see what I mean."

"I like to run and every chance I get I try to make a circle around the neighborhood. This is a great place to run. Do you run?"

"Every morning at five-thirty. I have a five-mile loop mapped out around my house. It usually takes me an hour to make the circuit. I don't have time to go to the gym, so running allows me to indulge in things like Mrs. Davis's fantastic pie." He made sure he said it loud enough for the housekeeper to hear.

The doorbell rang and Todd Madison stood up. "Mrs. Davis, that's most likely the attorney. If you'll allow me to go to the door, I'd appreciate it if you would ask Alli to join us."

"Young man, you go sit in the living room. I'll take care of the door and Alli," Mrs. Davis said indignantly. "I can do my job, sir."

Sunni and the detective grinned at each other and walked to the living room. "I like that woman. Is she always so bossy?"

"She runs this place and don't you forget it." Sunni pointed her finger toward the housekeeper and gave the detective a smile.

As they settled into chairs in the living room, Elena Martinez walked in. "Hello, Detective Madison. And, I'm taking a guess, but I think you're Sunni, right?"

"That was good, Ms. Martinez. It usually takes people time to tell us apart. What gave me away?" Sunni laughed. "Have a seat, please."

"The running shoes gave you away. I can't imagine your sister as a runner." Elena's sarcasm wasn't missed by the others in the room.

Alli walked in the room and sat down near the French doors. "I'm here. Who wants to see me?"

"I have a few questions, Miss Anderson." He turned to Elena. "I would like to record this session; with your permission, of course.

Elena nodded. "I agree. But I warn you I will stop any line of questioning that even hints of entrapment."

"That's fair." He walked over to the chair where Alli was sitting. "Now, Miss Anderson, please tell me once again what you were doing in a boat on the bay at four o'clock in the morning the day Mr. DaSilva disappeared?"

"I couldn't sleep. I needed some fresh air. That's it." Alli rolled her eyes and slouched down in the chair.

"Last time we talked, you told me you hadn't been in the boat. So I'm guessing from your response today that you were mistaken the other day? Is that something you do frequently? Go out in the boat, that is?"

"Every chance I get. I have a boat, I live on the bay, and I like to be on the water."

"Do you usually take the boat near Key Biscayne?"

"Sometimes." Alli's answer was terse.

"Okay. Now let's talk about you and Mr. DaSilva. What was your relationship with the deceased?"

Alli moved awkwardly in the chair. "I didn't have a relationship with the man. He was my mother's houseguest, not mine."

"You were in the house for over a month before your mother and sister returned home for the summer. You and Mr. DaSilva must have had some kind of interaction during that time, right?"

"We politely shared space if we happened to be in the same room at the same time. Is that what you mean?"

"Miss Anderson, did you have a sexual relationship with Mr. DaSilva?"

"Enough! Question time is over, detective. Alli, do not answer that question." Elena jumped up and interrupted before her client could answer. "You know better than to ask that kind of question. Unless you're charging her with a crime, there will be no more questions."

"Mrs. Martinez, isn't it better for me to ask these questions than the Grand Jury?"

"I think interview time is over. Sorry."

*****

After the detective left the house, Elena looked from one twin to the other. Sunni sat in stunned silence while Alli looked amused. She asked Sunni if she could have some time alone with Alli. "I need to go over some things with your sister. This is preliminary stuff, Sunni. Don't look so worried."

After Sunni left the room, Elena gave up all pretense of politeness and looked sternly at Alli. "Young lady, the expression on your face confirms that I'm dealing with a child, so I'll try to remember that even though you're eighteen, I'm not really dealing with an adult."

A moment of surprise crossed Alli's face, but she caught herself before she reacted.

"Do you have any idea why that detective was back here this afternoon?"

Alli shook her head and Elena continued. "Someone thinks you either murdered that man or have some knowledge about who did. They will probably try to take this to the Grand Jury for an indictment and when they do, you will be arrested. To make this very clear, you will go to jail."

"Arrested!" Alli shouted and moved forward in her chair. "For what? I didn't do anything but take a boat out for a ride. Is everyone crazy?"

"We need to have some serious conversations about you and Mr. DaSilva. That detective thinks he knows something or he wouldn't have come back here today." Elena was calm but emphatic. "Who do you want to talk to Alli? Me or the Grand Jury?"

"And, what do you think you know that I haven't already told you, Ms. Martinez?"

"I know that you're not helping your cause with your attitude, Miss Anderson. And, it may come back at you in very unpleasant ways." Elena picked up her things and headed out of the room. "By the way, I didn't bring it with me, but I have a photo you might be interested in seeing." She turned to give Alli a knowing glance. "I can see myself out."

*****

When Elena stepped out the front door of the estate, Madison was waiting for her in the driveway. "Do you have a few minutes, Ms.

Martinez? There are a few things I'd like to tell you. We can sit in the shade on that bench. If that's all right with you?"

Hesitating, Elena finally looked at the detective and agreed to the impromptu meeting. "What do you need to talk to me about? You've already tried to trap my client." She wasn't going to give an inch.

"Hey, I'm not the bad guy here. I'm trying to see if there's any way we can keep this from going to the Grand Jury."

"You know you don't have enough to make a case. Why do you keep harassing Alli Anderson when there is a murderer on the loose? She didn't have anything to do with this and you know it." The detective was playing games with her and she didn't like it.

"I don't know how this family got involved with DaSilva, but there may be some very unsavory people out there who think that young lady is fair game. Sam Baxter has extra security on 24/7 here at the house and at the facility where the mother is staying. I just think you and your husband need to know, since you're closely involved."

"Are you telling me I'm in some kind of danger?" Taken by surprise, Elena shifted her weight on the bench and leaned forward where she could get a better look at the man. "Do I need to have security, also?"

"I'm just telling you some of what I know. It may be important for you to be cautious."

"Thanks for the heads up. I'll discuss this with Eric and Jeff Cannon. He's our other partner." She stood up to leave. "Is there any other information you can give me about these people?"

"I don't have names. All I know is there's an underworld connection that we all need to be aware of."

As she drove out the gate, she wondered if Madison had tipped his hand too much by giving her this warning.

Chapter Twenty-one

Rio de Janeiro, Brazil, July 1980

John Avery

Gazing out the hotel window, John Avery never tired of looking at the lights of a city. The sparkle always hid the ugliness. He stared at the statue of Christ the Redeemer looking down over Rio de Janerio and found it ironic that the Protector of this city didn't do anything to ward off the shattering poverty.

Rio was a city that had grown quickly in the past twenty years and he was sure that many of the newcomers probably wished they had stayed on the farms. Today, when he rode through sections of the city, he was almost brought to tears by the sights of dirty, hungry children begging for scraps. Then he stood in front of the lavish estate of Paolo DaSilva and wondered how many families might go to sleep with full stomachs if they had the crumbs from under the tables of the families in DaSilva's neighborhood.

A knock on the door changed his thoughts and his focus. He became alert and suspicious as he walked across the room and said through the door, "Sim, Quem esta?"

"Abra a porta, senhor!"

Cautiously, John opened the door and was pushed aside by four men who forced their way into the room. He moved out of the way and waited. Three of the men looked behind curtains, doors, and furniture, while the fourth man motioned for him to sit down. So far there were no guns visible.

"Do you speak English?" John asked as the man shoved him toward the chair.

"When I have something to say, you'll know it." The burly man spoke English with a heavy Portuguese accent. "Why are you in Brazil?"

"I'm on vacation and, I might add, you're a strange welcoming committee."

"I'll ask you again. Why are you in Brazil?" The man took a threatening stance and leaned over John. The threat in his behavior was more than implied.

"I've already answered that question. What else do you want to know before I call hotel security?"

"Mr. Avery, I suggest you answer my question. My boss wants to know why you are nosing around in Rio."

"Who is your boss?"

"Eduardo DaSilva."

"Ah, yes. I know his name." John was quiet for two seconds. "Tell the gentleman that I love this city and I'll be doing some more sightseeing tomorrow." He stood up and walked to the door. "Now if you'll leave, I was planning to watch some television."

"We're watching every move you make, Mr. Avery. The boss wants to know why you're here and what you're looking for. He's not through with you, if you get my drift." The man motioned for the others and they started to leave.

John hadn't realized that he had attracted any attention and decided that his next move would be to contact Mr. DaSilva.

"By the way gentlemen. Tell your boss I'd be honored to meet with him."

*****

The next morning John's hotel phone rang. He listened to the caller.

"Yes, Mr. DaSilva. I'll wait for your car in front of the hotel in ten minutes."

*****

The chauffeur opened the door to the stretch-limo for John and he climbed into the back seat. A distinguished, elderly gentleman sat stone-faced staring at him, but before the car left the curb the man spoke to him in perfect English.

"You wanted to talk, Mr. Avery. So, talk."

"Mr. DaSilva, I'm looking into the death of your grandson and I'm hoping you can answer some questions for me."

"Who do you represent, Mr. Avery? And, why do you think I can tell you anything about this tragedy?"

"I work for an attorney who is representing the Anderson family. For several reasons they want to find out why your grandson was killed."

"Ah, yes. The lovely Margo. You know my grandson was in love with her. But I understand she was hospitalized before Paolo was killed, so why are the police investigating her?"

"Actually, Mr. DaSilva, the police think they can build a case against her daughter, Alli."

The man threw back his head and laughed. He slapped John Avery on the leg as he chuckled. "Do you know how absurd you sound? That is a joke, right?"

"I agree. It sounds preposterous. But never the less, she is under scrutiny and the prosecutor plans to take it to the Grand Jury. They don't have anything else and there is some damaging evidence against her. She was seen out in a boat around four in the morning the day that your grandson disappeared. And, then she lied about it."

"We both know she didn't have anything to do with this. But, why should I cooperate with you or with the police? My grandson was killed while he was a guest in Miami. What did they do to protect him?"

Ignoring the elderly man's anger, John continued. "Do you know of any reason why your grandson would be the target of murder?"

"My grandson was a wealthy playboy with very healthy appetites. There are any number of men who would have enjoyed killing him." He shrugged. "Maybe even a few women. But do I know any of them? No."

Abruptly the car came to a stop. The chauffeur opened the door and motioned for John to get out of the car. "Would you mind telling me where I am?"

"Ah, Mr. Avery, you wanted to see the sights of Rio. Enjoy yourself."

As the car pulled away, two, maybe three men jumped him from behind.

*****

The next morning, he woke up in the hospital with his leg in a cast, bandages on his arms, a massive headache, and swollen lips. But, he didn't have one piece of new evidence or his wallet or money for that matter. He groaned.

"Good morning, Mr. Avery."

Opening his eyes, he stared at a younger version of Eduardo DaSilva. "Who the hell are you?" He groaned again. "I don't think there's an empty spot for you to beat on, if that's why you're here."

"My grandfather was concerned and sent me to check on you."

"You mean after he had me trashed, he wanted to see if I was still breathing?" John tried for sarcasm, but his lips were too swollen to be effective.

"You're all wrong. He heard about this unfortunate incident when the police called him this morning. He has generously taken care of your medical bills and will make sure that you have a safe return to

Miami when you are able to travel. He deeply regrets that you were injured, but some streets in Rio are not safe after dark. You must have wandered into one of those places last night."

"Who are you?"

"My name is Tomas Labato."

John's ears perked up when he heard the name. He knew from the police report that this guy had identified Paolo DaSilva's body.

The man continued talking as he walked to the door. "I live in Rio, but have traveled many times to the States. I really love Miami." He stopped as though he had forgotten something. "I've left my card on the table. Please call me if my family can be of further assistance."

Later that day, John asked one of the nurses to send a telegram to Randall, Martinez, and Cannon. HAVE BEEN IN ACCIDENT. STOP. WILL BE HERE A FEW MORE DAYS. STOP. NOT SERIOUS.

Chapter Twenty-two

Alli

The early morning breeze was soft against her cheeks and the orange and yellow glow of the sunrise crossed the eastern sky promising a beautiful day. The ripples on the bay caught the first rays of the sun and the light danced across the top of each small wave with playful energy. Alli sat on the bench outside the boathouse with her legs pulled up under her and watched. After a restless night, her thoughts were running wild. She was afraid and there was no one she could tell or ask for help. The bravado that had gotten her through all of her life had vanished and she had never felt so vulnerable.

Sunni wouldn't understand, her father would be shocked, and her mother hated her and had already told her she never wanted to see her again. She had tried to hook-up with Mark Sanders but he had actually brushed her off. Nothing in her world was working–not even alcohol. She needed a man. Her body was crying out to be touched, but she couldn't leave the estate.

The detective was making her nervous. He knew she didn't have anything to do with Paolo's death, so why was he hounding her? Even the attorney made her nervous. What photo did the lady have that could be so incriminating?

So far, she didn't think her mother had told anyone the reason for her suicide attempt, but she knew that piece of information would eventually be shared with the world. Margo's love of drama would trump concern for her daughter; and why not? Alli hadn't honored any family loyalties with all her affairs, particularly the affairs with Paolo and the other men in her mother's life. But what did it matter? She didn't even know her mother and, she rationalized, how could she have feelings for someone she didn't know? No, she didn't owe her mother any loyalty.

Stretching toward the warmth of the rising sun, she imagined Paolo's hands kneading and probing her body and she groaned. She missed his touch and the ache in her body reminded her that it had been weeks since she had felt a man's arms around her.

A splash in the pool told her she wasn't alone and she turned to see Sam Baxter swimming laps. Her eyes were drawn to his taut body as he glided across the length of the pool and she wondered why she had never noticed how muscular he was. Now is a good time to take a swim. She walked quietly across the lawn, stepped out of her shorts and shirt, and dove into the pool. The lace of her underwear clung to her in just the way she had intended as she matched her strokes to Sam's. When they reached the end of the lap, she pulled her body close to his.

"Good morning. Do you mind if I join you?" She lowered her eyes demurely and waited for his reply.

"Hey, it's your pool. I'll just swim a few more laps and be out of here." Sam didn't even look at her. He let go of the side of the pool and swam away.

Alli hurried to catch up with him. When she reached the other end of the pool she grabbed his arm. "Are you always so on task, Sam?"

"When I have a nearly naked teenager swimming next to me, I don't have a choice." Sam's expression didn't change. "Go swim, Alli, and leave me to do the same." He pulled away and continued down the length of the pool.

She swam to the shallow end and climbed out of the water. The sunlight on her wet underwear made it appear that she was nude and she made no attempt to cover herself. She stood at the steps where he would exit the pool and waited for him to finish his swim.

As he stood in the shallow water, she made herself even more available to him by walking down the steps so that her breasts were at his eye level. "Don't you ever get lonely, Sam?"

"Sweetheart, you flatter me. You've got a great body and I'm sure you're terrific in bed. But I'm not the guy for you." He smiled, wrapped a towel across his shoulders and walked past her toward the guest house.

Fuming, she whispered after him, "You're the only man around, Sam. I have plans for us."

*****

Later that morning, seated across from Elena Martinez, she waited to see what mumbo-jumbo they were going to throw at her today. The whole investigation thing was testing her and she knew she had to keep her guard up.

"Alli, I thought you should know everything we have in our files. Perhaps that will refresh your memory when it comes time for you to answer more questions for Detective Madison." Elena pulled a folder from her briefcase and opened it. "The first thing I wanted to ask you about is this picture." She handed Alli the photo that John had found at the club in Pennsylvania.

"Good, God. Where did this come from?" Alli was surprised and then quickly tried to cover her reaction. "So what? It's a picture of me and Paolo."

"It was on a bulletin board in a club in Pennsylvania. I understand you sang there on the weekends when you were in school. What was he doing there?" Elena wasn't going to tip her hand.

Staring intently at the photograph, Alli tried to think what to say next. She wasn't about to let her attorney trap her into saying something she would regret. "I don't remember the occasion."

"The club owner tells a different story. He seemed to think Paolo visited you frequently. So, it wasn't hard for us to find the apartment he rented for the past two years. I'm just wondering how you managed to keep this a secret from your sister. Didn't she question that you spent several weekends away every month?"

Alli's eyes widened and she hissed between her lips. "Who do you think you are?"

Elena folded her hands in her lap and gently replied, "Miss Anderson, I'm the attorney your family has hired to represent you. My dear, you are under investigation for murder, and I don't think you've started dealing with the reality of what you may be facing."

Alli threw the picture across the room and angrily swept the magazines off the table next to her. "What do you want from me?" Her mind flashed back to the last time she had said those words and she pictured Dr. Morgan, the psychologist at Brentwood Academy, giving her a knowing smile. To erase that image from her mind, she jumped up from the chair and began pacing.

"I know you're angry," Elena said quietly. "But I'm here to help you. You need somebody on your side, Alli. If this goes to the Grand Jury, you'll need me. As sophisticated as you are, I don't think you're ready for what a police or Grand Jury interrogation can do to you." She walked over to where the young woman was standing. "I'm not judging you. All I want to do is help you get through this."

Elena motioned to her, "Come sit down and let's find a way to make this as easy as possible. We've got so much ground to cover."

For over an hour the two discussed the allegations and anything Alli might know about DaSilva's dealings with the underground. Elena felt like she was dragging every word out of Alli's mouth and no matter what she asked, the girl skirted around a truthful answer. Finally, she looked at her and asked, "We've talked around the issue of you and DaSilva. I know there's more to this story than you're telling me. Someday soon you may trust me enough to let me help you. One omission in your story is your mother. Tell me about your relationship with her."

"That's simple, Ms. Martinez. I don't have a relationship with my mother. Never have and most likely, never will. Margo is a diva who decided before we were born that Sunni and I were of no consequence. She pays the bills and we stay out of her way. That's the beginning and end of our story. As far as Margo is concerned, my sister and I are nothing but the diva's shadow."

"Children deserve more than that. I'm sorry." Elena was almost afraid to ask her next question. "This may be a touchy subject, but how do you think you'll react when your mother testifies against you?"

"I'll do what I've done all my life. I'll look her in the eyes and smile."

*****

At two o'clock that afternoon, Detective Madison drove up to the gate at MarGrove and asked to be admitted to the property. When Mrs. Davis opened the front door for him, he told her he needed to see Alli.

Alli entered the room dressed in a sun dress that accented her tan and her hair was piled high on the top of her head. She greeted the officer politely and took a seat.

Todd Madison tried to keep his objectivity, but Alli Anderson was beautiful. Every time he saw her he was aware of her magnetism and he wished the circumstances were different.

"Don't I need to have my attorney present to talk to you?"

"Unfortunately, I'm not here to talk, Miss Anderson. I'm here to inform you that you are under arrest. You have the right to remain silent. Anything you say will be used against you in a court of law. You have the right to consult with your attorney and to have your attorney present during questioning." The stunned expression on her face stopped him. "Miss Anderson, I have been trying to prepare you for this possibility for days. I'll give you time to call your attorney and your father before we leave. Please ask them to meet us at the county jail."

“You can’t be serious about this?” Mrs. Davis moved between Alli and the officer. “This has got to be a mistake.” Her voice was ragged with emotion. “Let me call for Sam and the two of you talk this over. You can’t take this young girl to the county jail!” She hurried to the intercom and called for Sam.

“Please make those phone calls. I can only give you a few more minutes.” He handed Alli the phone. “Tell your father to go ahead and begin making arrangements for bail. You don’t want to be in that place any longer than you have to be.”

“Then why would you put me there? What are the charges? Oh, dear God!” Alli was struggling to breathe, but in her wildest imagination she had never prepared for this.

“Five more minutes, Miss Anderson. You’d better make those calls.”

Sam ran into the room shouting, “Madison, what’s going on here?”

“I’m here to arrest Alli Anderson for the murder of Paolo DaSilva. She has been read her rights and I’ve given her time to call her attorney and her father, but she doesn’t seem to want to make the calls.”

“You better hope you’ve got enough evidence for this arrest!” Sam shouted at Madison, but turned to Alli. “Go upstairs right now and change your clothes. Put on jeans and a long sleeved shirt. And, change into some sensible shoes.” When Alli didn’t move, he shouted at her, “Do it now!”

He motioned to Mrs. Davis, “Go with her and make her hurry. This is serious.”

Grabbing the phone, Sam dialed Michael’s number and advised him of the situation. He asked him to call the attorney’s office to let them know what was happening and to ask them the name of a bail bondsman.

He turned to Madison, “I’ll follow you downtown. The others will meet us there.”

Within a few minutes, Alli came down the stairs followed by her sister and Mrs. Davis. When Sunni started to speak, Sam motioned for her to stay silent. "Sunni, I'm going downtown with your sister. Your dad will meet us there. Everything is going to be all right. Do you hear me? It's going to be all right."

Detective Madison walked over to Alli, placed her in handcuffs, and walked her out to his car. She didn't look back at Mrs. Davis or Sunni who stood crying in the living room.

"Oh, Mrs. Dee, this is the worst moment of our lives," Sunni sobbed as the older woman held her in her arms.

Chapter Twenty-three

Boca Raton
Margo

"You again. Why don't you just move in here and make it easier on yourself?" Margo wasn't in the mood to meet with Lulu. It seemed like every time she turned around the woman was in her face.

"Girlfriend, you know you look forward to our little chats. I'm the one thing that's going to get you out of this place, so be nice to me." Lulu entered the room with gusto. Her multi-colored caftan was awhirl as she walked and she was talking more with her hands than her mouth. "It's a beautiful day and we have work to do, so let's get to it."

Margo groaned. "Are you always so jovial? You get on my nerves." She had just crawled out of bed for the ten a.m. meeting and she wasn't awake yet. "I need a cup of coffee."

"Pour me one, too. I need to brace myself for your bad mood." Lulu took a chair and waited. "Did you have a rough night?"

"You'd think with all the money I've got, I could pay you not to bother me." Margo took her place and glared at her counselor. "Which of my secrets do you want to know today?"

"Usually I let you choose a secret to tell me, but today I want you to talk about your girls. I'd like to know something about them." Lulu made herself comfortable in the chair and took the coffee mug that was slammed down in front of her.

"There's not much to tell. Michael and I had decided there wouldn't be any children, then I got pregnant and had twins. The girls have been in boarding school since they were eight and Michael takes care of the parenting. I'm not the motherly type. End of story, Lulu, let's move on to the next topic."

"Interesting story. But let's sit with it for a few minutes." There was a purposeful silence before Lulu said, "What are their names?"

"Michael named them. Some kind of play on my middle name. I'm Alison and he very cutely named them Alli and Sunni." She was bored with the conversation and had no intention of continuing to discuss her daughters.

"Tell me about Sunni? Is she as bright as her name?"

"She's a sweet girl. Michael tells me she's very smart, loves school and wants to be a writer. She traveled with us for a few weeks after she graduated from high school this past May."

"Ah, you went to a graduation recently. That must have been fun."

The comment irritated Margo. "Lulu, I don't do graduations. For that matter, I don't do recitals, birthday parties, or any other type of children's events."

"But you did spend time with Sunni this summer, right? What did you learn about her that you didn't know before?"

"She likes to read."

Lulu waited for Margo to go on, but the silence registered the woman's indifference. "Okay. Tell me about Alli."

"No." The expression on Margo's face changed and her features hardened. Her reaction was visceral and she was shaken by the emotions that grabbed her. Why am I having this violent reaction? What did Alli do that has me so upset?

"Whoa, sister. Back up and let's start again. What's going on in that pretty head of yours? I asked you to talk about your daughters, not confess your transgressions to the pope."

Taking a deep breath, Margo knew she had to defuse her emotions before she answered the doctor's question and her throat was really hurting. “Look, Lulu, I don’t have anything more to say about my daughters. They are people I barely know. Our lives don’t intersect but once or twice a year. Their father makes decisions for them. All I do is help pay their bills. They come to MarGrove in the summer; sometimes I’m there; most often I’m not.”

Margo turned and looked out the window at the gathering clouds. “Don’t you get it? I never wanted to be a mother. It happened and I’ve provided well for those girls. That’s my only obligation to them.” Her voice sounded tired and no matter how hard she tried, there was no way she could project any quality sounds.

“Are you telling me that you have no feelings toward Alli and Sunni? Is that it?” Lulu leaned forward and caught Margo’s eye. “You may be able to kid yourself on this one, my dear. But you’re not kidding me. Your emotions run pretty high when it comes to those girls and I think you need to explore where those emotions come from.”

“You don’t know what you’re talking about!” Margo ended the conversation by going into the bathroom and slamming the door.

*****

When she was sure that Dr. Sarsyn was gone, she walked out of the bathroom and crawled back in her bed. She tried to relax, but her body was tense and she couldn’t push the thoughts away. Never before had she felt guilty about her lack of interest in the twins, but today she couldn’t stop thinking about the reaction she had to Lulu’s questions. She was angry with Alli, very angry. But her mind wouldn’t hold on to why. Closing her eyes, she saw an image of her daughter in the pool house. Beautiful, exotic, sensual Alli. Chestnut hair falling softly around her face, big chocolate colored eyes dancing when she laughed, graceful body curving in the right places.

At eighteen years old, she looked twenty-five and possessed a natural magnetism that Margo had worked years to cultivate. Why do I see her in the pool house? Why can’t I remember? She slammed her fist against the pillow and kicked the covers to the floor. A rapid pulse and sweaty palms reminded her of the hopelessness she felt when she tried to remember. That image was locked in her mind but she couldn't go to the next frame; she couldn't find the answer.

*****

Hours later, she woke up crying. Tasting the salt from her tears and feeling the dampness on the pillowcase gave her a sense of release. She knew she had been crying long enough to wash away the anxiety she had felt before she fell asleep. How am I going to climb out of all this chaos surrounding my life? For the first time she asked herself the question, what happens to me if I've really lost my voice? Oh, God, I need help!

Michael opened the door and saw that Margo was still in bed and the covers were in a heap on the floor. "Hi. Nobody mentioned that there was a problem. Are you okay?"

Softly he walked over and stood looking down at his ex-wife. "Even with your hair uncombed, no make-up, and eyes puffy from crying, you are still the most beautiful woman in the world." Gently he pushed strands of hair away from her face as he whispered.

"Margo, are you going to sleep all day? Wake up and visit with me for a few minutes." Leaning down, he kissed her forehead and whispered. "You know you broke my heart and I've had to watch your self-destructive behavior. If only I knew how to save you. All I can do is hope that at some point you decide for herself that you are worth saving and finally take the steps only you can take. I'll wait for you, no matter how long it takes.

"Michael? What are you muttering about? What time is it? Have I slept all day?" Margo mumbled as she tried to wake up. "Are you my reward for good behavior?" She smiled and sat up, letting Michael fluff the pillows behind her.

"It's two o'clock in the afternoon. I think you slept through lunch. Your tray is still over there on the table." He pointed to the untouched food tray. "You look like you've had a rough morning. Want to talk about it?"

"That doctor is relentless." Pouting like a little girl, she aimed for some sympathy from Michael. "I want to go home. I'm fine. All I need to do is rest my voice for a few months and I'll be ready to go back to work."

"I'm glad you're feeling better, but you seem to forget that you tried to kill yourself. I don't think they'll let you go home until you've dealt with whatever you thought went wrong in your life." Michael kept his voice soft. "You've got to deal with reality.

"It was a mistake, Michael. I took all those pills by accident. I just wasn't paying attention."

"Sweetheart, save that song and dance for someone who doesn't know you as well as I do."

He smiled at her, but she knew he wasn't buying anything she said.

"I'm surprised you took so many, but we both know you zone out when you don't like what's happening in your life." He took her in his arms. "I wish I understood why you keep throwing it all away. You have it all, Margo, and you won't let yourself enjoy it."

Pulling away, she turned on her side away from him. "Don't start, Michael. I'm too tired to deal with you, too."

"I didn't come to lecture you. I'm sorry." He moved away and sat in the chair next to the bed. "There is some news that you need to know." His voice broke as he began. "Some hot shot detective has made up his mind that Alli murdered Paolo and she was arrested a couple of hours ago."

Staring at the ceiling, Margo shook her head. "That's insane! Hire a good attorney and bring her home." Then she quickly raised up on one elbow. "Do something, Michael! It will be all over the papers that I'm a lousy mother. You've got to run interference on this before it's out of control."

"This isn't about you!" He couldn't believe what he was hearing. "For once, think about your daughter." He hurled the words at her as he headed for the door. "For once, damn you, be her mother!" He slammed the door behind him.

Margo was stunned. Michael was acting like all of this was her fault. She picked up the phone and dialed Lulu's extension. "You've got to come up here right now." She tried to yell into the phone. "I don't care if you have another appointment. Cancel it! I'm in crisis and it won't wait." Slamming down the receiver, all she could think about was how good a vodka collins or a scotch on the rocks would taste.

The next thing she knew, Lulu was shaking her awake. Groggily she asked, "How long have I been asleep?"

"I have no idea when you went to sleep. But it was over an hour ago when you called me. Now get up out of that bed and talk to me."

Slowly Margo crawled out of the bed and took the seat by the window. "You should have come when I called. I told you I was in crisis." Her lips curled in a pout and she focused her gaze out the window.

"Margo, I'm not here to play games with you. Tell me what this is all about or I'm out of here. I've got other folks to see."

"Michael was here earlier and he was very ugly to me. He made me feel terrible."

"That's not true. Nobody can make you feel something. Now why don't you back up and tell me why you decided to feel terrible?"

Whipping her head toward the doctor, Margo's anger flared. "What is wrong with everybody today? I'm sick and you all are acting like I'm to blame for everything. Give me a break."

"If you don't have anything else to say, I've got people with real problems who need me." Lulu Sarsyn moved away from where Margo sat.

"My daughter was just arrested for murder and when it hits the papers everyone is going to blame me!" Margo was getting hysterical. She threw herself toward Lulu. "Do you know what that will mean to my career? I can't handle that kind of bad publicity."

The high pitch of Margo's frail voice and her frantic movements alarmed the psychiatrist. She grabbed both of her arms and held them tightly to her side. "Get hold of yourself." She said calmly. "Sit back down and let's talk this through. You're not doing yourself any good with this kind of frenzy."

Letting go of her arms, she gently pushed Margo back in the easy chair.

Never changing the tone of her voice, Lulu continued to soothe the situation. "Now, take a deep breath and tell me what's happened since I saw you two hours ago."

Words tumbled from Margo's lips as she relayed what Michael had told her.

"Margo aren't you concerned about your daughter and the tragedy that seems to have fallen on your family?"

"You don't know what you're talking about! The press will have a field-day with this news. They'll smear my name all over the headlines, not my daughter's."

"Calm down. Which daughter has been arrested, Margo? Let's start there."

Margo jumped up from the chair and threw a book across the room. "That little slut, that's who! She stole him from me and then she killed him!" She snatched up a vase and flung it toward the door before Lulu could stop her. Screaming, she ran for the door knocking over everything in her path. With each step her tirade became more frantic.

The doctor hit the emergency button on the wall and ran to get between Margo and the door. Lulu was stronger than her patient, so she wrapped her arms around her and held tightly. "Stop this now," she commanded just as the door opened and two male nurses entered followed by the security guard, Claire McGuire.

As Margo continued to scream profanities at all of them, Lulu ordered one of the nurses to get Margo a 10 milligram injection of Haldol and motioned for the other nurse to help her restrain Margo.

Turning toward the security guard for help, Lulu called, “Ms. McGuire, I’m going to let go and I need you to help the nurse hold her until we can get her sedated.”

Margo struggled against them and continued screaming. Within seconds the nurse returned with the syringe and Lulu administered the shot. It took only a few seconds for Margo to sag against the nurse and security guard and go limp.

“Let’s get her to the bed and then I think I’ll be able to manage.”

They stretched Margo’s body out on the bed and pulled the covers around her as she whimpered. Her eyes were wide open, but she offered no resistance.

“Thank you for responding so quickly. My arms were about to give out.” Lulu shook her arms. “She was bound and determined she was going to trash this place even if she had to go through me to do it.” She turned to the others in the room. “I need to try and talk to her, but don’t go too far away in case I need you again.”

The nurses nodded and left the room. Claire McGuire looked at Margo and seemed reluctant to leave.

“Dr. Sarsyn, I don’t think it’s a good idea for me to leave. Would it be okay if I went in the living room and closed the door?”

“Claire, the issues I need to discuss are very sensitive. It would be better if you waited in your room. I’ll be all right.” Lulu smiled her appreciation. “That’s a very strong medication and it won’t wear off for several hours.”

“If you’re sure? You know I’ll be right across the hall.” As she started out, she turned and looked at Lulu again. “That is one angry woman.”

Lulu sat on the edge of the bed and lifted Margo’s head in her arms. Her voice was almost a whisper and her tone was that of a mother comforting a frightened child. "Honey, you're safe. No matter what, we'll work out this mess. But, you've got to talk about it. Holding it all inside is tearing you apart."

The psychiatrist stopped talking, eased Margo back on the pillow and let her cry.

Margo mumbled something but her words were too indistinct to be understood.

Lulu lifted her chin and smiled. "There isn't too much I haven't heard before. And if it's too shocking for me to handle I'll just hold on to you until I recover."

As Margo looked into the deep brown eyes of the woman who had been holding her, she knew she could trust her. She covered her eyes with her hand as though she didn't want to see the words she was about to say.

"Alli and Paolo were…" her voice tapered off and tears began to flow. She struggled with the words. "Sex, Lulu. She betrayed me. Thought he loved me." She turned her head into the pillow and uttered a sound of complete despair.

Lulu scooped the shaking, sobbing woman up in her arms again and held her. "You've just done the hardest part, my friend. Cry all you want. Lulu is here and I'll help you find a way through what hurts."

Slowly she rocked her back and forth, patting Margo's slender shoulders softly as she continued to croon. "Honey, this is the breakthrough that was needed for you to begin to heal. Now the real work can begin. But, you're not alone, Margo. I'll be here with you."

Chapter Twenty-four

Alli

Nothing could have prepared Alli for the eighteen hours she spent in the Miami-Dade County jail. Absolutely nothing. It was the worst experience of her life and she knew she would do anything to never repeat it. She was scared and unsure for the first time since she had been shuffled off to boarding school at eight years old.

The moment Detective Madison placed the cold handcuffs around her wrist, she wilted. All of her bravado, courage, and recklessness vanished, and she wanted her mother. That scared her most of all. She had never needed or wanted Margo; she had defied her, betrayed her, ignored her, and often, hated her. But sitting in the back of the squad car brought her face-to-face with a raw desire to have her mother rescue and comfort her.

She remained silent on the short ride downtown but the minute Madison opened the car door to lead her inside the jail, she turned to him in panic. "What are they going to do to me in there? Please, you know I didn't kill him. Why are you doing this to me?" Her pleading was that of a child begging not to be spanked or sent to her room. She fought hard not to cry.

"Everything points to you, Miss Anderson. I've got witnesses. I've got evidence. I just need to know who helped you do this." Todd Madison's voice was unsympathetic as he led her toward the building.

"I know you didn't do this by yourself, but everything I've got says you played some part in the guy's death." He stopped and looked her in the eyes. "Just tell me the truth and we'll see if it can't go easier on you."

"How long will I have to stay in this place? Will I be locked up?" Each step closer to the door filled her with dread and fear. All her thoughts were focused on the people inside the building who could do her harm. Where was her father; where was Sam? Who was going to help her? Then it dawned on her that the man next to her was her only hope and she had to find a way to keep him from locking her up. She twisted away from his hold to get his attention. "Detective Madison, tell them I'm going to talk. Tell them you need to take me to a room where we can talk. I'll tell you everything I know."

Leaning her body into his, she softened her look and her expression showed a new appreciation for his manliness. This man could protect her if she let him.

"While you go through the booking process, I'll ask for space and call your attorney. But, you'll still be locked up until you've seen a judge and bond has been set."

He was not smiling. "My hormones won't keep you out of jail, Miss Anderson. So you can stop with the kitten looks."

Suddenly, from around the corner of the building, they were rushed by a stampede of reporters. Flash bulbs went off in their faces, microphones and cameras were shoved at them, and people were shouting her name, "Alli, did you kill your mother's lover?" Alli, why would you want to murder the man?"

Madison pulled her behind him and began to push against the crowd. "Out of my way. There is no comment. Out of the way."

Several uniformed policemen raced from the building to clear a path and shield Alli. Within minutes they had her safely inside and the reporters were being told they could not enter the building until Miss Anderson had been taken to booking.

Shaken, Alli looked at Todd Madison and whispered, "Thank you. I thought I was going to be crushed to death."

*****

The booking process took longer than she expected and there seemed to be a longer waiting time with each step of the ordeal. Detective Madison left her with a woman who took down her basic information, inventoried her personal items, and assigned her an ID number before leading her to finger printing, photography, and a clinic where they took a vial of blood and administered a TB test. Just as she was beginning to think it wasn't going to be too bad, she was taken to a room where she was patted down and strip searched. Dear God, was this really happening? From there she was told to take a shower and put on flip flops and a blue uniform that looked similar to hospital scrubs.

Sam had told her not to laugh or make any smart-aleck remarks, now she understood why. The people she was dealing with did not seem like the type to tolerate anything but a serious demeanor. Where was Detective Madison?

It had been hours since he left her with a promise that he would be back with her attorney. She was tired, humiliated, and afraid of what was coming next. She tried to ask a few questions, but gave up on the idea of being answered with anything other than a nod. Surely, I'm not going to be left in this place for much longer.

The guard-woman who had searched her and ordered her to the shower led her to her cell through a maze of corridors and electronically locked doors. Gasping for breath, she felt faint when she looked inside. The place was smaller than her closet–stark, smelly, austere, and joyless. Her eyes scanned the barren walls, the concrete slabs that were supposed to be beds, the one piece lidless toilet and small sink. A small slit at the upper end of the wall, that she guessed was someone's idea of a window, let in a modicum of light. There was no way she could exist in such a space.

Then she saw that she wasn't alone; God forbid, there was a woman lying on the bottom bunk. She turned in a panic, but the guard pushed her forward and slammed the door behind her.

Before she had time to fully realize the meaning of the slamming door, the woman on the bunk looked her up and down and greeted her in a raspy whisper, “Hey, little chick. Welcome to paradise.”

Frozen with anxiety and trepidation, her heart rate rapidly increasing, she took a step toward the bunk bed and tried to support herself against one of the slabs of concrete. It took her several minutes to calm her breathing and realize she wasn’t going to fall down. The woman didn’t say another word, but the noise outside the cell would have drowned out any conversation that might have occurred. Noticing a small metal stool attached to the wall, she moved stiffly to sit down. She held tightly to the things she had been given–toiletries, a roll of toilet paper, and a hand towel–and sat there staring at the door.

*****

Hours passed before the door opened and her name was called. She realized she hadn’t moved since she sat down and when she tried to stand, her muscles and joints felt tight and sore. Her body was cold and it took her time to feel her hands and feet. But, at least she was leaving this hell-hole.

“Bye, doll. See you when the lights go out.” The woman’s cackle sent a chill down Alli’s spine.

“Ms. Martinez, get me out of here!” she cried the moment she saw her attorney sitting at the table in the small room. “Please do something so I won’t have to go back in there.” She regained her composure when she saw Detective Madison and Eric Randall.

“Miss Anderson, sit down. The detective tells us you want to talk.” Eric was the first to speak and the tone of his voice was not friendly.

“Alli, we’re here to help. But I want you to think very carefully before you say anything to this officer.” Elena’s tone was more comforting, but the implied warning was very real.

“Ask me questions and I’ll try to answer. Right now I’m too rattled to think on my own.” Alli looked at the young man who, hours earlier, she thought would rescue her. She now knew that her chances of leaving this place before she had seen the judge were non-existent.

"What part did you play in this murder? Who helped you move DaSilva's body from the pool to the bay?"

"I've told you before. I didn't have anything to do with this. I was out in the boat because I couldn't sleep."

"Why are your fingerprints all over the pool house and Mr. DaSilva's things? Did he reject your advances? Is that it, Miss Anderson? Were the two of you involved and he decided to call it off?" He was firing questions at her quickly hoping to catch her off guard.

"Alli, do not answer these questions! Do you have anything to say that will clear you? An alibi? Some new information that you haven't shared? If not, then I am advising you not to answer."

Eric wanted to make sure his client did not implicate herself simply to get out of jail for one night. "You have a bond hearing before a judge at nine o'clock tomorrow morning. You will be out of here by this time tomorrow. That's the best we can offer you."

"We're sorry, but you'll have to stay here tonight." Elena tried to soothe things. "I know the horror you're feeling is not going to be relieved by my meager words. Just hang on. We're doing everything we can to get you out of here."

*****

Dinner time was a bad dream, but lights out was a nightmare. They called it 'lights out' but the harsh lights were never turned off. She crawled in the upper bunk and curled into a small ball. No matter what, she wasn't going to close her eyes. The noise of the place and her fears left her drained and the smell of the food had made her nauseous. The other women had frightened her with their loud curses, their threatening eyes, and their stares. How did anyone ever get used to being in this place? What if I'm convicted and have to stay in a place like this for years? Silent tears fell as she prepared for the worst night of her life.

She felt the presence of the woman before she saw her standing beside the bunk. Suddenly the air was sucked out of the room and paralysis gripped Alli. The woman was tall and very thin. She could have been thirty-five or sixty-five. It was hard for Alli to tell her age because her face was cracked and leathery. She had the look of someone who was rarely sober and never had enough to eat.

She leaned toward Alli and was inches away from her face when she whispered, "I got a daughter 'bout your age. You ain't got nothing to be afraid of from me. Ain't no way I'm going to bother you. You hear me? Some people out there will try to eat you for lunch, so you stick with me."

The woman returned to her bunk and within minutes, even with the constant noise, Alli heard her snoring. How can she sleep? Don't they ever dim the lights in this place? Don't those women out there ever shut-up? She never closed her eyes and the tension in her body didn't ease all night. Counting each passing second, she prayed for morning.

*****

In a daze, Alli was escorted to court, stood before the judge with Elena, and pleaded not guilty. The District Attorney stated Alli was a not a flight risk and the judge set her bond. It was over in minutes but it would take most of the day before she was released from jail.

When she saw her father, she fell into his arms and begged him to take her home. "Stay at MarGrove, Daddy." In the voice of a child, she pleaded with him, "Please don't leave me alone."

*****

Something changed and she couldn't explain it. The liveliness and spunk that had always defined her was missing. It didn't feel like depression or melancholia but rather a hollowness deep inside her that felt out of place and foreign. The night in jail had redirected her energy and she had spent a restless night looking at her life through new eyes. Was she really so shallow that she had allowed men, money and material things to guide her? How could one night tear down the fabric of her life and leave her feeling so lost?

She was grateful that her father had not challenged her when she begged him to stay at MarGrove. His presence was settling. It was not like he hovered over her, but he was there in a way she wasn't used to.

Had her perspective and demeanor changed or had his? All her life she had known her father was there, but as other men took on a larger role, had she displaced and taken advantage of the one man who genuinely loved and cared for her? Late into the evening, after she had been released from jail, her father had sat in the chair next to her bed and held her hand. He had talked quietly and reassuringly, and she had listened. It must have been after she fell asleep that he left, because she didn't remember him letting go of her. How protected she had felt in those few hours, but how did she know if it was real? No one had ever tried to protect her before and she was afraid to trust what she experienced.

She looked across the room and realized her sister was curled up in a chair reading. How strange that she hadn't noticed her when she had first awakened.

"How long have you been sitting there? I didn't see you when I woke up."

"Hey there. Finally, you're awake. I was beginning to think you were going to sleep for days." Sunni put down her book and crossed the room to sit on her sister's bed. "You look a whole lot better than you did when they brought you home yesterday."

"Sunni, I wish I could wake up and this would all be over. That place was gross. It's ghastly." She lifted herself up on her elbow and made eye contact with her twin. "You can't imagine what it was like and I hope you never have to." She shuddered to think about her sister having to go through a strip search. "You know I didn't have anything to do with Paolo's death, don't you?" She wanted an affirmation from the person she trusted most in the world.

"I believe you about his death, Alli. But I know there's more to this story than you've told me and it's making me nuts." When there was no response, she asked her to join her on the balcony for breakfast. "Mrs. Dee went to special trouble this morning to fix everything you like. There's French toast with cinnamon, fresh papaya with yogurt and honey, and a pot of coffee. Since you didn't eat any dinner last night, I bet you're starving."

Alli watched the clouds fly by as the storm began to gather. It was hurricane season and there was a tropical depression headed toward the Bahamas that would keep the Miami weather unsettled for the next few days. Other than the sounds of the choppy water and breeze rustling the palm trees, the balcony where they sat was a peaceful oasis. But she knew the storm surrounding her was more tumultuous and frightening than any hurricane she'd ever seen.

Long minutes of silence passed before she put her cup down and looked at her sister with pleading eyes, "Are you really ready to know who I am?"

"Alli, whoever you are, I love you. Don't you know that? And, I probably know more about your life than you think I do. I don't want a sugar-coated version of your story. I just want to know the truth."

"I've probably had sex with every man Margo has brought home. Did you know that?" She watched a small Blue Jay circle the avocado tree in the back yard as she waited for a response. "Did you hear what I just said?"

"I heard you, I just don't have anything to say, yet. Keep going," Sunni whispered uneasily.

"Paolo DaSilva and I were lovers for over two years. He came to Pennsylvania at least once a month, Sunni. All those weekends I told you I was staying over at the club's apartment because it would be too late to drive back to Brentwood, I was really at Paolo's apartment." This time she turned and looked directly into her sister's eyes. "I've betrayed Margo every chance I got. Do you understand?"

The dark circles under Sunni's eyes shocked Alli and it suddenly hit her that her sister was feeling the pressure, also, and trying to deal with the craziness that had invaded their lives. Selfishly, she hadn't considered that the drama was impacting anyone but her.

"I know you're disappointed in me." She reached for Sunni's hand. "Please don't hate me."

"You've done some damaging things, but you haven't told me what I need to know." Sunni's response was monotone and her face was expressionless. "I'll let you know whether I'm disappointed in you or not, when you've told me about the rest of this madness."

"Okay," she said with resignation. "That day is like a thousand years ago, but Margo caught me and Paolo having sex in the pool house and she freaked. She told Paolo to get out, then she disowned me. Sunni, she told me to leave and never come back." Alli leaned forward in the chair and covered her face with her hands. "I didn't know she'd try to kill herself, Sunni. Please believe me."

"Unfortunately, I believe you. More than that, I feel sorry for you." She stood up and left the balcony. She turned back to her sister as she reached the door. "Our mother has never tried to be our mother, but damn you, Alli, for never trying to be a daughter."

The solid thud of the closing door echoed in Alli's head. For the first time in her life, her twin had turned away from her and she wasn't convinced she could ever win her back. She felt hollow and empty and very alone.

*****

"Daddy, does all this mean I'm really confined to Miami? I can't go anywhere outside this county?" Alli was pacing. "How long will this last?"

"It'll last until the trial or until they find someone else to pin this murder on. I thought you understood."

"I need to see Elena Martinez. She's got to come up with a way to help me get out of all this." For a moment Alli felt a spark of fight return, then as quickly as it surfaced, it was gone and her shoulders drooped. "Do you think I'm guilty?"

"There is no way that you murdered that man! We'll find the truth, Alli. I know it." He hugged his daughter to him and she sensed his anguish.

Alli pulled away, and before she could catch herself, asked her father, "Do you love me?"

"I've loved you since the minute you were born. Nothing has changed that. Nothing can change that." Michael rumpled his daughter's hair and smiled at her.

"Don't count on that, Daddy."

Chapter Twenty-five

Randall, Martinez and Cannon

The corridor outside his hospital room was darker than it should have been. No emergency lights or exit signs cast a glow to guide the way. He listened for an occasional cough or the tacit heaviness of nurses walking back and forth. But there was no sound.

He was edgy. Every nerve ending was on high alert. Something wasn't right and he couldn't help himself. When he had gone to sleep earlier in the night, he knew the extent of his injuries, but now there was a difference. He was lying under some kind of canvas tent, there was a wide strap across his middle that was restraining his movements. He struggled to move his legs, his arms, to lift his head; but he couldn't move or reach the nurse's call button. A voice told him to leave the DaSilva family alone. In a panic, he shouted out for help. At first his cries were tentative, and after each call he listened for the sound of footsteps or the whispers of nurses or other patients. The silence got louder and seemed to be echoing across the room and down the hall. He yelled. The screams reached higher and higher pitches as he reckoned with the fact that no one was going to come.

"O que se passa Senhor Avery? Calma faz favor!"

The voice was imploring, the words unfamiliar. He screamed louder and fought harder. Couldn't they see that the tent was closing in around him and the strap was cutting off his breathing? Then he felt the needle in his arm and the blackness engulfed him.

*****

Bright light caused him to cover his eyes but the sharp pains in his leg reminded him that he was in the hospital. The doctor standing at the end of the bed was reading his chart and frowning in that way doctor's do when they are about to give you bad news.

"Bom dia, Senhor Avery. It looks like you've had a bad night. Your chart tells me the nurses had to call for a sedative around 3:00 this morning. They say you were quite agitated. I didn't think the pain would intensify that much."

"I don't remember three o'clock this morning, but I know the pain is coming on pretty strong right now in that right leg. It's much worse than it was yesterday."

"Senhor, the multiple breaks in that leg required extensive surgery to repair. We had to insert several pins into the femur, but I am certain with physical therapy you will regain full use. Until this morning you have refused the pain medication that was offered. Unfortunately, I think you've let the pain get ahead of you and we'll have to work a little harder to manage it now. I've ordered something a bit stronger for today and, hopefully, we'll begin to taper off tomorrow. But I highly recommend that you take these pills for the next twenty-four hours."

"Okay, doc. But what can you tell me about going home. I need to get back to the States as soon as possible."

The doctor gave him a benevolent smile. "Senhor, take advantage of our wonderful hospitality. You will probably not be able to travel for at least another week."

John Avery grimaced. "Is there anything I can do to hurry this process?"

"Sim, senhor. You can rest, take these meds, and try to relax." The doctor returned the chart to the hook before he looked at John. "You must have some friends in high places, senhor. All of your medical bills have been taken care of and you have a twenty-four guard outside your door." He shrugged as he turned. "We've even been given instructions to order you special food from one of the finest restaurants in Rio."

"What are you talking about?" John was now on alert. "Who would do this?"

"My understanding is that Eduardo DaSilva thinks you took this beating for him. These thugs were apparently after him. Enjoy the compensation while you're here. Yours will be a first-class-all-expenses-paid stay."

"Wait, doc. What about a phone? Is there any way I can have a phone in this room? I need to make several calls."

"I'm sorry. But there's no phone available for this room. If you give one of the nurses your information she can make the call for you. Tchau, senhor."

I was careless and now I'm caught in a trap. I've got to get a message to Eric and Elena without arousing DaSilva's suspicion. Something really strange happened in this room during the night and now I have a security detail.

He opened his eyes to the piercing glance of Tomas Labato. "Mr. Avery, I do hope you are feeling better today. My grandfather is hoping that his efforts to make you comfortable are beneficial."

"Mr. Labato, thank your grandfather for me. But, as soon as the pain eases I'm going to make arrangements to fly back to Miami."

"When its time, my grandfather will have you flown home. Right now, relax and enjoy your time in Rio."

"Tomas, why do I have a security detail? What happened in this room last night?"

"All I know is the hospital called my grandfather around three this morning. Apparently you became overly distraught because someone was in your room. One of the nurses heard your screams and saw someone running down the hall. My grandfather doesn't want an international incident, so he had some of our security people posted in the corridor for your added protection."

"So it wasn't a dream." John pondered the seriousness of his situation but realized that at the moment he was helpless. "Tomas, before I met with your grandfather I received some disturbing news. Did you know that Alli Anderson has been arrested for your cousin's murder?"

"Oh meu Deus! How absurd." Tomas began to laugh. "What idiot brought those charges against the girl? There is no way she could have killed Paolo."

"My sentiments exactly. The cops are fishing for an accomplice and they'll try to break her in order to get information that will help them. They've got eye witnesses and finger prints, but even the investigating detective knows she doesn't have the strength to have done this." John hesitated before he continued. "What can you tell me, Tomas, and why doesn't your grandfather want me to try and find out who killed Paolo?"

Tomas held on to the bed railing until his knuckles turned white before he replied. "The answer isn't in Rio, my friend. I'll tell my grandfather what is transpiring in Miami and I'm sure he will hasten your return home. Avery, who do they think helped the girl?"

"Can't say, Tomas. But I'd think your family would want to know the truth, wouldn't you?" For the first time, John sensed apprehension in Tomas. There was more here than he had suspected, but the pieces weren't coming together. "Can you get me a phone? I've got to make some calls to the States."

Tomas nodded as he hurried to the door, but John didn't know if the nod meant yes or no.

*****

Two days later without another word from the DaSilva family, John Avery was transported to Miami on a chartered jet and taken by ambulance to a small rehabilitation facility in south Miami. He was rolled on a gurney to a private room where Eric Randall was waiting for him.

"Looks like this vacation didn't agree with you, John. What in the world happened?"

"First, do you know why I'm here? I don't need this place." John was angry that he had lost control of his life.

"Hey, pal, enjoy. My understanding is Eduardo DaSilva is footing all of your expenses until you're released from rehab. I got a call this morning from his secretary that you were on your way here and I was to meet you. The woman told me all expenses were being covered until you could walk away on your own."

"DaSilva has me beat up and then he tries to buy me with all of this. What a bunch of crap." The pain medication that he had been given prior to leaving Rio was wearing thin and he needed to rest. "Eric, could you get the nurse in here? I'm really starting to hurt."

*****

"You think you can talk for a few minutes, John? I need some answers." Eric waited until the investigator seemed more at ease. "I want to know what happened in Brazil. My wife's been a basket case since we got your telegram."

"I'm sorry, but they wouldn't give me a phone and I had no way to get information to you. Long story short, I met with Eduardo DaSilva, we rode around in his limo until he decided to drop me off in the middle of the slums of Rio. Within two minutes of getting out of the car, I was jumped by two, maybe three men and worked over. The next thing I knew, I was trapped in the hospital being treated like a king."

"How bad are you hurt? You look like those goons really worked you over."

"Concussion, lacerations, ruptured spleen, broken leg. Not to mention bruised ego." John lamented. "When Tomas Labato came to visit, I knew I'd been set-up. It was after I told him they were using Alli as bait, that I began getting the royal treatment."

The pain medication was beginning to slow him down and there was still so much he needed to tell Eric. "I think the grandfather is trying to protect the family name, but there is something about Tomas that makes me want to dig deeper into who he is and what he's been up to for the last few years."

"You think he's behind his cousin's death? Is that where you're going with this?" Perplexed, but curious, Eric continued. "John, the girl has been released on bail but we think the police are looking seriously at Michael or Sam as her accomplice. I know you're out of commission, but I need you to guide me on who to talk to and where to look for information."

"Eric, I'll do the best I can from here. As soon as I can get to a phone, I'll call Maddie Sonnett. She's worked with me before and she's good. She's an ex-cop, worked in the forensic lab for a lot of years and she's going to law school. You'll like her."

Thinking of his colleague made John smile. Maddie was a looker who knew what she was doing. He sent work her way as often as possible to make sure she could pay for school. "After I fill her in on what I know, I'll ask her to call you."

"You'll have a phone in here before the day is over. It's already been ordered."

*****

Maddie Sonnett walked into the law offices of Randall, Martinez and Cannon like she walked everywhere–with confidence. Her long, curly, red hair bounced around her beautiful face, announcing her arrival and catching everyone's attention.

The short skirt emphasized her long legs and her sex appeal, but the blazer and briefcase made a statement for her professionalism and said she had come ready to go to work. At thirty-three she loved her life and it showed. She had worked with the Miami police force to put herself through the university and was now working part-time as a private investigator so she could devote more hours to her law school studies.

At nineteen, she had married her high school sweetheart and they had gone through the police academy together. At twenty-nine, she was widowed during a South Beach drug raid that had gone bad and she decided there had to be another way to serve law enforcement. After months of sitting in a court room frustrated by what it took for her husband's killer to be convicted, she quit the force and enrolled in law school, determined to become a top-notch prosecutor. Her husband's death would serve some purpose.

"Hi, I'm Maddie Sonnett, here to see Eric Randall and Elena Martinez. John Avery sent me." She smiled at the receptionist and placed her business card on the desk.

"I think they're expecting you. Follow me."

Chapter Twenty-six

Sunni

"Fifty-one, fifty-two, fifty-three," Sunni counted the waves crashing against the seawall. The storm was strengthening and counting the waves helped her calm the anger she felt. Doing something mindless was a defense mechanism that she frequently used to avoid dealing with the anxiety produced by her dysfunctional family. The knock on the door surprised her and she prayed it wasn't Alli.

She wanted to isolate herself from the chaos that swirled in her mind–her mother, her sister, Mark. Reeling in her feelings, which she could usually do with no problem, seemed beyond her ability today. She sighed. Maybe a distraction would do more good than being by herself, so she called out, "Come in."

When Mrs. Davis walked in the room, she was relieved. She was her friend and confidant. A chat with her would be good.

"Sunni, that young man, Mark, has called you for the umpteenth time this afternoon and you keep refusing to take his calls. Honey, you can't punish yourself for the trouble in this house. Why don't you see what he wants? It would do you good to get out for awhile. It wouldn't change anything if you had some fun and it might help you."

"Mrs. Dee, you don't understand. Mark has a girlfriend. A serious girlfriend. My not talking to him has nothing to do with Alli or mother. But, thanks for being worried about me."

She loved the older woman like a grandmother and knew that Mrs. Davis cared for her. She had been her comforter for many years, but nothing she said would change the situation between Mark and

Jocelyn McDeal. "I was falling for him, you know that, and under the circumstances, that would have been disastrous."

"Why in the world was he hanging all over you if he has somebody? Shame on him! I'll never understand men."

"It's a long story. But I've made up my mind not to be friends with him anymore. It hurts too much. Besides, as soon as Lara can make the arrangements, I'm going to leave for Sarah Lawrence."

She watched as a sadness crossed the housekeeper's face. "I've got to leave, Mrs. Dee. Everything that's happening around here has me tied in knots. So I might as well go sooner than later. I've accepted that Alli won't be going with me. It may take some time, but I know that her attorney will be able to get these ludicrous charges dropped." She tried to put a good spin on her story. "You know, I really don't think Alli will ever join me at Sarah Lawrence anyway, so I better get used to living alone."

"I think you're probably right about that. Alli is her mother's daughter and she'll be the next star in this family if she can get her head on straight." Mrs. Davis seemed relieved. "Back to you, young lady. I've never known you to run away, Sunni. Why do you want to start now?" Mrs. Davis had her hands on her hips and her stance was one of determination.

"I'm not running away. I'm just getting started early, that's all." She could feel Mrs. Davis' eyes scrutinizing her thoughts and movements. "Don't look at me like that, please. I'd like you to support me on this."

"Can't do it, missy. I understand that you think you've got to get away. But, what you need is to stay here and fight for what you want and who you are. Running away isn't going to make your life easier." She brushed her hands together. "And, that sister of yours can't handle this by herself. Whether she knows it or not, she needs you."

"What are you talking about?" Mrs. Davis had never said things like that and it startled her.

"It's time you showed some gumption instead of always walking a step behind. That's all I came to say 'cause I've got to go start dinner." Mrs. Davis walked out leaving Sunni standing open-mouthed.

*****

Three hours later when the phone rang, Sunni accepted the call. "Yes, Mark, I'd like that." She put the phone down and went in search of the housekeeper.

"You win, Mrs. Dee–I'm going to meet Mark at a cafe in the Grove in thirty minutes. I'll have a glass of iced tea and see what he has to say. But that's it."

"Honey, that's more like it. Listen to what the man has to say. You just might get a surprise." Mrs. Davis couldn't hide her delight.

*****

Waiting for Mark to show up was like waiting for a mystery to be revealed. She hadn't seen him in several weeks and with every day that passed she had tried harder and harder to remove his image and his voice from her mind.

She spotted him when he was still a block away and the sight of him affected her the same way a rainbow did after a storm. Hope and serenity washed over her before a sense of excitement jarred her. Is this what love feels like? Her eyes measured every step he took and she could scarcely wait to hear his voice. Was he as handsome as she thought? His hair pulled back neatly in a ponytail, his bright brown eyes greedily drinking in everything they saw, his crooked smile making her think he had a secret he wanted to tell her.

Yes! She answered her own question. He is very handsome and I'm not the only one who thinks so.

"It's so good to see you." Mark scooped her up in a big hug. "I've missed you."

"Put me down before people come to see if I need to be rescued." She laughed and held on tighter. "I missed you, too." By then her feet were back on the ground and Mark was holding her at arm's length.

"Sit down and tell me what you've been up to for the last few weeks." She needed to get things back on a level that she could deal with before she said something she would regret.

"The band's working on some new music that I know your mom is going to love, and I've done some surfing. Last week Jocelyn and I went to California to see Rosanna, AKA my aunt, her mother." He smirked at the awkwardness of that last statement. "And, I've been helping my dad with some landscaping. You know, the stuff of summer." His eyes never left her face. "How are things at your house? Really?"

"Like something out of a bad novel. But what's new?" She didn't want to talk about her family. "Alli's finally calming down after her night in jail, Mom's still in rehab. You know–the usual things that happen in every family." She laughed but it wasn't with any sense of joy.

"I wish you weren't so beautiful." His look made her long for more than he could offer her and she knew she should get up now and walk away.

"Jocelyn and I have decided to cool it and see what happens. We did a lot of talking on our trip to California. We talked to Rosanna, and she is still adamant that, as first cousins, we can't get married. We've been trying to work this out for years and we're going in circles instead of forward. When Jocelyn said she wanted a break, I was relieved. I told her honestly that I was going to ask you out–that I needed to see if there was anything to the feelings I have for you. So stop your worries, she knows that I want to see you."

"Mark, is this some kind of contest? Are you trying to see if I can surpass Jocelyn in your heart and mind?"

"I guess I said that wrong, didn't I? Let me try again." He looked at her for understanding. "For years I knew what I wanted and I was willing to wait until Jocelyn felt the time was right. Then I met you and it all changed. Jocelyn has someone else in her life that must have done the same thing for her. We both need to see if our relationship is simply a habit or if we really are ready to move on."

He leaned back in the chair as though he needed some distance from her. "It's not a contest. You know my history; you know the chance you might be taking to get involved with me. But, Sunni, I can't get you out of my head."

"You make me crazy!" She laughed sadly. "I want a relationship with you. I want to be part of your life. But, all I can think of is how much it's going to hurt when you decide to walk away."

"Or, how 'bout how great it's going to be if what we have is the real thing?" he offered.

Was Mrs. Dee right? Was she supposed to take a chance and fight for what she wanted? Was Mark Sanders worth the risk?

"My heart says yes, my head is screaming no."

She turned to call to the waiter–she needed a distraction. After they ordered, she looked him in the eyes. "Let's see where this takes us. I want you in my life."

*****

Sitting on the balcony watching the sunset gave her time to think about what had happened earlier in the day with Mark Sanders. She couldn't get Jocelyn out of her mind. Was there really someone else in Jocelyn's life or was Mark's first love trying to find a way out of a no-win situation? The longer she thought about it, the sorrier she felt for Jocelyn and Mark as a couple and she wondered if she would ever be able to believe that Mark had chosen her over Jocelyn. Maybe she needed to talk to Mrs. Davis before she let her imagination ruin the best thing to come into her life.

As she walked downstairs to the kitchen, her father called her to join him on the patio.

"I haven't seen you all day. Come sit with me for a few minutes." Michael stood up and gave his daughter a hug. "Were you out shopping?"

"No, I had lunch with Mark Sanders and then I did some window shopping." She laughed. "Miami is not the place to buy clothes to wear at school in New York. I don't think sleeveless dresses will get me through the winter."

"Do you want me to ask Lara to go with you to New York to shop? I'm sure she would enjoy spending the time with you."

"I'll think about it. But doesn't she have a life of her own? Why in the world would she want to take her vacation time to go to New York with me?" Sunni had often wondered if Lara had a boyfriend, but had never asked.

Michael looked at her with a quizzical expression before he replied, "I didn't think it was a secret, but Lara and Sam have been, how do you say it? They've been an item for a number of years."

"Are you kidding? Our Lara and our Sam? Wow! I would never have figured the two of them were together." She scratched her head. "He's always here and she's never here. Are you sure?"

"Oh, Sunni, your naivety is refreshing." Michael gave her a loving smile. "Sam spends a lot of time at her place and almost every time he goes away, they are together. They just aren't ready to broadcast their relationship." He watched his daughter as she tried to put two and two together. "In fact, they were in Costa Rica last week."

"Good grief! Am I always the last to know everything?" She groaned and then broke into a wide grin. "Bet you didn't know that Alli has a great voice and wants to be on the stage like Mom?"

"You pulled one out of the hat on me, Sunni. Tell me more."

"She's never been interested in Sarah Lawrence or any other college. She wants a singing career. And, she's good, Dad." She looked at the mischievous grin on her father's face. "You're kidding me, aren't you?"

"You're so easy to kid, honey. I guess it would surprise you to know that I've slipped into that club near Brentwood on several occasions to check her out for myself. You're right. She's very good."

"Good enough for you to take on as a client?" Sunni was serious. If her dad said yes to this question, then she would know her sister would never join her in college.

"She needs some coaching, but I think she has what it takes." Michael walked to the edge of the pool, reflecting on something. "When this mess is over, I'll see what I can do to help her." He turned and looked at Sunni. "Now was there something you wanted to talk to me about beside your sister?"

"I don't think so. I was on my way to talk to Mrs. Dee if she's got some time." She gave him a hug. "I'll see you later, Daddy."

Sunni felt excitement for Alli. If their father was serious, and her sister would give up her notion of doing it all on her own, then her career might actually start in the near future. She might have known that her father kept closer tabs on them than she had suspected. But, did that mean he knew other things, too?

"Mrs. Dee, have you got a minute to talk? I need some advice." Sunni hopped up on the kitchen stool and waited for Mrs. Davis to look her way.

"Got a second or two before I have to baste that roast again. What can I do for you?"

"I took what you said earlier seriously and now I'm having second thoughts. I told Mark that I wanted him in my life and he said that's what he wanted, too."

"You must have left out the part about his girlfriend. Did I miss something?"

"He told me that she wants to see someone else. They need to see if their relationship is a habit or if it's real. That's where I get scared. What if I really get involved with him and he goes back to Jocelyn?"

"Honey, life is about taking risks. You like this young man and he likes you–now you have a chance to see if you're short-term or long-term. If I were you, I'd enjoy the ride. If it ends, you'll be hurt, that's for sure. But I bet you'll be able to tell me that you had a great time while it lasted. I'm pleased that you're even considering taking a chance. You worry too much and don't enjoy enough. Now get out of my kitchen so I can finish this dinner." She turned back to the stove, but called over her shoulder, "Call him and see if he's busy. I've got enough food to feed an army."

"Great idea! I'll go do that right now."

*****

Alli walked into Sunni's room later that evening and sat on the edge of her bed. "What did you tell Dad about my singing?" She didn't sound angry, just curious.

"I asked him if he knew how good you were and he said he did. He thinks you've got talent." Her sister had a puzzled expression. "Alli, he said he heard you singing in the club. Don't look so shocked. I think he kept pretty close tabs on us."

"I wonder why he never let me know he was there." Alli thought about it and then shrugged. "Oh, well. Do you think he's serious about taking me on as a client?"

"If you'll let him."

"I'm going to have to think about this. I never wanted it to happen because I'm Margo and Michael's daughter."

"Your choice. But today's music market is crowded with great voices just waiting for their chance and they never get it. He could open a door here and there that might make all the difference. I don't think he'd consider working with you if he didn't think you were a winner."

"If I go to jail, all bets will be off, don't you think?"

"You're not going to jail! Something is going to break in this case and they'll see that you weren't even involved."

"Always the Pollyanna, aren't you?"

"No, Alli. But I believe in who you really are."

"Right!" Sarcastically she replied to her sister's affirmation. "Now tell me what's changed between you and lover-boy. I thought he had a major love interest, but if he's back on the market, he's fair game, right?"

Sunni gave her sister a look that convinced her to back-off. "Hey, I'm only kidding. He's way too young for me, anyway."

Chapter Twenty-seven

Margo

What a hard, hard week....

Alli arrested, Lulu pushing harder than usual to uncover her issues with the girls, and now the specialist was coming from Miami to review the test results about her voice.

All she wanted was peace, and instead she was bombarded with heartaches. She had asked Michael to be with her when the doctor came, but he hadn't given her a definite answer.

Michael, she thought, what would I do without you and what have I done to deserve you? You've stuck with me, even when I've treated you like dirt. Maybe some day I'll be able to understand. Did I ever make you happy?

The knock on the door brought her back to reality and as she started to answer it, the door opened and Michael and Lulu walked in laughing and talking like they were old friends.

"You two look like you're up to no good." A hint of jealousy tinged her words.

"Your doctor is really very funny, Margo. I bet your sessions are a laugh a minute." Michael said with a cautious smile.

"Michael, how perceptive of you," said Lulu. "We make everything fun, don't we Margo?"

"You're the joke, Lulu. The more I suffer, the more fun you have."

"See, Michael. You're ex-wife loves to have me around."

Lulu was dressed in a conservative skirt and blouse and she didn't have on her usual flashy jewelry.

"You look like a real doctor, Lulu. Who're you trying to impress?"

"Hey, I clean up nicely for the good doctors from Miami. It's not every day that we have a nationally recognized specialist come to visit." She took a chair close to Margo. "On a serious note, are you sure you're ready for this visit?"

"What's he going to say that I haven't heard before? Rest your vocal chords, my dear. Stop the drugs and alcohol, my dear. All will be well, my dear. I know the drill, Lulu."

She looked from one to the other and then spoke to Michael. "I appreciate that you're here."

"Margo, I'm always here. You know that."

"I know, Michael. I just wanted you to know that I appreciate it."

She watched his face soften and thought she saw tenderness in the way he looked at her.

*****

Michael stood when he heard the knock on the door, then welcomed Dr. Mellon into the room. "Thank you for driving all the way to Boca to meet with us, Dr. Mellon. Won't you come in and have a seat?"

The doctor shook hands with Michael and was introduced to Dr. Sarsyn before he turned to greet Margo. "Mrs. Anderson, there is much for us to discuss. May we get started?"

"Of course, Dr. Mellon. What's first?" Margo was sure the session would be over before the man had a chance to get comfortable. She was used to people falling all over themselves when they met her, but this doctor didn't seem to care if she was a celebrity.

"First, let me tell you that I have gone over all of your test results very carefully and I have consulted with colleagues across the country. I don't have the best news for you." He pulled out a folder of charts that he placed on Margo's lap. "I'd like for you and Mr. Anderson to look at these while I try to explain what has happened to your vocal chords. Please stop me any time you have a question and I'll try to clarify anything that you don't understand."

Margo sat in stunned silence as the doctor proceeded to explain that alcohol and cocaine abuse, smoking, and overuse of her vocal chords had created the perfect atmosphere for cancer of the larynx to develop.

"The tumor must be treated as soon as possible if you are to hope for any kind of voice recovery. I am recommending surgery followed by a series of radiation and chemotherapy treatments. I must warn you that this process gives you no guarantee of voice recovery." He looked at her with sympathy. "I would advise you to retire from professional singing in order to protect your ability to speak once the treatment is complete."

Her voice was a whisper. "You've got to be kidding me. There's no way I can stop singing."

"Mrs. Anderson, I'm sorry. I know this is devastating news, but I'm not kidding. All of the substances you have used over the years are irritants to the vocal chords. You have a tumor affecting more than one area of your larynx, and the biopsy of the lymph nodes was inconclusive. However, we don't think the cancer has spread to other parts of your body. I'm optimistic that with proper and immediate treatment you will have a full recovery. But it is unlikely that your voice will maintain its strength or range." He waited for someone to ask another question, but their shock was too intense for questions.

"I would like to consider scheduling some additional tests and setting a surgery date for the last week of this month. If Dr. Sarsyn agrees, I'd like to have you transferred to Jackson Memorial no later than next Thursday. That way the tests that I need can be run; I can get the results quickly; and surgery can take place without further delay." He looked to Lulu for some confirmation.

"Dr. Mellon, I'd like to speak to you privately after you're finished here. But, yes, those arrangements can be made quickly. I will commute from here to Miami to make sure that Mrs. Anderson has the support she needs." Lulu walked over and took Margo's hand in hers. "Sweet lady, we'll get through this. I know this is a shock and it's going to take time to process it. But, you can do this."

Tears ran down Margo's cheeks as an all-consuming sadness hit her in the gut. She looked at Lulu and had no words. Just when she thought she couldn't bear it another minute, Michael lifted her gently out of the chair and held her as though he would never let her go.

*****

Lulu ordered a mild sedative for Margo and watched as Michael tenderly led her to the bed. She listened as he gave his ex-wife words of loving assurance that everything would be all right, that he would never leave her, that she would make it through even this unfortunate event. When Margo had fallen asleep, Lulu took his arm and led him out in the hall.

"Michael, I'll be here to help in any way I can. You don't have to do this alone."

As soon as the words were out of her mouth, Michael hugged her. "She doesn't know anything else. Singing is what she's all about. She has no friends. She has no life apart from what she does on that stage." Tears filled his eyes. "Lulu, if she was fragile before, I don't know how she'll manage this. Dr. Mellon just put the nails in her coffin."

"She's stronger than you think. We can help her find a new life and maybe that life will finally include the people who really love her." She paused. "Did she tell you her mother came to visit last week or that she's had several phone calls from her brothers? And, we were on the verge of a break-through about the twins. It will come together for her, Michael. It just won't be like it was before."

"She must be better if you're allowing visits and phone calls," he said.

"Very limited on both counts. I talked with her mother and her brothers before I agreed. You're the only person that has permission to visit on a regular basis. For some reason the two of you have this strange connection and you seem to have a calming effect on her. So, I don't monitor you as much as I would someone else."

"Thanks, doctor. How can I help?"

"Just continue to do what you're doing. Somewhere in the back of her mind, she knows that you love her. I think that's what has held her together all these years. You're the one constant in her life."

Suddenly, he looked crestfallen. "What am I going to tell the girls?"

"You'll figure it out. You're the one constant in their lives, too. You'll find the words you need." She started to walk away. "She is more than a voice. You know that, don't you?"

*****

When Margo woke up hours later, Lulu was sitting in the chair beside her bed. In the twilight, she saw that Lulu was dressed once again in one of her outrageous caftans, the pearl earrings had been replaced by long flamboyant dangles, and all the bangle bracelets were making music on her arms. Margo pulled herself to a sitting position. "What are you doing here so late?"

"Didn't have anything better to do than sit here and listen to you snore. How're you feeling?"

"Did I have a bad dream or was Dr. Mellon really here delivering my death notice?"

"He came to see you, but I didn't hear him say anything about you dying. I think he said your life is going to have to change, but he sure didn't tell you to call it quits."

"How do you think I'm going to live the rest of my life as an ordinary woman in the suburbs? Have you forgotten who I am?"

"No, I'm not the one who's forgotten. You created Margo a long time ago and you think she's all you've got. But I'm asking you to take a good, hard look at Margaret Alison Anderson and try to make friends with the fabulous woman that she can become. She's the real person behind all the fluff and you've let yourself forget that."

Chapter Twenty-eight

Randall, Martinez and Cannon

Maddie Sonnet poured over John Avery's notes, read and reread the files that she had been given by the law firm, and studied the police reports until her eyes blurred. The package was too neat, too scripted, which told her that something was missing. She had made a checklist and had tried to read between the lines of what she knew to be fact. But it wasn't coming together.

Yes, Paolo DaSilva was a playboy heir with dubious morals. He drank too much and fooled around with cocaine. He liked the celebrity that dating Margo afforded him and by dying, he had skirted jail for having sex with the daughter when she was under aged. But she couldn't find anything on him that would lead to murder. And the whole notion of some kind of crime of passion didn't add up.

Yes, Margo, probably had a reason to kill him, but she was in the ER at Mercy Hospital at the time and there was no way that either of the daughters had carried it off. The idea that Alli Anderson might have an accomplice was ludicrous.

Yes, Sam Baxter was a former Navy SEAL and had the skills to take the man out, but he didn't have the motive. Alli Anderson's honor and Margo's anger would not have been enough for the SEAL to go after him. And, if he had done it, the body would never have been found. So, he was out.

Yes, Michael Anderson had reasons. But he had a proven alibi with more than one witness to corroborate that he was at the hospital with his ex-wife. He left the hospital for several hours to take a shower and catch a nap and both the doorman at his apartment and the nurses at the hospital backed up that story. And the time frame didn't match up with the medical examiner's report. So, he was out.

Then there was Paolo's family. Tomas Labato, Paolo's cousin and business associate, had been questioned by the police and had apparently been dismissed as unimportant to the case. The big question mark on her checklist was Eduardo DaSilva, the powerful grandfather who had been instrumental in John's assault.

As she made doodles in the margin of her checklist, she couldn't get past the names of Tomas and Eduardo. Was there something there that the police had failed to pick up on? Why was Eduardo so anxious to derail John's investigation? And, where did Tomas fit in?

She picked up the phone and dialed a familiar number. "Do you have plans for lunch today? I've got a new case and I need to bounce some ideas off you. How 'bout meeting me at Wolfie's around one?"

*****

He was sitting at a window table watching the people stroll down Collins Avenue when she arrived. Distinguished even in khakis and a polo shirt, his white hair was styled, and his mustache was trimmed.

"Hello, my beautiful, dear Maddie. You are a sight for sore eyes." Lawrence Fitz spoke in a clear Virginia accent and stood to seat her at the table.

"Ah, you'd think I was young enough to be flattered by your good manners and foolishness!" she teased. Lawrence was her friend and mentor. The former FBI agent, who was spending his retirement writing crime novels, had been her father's partner and best friend for more than forty years. He was a man she could trust and his insight was invaluable.

"What are you working on that needs my attention?" He began quizzing her as soon as she sat down. "It must be something juicy if you want to talk to me about it."

Pulling out her checklist, she began to give him some background for the case.

"Wait a minute. Are you talking about the case where Alli Anderson was just arrested? If so, I know a bit about it. My assistant, Jocelyn McDeal, introduced me to the twin sister a few weeks ago."

"One and the same. Good, you already know some of the players."

"Not really, although I'm a fan of Margo's and have seen her perform on numerous occasions. Continue with your information." He smiled when she pulled out the checklist that he had created years ago. "That checklist never failed me, but when I shared it with you I wasn't sure you'd ever use it."

"Best thing you ever did for me, my friend. It keeps me focused." She nodded her affirmation. "Lawrence, I keep going back to Tomas Labato and Eduardo DaSilva. There's got to be something with these two that I'm missing. I've got copies of police files, attorney files, and files from John Avery. You remember him? He's the PI that I work with sometimes. Anyway, I've brought you copies so you can read up if you're interested."

"Thank you, Maddie. I'll be happy to help you. Maybe I'll be able to see some correlations that you missed. I know the girl didn't murder DaSilva and it was a shame the police put her through what they did. I understand nothing new came from that little charade except giving the media something to headline for several days."

"Apparently, the girl did tell them she'd been sleeping with the creep for years. But that's the only new bit."

"Why do you have the case instead of Avery?"

"He went to Rio to see what he could find out about the DaSilva family and somebody, he thinks it was the grandfather, had him worked over–badly broken leg and ruptured spleen. He was just transferred from Brazil to a rehab center here in Miami. It'll be several months before he can be back on the job, so he asked me to take over."

"Interesting. I'll take a look and get back with you in a day or two. Now, let's order lunch. I'm starving and I want to hear about your law classes, your love life, and what your father's been up to that he hasn't told me about."

"And, I want to hear all about the new book you're working on."

*****

Lawrence called her back two days later. "I've done some checking and we need to talk. Do you think we could meet with John at the rehab center?"

"I'll set it up for two o'clock this afternoon. He's at the South Dade Physical Therapy Center on Dixie Highway." She rattled off directions, then suddenly stopped. "I'm sorry. I forgot you don't drive. I'll pick you up at one-thirty."

"That's kind of you, Maddie. But my assistant is here today and she'll drive me. I'll see you at two."

*****

"John, it's good to see you again. Looks like you are recovering nicely from your unpleasant ordeal in Rio. Looking at how battered and bruised you are, you must have been really out-numbered." Lawrence said. "This is my assistant, Jocelyn McDeal."

"Pardon my manners, but it's a little hard for me to get up right now." John tried to make light of his injuries. "I'm still out of commission, but I can tell I'm almost back to normal."

John turned to Jocelyn. "Nice to meet you, Miss McDeal. Okay, Lawrence, what have you got for us? Maddie seemed to think it was important." He glanced at Maddie and motioned for all of them to take the various seats in the room.

"Maddie gave me copies of the reports she had and I went over them thoroughly. A couple of things tweaked my interest and I started making calls to some of my old contacts in the area. It took me awhile to find anybody that could help, but I scored big with a guy I used to tap when Myer Lansky was in his hey-day with the gambling operations on the beach."

"You think Paolo was involved with the mob?"

"First, it's not the mob. Second, it's not Paolo, but Tomas. And, third, there's a drug angle in there somewhere. Seems he is heavily in debt to a group that run some high roller games at hotels on the beach. My contact seemed to think some big threats had been made by the Empress and Tomas had told her people he was going back to Rio to get the money from his grandfather. When that didn't happen they told him to expect a visit."

"Are you thinking they hit Paolo by mistake?" John got excited. Maybe it was the missing piece in the puzzle. "If that's truth, why do you think Eduardo went after me?"

"I don't think it was Eduardo. I think it was Tomas." Lawrence looked at his notes. "I think the young man mistakenly thought you were one of the hit men and didn't want you talking to his grandfather. The police report said they found a telegram from Eduardo in Paolo's desk at MarGrove that indicated the old man was angry about some missing money and wanted both of them to return to Rio immediately. We also know that the two of them were leaving Miami. The police found airline records to indicate they had reservations to leave the next day."

"You think Paolo knew what was going on and Tomas killed him?" Maddie jumped up and walked across the room. "Lawrence, that's genius."

"Slow down, Maddie. I didn't say that was my conclusion at all." Lawrence looked at Jocelyn. "What else did we find on Tomas Labato?"

Jocelyn spoke for the first time. "You found that he also had some heavy debts in Las Vegas. He entertained pretty lavishly when he stayed out there and spent a large amount of money on a call girl named Naomi Peacock. Also, he was in debt big time to the group here for some trendy recreational drugs. My informant thinks La Emperatriz de cocaina had Labato's name on one of her hit lists."

"That woman's lethal. How did he get messed up with her?" John looked at Lawrence.

"I'm not entirely sure yet. We'll do some more research on it and hopefully we can find the connections between Tomas and the cocaine empress." He shared a worried glance with John. "I wanted the two of you to have this information. For what it's worth, it needs some more investigation. I've just scratched the surface."

John knew the elderly man loved what he was doing. Lawrence had lived his life as an FBI agent and hated when age forced him to retire. He lived vicariously through the crime novels he wrote and the little assistance he could offer Maddie and several others in law enforcement around the country.

"Maddie, I'm going to leave all these notes with you and John. I made my own copies that I'll continue to ponder. If I come up with anything else I'll give you a call." He motioned for Jocelyn to hand over her folder.

"Lawrence, you've given us a new way to look at this. I'll call the attorney group that I work for and let them know we've got a new angle."

"Which group is that, John?" Lawrence inquired.

"Randall, Martinez and Cannon. They have an office downtown and primarily do defense work. Right now they represent Alli Anderson."

"Ah, yes. That would be a lovely lady named Elena, if I'm not mistaken. Please give her my regards." Lawrence and Jocelyn both smiled at the mention of the attorney who had worked so hard to have the kidnapping charges dropped against Jocelyn's father, Carter McDeal.

As soon as Lawrence and Jocelyn were out the door, John asked Maddie to call the law office to see if Eric and Elena could meet with them that afternoon.

"Maddie, if Lawrence's hunch is right we're going to have to move fast."

Chapter Twenty-nine

Michael

Could it get any worse?

Michael was overwhelmed by the waves of trouble in his life. Alli arrested for murder and Margo diagnosed with a form of cancer that had destroyed her voice. Even though it was only two in the afternoon, he mixed himself a vodka collins and walked out to the patio.

The stiff breeze did nothing to counter the heaviness of the humidity, and the falling barometric pressure matched his mood. It reminded him the weather man was still watching a tropical storm somewhere off the coast. But he had too much on his mind to worry about a storm. How was he going to tell his girls, how was he going to give this news to the press, how was he going to dissolve the machine that made Margo's tours and shows run so easily? My God, a lot of people are going to lose their jobs.

He had asked Sam and Lara to meet him for a drink before dinner and had asked Mrs. Davis to prepare a special meal. He would tell the three of them at dinner, but he knew it wouldn't be fair to tell the girls in such a public way. Gulping down the last of his drink, he fortified himself and headed upstairs. Knocking on Sunni's door, he called for her to meet him in Alli's room.

The girls climbed on Alli's big bed and looked expectantly at their father. His hair was disheveled and he looked haggard. "What's eating you, Dad?" asked Alli. "If I didn't know better, I'd think you'd been on a bender."

"Good grief, Alli, leave him alone. There must be a big problem for Daddy to look like this." Sunni jumped to defend her father.

"Do I really look so bad?" Both girls nodded their heads and Michael wiped the sweat off his upper lip before he spoke again. "You're right, Sunni. I'm afraid I've got some more bad news."

"Are we cursed or something?" Alli grabbed one of the pillows on the end of the bed and hugged it to her.

"I hope we're not cursed, but it does look like we're being bombarded with some temporary set-backs." He tried to sound reassuring.

"I've just left your mother and her doctors, and the news is not good. You know since she's been hospitalized she's had trouble with her voice."

"Oh no. I don't think I want to hear this." Sunni grabbed the other pillow.

"I can't think of a way to make this any easier, so I'll just tell you the truth. You mother has cancer and it has impacted her vocal chords. She's facing surgery, radiation, chemo, the whole treatment."

"Poor, dear Margo. She must really be upset that she won't be able to start her next tour on time." Alli said sarcastically.

Michael wanted to slap her, but he sat and looked at her as though he didn't know her. "Alli, your mother will never sing again. Do you hear me? She will never sing again." He tried to swallow his anguish. "Her career is finished and she has a hard road ahead of her. I would think you could feel a little bit of sympathy for her."

Crying softly, Sunni looked at her sister with disgust. "No matter what, she's your mother. She has cancer, Alli. Nobody deserves to have cancer."

"Okay, okay. But, you're acting like it's the end of the world." Alli's tone of voice hinted at her indifference.

"It might be the end of the world as we know it, Alli. Have some compassion, for crying out loud."

"Okay, okay. You're right, both of you. I'm sorry, Dad. How is she dealing with this?"

"Not well, I'm afraid. She's fragile and this is one more blow."

"What's going to happen now? When is the surgery?" Sunni wanted answers.

"She's going to be transferred to Jackson Memorial in a few days. They need to run some tests and as soon as she's cleared, they'll do the surgery. From everything I've heard, Dr. Mellon is one of the best in the country."

"Why aren't you getting a second opinion?" Alli finally entered the discussion.

"Dr. Mellon sent her information to five or six other doctors and I think the decision he brought us today was by consensus. If the two of you want to talk to Dr. Mellon, I'll make the arrangements. You deserve the best information available and I can only give it to you second-hand."

"I trust you, Dad. I don't need to talk to the doctor. How about you, Alli?"

"I'm good. If I have a question I'll come to you."

"Now that you've been told, I've got to tell Sam and Lara, the band, all our technicians, and the crews." His shoulders drooped. "The list is endless. So many good people are going to lose their jobs."

"I know this isn't the right time to ask this. But could I work out with the band before you decide to dissolve everything?"

Michael knew his daughter was self absorbed and he should be angry that she would even suggest that she was good enough to work out with her mother's band. But, as he thought about her request, he realized it might be her only chance if the empire he and Margo had built was coming apart.

So, he agreed without further hesitation. "I'm not guaranteeing anything, Alli. But give it a shot and we'll see what happens." He gave his daughter a troubled glance. "Don't mention this to your mother. I mean it, Alli. If you tell your mother that you're doing this, it's over before it begins." He hoped she understood just how serious he was.

As Alli nodded her agreement, Michael remembered a younger Margo. His daughter had the same drive and ambition, and he knew that with his help or not, she would somehow make her way to the top of the music industry. His heart was heavy as he thought about all the lessons she had yet to learn.

"Sam and Lara will be here for dinner. I intend to tell them and Mrs. Davis. Then we will all have to talk about our plans for going forward." He stared out the window at the choppy, blue water of the bay and took a deep breath. "I know she hasn't been there for you and I'm asking a lot to ask you to be there for her. But that's what I'm doing. I'm asking you to give your mother support, love, and encouragement. You don't want to live with the regret of not doing that."

*****

Dinner was being served and Michael was amazed that the conversation at the table was so casual. Life could be falling apart, yet, the world continued to turn and people could act as though nothing extraordinary was happening. When Mrs. Davis finished serving and started to return to the kitchen Michael stopped her.

"Mrs. Davis get a plate and join us, please."

"Oh, no, Mr. Anderson. I've got my food in the kitchen. But, thank you for asking."

"Mrs. Davis, this is a family meeting and I need you to be at the table. Please, take a seat." Michael insisted.

Mrs. Davis sat down and put some food on her plate. When everyone was eating, Michael started the conversation.

"Since June, this family has had one crisis after another. We're doing a good job of dealing with everything that's happened, but I have some more bad news to share. I'm afraid this news is going to impact all of us and we'll need each other to get through it."

"Michael, you're scaring me. What in the world do you have to tell us?" Lara folded her napkin and placed it on the table. "Curiosity and dread are about to get the best of me."

Looking around the room, he focused on each face at the table. He knew these were the people he could call on when he needed help. And, he was going to need everything they could offer. "I've already talked to the girls, but I have to tell you the doctor's report today was not good. Margo has cancer and it has impacted her vocal chords. She is facing surgery and treatments that will probably mean the end of her career." He watched the looks of disbelief on the faces of Sam, Lara, and Mrs. Davis.

Sam spoke first. "Michael, I'm sorry. It's going to take me some time to fully comprehend what this means." He sighed. "How is Margo? She must be devastated."

Lara reached for Sam's hand. "What do you need me to do, Michael? We've got a full schedule starting in October. The band starts rehearsals next week. I've got all the backup ready to start work at the same time. Scenery, costumes are already in production. Wow, I feel sick. This is awful for all the people who depend on her for their livelihood, but I can't begin to imagine how she's dealing with it. When can I see her, Michael?"

Lara talked fast and jumped from one subject to another. "As the person who carries out the plans, the next few weeks will be horrendous and costly. Contracts will have to be broken, lives will be changed, and fans will be disappointed." She took a breath. "I'm babbling, aren't I? If I stop to really think about it I'll probably fall apart, but not tonight, not this week." Tears formed in the corner of her eyes. "Margo is my boss and friend. Michael, you and the girls are part of my life. Just tell me what you need for me to do. I'll help in any way I can."

"Lara, I know how much you care. Thank you." He'd come to love these people. "We're all in shock. It will take time for us to grasp how this is going to change Margo's life and ours. But we'll get through it. I'll try to get the rehab center to make an exception to their rules so you can visit her. Surely in light of all that's happened, they will let her have her family and close friends around."

Michael closed his eyes and groaned. "I just remembered, I haven't told her mother. Right after dinner I'll have to go see her. I should have invited her to be with us. I'm not thinking straight."

"I'm sure grandmother would rather hear this news in private, Daddy. It's for the best that she's not here." Sunni tried to offer him some comfort. "If you'd like, I'll be glad to go with you."

"Thanks, Sunni, I'd like that. Sam and Lara, let's meet first thing in the morning. Mrs. Davis, would you mind if I joined you for lunch tomorrow? We have some household things to discuss. Sunni, don't say anything to Mark. I'd like to meet with the band and tell them all at once. I'll meet with Twin Palms tomorrow afternoon and find out how to get you all in to see Margo."

Taking a break, he caught his breath. "Anything else I need to cover right now?" Michael was on-task. Ticking off all the things that had to be done prevented him from thinking about Margo.

Mrs. Davis walked around the table. She hugged each of the girls, then stopped at Michael's chair and put her hand on his shoulder. "You know I'll help you any way I can. I'll count on you for meals from now on and I guess you'll be staying here quite a bit."

"We'll see, Mrs. Davis. At least, for Alli's sake, I'll be here tonight as planned."

*****

The next day Michael continued to check off the items on his list. It was going to be hard work to cancel tours, recording dates and the events that kept Margo in front of her public. The day had drained him emotionally and physically. So far, nothing had leaked to the press, but he knew that he had to go on the offense to make sure the rumors were controlled.

He and Lara had worked out several press releases and had strategized all morning on the best way to go about closing out Margo's shows. By the end of the week the world would know that Margo's voice might be lost to them forever. He had to stay busy or the waves of grief would knock him down.

Telling Margo's mother had been easier than he thought. She had never wanted her daughter to be a star and seemed relieved that Margo would finally be out of "that horrible life."

"I know she can beat this illness," her mother exclaimed. "I've never been sure she could beat the life that got her in all the trouble she's in today." She shook her head. "I know you hid the worst of it from me, Michael, but I know she's had more than her share of problems. I know you think I'm crazy. But I want my daughter back and I bet you'd like to have your wife back."

Thinking about his former mother-in-law's words was hard. She had always blamed him for the divorce and Margo's lifestyle because she had no idea of the choices her daughter had made. Even though he had given up long ago on ever having Margo back as his wife, her mother seemed to be hanging on to the dream.

He couldn't afford to get hooked back into Margo's craziness, but it would be wonderful if the set-back finally released her from her demons and created a new relationship for them.

Chapter Thirty

August, 1980
Margo

"Who are you? How did you get this number?" Margo's voice shook as she replied to the threat she had just heard.

"Who are you? What is this all about? I don't owe anybody money." She knew she had to remain calm. "Please tell me why you're asking me for money."

"I don't owe anybody a million dollars and who is this woman you're talking about?"

She gripped the phone tighter. "You're giving me three days and then you'll hurt my daughter. This is crazy!"

Listening as the voice got more agitated, she sensed danger. "Paolo's dead and my Alli will be next if I go to the police. You're not serious."

Then she laughed. "Do you know that I'm in a facility that won't let me out the front door? How do you expect me to deliver money to you on Friday? Besides, I'm not going to give anybody money that I don't owe." The phone went dead and Margo panicked.

Pushing the alert button, she called for Claire McGuire to come to her room. She tried to stop her hands from shaking so the woman wouldn't see how upset she was.

"Claire, a man just called demanding money. He said his boss wants a million dollars or my daughter will be killed. This has got to be some kind of joke."

Sitting with the phone still in her hand, Margo wanted Claire to agree with her that it was a joke. But instead, the woman took the phone and began dialing.

"Sam, this is Claire. A disturbing thing just happened. Margo received a call demanding $1,000,000 or her daughter would be killed." Listening she turned to Margo. "He wants to know if you could detect anything familiar in the voice or if the person who called had an accent?"

"Let me talk to him." Taking the phone she relayed everything she could remember. "He said I had until Friday and if I called the police I would be sorry."

She hung up the phone and told Claire that Sam would join them in an hour. "Do you think this is some kind of prank?"

"I'm not sure, but it's very alarming that the caller has this phone number. Only three people know it--Sam, Michael, and your mother. I don't think there is anyone else."

Margo looked sheepish for a moment. "Claire, I gave the number to Tomas Labato. I called him one day to find out how Paolo's family is doing and he asked for the number so he could call and check on me. It's strange that he's never called me back, so he most likely threw the number away."

Claire snatched up the phone and redialed the number. "Sam, I'm glad I caught you before you left. Check on Tomas Labato. See if he's in Brazil or the States. Margo gave him this phone number." She listened to what Sam had to say and hung up the phone.

"He'll check on Tomas and then he and Michael will be on their way here. We aren't to answer the phone or the door for anyone. He wants me to call Dr. Sarsyn and ask her to put the building security on alert."

"Sam doesn't think this is a joke?"

"Definitely not a joke. If someone has this number, all your security has been breached. Let me call Dr. Sarsyn and then I'll begin to see what I need to do to make sure this apartment is safe. Sam is relocating your girls."

Within ten minutes, Lulu Sarsyn let herself in the door. "Claire, I've called security and they'll meet with Sam as soon as he gets here. How are you doing, Margo?"

"I thought this was a joke, so at first I wasn't too concerned. In my business there are a lot of nuts who do this kind of thing. When Claire reminded me that I have a secure phone number, I started to get nervous. But, Sam is already taking steps to protect the twins."

"You're lucky to have him on your team. I don't know how you celebrity types handle this day in and day out." Lulu turned to Claire. "Is there anything for me to do here? If not, I've got two patients in crisis who need me."

"Doctor, until Sam gets here all we're going to do is sit and wait. When he arrives, I'm sure he'll want to talk to you." Claire was seated where she could see the front door of the apartment and the sliding glass door to the balcony. "We'll put all the locks on once you leave and I've got the alert button for the building's security team where I can reach it in a hurry. We're fine and, I think you'll agree, it would be quite a trick for somebody to get to us on the tenth floor."

Margo had started pacing the room, but Lulu motioned for her to take a seat. "Don't work yourself into a frenzy. It won't help you or anyone else. Sit down and try to read or talk to Claire until Sam gets here. I'll come back as soon as I can."

*****

"Start from the beginning, Margo. Tell me everything you remember about the phone call." Sam asked for the third time.

"I've told you everything I can. Where are the girls and what are you doing to protect them?"

"The issue with Alli not being able to leave the county threw me a curve. I wanted to have them on a plane out of Miami but that's not possible. Right now I've split them up. Alli is with your mother and Sunni is with Lara. I called Eric Randall and Detective Madison to see if we could get the judge to issue an emergency order to move Alli out of Florida. They're working on it."

"Do you have security at Mom's and Lara's? I know both of them live in buildings where guest have to be buzzed in, but neither of those women would be any good in a fight. Hire more people if you have to." The more Margo talked, the faster her words came. She was getting worked up.

"You've got to relax. You know our drill. We've gone over and over situations like this." Sam's voice was firm but reassuring. "There is a security detail at both sites and they know what to do. Trust me; I won't let anything happen to them." He went over the plans with her again to try and alleviate some of her concern. "Back to the phone call. Is there anything about the voice that reminded you of Tomas or anyone else?"

"Sam, the voice was disguised. There wasn't anything significant about it that I can remember." Tired and tense, she tried to think.

"Michael and Claire will be here with you. The house in the Grove is vacant for now. I sent Mrs. Davis to her sister's for a couple of days. I'll be at Lara's and one of our guys, Tim Elwood, will be at your mother's. I have men on the perimeter at all three places and so do the police."

He walked over to the phone. "Margo, a team will be here soon to put tracers on this phone and they are also monitoring the phones at MarGrove. Every in-coming and out-going call will be recorded. Don't answer this phone unless Michael or Claire is in the room with you, and when the person calls back you have got to keep them on the phone as long as possible." He knew she wasn't paying attention when he saw the glazed look in her eyes. "Do you understand?"

"Oh, Sam! They're going to move me to Jackson Memorial in a few days. How in the world can you protect me in that place?" She looked at Michael in a panic. "Michael, you'll have to call Dr. Mellon and tell him we have to postpone the move. I'd never feel safe in that huge hospital."

"You're right, but we'll see what he has to say. Your tests and surgery are of primary importance. He may not agree to postpone."

"Tell him I won't be moved! I need a drink. This is all too much."

"I know how you feel. But, you can't start going backwards, Margo. A drink is the last thing you need." Michael hesitated. "I confess. I grabbed a drink when things were weighing me down two days ago and it didn't help one bit. You can get through this without alcohol and so can I."

Kneeling down in front of her, Sam took her hands in his. "You trust me, don't you? I have always taken care of you and if they have to move you, I'll deal with it. Jackson Memorial won't stop me from protecting you." Compassion filled his voice and the look in his eyes reassured her to some extent.

*****

After Sam left and Claire had gone to her room, Michael took Margo in his arms. "Our girls are safe, you're safe. Sam has everything under control."

Nuzzling her head against his neck, she whispered, "Michael, I'm sorry."

"What are you talking about?"

"I've made so many bad choices. It's my fault this has happened and I'm sorry. I have years and years to be sorry for. Oh, Michael, you've got to believe me. I never saw how my decisions were impacting you and the girls. Never! Not once did I stop to think about any of you and now I've made a mess of everything."

His strong arms wrapped around her didn't lessen the anguish she felt deep in her bones.

Chapter Thirty-one

Randall, Martinez and Cannon

Eric hung up the phone and then glanced at each face in the room before he spoke.

Elena looked anxious, Maddie seemed ready to fight, Lawrence appeared calm, and Sam was wound tight.

"That was Madison. They've checked and Tomas Labato appears to be in Rio. The police think it would create an incident if they send someone to Rio. They're hoping we have someone who can go and talk to Labato. Based on what we find out they'll start an investigation or they'll discount him."

He frowned as he scanned the group. "After what happened to John, I don't want to send Maddie." He looked at Sam. "Any ideas?"

"If Maddie is willing, I think she and I should go to Rio as soon as we can get a flight." He continued talking as he glanced her way. When she nodded yes, he continued. "We can cover a lot of ground in a short time and she can handle things that won't put her in danger."

Eric picked up the phone and called his secretary. "I need for you to book two round-trip tickets to Rio leaving this afternoon, returning Friday. One for Sam Baxter, the other for Maddie Sonnett. Call me back when you have the details. Thanks."

As soon as Eric hung up the phone, Maddie said decisively, "I'm not afraid to go to Rio, Eric." Then she whirled around to Sam. "I don't need a knight in shining armor, but thanks for offering."

Sam laughed. "Hey, no offense intended. I just don't think you'd look good with your arms and legs in a cast."

"You guys be serious for a minute," Elena intervened. "What do you think we can accomplish in Rio, Sam?"

"Elena, we need to find out how, not if, Tomas is involved. There's no doubt in my mind that he is pivotal to this case. First, if he's involved, he'll know where these threats are coming from. That information alone may help us prevent a disaster. Second, we need to know how much the grandfather knows."

"Sam," Lawrence said," my contacts are certain that Tomas owes a large amount of money. They think it's even more than the million that's being demanded. Right now they haven't narrowed down the source and they don't know if there's a connection between the debts in Vegas and the debts in Miami. They keep feeding me information as they uncover it." Lawrence closed his notebook and looked at Maddie and Sam.

"DaSilco is a powerful entity in the world and the family assets are enormous. Why can't Tomas cover his debts? I have a suspicion there is more to this story than Tomas's debts and Paolo's murder. No one has come up with a motive for the murder and the grandfather may hold the key." Lawrence sighed. "I'd love to go with you to Rio, but alas, my mind and body don't work at the same speed anymore."

"You're helping immensely right here, Lawrence. I know you've got contacts all over the place. Once we've talked to Tomas, I'll let you know what questions we need answered."

Frowning, Elena looked at her husband. "Eric, is this investigation into the DaSilva family really necessary for our defense of Alli?"

"Elena, I believe it is–for two reasons. First, we're defending our client on a possible murder-one charge and then, we're trying to prevent her possible kidnapping and murder. I think we have a legal and moral obligation to pursue every avenue that's open to us. Right now our job seems to be to coordinate all of the resources we have available to us." Eric put down the papers he was holding and gave his wife a stern look. "The only defense we've got right now is the question of whether Alli could have lifted Paolo in and out of the boat. Not a very strong defense, don't you agree?"

"I can go along with you up to a point. Just remember, we've already got one investigator in the hospital." She shook her head and decided to drop the subject. "I'm not challenging your decision. I just don't want another incident."

Lawrence jumped to Elena's defense. "You are wise to be concerned, my dear. We may be dealing with unsavory and dangerous people. To ease your mind, remember we're not working outside the law. What we're doing is only part of what's going on. The police and the FBI are also carrying out full blown investigations and anything we discover will be communicated to them."

Elena smiled at Lawrence and nodded her appreciation for his support. He had managed to diffuse the tense energy that had developed in the room. "Changing the subject. Sam, what kind of protection do you have in place for the twins?"

"They're safe. My team and the Miami police are covering them 24/7. My biggest concern right now is Margo. If they can't postpone her surgery for a few days and she's moved to Jackson Memorial that will complicate things."

"I forgot about her." Elena's scowl deepened. "That hospital is a maze. Security there will be a real challenge. I wonder if her doctor has privileges at any of the other hospitals?"

"The hospital isn't the only problem, Elena. We need Margo to be able to take those phone calls."

Eric chimed in. "I know the doctor wants this surgery done as soon as possible, but surely it can wait until after Friday. Isn't that our deadline? That gives us three more days."

Sam stood up and started pacing the room. "If Maddie and I can get to Rio tonight, we'll have approximately forty-eight hours to cover a lot of territory."

When the phone rang, Eric picked it up, "Yes, that's great. Thanks."

"Everything is set. You're on flight 1280 from Miami to Rio leaving at three forty-five this afternoon, returning Thursday night. Two rooms booked at the Rio Palace. See Wanda on your way out. She's got all the information."

As his eyes met Maddie's he became more purposeful and intent, "You be careful and don't take any unnecessary risks." His eyes didn't move off her face as he spoke to Sam. "Take good care of her, won't you?"

Eric realized he had stared at Maddie a moment too long when he caught the expression on Elena's face.

*****

The first part of the flight to Rio was rough as the plane skirted the edge of a tropical system that swirled in the Caribbean. Maddie loved to fly but she was working hard to maintain her composure as a series of jolts catapulted them up and down over the turbulent air. At one point she had almost grabbed Sam's arm, but instead, steadied herself by clutching the arm rest.

"I asked the stewardess to bring you a ginger-ale with a touch of bourbon. That'll calm your stomach and settle your nerves." Sam was holding on to the overhead bin as he tried to resettle himself in his seat. "I hate flying when it's like this. I forgot we've got this tropical system all around us."

"Do you think it will be like this all the way to Brazil?" Maddie's voice was almost a whisper.

"We'll probably be out of it soon. Once we're across the Florida Straits, it should get smoother." He handed her the drink the stewardess was offering. "Take a couple of sips and see if it doesn't help."

Trying to change her expression from sheer terror to small fright, she took a quick gulp of the drink. Feeling the heat of the drink as she swallowed, she closed her eyes and waited for the bourbon to do its job.

"Maybe if we talk business it'll take your mind off this roller coaster. As soon as we land, I'm going to take a cab to Tomas's apartment. I want you to go to the hotel and rest. In the morning I want you to go to the government building, start with corporate revenue, and check on Tomas's role in the oil company, his salary, anything you can find that will give us a hint about his economic situation. Lawrence had a good thought when he asked why a man who is worth a fortune can't pay his debts?"

There was no reply from Maddie. She was sound asleep.

*****

Sam made sure Maddie was on her way to the hotel before he hailed a cab to take him to Tomas Labato's apartment. He wanted to take Tomas by surprise.

The apartment was in a modern high rise on the beach in Ipanema, one of the most affluent areas in Rio made famous by a hit song in the 1960s. The facade and lobby of the building shouted wealth and privilege. The doorman indicated that he spoke no English, so Sam tried his limited Portuguese.

"Chama o Senhor Tomas Labato, faz favor." It surprised him when the man understood him and picked up the house phone to call Tomas. After a very brief conversation he was directed to the elevators and given an apartment number on the tenth floor.

Tomas was waiting when the elevator opened. "Mr. Baxter, what a surprise to see you in Rio. I hope this is a social visit." Tomas's eyes reflected his caution. "Come in and have a seat. Let me fix you a drink."

The living room was ultra-modern with a minimal amount of well-placed furniture that took advantage of the wall of windows overlooking the ocean. "Beautiful view, Tomas. I'll take that drink but this isn't a social call. I'm here because I need your help."

"Tell me more, but it's unlikely that I will be able to assist you. Unless, of course, you need recommendations for a good restaurant or the best nightlife in Rio." Tomas handed Sam a drink and took a seat across from him.

"It's a bit more complicated than that and I need some quick answers." Sam took a swallow of the drink and put his glass down on the coffee table. "Margo has received a threatening call from someone who wants a million dollars or one of the girls will be murdered."

Tomas shrugged. "I'm sure people are always trying to capitalize on her fame and money. Is this threat unusual?"

"The caller said this was payment for a debt and Margo's boyfriend had already been killed because of it."

As the color drained from Tomas's face, Sam knew he was on target. That reaction proved to Sam that Tomas knew all about the reason for the call.

Recovering quickly, Tomas stood and walked to the window. "I don't see what this has to do with me and I can't imagine that Paolo was killed over a million dollars. That thought is ridiculous." He turned back to face Sam. "Why are you telling me all of this? You should be working with the Miami police."

"I assure you the police and the FBI are working this from every angle. But I think you're the key, Tomas. I think you know exactly what I'm talking about and I need names. I need to know who you owe all this money to and why."

Tomas began to laugh. "You are being very blunt, aren't you? I can save you a lot of time. Let me bring this conversation to a close right now. I don't know what you're talking about."

"I've got the info on your debts and so does the FBI. What has me baffled is why. You have tons of money and resources, and for some reason, you are in over your head. I'm sure a million is nothing to you."

"Please leave now, Mr. Baxter. I have nothing to say to you on this matter." Tomas's eyes betrayed his anger, even though his tone of voice was very controlled.

"I was hoping you could help me out. Perhaps I'll have better luck with your grandfather when I see him." Sam stood and headed to the door.

"It would not be in your best interest to approach my grandfather."

"I've got until Friday to get some answers. I don't intend to let anything happen to Margo or her daughters because of your debts. Do I make myself clear?" The threat hung in the air as Sam spoke.

Tomas stood still as a statue for almost a full minute, holding Sam's glare. With a slight bow, he sneered. "Dario Vincetti. Find him and you've got your answers. Now leave before I call security."

As Sam closed the door he saw Tomas pick up the phone.

*****

Sam called Lawrence Fitz the moment he got to the hotel. "Lawrence, check out Dario Vincetti. The name is all I've got."

"I know the name. He's a small time racketeer who runs games for the Empress. I'll see what I can find out."

*****

"Maddie, we're being followed," Sam whispered as he grabbed her arm and steered her into one of the street-side cafes. The plan was to see Eduardo DaSilva this morning but it was possible that plan would be detoured. "Let's take a table outside and see what happens next."

"This story doesn't add up, Sam. Why in the world doesn't Tomas go to his grandfather and borrow the money? Or better yet, why doesn't he use some of his assets? From what I can tell, the guy is worth millions and now that Paolo is dead, he stands to inherit everything."

Her eyes brightened as she finished the sentence. "Is that the motive here? Did he have Paolo killed in order to remove the heir?"

"I've gone over this so many times in my head that I'm losing track of what's what. That's an obvious answer, but somehow I don't think that's the right one." Sam picked up the menu and glanced over the top of it at the man across the street. "Is that guy going to stand there until we've finished lunch?" He chuckled. "Is this some kind of intimidation strategy?"

Maddie lifted her head and stared directly at the tall stranger leaning against the wall of the building that faced the cafe. "Do you want me to go ask him?"

Before Sam could stop her, she raced across the street and stopped in front of the startled man. He watched as she pointed her finger at the man and seemed to be giving him a piece of her mind. In less than a minute, she walked back to the cafe and settled into her chair. They watched as the man moved on down the street.

"That was easy," she said in an off-handed way. She didn't look at Sam, but picked up the menu to make her decision for lunch.

"You are either crazy or stupid!" Sam meant to let her know that he was not pleased with what she had just done. "What the hell did you say to the man? Or better yet, what did he say to you?"

Very calmly she looked up from the menu. She batted her eyes and gave him a flirtatious smile. "I couldn't understand a word he said. If he was speaking Portuguese, it was mixed in with some other dialect." She put the menu on the table and reached across to take his hand. "I've decided what I want for lunch, how 'bout you?"

Startled once again by her action, his face flushed red. He was getting angry with her flippant attitude and he wanted it to show. "Maddie, what did you say to him?"

Continuing to hold on to his hand, she didn't flinch. "I told him he was spoiling my lunch and I didn't want him to follow me anymore. Then I told him my husband was a very jealous man who could put a bullet between his eyes at three-hundred yards."

Sam laughed until tears rolled down his cheeks. “You are one gutsy broad! Let’s go–you’ve bought us a few minutes.” He stood up and moved away from the table.

“Hey! What about lunch? I’m starving,” she complained as she moved in his direction.

*****

They walked into the DaSilva building and headed to the elevator. Sam pushed the button and the elevator door opened on a surprised Tomas Labato.

“Senhor Baxter, what a surprise. I didn’t expect to see you here.” He grabbed Sam’s arm as he walked out of the elevator and prevented him from following Maddie inside. As the door closed separating them, Sam silently wished her good luck.

“What is it with you, Senhor? Every time I turn around you are in my way.” Tomas hissed the words between gritted teeth.

“I told you I’m on a tight deadline. I need answers now.” Sam pulled away from Tomas’s grip and shook his arm to release the tension.

“You won’t find the answers here. Go back to Miami.”

“Há um problema, Senhor Labato?” A security guard approached and stood close to Sam.

“Não, Jose. Não há problema.” Tomas said. “O senhor estava saindo.”

“I suggest we leave the building together, Mr. Baxter. I’ve told the guard you were leaving and you wouldn’t want to upset him.”

Sam turned and walked out of the building with Tomas beside him. Once they were out on the sidewalk, Tomas became more menacing. “I told you to leave my grandfather out of this. He is still in mourning for Paolo and I’ve told you he knows nothing. The people you want are in Miami.”

"The person I want is standing right in front of me. Pay your debt, Tomas, and solve this problem for everybody. Then tell the authorities what you know about your cousin's murder." Anger flashed in Sam's eyes and he wanted Tomas to know that he wasn't cowed. "You've put innocent people in danger and I want to know why!"

"You know nothing! So get out of Brazil and leave my family alone."

Sam grabbed Tomas by his shirt collar and pulled his face close. "You scum. I think your cousin's death is already on your hands and if you don't do something soon to clear up this mess, the death of Alli Anderson may be on your hands, too." He let go of Tomas and brushed his hands as though he had touched something dirty. "If anything happens to that girl, there won't be a place on this planet for you to hide."

Eyes burning with rage, Tomas walked around Sam and entered the coffee shop across the lobby.

*****

Maddie knew the questions she wanted to ask Eduardo DaSilva and thought she would probably have better luck without Sam. She was certain her request to see DaSilva would be negative. So, she would have to figure out which office was his. If she knew that, then she could find a way to get inside. Watching every movement in the hallway, she waited to see which door the receptionist entered. It didn't take long for the tall, shapely brunette to return to the reception desk and motion for Maddie to follow her.

"Senhora, please go to the third door on the left. Senhor DaSilva will see you now."

Hiding her surprise, Maddie walked confidently down the hall.

*****

She entered an office that was austere and cold, literally and figuratively. The room had two walls of floor-to-ceiling glass, two walls painted white with no adornment, white carpet and chairs, and a wide mahogany desk. The thermostat was turned down to arctic and she wasn't dressed for ice and snow. Eduardo DaSilva, dressed in a black three-piece suit, sat in stark contrast to his environment. Wow, she thought. The effect was dramatic and didn't invite guests to linger.

"How may I help you, Ms. Sonnett? I assume you are here for some important reason."

His voice was not unkind, but he didn't ask her to take a seat and he didn't stand when she entered the room.

"Mr. DaSilva, I need information. It is literally a matter of life and death." She walked forward and stood directly in front of him. "My clients are being threatened as a result of your grandson's debts, and so far he is being very uncooperative." She rested her hands on his desk and leaned forward. "You, sir, are my last resort."

"Threatened? Ms. Sonnett that is a serious claim. Would you mind telling me who you work for and how you support this claim. What kind of threat are we talking about?"

"Margo received a phone call from an unknown who threatened to kidnap and possibly kill one of her daughters if the million dollar gambling and drug debt that Tomas owes is not paid by Friday. The man who called told her that Paolo was already dead because of it and one of her daughters would be next. Naturally, we now believe there is a connection."

He startled her by jumping up from his chair and she stepped away from the desk. "This is absurd! Are you telling me that Paolo was killed because Tomas owes someone money? Is that what you're saying?"

She knew he hadn't meant to display such a reaction as she watched him quickly recover his composure.

"I'm telling you what the caller told Margo. We've tried to discuss this with Tomas and we were blown off. He denies the debt and laughed when we told him what the caller said about Paolo. Our sources believe this is a legitimate threat."

"Young lady, you can't possibly believe that I'm going to hand over a million dollars to you." He laughed. "I've heard every scheme you can think of and this one has been used before. Now leave my office before I have security remove you."

"Mr. DaSilva, this is not a scam. Believe me I could come up with something a bit more creative if I was trying to con you for the money. I don't want your money–this is about information. We need names."

She watched as Eduardo, who was used to being in control of every situation, slowly returned to his chair. She softened the tone of her voice but she did not back down. "If I were you, I'd be concerned that my grandson died for this piddling amount of money and the life of an innocent girl may be in jeopardy. Why don't you call Tomas and ask him to come here and confront me about this accusation?"

"Who sent you here?"

"I work for a law firm that represents the Anderson family. Let me assure you that I'm not working independently. The FBI and the Miami police are actively involved but are trying to avoid making this an international incident. The head of security for the Anderson's, Sam Baxter, is here with me and has tried unsuccessfully to discuss this with Tomas."

He picked up the phone and asked his secretary to find Tomas. "Díga-lo venha para o meu gabinete agora mesmo."

Chapter Thirty-two

Margo

"Lulu, I want to talk to my girls. Can that be arranged once I'm in the hospital in Miami?" She looked over her coffee cup at the woman she was learning to trust. "I thought about it all last night and I need to see them. I just don't know what to say to them."

"I can make those arrangements, but don't you think you need to talk about why you want to see them? Your daughters aren't used to mother-daughter conversations and it might not go as smoothly as you want it to. Margo, I think you're acting on emotion and it won't work if you're just trying to satisfy some selfish need. I know how angry you've been with Alli. Is this going to turn into a screaming match with her? 'Cause if it is, you better think twice about seeing her."

"My world is falling apart and I need to do something to pull it back together again. Shouldn't I begin with the two people I've hurt the most?"

"That would be noble if you were thinking about their best interests. You've got some things on your plate right now that need to be faced before you reach out to someone else. Don't you think we need to talk about what's happening to you right now? I haven't heard one word from you about the doctor's diagnosis or what it means to your career."

"What do you want me to say?" Margo felt like screaming. "Do you want me to fall apart in front of you, is that it?"

"You know that's not true. But, if you don't talk about this, it will blindside you when you're least expecting it." Lulu folded her hands in her lap and softened her expression. "Margo, I've watched your progress over the past month. Now that substances aren't controlling you, you've taken some remarkable steps toward healing. Don't let all the work you've being doing be for nothing. Keep moving forward. Stay in touch with your feelings and don't go back to running away. That's the only way you're going to stay sober once you leave the hospital. If something hurts, it's going to hurt and the only way through it is to deal with it."

The room filled with a heavy silence that hung between them. Lulu spoke first. "Your adult life has been about covering up your feelings with drugs and alcohol. It's a cop-out to say that you were only doing it to have fun."

"You think you know everything. I don't need to listen to this if I don't want to."

"So true. You can make your own choice about what you want for yourself. But, I'm asking you to think about making some smarter choices. Particularly if you're thinking about seeing the twins. Don't bring them in if you're not willing to deal with being their mother."

Lulu stood up. "I've said enough. You think about it and if you really want to see the girls, I'll make the arrangements." She turned and left the room.

*****

Margo looked up from her book when Michael entered the room. "Michael, why are you still here?"

He looked surprised. "Would you like me to leave?"

"I don't mean right this minute. I mean after all the hell I've put you through. Why haven't you walked away? It can't be about the money." She pulled her legs under her and curled up in the chair.

"Is this a serious conversation or do you want some flip answer? I could give you several reasons." Michael poured himself a cup of coffee and sat down on the sofa. "Why are you asking this question?"

"I want to know. I want you to talk to me about our life. I've lost me, Michael, and I don't know how to get back on track. Maybe if you answer my question I'll have a starting point." She knew her pain showed, but she needed an answer.

"There's no big mystery, Margo. The answer hasn't changed since you were eighteen years old. I love you." He whispered the last three words, but he didn't take his eyes off of her.

"After all I've put you through. I don't understand."

"That's the difference between us, Margo. You have to know what love feels like to understand why I've stayed. I'm not sure you've ever let love really touch you."

"That's nonsense. I know what love feels like. There are fans all over the world who love me." She walked over to the glass doors and looked out at the ocean. "Love feels good, Michael." Her voice was low and seductive. "Come with me to the bedroom and I'll prove to you that I know what love feels like." She walked over and took his hand.

"You've made my point, Margo." He stood up and started for the door. "Having sex won't answer your question."

"Wait, Michael. Why are you leaving?" His response confused her.

"It hurts too much to stay." He closed the door quietly as he left.

The fear of being alone swept over her as she stared at the closed door. He was hurt but she didn't know why. She had offered herself to him and he had walked away. Maybe he was the one who didn't know what love was. She picked up the phone and dialed Lulu's number.

*****

Several hours later, Lulu walked into Margo's suite. "Okay, what's the big emergency? You look like you've lost your best friend."

"It really hurts my throat to talk today, but I need you to tell me about love." Holding her hands around her throat made it easier to talk. For weeks she had dealt with a sore throat but today the rasping was worse than ever.

"That's a big topic, honey, and I can only tell you about my experience of love. I can't define it for you. What brought this up?"

"Michael doesn't think I know what love is. That's absurd, of course. We were talking about it earlier and I thought things were going well. Then all of a sudden he told me it hurt too much to stay and he left." Exasperation filled every word. "How could he say that to me?"

"You're leaving something out. What were you talking about just before he left?"

"I told him I knew what love felt like and I asked him to come in the bedroom so I could show him."

"Well, that's a starting point. Why don't you define love for me and we'll go from there."

"That's the question I asked you. Apparently, I don't have the right answer." Margo threw up her hands and gave Lulu a quizzical look. "I thought love was about being attracted to someone, but I guess my idea isn't good enough for Michael."

"That's part of the answer, Margo. But, let's explore some other aspects and maybe you can add to your understanding of something that's often complex."

Lulu walked around the room and picked up a small, crystal vase. "When I look at this vase I see something beautiful and I'm attracted to it. Do you think that's love?"

"Of course not. The vase is an object."

"Right. I'm attracted by its loveliness and I would like to show it off in my home. But there is no love involved between me and the vase. I can hold it, caress it, admire it, obsess over it, use it to enhance my home, but if I say I love the vase, it can't love me back. We can't have a relationship, we can't connect in any way that's meaningful. But it gives me pleasure to see that vase."

She replaced the vase and sat down across from Margo. “Some people might think my attraction to the vase is love. But is it?” She waited before she added, “I certainly have feelings about the vase. I want to make sure it doesn’t get broken. I want to keep it show-worthy. I care about what happens to it. So, what’s missing?”

“You tell me.”

“I don’t have the right answer, so I’ll quote a few people who have more wisdom than I do. Erich Fromm came up with a definition that has pointed me in the direction of love on numerous occasions. He said, “Love is the attachment that results from deeply appreciating another's goodness.” Or, how about this one from M. Scott Peck, “Love is not a feeling. Love is an act of will.” Picking up a paper and pen, she began to write. “I want you to think about these two quotes, so I’ve written them down for you. They’ll give us a shared language that may open up a great conversation on the subject of love.”

“If you say so.” Taking the offered paper, Margo looked at what her doctor had written and shook her head. “Is this my homework?”

“No, Margo. I think this would be called lifework.” She laughed. “It’s always your choice. I’ll leave it with you and you decide what you want to do with it.”

“You think Michael understands what these men are talking about and I don’t, right?”

“You asked me to define love and I’ve tried to come up with some language that may help you form your own definition. If this helps, great. If it doesn’t, we’ll go in another direction.”

She walked over and put her hand on Margo’s shoulder. There was tenderness in her voice when she spoke. “One thing about you, you never ask easy questions. We’ll talk later, okay? I’ve got another appointment.”

Staring at the words on the paper, Margo felt even more lost and confused. Had she ever loved anyone? Or had she confused lust with love? Could she learn to be loving?

"Everything was so much easier when I could take a drink and not think about things like this."

*****

Hours later she stood on the balcony and watched the storm clouds gather on the horizon. Another tropical depression hugged the coast even though it wasn't supposed to hit south Florida. The sky looked ominous and the air felt heavy because of the falling barometric pressure. It matched her mood.

The sliding glass door opened and the scent of aftershave told her Michael was behind her. She was grateful that he had returned.

"You're not mad at me anymore?" Turning away from the ocean to look at him, she felt a sense of relief. "I'm glad you're here."

Then she looked at his face and knew the visit had nothing to do with her. "Come inside, Margo. I have some bad news."

Quickly she walked into the living room and sat down in her chair. "You look awful. What could possibly be so bad?"

"Alli is missing. Tim Elwood said the last time he checked both your mother and Alli were asleep. That was around two o'clock this morning. He stretched out on the living room couch with the television on to watch some reruns. Your mother usually gets up about eight and Alli sleeps in until ten or so. When your mom didn't get up at the usual time he checked but she was still asleep and he didn't wake her. He didn't check on Alli because he knew she didn't get up early. When your mother woke up and called Alli for breakfast was when they discovered she was missing."

Fear gripped Margo and she tried to ask Michael a question, but there was no sound when she opened her mouth to speak. She balled up her fist and pounded the arm of the chair. Suddenly, she jumped up and ran to Michael. She threw her arms around him and held on as tightly as she could.

Michael held her until she stopped shaking then he told her the rest. "Your mom's condo is in a secure building and she lives on the ninth floor. There was no sign of forced entry, no one passed the security in the hall, and the guys guarding the perimeter of the building didn't see anything suspicious. No one heard or saw Alli leave."

He walked Margo back to her chair. "Sit down. I've talked to Claire and Lulu and they'll be here any minute." Holding on to her hand, he took his other hand and lifted her chin. "She's going to be all right. She probably slipped out to get some fresh air or something. You know Alli, she doesn't think any of this is serious."

"I don't know Alli," Margo whispered.

"Those are the saddest words I think I've ever heard you say."

"I don't know my own daughter." Her throat hurt and she wasn't sure if Michael could even understand what she was saying. "It's not Friday. That man said we had till Friday."

Eyes closed and clutching her aching throat, Margo felt totally beaten. Emotions hit her from every direction–fear, sadness, regret–and a physical ache caused her to double over. Again, she tried to talk and the raspy whisper was even less understandable than it had been when she had gotten a few words out just a few seconds before.

The phone rang and Michael reached to answer it. "Hello. Margo can't come to the phone." He listened to what the voice on the other end of the line was saying and knew this was the caller that he needed to keep talking. "I'm Michael Anderson. What do you want?"

Margo could hear the muffled voice of the man who had called her earlier in the week and she wanted to scream, hit him, make it all stop.

"What are you talking about? Wait, do you have my daughter?" Michael's voice got louder with every word. "If you don't have her, then where is she?"

"I understand, but you told us we had until Friday. We're doing everything we can to get your money. We sent people to Brazil to ask Eduardo DaSilva for the money and they won't be back in Miami until tomorrow."

He was calmer and the words were more matter-of-fact. "But I need to know where Alli is." Looking at the clock, he knew he had to keep the man on the line for at least two more minutes. "How do I know she's safe?"

He listened and turned to Margo. "He says Alli is all right. They didn't take her but they know where she is."

"If you know where she is, tell me!" As he listened he didn't take his eyes off Margo. All of a sudden, he frowned and slammed down the phone.

"Seems our Alli walked back to MarGrove around six this morning. She doesn't have a clue what kind of danger she's in." He put his head in his hands and his voice betrayed his weariness. "They know where she's staying and someone followed her to the house. Ah, Margo! What is happening to us?"

Picking up the phone, he called Todd Madison with the Miami Police. He explained what was going on and learned that the FBI had been able to track the call to a pay phone at a marina near South Beach. But the man was gone by the time they got there. As soon as that call ended he dialed the attorney's office and explained what he had just learned.

"Elena, you've got to get the judge to agree to let us move Alli out of Dade County. Now. This minute. We can't wait any longer."

A knock on the door made him jump. "It's okay. It's just Lulu or Claire." He turned to Margo who sat frozen. "It's okay." Mouthing the words, he held on to the phone as he walked to open the door. Lulu and Claire stepped inside the apartment and waited for him to hang up the phone.

"Elena, call me as soon as you know something. I'll be headed back to Miami in a few minutes. Yes, I called Todd Madison and the police are going to pick Alli up at MarGrove." He listened and then responded, "Yes, the police have notified Tim Elwood and Margo's mother. Yes, Sam and Maddie are supposed to be on a flight back to Miami this evening. And, yes, I will check in with you once I know that Alli is safely at her grandmother's. Call me when you hear from the judge."

Margo handed Michael a sheet of paper that she had written on. "Let me come with you. Tell Lulu I need to do something. I can't just sit here and worry." She watched him read it, then in a raspy voice she whispered, "Please."

Michael read the note and handed it to Lulu. "What do you think? She could go with me to Miami for a couple of hours and we'll be back here before dark. Claire can ride with us and I'll have a security guard meet us at MarGrove."

"I don't like the idea, Michael. Those people have eyes everywhere and they could get a lot of leverage by kidnapping Margo."

"I don't think they want that much publicity, Lulu. The threat to Alli is a scare tactic. Those people want the money."

"You're being naive, Michael. But, Margo's right. It's no good for her to sit here and worry. Why don't the four of us take a ride to Miami?"

Margo sneered at Lulu as she handed her a note. "You're not my mother!"

"Lord help you, sweetheart, if I was your mother. Those are my terms. Take it or leave it."

Chapter Thirty-three

Alli

The moment she slipped out of her grandmother's condo building a weight lifted off her shoulders. She smiled when she thought about how easy it had been to escape. The security guard had fallen asleep on the couch and she waited until she heard him snoring before she tiptoed passed him to the front door. She wasn't sure how she eluded the watch dogs outside the building, but she felt sure that no one had followed her.

For two days she had walked around the condo with an in-prison heaviness and all she dreamed of was getting away for a few minutes. Her grandmother was doing everything she could think of to make her feel at home, but the woman was hovering and Alli felt trapped.

It took her ten minutes at a brisk walk to go the distance between the condo and MarGrove. After she had punched in the gate code and let herself in the front door, it dawned on her that she had never really appreciated the house. The high ceiling of the foyer and the spaciousness of the living room amazed her. It's five times the size of the condo. No wonder I was suffocating. Looking around, with the early morning light coming through the windows, it was easy to see why her mother loved the place. The house had been designed to capture the best of Florida, blend with the tropical setting, and invite guests to linger. The rooms were elegantly furnished in soft turquoise, sea green, and cream. She had to admit that her mother had good taste.

There was no hurry. She figured she had hours before she would be missed, so she curled up in one of the big chairs near the fireplace and stared out at the bay. There was so much to think about. She knew she wasn't going to be tried for Paolo's murder. How could anyone even think she was involved? But, this latest little kidnapping wrinkle was keeping her from practicing with the band and she had to figure out a way to get to rehearsals. All of her time and energy needed to be focused on convincing her father to let her take Margo's place on the tour. She knew she was good enough and she was confident she could win over any audience.

Picking up the phone, she called and woke up Mark Sanders. "Sorry to wake you, but I have a million questions and a few favors to ask."

She could tell that he didn't appreciate being awakened so early.

"Mark, I need to talk to you about the new music for Margo's tour. There's a big chance I'll be taking her place and I've got to start working with the band, the back-up singers, and the dancers."

He still didn't sound awake enough to understand what she had said. "Wake up, Mark. For starters, I need to know about the new music, when I can get together with the band, how many of the songs are production numbers, and how many of the pieces for this show are on her latest album."

"That's exactly what I said and you've got to help me. So, stop laughing and tell me when we can start rehearsing."

Agitation was creeping into the tone of her voice. "Don't you hang up on me! I'm serious. Margo's sick and I'm going to take her place. So you better get used to having me around."

Alli was shocked when he hung up. She had been so certain he would be eager to work with her. Be careful, Mark. You just hung up on your next boss.

She started upstairs when the phone began to ring. Good. He's calling back to apologize.

"If you're calling to apologize, make it good," she snapped.

"Stop yelling at me about what I'm supposed to do or not do. I needed some fresh air, detective. No need to get all upset."

She listened as the detective continued. "Are you telling me you could put me back in jail for taking a walk? That's absurd and I'm not in danger! All of you are going over-board with this thing." She walked over and looked out the window. "Yes, I see you. Let me open the gate."

She groaned and put the phone down. "Why can't they understand what I need?"

She opened the gate and the front door to look eye to eye with an angry Todd Madison.

"Let's go inside and close this door. Apparently the people who are threatening to kidnap you are watching this house and know you're here."

He moved her out of the doorway and steered her toward the living room. "Please take a seat away from the window."

"Why in the world are these people after me? I didn't do anything to them," she whined.

"We don't have it all figured out, but money is owed and somebody thinks your mother should cover it. Look, I know this isn't easy, but you've got to do as we say until we catch these guys." As he talked, she watched him check the doors and windows.

"We need to move you again. It's not safe for you to be at your grandmother's. Sam and your dad are waiting to hear if the judge will let us move you out of Dade County. Once I hear from them you will be moved to a safe house out of this area."

"You can't do that. I've got things to do here. I won't go! I've got music to learn and rehearsals. I can't leave town now."

"Sorry to mess up your plans, but my job is to make sure nothing happens to you. You tipped our hand by leaving your grandmother's, and lucky for us, they wanted us to know it." He changed his tone of voice and tried to reason with her. "I'm the only one who will know where you are. You won't even know a physical address. Trust me, this is for your own good."

"What about Sunni? What are you going to do to make sure they don't get her by mistake?"

"She and Miss Finley are already on their way to the airport. I've got a car picking up your things at your grandmother's, but if there is anything else you'd like to take with you I suggest you get it now. As soon as that phone rings we're leaving."

*****

The car pulled into the garage and the door lowered behind them. Sam told the women to wait until he had spoken to the detective before they came in the house. He asked Michael to stand at the kitchen door while he went inside.

"Is Alli in the house, Michael?" Margo called from the car window.

"Yes, it sounds like she and Detective Madison are in the kitchen. I can hear Sam talking to them." He walked over to the car and opened the back door. "Margo, are you sure you want to go inside?"

Lulu reached over and took her hand. "It's okay if you're not ready. You can do this later, Margo."

"You're right. I thought I was ready to see her, but I'd only make a mess of things. I think I should wait for a better time."

She looked up as Sam came to the door and motioned for everyone to enter the house.

"Sam, I'll go with you. Margo and Lulu have decided to stay in the car. Clair can stay with them," Michael said.

*****

All the curtains in the house were closed and the only light was the lamp over the kitchen island. When Alli saw her dad, she rushed over to him and began to plead like a five-year-old.

"He wants to take me away to some safe house. Tell him I can't go. Tell him I've got rehearsals. Make him understand how important this is."

Michael stared at his daughter in disbelief. “I’m afraid for the next few days you don’t have a choice. The rehearsals will wait.” His volume increased with his anger.

“You’ve just pulled a stunt that shows us how little regard you have for yourself or any of us. You may not be mature enough for a music career. You will do as the detective says or I can assure you there will be no tour. Do I make myself clear, Alli?” He grabbed her arm and pulled her closer to him. Locking his eyes on her, he spoke through gritted teeth. “You will do whatever you’re asked to do.”

“You give me no choice. Now let go of me. You’re hurting my arm.” As he loosened his grip, she shook her arm free and turned to Sam.

“Who will be going with me to wherever it is I’m going? And, where is my armor?”

“Stop with the sarcasm, Alli. You created a dangerous situation this morning and no one’s amused,” Michael warned.

“Fine. Let’s get this over with.”

“We can’t leave if the judge doesn’t sign the order, so everyone needs to sit down and relax until that phone rings.”

Madison whispered to Michael that he appreciated his help. Then he turned to Sam. “Is she always this stubborn and defiant? I think you all are mistaken about her capabilities. She’s proving my case, not yours.”

Ignoring the others in the room, Michael spoke to Alli. “Your mother is in the car. She was concerned about you.”

“You’re kidding. She’s worried about me? That’s a first.”

“Maybe you’d like to talk to her.”

“Sorry, dad, but I don’t think it would be a good idea for me to see her right now.”

She didn’t need a confrontation with Margo that might confirm, in front of her dad and Sam, that she had been disowned.

*****

The ringing phone broke the tension between Alli and Michael and gave them an excuse to end the discussion. Sam spoke with Elena and gave the others the sign that the judge had approved a supervised move.

"I've made all the arrangements for the safe house," Madison said.

Alli saw a look of concern cross her father's face before the detective continued. "She'll be protected where I'm taking her and I promise you'll get a call every day to reassure you."

He turned to Alli. "It's time. When you're ready I'll help you carry out your things."

Picking up one of the suitcases, Madison turned to Sam. "Plan A is in place. Thanks for suggesting that I use one of the cars in the garage. It's good that you celebrity types have cars with tinted windows." He smiled. "A patrolman will pick up my car later this afternoon and will call to let you know where to pick up this one. Once we're at the safe house, someone will be in touch. Give me a fifteen minute lead before you leave the house."

Alli kept her head down as they walked past the car where Margo was seated. When this nightmare was over, she knew she would have to face her mother, but now wasn't the time.

Chapter Thirty-four

Tomas

"Ms. Sonnett, I would like to talk with my grandson alone. Why don't I call you later at your hotel?"

"I'm sorry I brought you bad news, but you understand the urgency of the situation. I'd appreciate a call as soon as possible. We're staying at the Rio Palace."

"Good day, senhora."

Tomas spotted the woman as he stepped off the elevator. He stopped and leered at her so she would understand his disrespect and disgust. If he had more time, he would arrange to spend some very "special" time with her.

But his grandfather was waiting. It was never wise to keep Eduardo DaSilva waiting.

He tapped on his grandfather's door and walked into the office. The old man was deep in thought as he sat at his desk looking out at the mountaintop statue of Christ the Redeemer. From past experience he knew to stand quietly until he was acknowledged.

"I have lived in the shadow of the Christ on Corcovado Mountain all my life and for all my many years, I have believed that He protected my family from evil. Now I don't know what to believe."

His voice was steady and calm, but when he turned around, the fire in his eyes caused Tomas to take a step back. "Evil has come to my house, Tomas. Wouldn't you agree?"

"I don't know what you're talking about, avó. I don't understand." All of Tomas' senses were on alert as he tried to hold eye contact with the man who was his idol. “Has something happened that I don’t know about?”

Eduardo stood up to his full height of over six feet and approached his grandson. With each step, he seemed to grow taller, and Tomas felt his own stature shrinking. He opened his mouth to speak just as his grandfather’s open hand slapped him across the face.

“You have brought disgrace on our family. You have shamed me!”

The sting of the slap and the intensity of the words took Tomas off guard but he knew better than to try and defend himself.

“Avó, what have I done?” His whisper could barely be heard as he rubbed his cheek and struggled to recover his dignity.

“I will discuss this with you only once, Tomas. Then I will do what must be done to protect Margo’s daughter. After you answer my questions I will decide how to deal with you. How heavily are you in debt to those people in Miami? How much money did you embezzle from this company? And, God forbid, how does Paolo’s death figure in all of this?” With each question, Eduardo’s voice got stronger and louder. “Answer me now!” he roared.

“It’s a little thing, Avó. It’s not what you think,” he stammered. “I am repaying my small debt. There is nothing for you to worry about.”

“You dare to stand there and lie to me! Don’t you think I’ve seen the books? Did you not know that I had called you and Paolo home because of discrepancies that had been found? I kept hoping it was a mistake, Tomas. I kept praying that you had not betrayed me. Now I want the truth. No more lies, Tomas! No more lies!”

The room closed in on Tomas. It felt icy, and even though he knew every inch of the office, it suddenly felt foreign. He reached for his grandfather’s hand but the old man pulled away.

He dropped his head in shame. “I owe several million dollars, but I have tried to repay it.” His body began to crumble under the intensity of his grandfather’s scrutiny. “I beg you to understand. I tried to repay it but I couldn't. I used all my resources and then they told me they would kill me if I couldn't come up with the rest of the money."

All his life he had yearned for his grandfather's approval and praise, but it had always gone to Paolo. Tomas was the forgotten child. All his life he had watched as Paolo was groomed to one day head the business. He had watched with envy when Paolo was taken on trips, when Paolo was given gifts, and when Paolo had lived the life that Tomas wanted.

He held his tongue and complied when Paolo lorded over him. From an early age, he had worked hard to keep his hatred for his cousin under control. Now, years of anger welled up inside him with such ferocity that he could not contain it.

Fists clenched at his side, he approached his grandfather until they were merely inches apart. "I went to Paolo for help and he laughed at me. He laughed at me," he roared, spittle spraying as he raged.

"I had no choice! Do you hear me? I had no choice! You never knew I existed, but I watched you and learned from you. I knew how to access your accounts. I forged your signature and withdrew enough funds to buy me time. But it wasn't good enough and they told me they were coming for me."

His anger spent, he retreated from Eduardo as tears streamed down his face. He hid his face from his grandfather's stare. "They were coming for me. What could I do?"

"What did you do?" Eduardo screamed. "What did you do?"

"I told them it was Paolo's fault. I told them I would go to Paolo one more time and make him give me the money. I told them Paolo was at MarGrove."

"So you led them to your cousin and betrayed all of us. Is that how it happened? Tell me, is that how it happened?" Eduardo grabbed Tomas's shoulders and began to shake him. "Answer me!"

Simpering in fear, Tomas nodded.

Eduardo pushed him away. “Who did this? Give me a name.”

“Dario Vincetti,” he whispered in ultimate defeat.

“Meu Deus. What have you done to us, Tomas?” Eduardo closed his eyes. “Were you also responsible for the American investigator who was beaten?”

“He was making trouble for the family,” Tomas said, raising his head.

“Leave this building now. Go tell your mother the shame you have brought on this family and never return here again. I am finished with you, Tomas.”

Tomas stood in disgrace as his grandfather turned away from him. In a whisper, he told Eduardo that he was sorry and then he quietly walked out of the room and closed the door.

*****

Eduardo knew the moment that his grandson surrendered. He watched the light go out of his eyes and his shoulders slump in defeat.

But he knew he could not relent or forgive, and his heart ached. Both of his grandsons were lost to him but he had to stand firm and fight against Tomas’s betrayal.

He walked behind his desk, reached for the phone, and spoke the name of Dario Vincetti.

*****

Hours passed before the hotel phone rang. Maddie stopped pacing and jumped to answer it. She listened as Eduardo DaSilva’s voice calmly, but sadly, spoke to her.

“The problem will be taken care of. Go back to Miami and assure Margo that her daughter is no longer in danger.”

Then the phone went dead.

Chapter Thirty-five

Alli

The helicopter landed in the middle of a grassy field on a small island. She was sure they had headed west because they were flying over water that looked more like the Gulf of Mexico than the Atlantic Ocean. But she was clueless about her actual location.

"Where in the world have you brought me? This looks like the last outpost of Christopher Columbus."

"Miss Anderson, I only take you to the finest places. I think you will enjoy this island for the few days that you'll be here."

"Oh, yes. Jail was the most delightful place," she snarled. "But this? You've out done yourself." Curling her lip in disgust, she continued. "You're wrong, detective. I hate it, already."

From what Alli could tell, the access was limited and there were only a few residents. There was certainly no place to shop. A car had met them when the helicopter landed and within ten minutes they had moved from the airfield to a cottage set far back in the piney woods not far from the water. The helicopter would return for them when Miami-Dade PD gave the all-clear.

"Welcome to Paradise," he kidded as he and Alli approached the front door of what looked like an authentic Cracker house. There was a wide covered porch on three sides of the wooden structure, a metal roof, raised floors, and a hallway that ran from the front to the back of the house.

He dialed a security code which unlocked the door, then swung the door open wide. Alli climbed the steps, crossed the porch and stood just inside the doorway.

On one side of the hall was a small living and dining area with a kitchen. On the other there were three bedrooms and probably a bath. She could see a back door from where she stood.

"You can't expect me to stay here." Alli said as she stared at the rustic conditions. "There's no air conditioning, no TV, no anything!"

"For as long as we have to stay, this is home. Get used to it. I didn't bring you here for a vacation."

He carried her bags and his duffle inside. "Do you want the front or the back room? Agent Clark will be staying in the middle room as a sort of chaperone. Don't worry, she's FBI and will watch us like a hawk."

Alli groaned. "Is there even any food here? This place looks like it's abandoned." She walked over to the kitchen and opened the refrigerator.

To her surprise it was full of casseroles, milk, eggs, and even a chocolate cake. The freezer was full of meat and packaged vegetables. As she opened the cabinets, she realized that the house had been stocked with enough food to last them several weeks. "Somebody made sure we wouldn't starve. Southern hospitality at its finest." Sarcasm was her only defense against this latest disappointment. Instead of singing with Margo's band, she was locked up against her will in a shack a million miles from nowhere.

"You might as well make yourself comfortable. If you think you can walk away from this place like you did your grandmother's, you're mistaken. And, it's a long swim back to Miami. Since you didn't choose, I'll take the front room and you can take the back." He dropped her suitcase in the doorway of the back bedroom. "Hey, come check this out. You've got a great view from this room. If you hold your head just right you can catch a glimpse of the Gulf."

"Did you forget I live on the bay? I see the water every day." She flopped down on the sofa, slipped off her shoes, and picked up a magazine. "Who's going to cook and clean?"

Surprised, Todd turned around and pointed at her. "I guess the three of us will divide up those duties, Miss Anderson. There's just us and I doubt that Agent Clark plans on being your maid while we're here."

*****

For the rest of the afternoon, Alli pouted and dreamed of escape while the detective checked out every aspect of the house and the surrounding grounds.

As she unpacked the few things she had brought with her, she became upset when she looked down at her right leg and noticed the gold anklet she always wore was missing. Paolo had given it to her last year and she had thought it special until she saw her mother wearing one just like it.

Instead of being angry with him, she enjoyed knowing he branded his women and she was one of them. As she tried to remember where she might have left it, her stomach began to growl.

She stomped into the kitchen and put one of the casseroles in the oven. Taking down dishes, she began to set the table. Why couldn't they have sent me to a hotel with room service? Sunni's in New York living it up at the Plaza and I'm stuck in the Everglades.

She called to the detective and told him dinner would be ready in twenty minutes. "When is that lady supposed to be here? Do we have to wait for her?"

As they sat across from each other at the table, Alli had to admit the casserole wasn't too bad and her jailer could hold a decent conversation. He was nice looking and she decided he was probably in his early thirties. Checking him over, she liked his black hair, his trimmed mustache, and his greenish eyes. He was over six feet tall and she liked his build. Even though he had rebuffed her the day he took her to jail, there might be some potential for fun, after all.

"May I call you Todd? It seems silly for me to walk around here calling you Detective. And, please, call me Alli. I'm tired of the 'Miss Anderson' bit."

"I guess we can break the rules while we're here. I wonder who made this casserole? It's actually pretty tasty."

"Tell me about life as a Miami cop. Is it exciting or do you always end up on babysitting duty?"

"You're my first sitting job." He smiled at her. "Most of the time, I'm out there dealing with the bad guys."

"Are you married? Have kids? Who are you, Todd Madison?"

"Alli, I'm a regular guy who likes to see the bad guys lose. I'm not married, no kids, no obligations. I grew up in Miami and plan to stay there forever. I like my life." Todd leaned back in his chair and tried to relax. "What about you? Do you have some big plans for the future?"

"Oh, I have giant-size plans. As soon as you set me free, I'm going on tour. I'm a singer and I plan to be at the top of the charts very shortly."

"You certainly have the credentials. Your mom and dad can make some big things happen for you with all their connections. But what about college?"

"No way. That's Sunni's thing." She stood up and began to clear the table. "Are there any rules that say I can't walk the beach?"

"Only if one of us is with you. I'd be glad to walk with you, but you can't go by yourself."

She looked at him, then shrugged. "Hey, here's the deal. I cooked but you have to help me clean up. You wash and I'll dry. Then let's walk."

"You've got yourself a deal."

*****

The afternoon passed slowly, but the walk on the beach made her feel less stressed. She decided that Todd Madison wasn't so bad after all and maybe the next few days could be turned into pleasure if the lady agent didn't get in her way.

It was almost dark when a car pulled up in front of the house and dropped off the FBI agent. Donna Clark was mid-forties, had grown up on a farm in Minnesota, and had no time for nonsense.

She walked to the porch, said hello, and asked which room was hers. When Todd offered to carry her bag she brushed him out of her way.

"No thanks. I can manage." She walked down the hall to the door of her room before she turned back to the stunned couple.

"I'm exhausted. I'll see you in the morning." She glared at Alli. "Young lady, I understand you like to play escape games. Don't try it on my watch. I can hear a pin drop when I sleep."

After Agent Clark had closed her bedroom door, Alli looked at Todd and tried not to laugh. "I guess she told me. Where do they find these people?"

*****

Later that night she waited until she heard Agent Clark softly snoring before she walked to Todd's room and crawled into bed beside him. Startled, he jumped up and grabbed his gun.

"Whoa, Todd," she whispered in alarm. "It's me. Put that thing down."

She scrambled off the bed and walked to the window. Standing in the moonlight, she knew her silky nightgown glimmered in the light and showcased all the curves of her body. Seductively, she leaned forward, "Do you always react that way when someone gets in bed with you?"

"Only when they're not invited. Don't do that again, Alli. I'm on duty and you are in my charge." His voice softened. "If you're ever in bed with me it will be by my invitation."

"You're no fun. What are we going to do for the next few days?"

"We'll think of something. Now go back to your bed and get some sleep."

Opening the door, Agent Clark was waiting for her in the hall and wordlessly she watched until Alli had closed the door of her bedroom behind her.

*****

For two days, they danced around each other as the sexual energy continued to build. Alli used every opportunity to tempt him and was astonished at his power of resistance. Every time she thought Mrs. Clark wasn't looking, she became kitten-like and tried to rub up against him.

And, it became part of the game for him to blush and quickly move away. Quietly he would shake his head at her or whisper, "Stop doing that." But as the hours passed, she noticed he was becoming more playful and less businesslike.

I'm making progress.

Sitting on the front porch eating lunch, they watched a sailboat on the horizon. "How much longer do you think we're going to be here? I'm missing out on rehearsal time with the band."

"I didn't know you were part of your mother's group."

"I'm not. I'm taking her place."

"What do you mean, you're taking her place?"

"She's sick and they were going to cancel the tour, but my dad asked me to take her place. It's a long shot for him, personally and professionally, so I've got a lot to prove. If we can keep even a few of the venues, then I'll get my chance."

"That's ambitious–replacing a major headliner with an unknown. Wow. Your dad's got some kind of chutzpah." Todd shook his head.

"Thanks for that vote of confidence!" Alli felt a moment of doubt. "Whether you believe it or not, I can do it. I'm good and I plan to be as big or bigger than Margo."

Stomping into the house, she slammed the screen door behind her. "You wait and see, Detective Madison. Just wait and see."

"I'm sorry," he called after her. "You took me by surprise, that's all. Don't be mad."

She walked back to the porch, hands on her hips, eyes blazing. "Why don't you come with me? I'm going to need security and you can be my body guard. That way you can witness my success first hand."

"Whoa! You don't even know if there's going to be a tour and you're offering me a job. You are something else, Alli Anderson."

"Think about it Todd. It has to beat any offer you could get from the police department."

Chapter Thirty-six

Margo

"Lulu, I got really angry again when I saw her. How am I ever going to get past how I feel? I've never felt motherly toward her and now I've got to learn to be her mother and forgive her, too." She looked to her psychiatrist for some answers. "You're asking too much."

"Margo, I'm not asking you to do or feel anything. What I'm asking is for you to continue to recognize and deal with how the people in your life make you feel. For too long you walked away from everything that caused you to feel. You masked it all with alcohol, drugs and sex, and you'll do it again if you decide to give in to your old escape tactics. Then you'll never get well. It's your choice. Do the hard work or go back to the easy out."

Lulu's voice was tender and Margo realized that her doctor cared about the choice she was being asked to make.

"So–you do like me a little, right, Lulu?"

"Honey, it's not about me. Do you like you? That's a better question and one you haven't had the courage to face."

She folded her hands in her lap and took a deep breath. "I always thought I liked my life. I'm a star, millions of people know my name and there are even those who adore me. I live lavishly. I work hard, but I'm well rewarded." Thinking about all she possessed had always brought her pleasure, but that was gone. "I have the kind of life most people can only dream about. It's madness for you to think I haven't been happy or that I don't like myself."

"You don't have to defend yourself, but tell me one thing. If this is the life you want, then why did you try to end it?"

"That was an accident. I keep trying to tell you that it was an accident."

"You're lying to me and you know it. Don't go backward, Margo. Take off the mask and talk to me about why you were hurting so much that you didn't want to live anymore. That's the kind of conversation we need to be having. Did you think about those notes I left you on love?"

"Yes," she hesitated. "No, not really. I've had too many other things to think about."

"Excuses and defenses again. What are you afraid of?"

Margo pulled her feet up under her and curled herself tightly in the chair. She hugged herself and dropped her head so her chin touched her chest. How could she answer that question? How could she reach so far inside herself for answers she had tried all her life to hide or deny? How could she say what had to be said?

"I'm a fake," she whispered and held herself even tighter. "I'm not real. All I am is a voice. There's nothing else." Squeezing her eyes shut didn't drown out the words. The words she had been afraid to face all of her life. "All I am is a voice."

"Well done, Margo. Maybe you have finally let go of the fear that has controlled your life. You've said it out loud and defused its energy. You didn't vanish into thin air–you're still her and you're alive. How does that feel?"

"I'm scared, Lulu. I'm scared that no one will love me if I'm not Margo. The crowds will disappear, the applause, the adoration will all be gone and then what will I have?"

"What will you have, Margo? Think about it and tell me what will be left when that is all gone."

The mournful music of silence played on as the two women waited for Margo to make her choice. When she finally spoke, the sadness in her words came from a heart that was breaking.

"There will be nothing. I've ruined any chance that Michael or the girls will be there. I will be alone and I don't know how to be alone, Lulu. I don't know how to be alone."

There were no sobs, there was no drama. There was only the long shadow cast across the room by Margo's poignant words of truth.

Chapter Thirty-seven

Randall, Martinez and Cannon

Elena sat across the breakfast table from Eric and listened as the television reporter broke the news.

"Dario Vincetti, an alleged henchman for the Empress of Cocaine was found critically wounded late last evening on the steps of the Miami-Dade County Police Department headquarters. Vincetti had suffered numerous gunshot wounds and was semi-conscious when his body was discovered by an unnamed police officer. Sources at the department report that Vincetti was holding a copy of the newspaper reporting Paolo DaSilva's murder. Vincetti died in the emergency room at Jackson Memorial Hospital. A full investigation is underway to determine the possible connection between Vincetti and the Empress, and their role in the murder of DaSilva. It is reported that a message was scribbled across the newspaper that read, 'We're even, Eduardo'.

"What do you think about that? When Maddie called to let us know that Eduardo DaSilva was going to take care of things, I never figured he was going to have the guy killed."

Eric folded the newspaper he had been reading and placed it on the table. "Call that detective, Todd Madison, and see if you can find out any of the details. I'm going to call and see if Maddie and Sam are back in the country. We need to meet with them and get the whole story. Vincetti changes things dramatically for Alli Anderson."

He left the room and Elena wondered what the real impact of this news would be on the Anderson and DaSilva families. Was Dario Vincetti behind the threatening calls? Did he really kill Paolo

DaSilva? Had the debt been paid or was someone still out there waiting to collect a million dollars? In her opinion, it was too soon for anyone to let their guard down.

*****

Maddie and Sam's plane landed around midnight and after a few hours of sleep, they planned to meet at the law office to discuss their options. Then Sam would head to Boca Raton to be with Margo if and when she received the promised Friday phone call.

*****

"Sam, what's your take on Vincetti's murder?" Eric addressed his question to Sam, but he couldn't take his eyes off Maddie.

His attraction to her was heightened and he knew better than to let his imagination run wild with Elena sitting next to him. But, the woman looked too gorgeous for him not to notice in her tight black jeans and bright yellow shirt. He brought his attention back to the room when he realized that Sam had stopped talking and everyone was staring at him.

"I'm sorry, would you say that again, Sam? I lost my train of thought for a moment."

"Maddie is the one who spoke with DaSilva. She can tell you more about that than I can." Eric caught the look on Sam's face and knew he would have to be more careful. It wasn't smart for him to ogle another woman with his wife sitting next to him.

"When I met with Eduardo DaSilva, I was unprepared for how little he knew of Tomas's activities. I think I took him completely by surprise with my questions and his anger was close to the boiling point by the time he asked me to leave his office."

"Was he angry with you?" Elena asked.

"No, not at all. It was directed at Tomas. He asked his secretary to find Tomas and have him come to his office and then he asked me to leave. He wanted to talk to his grandson alone and he said he would call me at the hotel later. With the amount of rage I suspected was just under the surface, I was more than happy to leave his office." Maddie looked at the others at the table and smiled at Lawrence Fitz.

"You know, Fitz, I always like to leave before the fireworks begin."

"Then what happened, my dear?" Lawrence asked. "I had expected the elder DaSilva to be in the dark about his grandsons' activities, but I'm surprised that the man would let on to you that he didn't know. Did he say or do anything threatening?"

"Not at all. His demeanor was aloof and aristocratic, almost cold, except for a few seconds when he forgot that I was there. He reacted to something I said and then quickly recovered. But that little slip told me he was shocked and angry."

"What happened when he called you at the hotel?" Eric asked.

"The call was all one-sided. He simply told me it would be taken care of and to tell Margo her daughter was safe. Then he hung up. His voice was the saddest I think I've ever heard."

"This morning when I heard that Dario Vincetti had been murdered, I figured that DaSilva had evened the score." Sam added. "We can't take any chances, but I'm betting that Eduardo found out that Vincetti killed Paolo and had him iced."

"Do you think he has those kinds of connections?" Eric was still trying to put the puzzle pieces together.

"Eric, I wouldn't be surprised at anything Eduardo DaSilva could accomplish. The man is powerful and his name carries weight in many different arenas," Lawrence offered.

"Whoa! Are you saying the man has connections to the mob?"

"I didn't say that. His power isn't just in the oil business and let's just note that he could take care of a two-bit hoodlum like Vincetti in any one of the worlds where he has influence."

"Unbelievable. I've never really comprehended the vastness of the underworld and how people operate within that sphere. More often than I'd like to think about, our work is forcing me to acknowledge that the tentacles of that world can reach into the peaceful corners of my life," Elena said.

"Sad, but true, my dear," Lawrence agreed.

"The business at hand is whether Margo gets a phone call today and how it will be handled." Eric interjected. "Has anyone talked to Todd Madison? Do we know that Alli is really safe where ever she is?"

"I haven't heard directly from Madison, but I've talked to his supervisor and apparently they feel confident that Alli is protected. I also talked to Lara, and she and Sunni are fine in New York. I think we need to proceed as planned and see what happens. What do you think, Lawrence?"

"You're right, Sam. You and Michael need to go to Margo's. The FBI and police are ready for the call when it comes in and you've done everything possible to protect Alli and Sunni. If there's no call, and I don't think there will be, then we know that Vincetti was our man."

"What about his boss? Wasn't there a woman involved according to the caller? If the money hasn't been paid, will someone else come after Margo and Alli?" Elena looked worried. "What if we're oversimplifying the situation?"

"Elena, if DaSilva is true to his word, he has covered everything and this ordeal is over. We'll know soon enough." Lawrence tried to reassure her. Then he looked at everyone in the room. "The one unanswered question is Tomas Labato. He's a loose cannon."

"Fitz, what do you mean?" Maddie turned to her mentor with concern. "Don't you think if DaSilva took care of Vincetti, he'd make sure that Tomas didn't do any more harm?"

"It's probably nothing, but I can't get the man out of my mind." Lawrence picked up his folder and started to leave the room. "Forget I said anything. Chalk it up to an old man's ramblings."

Elena wrote herself a note. "For everyone's peace of mind, I'll check to see if Tomas left Brazil."

"And, I'll see if I can get through to Eduardo DaSilva. Thanks for your ramblings, Fitz. Better safe than sorry." Maddie smiled and nodded to Elena. "I'll call you when I know something."

*****

Lawrence Fitz was very concerned about Tomas Labato. As he and Maddie walked out of the building, he expressed his anxiety.

"Maddie, I don't mean to be an alarmist, but I have this nagging feeling that we haven't heard the last of Labato. My hunch is his grandfather has cut him loose and that means no resources. The man is accustomed to a very lavish life without having to work for it. Get as much information on this as you can and we'll keep hoping that it was a waste of your time." They had reached the sidewalk when he placed his arm around her and gave her a hug.

"Maddie, some personal advice. Watch out for Eric Randall. The man nearly fell off his chair when you came in the room. I like you and his wife too much for him to lose his integrity over you."

"Fitz, you're funny. I think your imagination is working overtime. The man hardly knows I'm alive."

Chapter Thirty-eight

Margo

All morning strangers paraded in and out of her room with wires, metal boxes, headsets, and a number of items she couldn't name. They were beginning to get on her nerves.

"Why are you redoing what you did two days ago?" she asked one of the men who was working on the phone. "This seems like overkill if you ask me."

"Sorry to bother you ma'am, but I'm making sure it's all working the way it should. I'll be out of your way in a few minutes."

"I need to make a call. May I use the phone?"

"If you'll make it a short call." She knew the man was annoyed that she kept interrupting his work. But he stepped away from the phone.

"Lulu, I need to see you." She waited for a response. "No, it can't wait." She hung up the phone and walked out to the balcony. She was melancholy and wanted to go home. Lulu was the only one who could make it happen.

*****

"Lulu, I'm homesick and I want to go to MarGrove for a day or two before they move me to the hospital." Seeing the look on Lulu's face, she added, "Now before you get all excited, listen to me." Margo needed to have a convincing argument if she was going to succeed. She knew Lulu would question everything she said.

"So, you've made your diagnosis and have come up with a treatment plan?" Lulu sat down and stared at her.

"I just want to go home. There's no crime in that, is there?"

"Margo, you've got some real health issues, and I'm not just talking about the physical problems you're facing right now. You aren't ready to go home and you know it."

"I know I'm not ready to go home for good. I just want to sleep in my own bed, see my things, and talk to Mrs. Davis. You know what I mean."

"I'd understand what you mean if you were a dying woman making your last request, but you'll be able to do all those things in time. You're not ordering your last meal for goodness sake." Lulu laughed and then looked at her client with tenderness.

"Margo, everything that's wrong with you is fixable, but you've got to give it time. If you don't, you'll be right back where you were six-weeks ago." When Margo's only response was silence, Lulu began again. "I'll make a deal with you. Let's get this phone call business behind us. Let's see what kind of arrangements Dr. Mellon has made at the hospital, and then we'll talk. If all goes well today, I expect Dr. Mellon will want you at Jackson Memorial tomorrow."

"All I want is one night at my own house! Did anyone ever tell you that you don't make it easy on your patients?"

"Only you, and that's most likely because my other patients don't make the kind of demands you do. Did anyone ever tell you that you whine a lot?"

"Touché."

All afternoon she and Michael sat and stared at each other. They read, they snacked, they talked about nonsense, and they waited. Waiting was hard on Margo. She was a woman used to having her whims met and her demands acted upon. She picked up the notes on love that Lulu had given her and read them again, trying to make sense of the concept they expressed.

"Michael, have you ever heard of Erich Fromm?"

"Yes, why?"

"Are you familiar with his ideas on love? Or, M. Scott Peck's?"

"I've read books by both of them, but I can't quote them. Are you reading their work?"

"Lulu gave me some quotes by each of them and asked me to think about them. I was just wondering if you knew anything about them. One of the quotes really hit me and made me think. Fromm said that love is about appreciating the goodness in someone. That sounded simplistic until I thought of you. You're a really good man and I missed seeing your goodness. From the first time you talked to me when I was a teenager, you were a good man and all I could think about was your ulterior motives. I've always thought you were using me for your own success, that you were controlling and smothering me. I never thought that you had my best interests in mind and I've hurt you too many times to count. Haven't I?"

He sat silent for a moment, then gave her a gentle smile. "I always wanted the best for you, but you had your own ideas. When you first got to New York, you were so young, so vulnerable and there were vultures waiting to capitalize on you. I just wanted to protect you. It's taken some counseling over the years to make me see it, but I finally realized that everything I did to protect you caused you to feel like a victim. I realized I couldn't make you see it my way, so I had to change my role. I couldn't be the long suffering husband–I had to give you the freedom to choose for yourself. I had to become the detached manager so we both could survive. Even when I saw you destroying yourself, Margo. And, for the most part, I've been able to hold the line on my feelings for you."

"But you still come to my bed every now and then. Doesn't that make it harder on you?"

"I'm human, Margo."

"If loving someone is appreciating their goodness, what good do you continue to see in me?"

He leaned forward, rested his elbows on his knees and his chin on his folded hands. "You hide it away sometimes. But, I see who you are when you're sober and there's a lot to like about the person you are then. You're kind to the people around you, you make people feel at ease, you're generous, and you laugh. I see so much good in you that you don't see about yourself."

He sighed. "I've let go of my hurts, but I see the hurt in our girls' eyes. I see their longing for your love and approval, and that gets to me. More than anything, I wish you could love your daughters. Even Alli, with all her flaws, needs your love. She has hardened her heart to you and acts like she doesn't care, but everything she does is to get your attention. Even the things that hurt you." He stood up and started to walk toward her when the phone rang.

They looked at each other in alarm. "Oh, God. It wasn't supposed to ring," Michael gasped.

He looked at Margo who seemed frozen to her chair. "You've got to answer it. Remember what the FBI agent told you, Margo."

Holding her breath, she picked up the phone. "Hello."

She listened as the voice on the other end began shouting demands. "Slow down. I can't understand you. What are you talking about? How could I have ruined your life? I don't even know you." She was silent as the ranting stopped and the man outlined his demands. "Let me see if I understand you. You want two million dollars in small, unmarked bills delivered where? And, if I don't comply, what did you say is going to happen?"

She turned ashen as she listened. "You what? What did you say? Wait, don't hang up. I need you to explain what you're talking about."

Stricken with fear, she hung up the phone and looked at Michael.

The door opened and Sam, the FBI agent, and a Miami-Dade policeman entered the room.

"What did he say, Margo?" Michael's voice was tense with fear.

"Sit down, Margo, and let's talk this through," said Sam. He led her to the sofa and pushed her gently onto it. "You did a great job of keeping him on the phone. They're working on pinpointing location right now and they've sent people to protect the house."

"Somebody tell me what's going on?" Michael's tone was impatient.

"Margo, think hard. Was it Tomas?" Sam tried to get Margo to focus. "Sit down, Michael, and I'll explain everything in just a minute."

"I couldn't tell. It sounded like him but I'm not sure. I do know it wasn't the man who called before. I'm certain of that."

"Let's talk about what he said. I'll repeat what I think I heard and you add to it or disagree if I'm wrong. Okay?"

Margo was still shaken, and glad that all she had to do was nod.

"He wanted two million dollars, right? He wants it delivered to an industrial park in Hialeah tonight at ten? He wants you to deliver it alone?"

"Yes, that's what he said, but how can I do that?"

"That's for the FBI to figure out," Sam continued. "The man said he would burn MarGrove to the ground, right? And, then he said he was looking for Alli and Sunni? That's good, Margo. That means he doesn't know where they are."

"He said he had some unfinished business with my girls. What did he mean by that, Sam?" Her voice was getting raspier and her throat seemed to be closing as she tried to speak.

"He won't find them, Margo. Hold on to that thought, please. If it's Tomas, he's an amateur. He won't know where to start looking for them."

Sam turned as the FBI agent handed him a note. "Margo, they've pinpointed the call to a pay phone in Coconut Grove. They've got a description of Tomas and they'll find him."

Picking up the phone, he dialed Elena's number. "Hi, it's Sam and we did get a call. What did you and Maddie find out about Tomas?" He listened to Elena and then hung up the phone.

"Maddie discovered that Tomas flew out of Rio late last night and entered Miami at noon today. So far, there is no record of him renting a car. She talked to Eduardo and all he would tell her was he was finished with his grandson. My guess is Tomas is looking for funds to tide him over until he can manipulate the company books or get back in the good graces of his grandfather."

"Somehow the tumors in my throat are becoming less and less important," she whispered. "Don't let him hurt the twins, Sam. That's all I ask." She walked over and hugged him. "Thanks for all you do, Sam. Have I ever told you that before?"

She smiled and turned to Michael. "I'm so tired. I need to lie down. Please call and ask Lulu to come see me. If I have to go to Hialeah tonight, I'll need some coaching on what I should do."

Moving toward the bedroom, she brushed her hand across Michael's arm and whispered, "Please stay with me."

Sam phoned Lara, Miami-Dade contacted Todd Madison, and soon teams of police and FBI agents were spread out over the city looking for Tomas Labato. The Coast Guard was alerted to patrol the bay side of the estate and Miami-Dade officers would be stationed inside and outside the house.

The FBI and Michael worked with the bank to gather the funds to be used if the drop was necessary. A network would be in place and plans were in motion to protect Margo, her daughters and MarGrove.

*****

"Lulu, I'm exhausted. For months it's been one crisis after another and it's worn me out."

She had taken a good look at herself in the mirror. She looked as bad as she felt. The dark circles under her eyes and the dullness of her hair made her appear older. Illness and stress had taken a toll on her body and her spirit.

“I’m afraid my life will never feel normal again.”

“You’re under duress and that never feels normal. A few days of rest should do the trick.”

“No, Lulu. I don’t think rest is the answer. You’ve done this to me.” She smiled at Lulu and closed her eyes.

“A few weeks ago I would have poured myself a stiff drink and let someone else take care of whatever was going on in my life. I would never have gotten my hands dirty. That’s what I paid everyone else to do.” She covered her face with her hands. “I am one self-absorbed, uncaring shell of a woman, aren’t I?” She dropped her hands and looked into the kind eyes of the psychiatrist.

“You’ve made me see that, Lulu, and it hurts.”

Lulu held her gaze, then spoke softly. “I know it hurts and that’s not a bad thing. It’s been a long time since you allowed yourself to feel anything at all, and if you’re going to get well, you’ve got to muddle through. Feel what you feel, Margo, and be grateful that you’re not hiding from your own life anymore.”

“You really want me to shed Margo, don’t you? You don’t want her to exist anymore!” Anger rose inside her. “You’re going to keep pushing me until Margo has totally disappeared. And, then what will I have? Who will I be if Margo is gone?”

“Margo, I’m not pushing. You’re finally seeing your own shadow and it’s decision time. You get to choose who you want to be. It’s never been my decision to make. All I’ve tried to do is help you see that you really do have a choice.”

Lulu smiled as she turned to leave the room. “Now get some rest. You’ve got a job to do that’s going to require all the strength you’ve got. And, honey, the hard part starts after you’ve taken that bag of money to Hialeah tonight.”

*****

The look on Sam's face told Michael that something bad had happened and he braced himself for the worst.

"We didn't get there in time, Michael. We just got a call that a fire was reported at the house. It looks like the only damage was to the guest house but from the look of things, this guy intended for the whole place to burn. The fire department found incendiary materials all around the exterior of the main house, the pool house, and the dock! Apparently he had set all this up before he made the call."

"The man is crazy! He's got to be stopped. Why are we sitting here doing nothing?"

"They're trying to make sure it was Tomas. Calm down, Michael. Let the cops and FBI do their work." He turned and looked at Margo's closed bedroom door. "Do we tell her or do we wait?"

"We wait. There's no point in upsetting her more."

"Okay, but I'm praying they catch him before she has to make that drop tonight. As sick as she is, this could be a disaster. Does she know how sick she is?"

"I think it's all beginning to sink in, Sam. This last episode kicked her while she's down and she's exhausted."

"What's the news from Dr. Mellon?"

"He's insisting that we bring her to Miami tomorrow even though I've tried to explain the situation. The man keeps telling me the surgery can't wait."

"We're lucky he gave us a few extra days. But, if he says tomorrow, then we'll get her there. Is he still insisting on Jackson Memorial?"

"Yes, but if you don't think that's safe, she's not going." Michael was emphatic.

"Let's wait until we see what happens today. If this is Tomas, and I think it is, he'll make mistakes and they'll find him." The phone began to ring and Sam motioned for Michael to answer it.

"Identify yourself first and see what happens."

“Hello, this is Michael Anderson.” Expecting the caller to hang up, he waited before he said anything else. “She’s resting, but I’ll take a message.”

“Keep him talking,” Sam whispered.

“Do you want me to see if I can wake her?” No response. “I’ll be glad to wake her if this is important. What did you say? Don’t hang up!”

When the phone went dead, he turned to Sam, ashen-faced. “Oh, my God. The man is crazy.”

“What did he say?”

“He says he knows where Alli is and he will make good on his promise if the money isn’t delivered. He said the fire was a warning that he means what he says.”

“I don’t believe him. There is no way he would know where she is. Absolutely no way. He’s bluffing, Michael.”

The police officer walked in the room and looked at the two men. “He’s right, Mr. Anderson. There’s no way he can get to your daughter. Sam, can I talk to you?”

Michael sat down in stunned silence. “It’s one thing for him to burn the house, I can cope with that if I have to. But, not my daughter. He can’t hurt my daughter.”

*****

The officer spoke quickly but calmly. “We traced that last call to somewhere on Tamiami Trail. There’s no way he can know where the safe house is. We’ve contacted Madison and he and Alli are moving north. We’re sending a car to pick them up and they’ll head to another location across the state. This guy knows he has to be in Hialeah tonight, so there’s no way he’s going to start tracking them. I’m waiting for a report on some fingerprints that were on a kerosene can found outside the gates of MarGrove. The guy is careless, Sam. We’ll get him.”

"Did they find anything else that we could use?" Sam inquired.

"A neighbor noticed a black Mercedes parked outside the gate just before the fire started, so we've got a chopper headed west out of the city looking for the car. We were too late to stop the fire, but we'll get him before he can do any more damage."

"Anything else on Vincetti?" Said Sam.

"Not a thing. If DaSilva had him killed, he used a pro. We're still investigating and forensics is working overtime. Something'll turn up eventually."

*****

Sitting down with Margo and Michael, Sam relayed everything he had been told by the police and the FBI.

"Margo, they're tracking Tomas and doing everything possible to make sure Alli is safe. It will all be over before you leave for the hospital in the morning. I think they've worked out a way for someone else to make the drop tonight. That's kind of tricky but they're working on it."

"I hope that's true. The thought of going through with this is driving me nuts." She smiled. "Well, nuttier than I already am."

"No matter what happens, you know Sam won't let anything happen to you." Michael turned to Sam. "Don't know how we would have handled all of this without you."

Sam brushed off Michael's remark and turned back to Margo. "If they can't find a decoy, you'll have to do it yourself. Someone will be here this afternoon to get you ready. They'll walk you through it step by step. And, you know you won't be alone. Not for one second."

"Thanks, Sam." Margo knew that her bodyguard and friend would do what needed to be done to keep her safe, but her nerves were frayed. There was so much going on in her head that it was giving her a headache. If Sam and Michael knew she was more afraid of facing her daughters than she was of dropping off a bag of money for a lunatic, they would really think she was insane.

She looked at the two men seated across from her and knew they would do everything possible to keep her safe. They were old friends, the three of them, and they had traveled some tough roads together. Michael and Sam were always there when she needed them. They took care of her life so she could indulge in her idea of pleasure. They took a back seat so she could be in the spotlight. She knew she had taken advantage of them and, for a moment, she felt ashamed. How had she missed what they had offered?

Her thoughts were interrupted by the ringing of the phone and she nodded to Michael to answer it. When she saw him smile, she knew it wasn't bad news and she sighed in relief.

"Who was that, Michael?"

"It was Lara. She wanted us to know that she and Sunni have spent a ton of money on a new wardrobe and they were able to find Sunni her own apartment close to campus."

"What are you talking about? Sunni and Alli already have an apartment there," Margo said with confusion in her voice.

"Our Sunni wants to be alone. Apparently eighteen years of being Alli's shadow has finally worn thin and she wants her own place. Can you blame her?"

"I didn't realize that's how Sunni saw herself." She was close to tears and she took Michael's hand. "Do you think it's too late?"

"Too late for what?"

"For my daughters and me to ever be close–to be a family?"

"It all depends on how much you're willing to try and how much patience you've got. I don't think it will be easy, Margo. But if you're sincere, I think they'll give you a chance. It's worth a try." Michael said.

"Your daughters are great people. I think you'll really like them when you get to know them a little. Alli's just like you, so she may take some taming before she'll let you in, but Sunni will welcome you with open arms." Sam said.

"You know, I never gave it a thought before, but Alli is like you and Sunni is like Michael." He laughed. "Is the world ready for two Margo's?"

Chapter Thirty-nine

Tomas

Sitting in the car outside the small airport hangar, he tried to think clearly about his options. He could hire a small helicopter to pick him up in Hialeah and take him to a major airport--maybe Orlando or Tampa. But he knew the police and FBI would be watching all the transportation outlets.

He could drive to Mexico using the car that was registered to his friend, Naomi Peacock, but she would probably report the car stolen if he didn't return it by tomorrow. His body responded at the thought of her and he regretted not having time to take her to bed. He had awakened her this morning when he arrived in Miami and she had welcomed him with her usual ardor and passion. He never got enough of her, but it was too dangerous for him to go back to her apartment. At the moment, he needed her car more than he needed her body.

A tap on the window of the car brought him out of his reverie. "Hey mister, you need some help?" An elderly man dressed in a mechanic's uniform was trying to get his attention. "This isn't a parking area, so you need to move your car."

"Sorry, I got confused about which hangar I should go to if I want to rent a helicopter."

"You a pilot or a passenger? Makes a difference where I send you, you know."

"I'm a passenger. Please point me in the right direction."

"See that hangar across the way? Cross the tarmac and go in that side entrance door. That's the office for Lance. He'll tell you all you need to know."

The elderly man moved away from the car and Tomas started the engine. He had to control his thoughts and figure out his next moves or he was going to be in trouble.

Finding the office empty, he walked around the building and entered the hangar. "Anybody here?" he called.

"Over here. How can I help you?" A young man came around from behind the small helicopter and extended his hand. "I'm Lance."

"I need to inquire about renting the helicopter. Are you the pilot?"

"That's me. Let's go in the office and see if I can answer your questions."

They sat down in the small office and Lance began to explain the services he could offer, but Tomas interrupted him.

"I'm thinking I need to be flown to an industrial park in Hialeah tonight and then returned here to pick-up my car. I'm going to be picking up something valuable and don't want to be driving around the streets of Miami. Is that possible?"

"Whoa, man. I'm not going to get involved in anything shady. I need this business too much to go to jail." Lance stood up from behind the desk and started moving toward the door. "Plus, we've got a tropical storm off shore that's kicking up some wind. Don't know if I'll be able to get my bird in the air tonight."

"You have misunderstood. There is nothing illegal about what I need to do. But, I can see I've made you nervous. I'll find someone else." Tomas stood up to leave and something shiny caught his attention. He walked over to the bulletin board and removed the small anklet from where it was tacked on the board. Turning it around in his hand, he found the initials AA that he knew would be engraved on the front side. His cousin Paolo had given a piece of jewelry like this to every woman he was serious about. The design was always the same, only the engraved initials changed.

"Where did you get this?" he asked.

"Why do you care?"

"I think this belongs to a friend of mine. A young woman about twenty or so, dark chestnut hair, green eyes."

"Yea, that's the girl. I flew her out of here a couple of days ago and she left it in the chopper." He eyed Tomas suspiciously. "I'll give it back to her when I go pick her up."

"Where did you take her? I didn't know she was out of town." Tomas rubbed the anklet back and forth in his hand. How lucky can I get? "I'll just take it with me and give it to her when I see her."

"Nothing doing. She'll be back in a couple of days and I'll give it to her myself."

"You're right. You should be the one to return it." Tomas walked out the door. "Sorry we couldn't do business." He smiled as he got in the car and drove away from the airfield. When he had the money he would come back here and force the pilot to tell him where he could find Alli.

*****

When Margo answered the phone, he almost gloated. Smugly, he knew his words would have a chilling impact.

"Does gold anklet mean anything to you? 'Cause I've got a pretty little anklet dangling from my fingers. I know it's not the one you wear, Margo. The initials on this one are AA. I may up the ante, but let's keep it at two million for starters."

Chapter Forty

Alli

"I'm not going! This is the stupidest thing I've ever heard of. Who in the world would look on this forsaken island for anything?" Anger made her voice crack. "Put my stuff back in that room! I'm not moving," she continued to rant. "Stop looking at me like I'm a spoiled child!"

"You'll do exactly what you're told. That temper of yours doesn't bother me in the least. We've been told to move and we will. One way or another!" Exasperated, frustrated and angry, he just shook his head. "There must be some kind of threat or they wouldn't be moving us. Don't you get it?"

"All I know is I've been living in a hell-hole for days and now I'm being moved to heaven knows where. Are you guys using this little story to create some kind of TV police drama or something?"

Agent Clark walked over to the car, "Alli, I've counted to ten about ten times. Get in the car!" She shrugged at the driver and climbed in the back seat.

"If she's not in the car in the next minute, leave her here. Madison, let's go!"

That did it! The thought of being left alone was more than she could handle. "Where are we going now?" she demanded as she threw herself in the back seat of the car next to the agent.

"Miss Anderson, our instructions are to get you off this island. We're supposed to drive you to Flagler Beach. That's all I know. Someone will meet us there and, hopefully, we'll hand you over to them."

The driver gave Alli that information without getting involved in her outburst. He whispered to Todd Madison who was seated next to him. "I've seen her type before–the little rich girl who's used to having it her way. Bet you've had an interesting week."

"Why are they jerking us around like this, Todd?" She leaned across the front seat and tapped him on the shoulder. "Is there an end in sight? I'm losing valuable time running all over the state of Florida. I've got things to do."

"As soon as they get this guy, you can go back to Miami. Until then, we do as we're told. You seem to forget you're not the only one being inconvenienced. This assignment has impacted my life. Not to mention, Agent Clark's, and the driver's. However, whining and tantrums are not our style."

He stopped talking and looked out the window as the car crossed the bridge and left Pine Island behind.

*****

When she woke up and looked around, the car was stopped in a parking lot across the street from the beach. People walking beside them were coming up from the water carrying chairs and umbrellas. They were laughing and talking as though they didn't have a care in the world. Alli groaned as she remembered she wasn't on vacation.

"Did I sleep the whole way or do we still have more to go?" Groggily, she tried to get some information.

"We're in Flagler Beach ahead of schedule. I just called Miami for instructions and they said to tell you to enjoy the sights."

"Right." She sighed and leaned her head against the window. She played the music from the tour over again in her head. There were words to memorize, dance steps to learn, music beats to master, and here she was in the back seat of a stranger's car waiting for some maniac to carry out his threat. Voices and surf sounds kept interfering with her concentration and she gave up.

"Todd, do they think this guy is really going to come after me? I thought all he wanted was the money."

"I've got some news for you that I was going to tell you later, but you need to be aware of what's going on. Things have kind of taken a different turn." He turned around in the seat where he could see her face.

"Are you missing a piece of jewelry?"

"I don't think so, why?"

"Are you sure? Don't you usually wear some gold thing around your ankle? I don't know what they call it."

"My anklet! Yes, I lost it a couple of days ago. I missed it when we got to the island, but figured I'd forgotten to put it on that morning."

"Could it have fallen off in the chopper?" Not waiting for her to nod or answer, he went on. "The person making the phone calls says he has it. But it didn't check out when they found it at the airport. However, this morning a guy was at the airport to rent a chopper and saw it hanging on the board. He told the pilot that it belonged to a friend and then he described you."

"How could he do that? I don't know this guy."

"You probably didn't know the original caller, but they think they found him dead yesterday. There's a new caller and you do know him."

"Are you kidding?"

"No, Alli. They are pretty certain the new caller is Tomas Labato."

She started to laugh, then caught the look on Todd's face and knew he was serious. "I don't think Tomas would hurt me. Why would he be involved in this mess?"

"I don't have all the details. But we have a face and we need to be on the lookout at all times. Don't kid yourself, Alli. They think he's desperate, which means he could and would hurt you if he thought you would keep him from the money."

She slumped in the seat and tried to imagine being afraid of Tomas Labato. When Paolo was alive, there had been nothing forceful about Tomas. He was like Sunni, always in the background.

But she had seen her sister's anger. When Sunni felt she had been pushed too far or someone was taking advantage of her, she could come on strong. Paolo had treated his cousin like a servant, so it was possible Tomas was a volcano about to explode and she didn't want to be around when that happened.

"What are your new orders? I'm hungry." She might as well make the best of things. It didn't look like she would be going home right away.

"We're on the move. They don't want us to be in one spot." Settling himself back in the front seat, he nodded to the driver to start the car. "We should be able to find a drive-thru somewhere close. I'll treat you to a burger."

"My hero."

Chapter Forty-one

Margo

Dusk enveloped the city and Margo was antsy. All day she had prayed for a way out. Driving to a deserted industrial complex at ten o'clock at night was not her idea of fun. But Tomas had warned her during the earlier call that he would be watching the site and would know if the FBI had set a trap for him. She would not risk her daughters being hurt–or worse.

Michael and the agent returned hours ago with the money she was to deliver; Sam had gone with the agents to do whatever they needed to do for her protection; and she continued to wait. Since this bizarre episode in her life had started, it seemed all she had done was wait.

"Are you going to eat some of that dinner, Margo?" Michael asked.

His voice brought her out of her reverie. "I'm not hungry. But, if you offered a jug of wine to go with it, I might reconsider." She knew her smile was wooden and empty, but that was how she felt. It was all she could do just to breathe.

"I know you're joking, but I could use a jug or two myself. Tell you what. I'll call down to the kitchen and ask them to make you a hot fudge sundae. How 'bout that? It used to be your favorite."

"You're trying too hard, Michael. I'll be all right. The waiting is getting to me, and I'm scared. Do you know how long it's been since I've driven a car? I'm not even sure I know how. Even the thought of a hot fudge sundae makes my stomach do flips." Stage fright had nothing on the terror that perched on the edge of her mind. Perhaps her past obsession could at least serve as a temporary distraction. "Michael, we haven't talked about the tour. I can't even imagine what's involved, but has everything been cancelled?" As she asked the question, it dawned on her that she was about to lose a tremendous amount of money.

"How much did we have to pay to break all the venue contracts? I hadn't stopped to consider the costs."

"I'm taking care of it, but there is still a lot to do. Don't worry about the money. We'll be fine."

"If you say so. But, I know this will hurt my bank account."

"Margo, no matter what happens, you have more money than you will ever need." He laughed. "You are a very rich lady, or have you forgotten that?"

"I haven't thought about money in years," she said.

"Strange how we take things for granted, isn't it?"

Looking at him, she knew he was talking about more than money.

*****

Sam sat down next to her and started going over the checklist. "You know you won't be out there by yourself. There are safety nets all around you, Margo. You won't be able to see them, but they're in place. Whatever you do, don't get out of the car. Turn the headlights off and on three times, roll the window down and drop the money bag in front of the designated spot, and then get the hell out of there. Drive back the way you came and Michael will be waiting for you at the corner of Palm Avenue and 49th Street. As soon as he's in the car, drive north until you get to the Palmetto Expressway. Get on the expressway and head for Boca. If you need him to drive, wait until you're on I-95 then pull over and change drivers."

"I haven't driven in over twenty years, Sam. I don't know if I'll be able to drive that far. What if I get the shakes?"

"I know this is hard, Margo, but this is the most important for you to remember. Don't get out of the car and don't stop in Hialeah long enough to change drivers. It's too dangerous. You can do this, Margo, I know you can."

He held her gaze until she nodded. "Roll the window down just enough to get the parcel through and once the parcel is out the window, gun the engine and go! Don't hang around to see what's going to happen. There are others who will handle that."

"This feels like an episode of Hawaii Five-O. Will Danno be around if I need him?" she asked with a shaky laugh.

"I can guarantee you that one tap of the car horn and you'll be surrounded by fifty real-life Dannos. Stop worrying."

*****

How long had it been since she and her brothers had drag raced through the streets of Hialeah? As teens they had been crazy about fast cars and there was always someone who thought their car was better. Her brothers would set up the other drivers with taunts of "Are you afraid of a girl? You think a girl can beat you?" And, nine times out of ten, she would beat them, look at the surprise on their faces, and challenge them to try it again.

Thinking about those days gave her more confidence and helped keep her focused on the road as cars whizzed by on either side of her. Nonetheless, the Interstate was terrifying.

If I survive, my next career could be race car driver! Then she smiled. Thank God, I have a driver. I don't have the nerves for this anymore. Not having to drive herself around was one more thing she took for granted. How easily she had forgotten all the things that money helped her avoid.

The directions to the industrial park and the leather carrying case with the money were on the seat beside her. Anxiously, she imagined what the scene would look like if she had an accident. She laughed openly as she pictured the sight of two million dollars blowing all over the highway like snowflakes.

The time went quickly and soon she approached the exit off the Palmetto Expressway that would take her to Hialeah. Nothing looked familiar and for a Friday night at nine forty-five there were few cars on the road once she left the expressway. She had to stay focused so she could find the right place for the drop. She slowed the car down to read each street sign and mentally checked off every mile she traveled. She could hear her heartbeat in her ears and breathing took more of an effort as she got closer to her destination.

She turned off the main road at the entrance to the industrial complex into near pitch darkness. The road meandered through a canyon of large warehouse buildings that cast eerie shadows everywhere she looked. Alone in the terrifying maze of steel, it was worse than she had imagined. The hair on the back of her neck stood up and her sweat-soaked hands slipped on the steering wheel.

Stay calm. You're not alone. She repeated the words over and over as she slowly drove to the third street and turned left. As the car turned the corner, she started counting the buildings. The fourth building on the left was the place. All she had to do was blink the headlights, roll down the window, and drop the case on the ground. She took a deep breath.

In a split second, she rolled down the window and threw the parcel out. As she started to pull her hand back inside the car, she was grabbed. God, help me. This isn't the way it was supposed to be.

Screaming, she fought to pull her hand free, but his grip tightened. Without thinking, she used her free hand to throw the gear shift in reverse and gunned the engine. She felt her wrist snap as the man tried to hold on to her, but the momentum of the moving car finally forced him to let go of her hand. Pressing harder on the accelerator once her hand was free, she gave no thought to controlling the car.

Suddenly, the back fender of the car ricocheted off the side of a building, shattering the car windows on the passenger side and crushing metal with a force that threw her body against the back of the seat.

Dazed and terrified, she tried to use her left hand to close the window, but searing pain shot through her arm. Forget the window, just get out of here! She pushed the gear into drive and started to move the car away from the building.

"Margo, stop! Don't move the car."

At the sound of Sam's voice she jammed her foot on the brake. Chaos broke out around her. Men shouted as a helicopter hovered above, the rotor wash almost deafening. Then the sound of a single gunshot. She threw herself down on the seat and hoped a stray bullet wouldn't find her. More gunfire, more shouts, search lights.

Sam put his arm through the half-open window and pulled up the door lock. "Can you drive?" he shouted. "We've got to get out of here."

"I think my wrist is broken and I can't stop shaking."

"Climb over the gear shift and let me get behind the wheel. Hurry! I've got to get you out of here."

He yelled and pushed her at the same time. She felt the gear jam into her ribs as Sam shoved her from one seat to the other. The car rolled forward as she pulled her legs across and sat down. She hooked her good hand into the door's arm rest and held on as Sam accelerated.

"Get down in the seat as far as you can," he shouted and pushed her head down. "Stay that way till we get out of here."

The car crossed a speed bump and her teeth jarred. The tires screeched as they took a turn, then abruptly Sam slowed the car down and she could hear the sound of traffic on a paved street.

"Can I get up now?"

"Yeah, I think we're good." Sam replied in a more normal tone. "Damn that man!" He hit the steering wheel out of frustration. "It was Tomas. I got a good look at his face. It'll be easy for them to get him now that they're sure who it is."

"When can I stop shaking?" Margo whispered. She straightened in the seat and struggled to catch her breath. "I don't think I've ever been so scared. When he grabbed my arm, I nearly fainted."

The car slowed down as they approached the corner and she recognized Michael waiting for them.

"My God, what happened?" he shouted. "You're late and I was beginning to panic." He struggled to open the crushed car door. "Sam, why are you driving? What went wrong?"

"Just get in Michael. We've got to keep moving," Sam directed as he pulled away from the curb. "Tomas grabbed Margo as she was making the drop and all hell broke loose."

"Are you all right?" Michael turned his attention and concern to Margo.

"I think my wrist is broken and I'll probably have nightmares for the rest of my life. And, I think my hair must have turned white. Other than that, I'm in perfect shape." She joked, hoping to gain some composure. "You loaned me your car for a few minutes and I've almost destroyed it."

"You're funny!" Michael said with a nervous laugh. "How are you really?"

"I was trying to be funny, but I wasn't kidding. I just told you. It was a harrowing experience." She looked over at Sam. "Where are you taking me? This isn't the way back to Boca."

"You're supposed to be at the hospital first thing in the morning, right? We're going to be a few hours early. Somebody's got to look at your wrist."

"What happened with Tomas? They got him didn't they?" Michael asked.

"I don't have an answer for you, Michael. All I could think of was getting Margo out of the way. There were several gunshots as we were leaving. If they didn't get him, they know who he is now and he won't get far."

"Margo, how did he grab you? I thought Sam told you not to get out of the car!" Michael exclaimed, leaning forward in the seat to get a better look at her.

"Whoa," said Sam before she could reply. "She did exactly as she was told. Tomas planned the drop point so he could grab her and use her as a hostage to get himself out of the complex. We considered that possibility and the team was ready. Margo reacted quickly so he didn't have a chance to open the car door, but he may have broken her wrist and I'm afraid one side of your car is pretty banged up."

Margo turned in the seat and glared at Michael. "Tomas had a choice to hang onto me and get dragged to death or let me go. I backed the car into a wall or something. The jerk did a number on my wrist before he turned me loose and your precious Mercedes will never be the same."

*****

Miles later, Sam pulled the car under the portico at the emergency entrance of Jackson Memorial Hospital and Michael went inside to prepare the way for her to enter. Once he made the arrangements, he returned to the car. "Sam, what's the plan?"

"I'm headed to the police station to see what I can find out. As soon as I know what's going on, I'll come back here."

As the car drove away, Michael shielded Margo's head with his coat so they could walk undisturbed into the building. He put his arm around her taking care not to hit her left wrist.

"Let's see if we can get through this without someone recognizing you."

"I'm not exactly at my best, am I?" she asked with wink.

"Oh, honey. You look gorgeous compared to the way you looked the last time you were brought to an emergency room. We're just not ready to answer any questions about why you're here this time."

He steered her passed the desk and quietly asked the volunteer to call for Dr. Mellon. "They found us a room where we can wait undisturbed. Hopefully, your doctor will be here soon and they're calling an orthopedic specialist to look at your wrist."

She looked at him and let her tears fall unheeded. "Don't leave me, Michael."

*****

Tomas lay on the ground with his face against the hard asphalt of the parking lot, his hands cuffed behind his back, his right shoulder throbbing with pain.

What had gone wrong? He had made such careful plans. Why had Margo reacted the way she did? Didn't she know he would never hurt her?

How long were they going to let him lie there? He was a Brazilian citizen and he would call the embassy. The Americans could not treat him in such a manner without being in jeopardy of causing an international incident.

He would make them pay for what they had done. Blood trickled down his face from the gash on his head and his knees were bruised from the fall he took when the cops tackled him to the ground. It seemed like hundreds of cops had surrounded him and he wondered where they had been hiding.

They would pay when his family found out about this treatment. Then his grandfather's words came into his mind like the gale winds before a hurricane.

"I'm finished with you."

Eduardo DaSilva always meant what he said. The words echoed between the buildings and hopelessness crept into every cell of his body. Silently he cursed the cops for not killing him.

"You're a piece of crap, Labato!" Someone kicked him in the ribs. "They're gonna bury you so deep you'll never get out of prison."

"Read him his rights and get him downtown. Book him on attempted kidnapping, assault, and extortion, while I try to figure out how to get him charged with second degree murder in the death of Paolo DaSilva."

Chapter Forty-two

Alli

"Hey, you! Wake up! You're almost home," Todd Madison called over his shoulder as the car sped through the early morning streets of a quiet Miami. "They got the guy, Alli. It's over and we're taking you to MarGrove."

Sleepily, she pulled herself upright. Her body ached from being cramped on the backseat of the car for hours. "What time is it? Have we been driving all night?" Her voice was raspy and her throat was dry. "Could we get something to drink? I feel like I've been eating dirt."

"It's around four-thirty and, yes, we've been on a grand tour of Florida. You fell asleep around midnight."

He turned to the driver. "There should be an all-night Burger King or McDonald's around here somewhere. Pull in and we'll treat the young lady to a soda."

"Thanks." She looked over at Agent Clark who seemed wide awake. "Can somebody tell me what's going on?"

"Simple. They've arrested Tomas Labato. You're safe." The woman didn't blink. Her words were clipped and even Alli could tell that the woman resented being in the car.

Turning her attention away from the bridled animosity, she directed her next question to Todd. "How do they know he's the one?"

"He tried to hurt your mom. She's in the hospital."

"Is she all right?" Alli caught herself. "I mean, what happened?"

"All I know is she's okay. I don't have any details." His voice softened. "We'll find out as soon as we get you home."

*****

The house was dark and, hopefully, empty. The driver and the agent had drawn guns and searched from room to room. It felt creepy to stand at the front door and be told she couldn't go inside until they had completed a thorough search. Without Mrs. Davis being there, it didn't feel very welcoming.

"Are you leaving me here alone?" Alli asked with a frown. When they drove up and she saw the damage from the fires, fear finally caught up with her and she shuttered. She used to be braver than she felt right now. "I mean, is anyone else going to be here today?"

"I think they told me Sam would be here sometime this morning. Your dad is with your mom at the hospital. I don't know when your sister and Mrs. Davis are coming back, but I'll check on that."

He carried her suitcase inside and placed it on the floor in the living room. "We'll stay until it gets light and then we've got to go. You got a few hours sleep while we were touring the state, but no one else did."

"Thanks, Todd, but now that we're inside, I think I'll be okay." She looked at the circles under his eyes, his tousled hair, and knew he needed sleep. "Our driver and the Gestapo lady must be exhausted, too. You all go on. I'll be fine."

He walked over to the phone. "I'll call and have Miami PD send someone over to stay with you until Sam gets here."

"Not necessary. I'll lock the doors and set the alarm. I need some real sleep, too." Her body felt sluggish and achy and she knew she looked grubby. Nothing a hot shower and the comfort of her own bed couldn't fix if they would just go away and leave her alone.

"Really. Now that I know the guy is behind bars, I'll be able to sleep. Why don't you call me later?"

He was too tired to argue, so he nodded and walked to the front door where the others were waiting. "You guys go on. She's going to her room and I'm going to crash on the couch until they send someone to debrief us."

Quickly, she took a step forward and grabbed his arm. "Someday I'll show you how much I appreciate you for taking such good care of me."

"For a bratty kid, you're okay, Miss Anderson."

*****

The steamy shower felt wonderful and she stood against the wall and let the water cascade over her achy muscles. Her skin felt dry and itchy from being in the same clothes for so long. What day was it anyway? She'd lost track of time. Had they been gone for three or four days?

I've got so much to do, but I can't think about it right now. Later. I'll think about it later. She rubbed her body dry, pulled on her nightgown and crawled in her soft, comfortable bed. Tired didn't begin to describe how she felt.

*****

"Alli, it's Mrs. Dee–wake up, honey, and come have some dinner. You've slept all day." She gently touched the sleeping girl's shoulder. "Welcome home, sleepy head. Get dressed and come downstairs. Your dad and Sam are waiting for you."

Slowly she opened her eyes and realized she was in her own bed. "What? Oh, Mrs. Dee, when did you get back?" She stretched like a kitten in the sunlight, then hugged her pillow as she looked around her room. "It feels so good to be home." She pulled herself up. "You said Dad and Sam. Where is Detective Madison?"

The housekeeper chuckled. "He was sleeping like a dead man until some policeman came to drive him home. He left several hours ago, but said he'd be back for a debriefing."

She looked at Alli with a curious expression. "Where have the two of you been for the last few days? Where you alone all that time?"

"You've been reading too many romance novels, Mrs. Dee," Alli said with a laugh. "We were on a forsaken island on the Gulf coast with a witch for a chaperone."

*****

All through dinner, Alli listened to the men discuss the events of the summer. Paolo, Tomas, murder, kidnapping, extortion. It went on and on.

"Does this mean they'll drop all the trumped up charges against me?"

"I hope that's already in the works. They knew you weren't involved," Michael said, quick to reassure her.

"We'll wait and see," Sam said. He didn't sound as sure. "They think Vincetti killed Paolo by accident and they think he was the original caller. But they've got to make sure of everything before they let anyone off the hook. The only thing they know for sure is Tomas was caught in the industrial park last night. He's in jail, but that's all they know."

She groaned. "Do you mean I'm still under all those court orders?"

"For the time being, you're still under the jurisdiction of the court. We need to call your attorney and see where we go next." Sam looked at Michael. "Do you want me to take care of that in the morning?"

"Good idea, Sam. Thanks." He turned to Alli, his brows pulled together in a frown. "You haven't asked about your mother?"

"Oh, right. How is she?"

"Tomas fractured her wrist, but that will heal. Her throat surgery is scheduled for Monday morning at seven. They're running some tests today and tomorrow, but Dr. Mellon doesn't expect anything to change."

"She has cancer, right? And, she'll never be able to sing professionally again? Even with the surgery?" Alli wanted to make sure she understood her mother's options.

"Never say never, Alli. Your mother is a very determined woman. We know she has to rest her voice right now, but who knows what the future holds." He seemed to be battling his feelings.

"Don't let your ambition destroy your concern for others, Alli." He cautioned. "I'm not giving up on your mother. I hope you understand that."

*****

After dinner she asked her dad to sit with her by the pool. "Let's talk tour. This whole ordeal has me really far behind, but I'm ready to get started. I've had a few days to think about the show and I've got some great ideas."

Michael looked at her and started to laugh. "Lighten up. I'll call everyone and set up a meeting for tomorrow. The band can determine a rehearsal schedule and we'll get busy. Sunni and Lara will be back in the morning, and Lara can begin working out details with you."

He turned serious. "You may have to save your ideas for another tour. Everything's pretty much set for this one." He watched her expression change. "There's no time to introduce new ideas. This show was planned out last spring. Your job will be to fit into the routines and give them a lead voice."

"I don't have a say in anything?" She said with a pout on her face.

"That's about it. Perhaps we can talk about your ideas later and work them in somewhere. But for now, you're going to have your hands full learning the numbers that the band and dancers have already worked up." He sighed and stretched his legs out in front of him. "I've only been able to salvage four of the venues. The others have pulled out. You're an unproven talent and they weren't ready to take a chance on you. But you've got a few concerts to prove them wrong."

Alli stared at him in disbelief, but swallowed her disappointment and opted to take the opportunity he offered her. She reached over and gripped his arm. "I can do it, Daddy! You know I can. After four shows the others will be begging to be put back on the schedule. How many shows at each venue?"

She rocketed out of her chair and danced around the poolside. She was too elated to sit down.

"In total, there are probably twelve shows. I'll have to check. You realize that if tickets don't sell, they may all pull out."

"That's not going to happen. We'll do all those shows and more." Failure was not in her vocabulary.

"There's one other issue, Alli. We need to talk about your mother."

Her euphoria evaporated and her smile disappeared. "What do you mean?"

"Margo isn't going to like this arrangement and you know it. She's the star, remember."

How could she forget? All her life it had always been about Margo, but she was determined to change that.

"Do you think she'll stop me?" Alli asked cautiously.

"Nothing will stop you, if you're serious. But you may have to find another way to make it happen for yourself if she says no. I'm not trying to dampen your enthusiasm, but I'm Margo's manager first. Somehow I've got to find a balance that your mother can live with, too. If she says no, I won't fight with her to change her mind."

"Talk to her. Tell her you've made a decision. Make her understand," she commanded.

"Whoa. I think you're close to stepping over the line, Alli. Don't give me orders." Michael glared at her until her gaze dropped. "I'm trying hard to remember that you're my daughter." Then his voice softened. "This is your mother's tour and if you want it, you're going to have to ask her for it."

"She won't talk to me, and for sure she isn't going to say yes to me!" She fought back tears as she felt her dream slipping away. "You don't understand! She hates me."

"Then you better find a way to make her like you! Without her approval, this tour isn't yours."

Anger rising, she snapped at her father. "You can't be serious! How can you do this to me?"

"I didn't do anything to you. Whatever's going on between you and your mother needs to be resolved by the two of you. I've done my part. You two need to work it out." There was a new tone to his voice. "I'm not going to back down. You're being offered the chance of a life time. Margo hasn't been the best mother and now I can see that you've never learned how to be a daughter."

He stood up and put his hands in his pockets. "Your choice, Alli. I can give you a chance to work with the band, but the tour doesn't leave without Margo's okay."

He walked back in the house and left her to her thoughts.

*****

Now what was she going to do? Her mother had disowned her, hated her, and would never give her permission to take her place on the tour.

Besides, how could she ever face her anyway?

BOOK THREE

Man must evolve for all human conflict is a method
which rejects revenge, aggression and retaliation.
The foundation of such a method is love.
~Martin Luther King, Jr.

Chapter Forty-three

Sunni

"I'm so glad to see you!"

Sunni grabbed her sister in a bear hug and twirled her around the room. "These last few days have been unbelievable. I've chewed my fingernails down to the quick worrying about you and mother. Tell me all about it."

"Stop twirling me around. And don't give me that sob story. You were in New York having a great time. I can't imagine you sitting in the hotel worrying about me when there are so many fun things to do in the city."

"I was worried. Why do you always have to act like nobody cares about you?" A sound of hurt crept into Sunni's voice and she moved away from her sister.

"I know you care. You're just making a big deal out of nothing. They shuffled me around the state for a few days and shut me away on some island off the Gulf coast. I've been bored out of my mind. One good thing, I got to know Detective Madison and he's a nice guy."

Looking sheepish, she continued, "I've asked him to go with me on tour as my body guard. What do you think of that?"

"It's definite? You're going on tour?" Sunni asked in surprise.

"It's almost a done deal. But Dad threw me a curve last night. Can you believe, he's going to make me ask Margo if I can take the tour?"

"Not a good thing for you, dear sister. Looks like I'll see you at Sarah Lawrence after all," she said sarcastically. "Mom will never agree and you know it." A scowl crossed Sunni's brow. "Why would Dad do that? He knows she won't agree." She thought for a second before she continued. "I thought this was a business deal between you and Dad?"

"It's her band, her bus, her tour. Sunni, how can I convince her to let me go? You've got to help me."

"No way! I'm not getting in the middle of this."

"You've got to help. She'll talk to you," Alli pleaded with her sister. "Come on, Sunni. If I asked you to do something, I can always count on it getting done." She got more emphatic with every word. "This is the most important thing in my life and you're turning me down? I need you. Don't act like this."

Sunni shook her head. "Alli, I'll stand behind you. You know that. But, I can't make this happen. I'll go with you, but you have to do the talking. You have to convince her that you won't be a threat to her career."

"What career? She can't sing professionally anymore! After the surgery tomorrow, her voice will be gone. Don't you understand?"

"It's only temporary, Alli. With therapy, she'll get it back."

"Not according to the doctor. This is it. The cancer has destroyed her career and now it's my turn." The determination in her voice made Sunni back away.

"You're kidding yourself, if you think she's finished. She'll come back. You wait and see." Sunni's voice quivered.

"Oh, Sunni. You're burying your head in the sand." She walked over and hugged her twin. "I'm not stealing anything from her. But I've realized that I'll get to the top faster if I capitalize on what she's already built. Can you blame me for wanting this?"

Tears filled Sunni's eyes and she hugged her sister back. "It's that serious? She won't sing again?"

"From everything Dad has told me it is very serious. Will you go with me to the hospital this afternoon? I can do this if you're with me."

Sunni dropped her arms from around Alli and walked away. Sitting in the armchair near the balcony doors, she leaned back and closed her eyes. The silence was heavy and Sunni knew whatever she said would define their relationship for years to come.

Slowly, she raised her head and looked in Alli's eyes. She saw her sister's flaws, her hurt places, her selfishness. She had lived with her demands and her fears. It was all there in that moment. But, so was all the love, all the times when they had clung to each other because they didn't have anyone else, all the disappointments of growing up without a mother's touch. She saw it all and wondered how she could deny her.

Sunni took a deep breath. "I love you more than anything, but I can't go with you unless you promise to ask for her forgiveness. Don't look like that, Alli. I know she hurt us, she ignored us, she left us to raise ourselves, and she owes us an apology. But, you've done everything you can think of to hurt her, and with the Paolo thing, you succeeded. If you're willing to own your part, I'll go with you. I'll fight for you. I'll do what I can to help you."

Alli stared at her sister as though she had never seen her before. Her eyes flashed with anger, her face flushed, and her hands fisted.

"You're right! She did all those things to us because she could pretend we didn't exist. Or, better yet, she could obliterate us with a life of sex, booze, and drugs. She didn't care if we lived or died! And yet, you sit there and ask me to apologize to her."

Shouting, her words spewed out like venom. "All our lives, not a kind word, not a moment of tenderness. She never celebrated our success, never dried our tears, never helped us get through the rough times. She was never there! And you want me to wipe all the years away and tell her it was okay! I can't believe you'd even suggest this?" She spun out of the room and slammed the door behind her.

*****

Stretched out on the bed, Sunni stared at the ceiling. Alli's tirade had worn her out and depleted her energy. Why is everything so hard? For once, it would be nice to have something go easy. She had thought this summer would be different and instead it had been more troublesome than any other time of her life. She managed a small smile when she thought about how she would answer when people ask her, "What did you do this summer?"

She thought soap operas were the imagination of screen writers, but she had lived one this summer. Maybe she'd lived one her whole life. She pictured herself standing in front of a classroom and telling her class mates the events of the summer.

"Well, it started with my sister betraying my mother and my mother trying to kill herself. Then we had a murder. Then someone threatened to kidnap my sister. Then someone burned down our guest house. And then, my mother, the best singer in the world, was told she has cancer and will probably never sing again. Oh, yeah, and I got to go to New York for a few days."

She probably had good cause to be depressed, and today she felt miserable about all that had happened. But her few days in New York with Lara had helped her put so much of her life in perspective. Lara was grounded and all the years of working with Margo had taught her to roll with whatever came along. Sunni had found it easy to talk to Lara and had felt safe sharing some of her concerns and fears with her.

"Lara, it's not easy being Margo's daughter and Alli's twin. Sometimes I feel like I don't really exist. I'm the invisible one."

"Why do you let them define you, Sunni? Why would you be content to stand in their shadows? I'm not trying to be judgmental. I just want you to see who you are not who they think you should be."

She remembered the look of kindness in Lara's eyes and how it made her feel to know that this woman really did see her.

"You're a lovely young woman with dreams of your own, Sunni, and I hope you don't let anyone diminish them. You've told me you want to be a writer; so write. Put all your hopes and fears into the words you put on paper and people will identify with what you're saying. You can choose to be invisible or not. There are so many ways you can use your talents to make a difference."

"Is that how you feel, Lara? Like you've made a difference?"

"Honey," she laughed, "I've used my talents to keep the people who work with your mother from killing her! I guess that would be called making a difference. I'm the mediator–the peacemaker. I'm everybody's mother when we're on the road. It's my business to make it all run smoothly and most of the time I succeed. I don't need the limelight, Sunni, and neither do you. It's not the limelight that makes a person successful–it's being the best you that you can be."

Thoughts of Lara and the New York trip faded as thoughts of Mark came to her mind. Yes, there were people who were making a difference in her life and she let her sadness float away.

She reached for the phone, dialed his number and waited for the sound of his voice to lift her away from the misery that hung over MarGrove.

*****

"Mrs. Dee, don't count on me for lunch. I'm going to walk to the cafe and meet Mark."

"That's nice, Sunni. Tell that young man hello for me."

"I know, I know. You're glad I'm going to see him. But, nothing is settled between us. Right now we're just friends." Sunni couldn't help but smile at Mrs. Davis's lack of subtly. The woman didn't hide the fact that she liked Mark and hoped the relationship would continue to develop.

"After lunch I'm going to the hospital. I'd like to visit with Mom before she has her surgery tomorrow."

"What about your sister? Is she going with you to the hospital?"

"I doubt it." There was resignation in her voice as she tried to deal with Alli's attitude. "See if you can't talk her into it. Maybe she'll listen to you."

Chuckling, Mrs. Davis replied, "That'll be the day."

"Mrs. Dee, were you afraid of Tomas?"

"Honey, I don't know if I was or not. I just hoped I wouldn't have to deal with him. From everything they told me, the man was desperate. And desperate people do stupid things. I was all too happy to leave for a couple of days. I'm really glad I wasn't here when he tried to burn the place down. Every time I look out the window at Sam's charred house, I get angry."

"They'll build it back, won't they?"

"Who knows what's going to happen around here. This has become a sad place." Wiping her hands on her apron, she picked up her coffee cup and took a sip. "I wouldn't be surprised if your mother sold the place."

"I hope not. I love this place." Not sure if she should say anything, she looked at Mrs. Davis with a childish grin. "Can you keep a secret?"

"My lips are sealed. What do you know that I don't?"

"I think Sam and Lara will be getting married soon. She kind of told me that while we were in New York. Maybe the guest house can be enlarged so they can live there."

"It's about time! I've been trying to wake Sam up for years. That lady is the best thing that ever happened to him." She smiled at her young charge and winked. "Once they're married, they might not want to live in our back yard."

"Probably not. But I'm going to suggest it anyway." She glanced at her watch and realized she was going to have to hurry.

"Mrs. Dee, gotta' go! I'll see you later."

*****

Mark was already sitting at one of the outdoor tables when she arrived and as she looked his way, she realized how much she had missed him. Everything about him cheered her up--his smile, the sunlight on his hair, and the navy blue polo shirt that showed the definition of his muscles. She felt giddy every time she saw him and her first thought was how good his lips would feel against hers.

Gathering her in his arms, he gave her a bear hug. "Hey, gorgeous! I've missed you."

Then the lips she had been missing were on hers.

"Wow! If that's the way I'm greeted when I've been out of town for a few days, I'll have to go away again."

"Oh, no you don't. You stay as close as possible and I promise to greet you this way every time I see you."

"Kiss me again and I'll consider your offer." For once in her life she wasn't worried about what other people would think.

"What a scary few days. I'm glad it's over and your family is safe. Guess we all misjudged Tomas." Mark's brow creased as he spoke. "What's the latest?"

"All I know is he's in jail. Sam told us the police think Paolo was killed by mistake. The people Tomas owed money to thought they could rough up Paolo and he would give them the money. But, it got out of hand and Paolo drowned." She shook her head. "That was the piece of the puzzle I couldn't figure out. It didn't make sense that they would kill someone who owed them money."

"I agree. But then we don't think like they do. Tell me about the house. I read in the paper there was a fire."

"Tomas burned Sam's house before he was scared off. Thank goodness he didn't get to the main house." She closed her eyes to block out the picture of MarGrove in a charred heap. "It really looks bad when you drive in the gate. All that's left of the guesthouse is blackened cinder blocks and ashes. That whole side of the yard is a mess. The grass halfway to the big house is burned to a crisp. So are some of the trees and the flower beds. It's pitiful looking."

"Where is Sam staying?"

"Guess I'm not the last to know."

"What are you talking about?"

"He's staying at Lara's."

"Lara Finley?" Mark's surprised look confirmed that he didn't know about Sam and Lara's relationship.

"I think they'll be getting married soon. Isn't that great?"

"Wow. I'd have never guessed they were serious. Good for them."

Lunch was over before she knew it. They had talked and laughed enough that she had forgotten her worries. As she gazed at Mark, she wished her time with him wasn't about to end. "You are really good for me. Being with you lets me forget all the things I've been worried about."

"Like what? You know they've scientifically proven that worry never helps anything."

Ignoring his last remark, she went on. "What do you think about Alli going on tour? That's one of the issues I'm trying to sort out."

"From what I know, that's not for certain. All we've been told is she's going to rehearse with us a few times. On the other hand, Alli's made it clear to me that she thinks she's taking your mother's place." He shook his head. "I don't know if I even have a job. There's been so much for your dad to think about that the band has sort of been left out of the loop."

"That's interesting. I thought he kept you all up-to-date on everything." When Mark shrugged she went on. "Daddy said four of the venues didn't break the contracts. But last night he told Alli she was going to have to ask Mom if she could go on tour in her place." She grimaced. "I think we're about to witness another world war."

"The band may have the last say in this. I'm not going to put my reputation on the line if she's not good."

"Oh, she's good, Mark. She's really good. With time and some experience, I think she'll be even bigger than Margo."

"I'm hoping this isn't a wild goose chase, but I'm willing to give her a try. Let's see what your mom and the rest of the band have to say. Now, what else are you worried about?"

"Mom's surgery is in the morning. What if she can never sing again? What if she tells Alli no? What if the cancer has spread? You know, little things like that."

"Sunni, brighten up. I think you're chasing trouble that doesn't exist. If your sister is good, she'll make her way even without Margo. You told me yourself that she never wanted to use Margo's name. If she's changed her mind, more power to her. And, your mom's a fighter. She'll be all right."

The warmth of his smile made her feel better and she took his hand in hers. "Thank you." She whispered. "Thank you for being here when I needed something positive to hang on to."

"Sunni, let's go walk on the beach. The sand and sea changes my attitude no matter what's going on in my life."

*****

He was right. Walking on the beach, hand in hand, Sunni felt peaceful for the first time in weeks. The brisk breeze, the waves lapping gently against the sand, and his touch had quieted her mind and renewed her energy.

"My apartment is right over there. Come with me," he whispered so softly she almost missed hearing him. She didn't need more words to know that she would follow his lead.

*****

As soon as he had closed the door behind them, he took her in his arms and drew her into an embrace. They had shared kisses in the past, but he had never kissed her with such passion.

Though she wanted to know what Alli knew, she wanted love to guide her. She wanted his touch and his passion, but more than that, she wanted his love.

"Mark, are we ready for this?" Breathlessly she said the few words and waited for his reply. "Do we have a future?"

He rested his forehead against hers, still holding her in his arms. "Jocelyn was my past. You're my present. And, neither of us knows the future. I want to make love to you, but I want you to want this as much as I do. I won't rush you or put any pressure on you. This has to be your decision." He took her face in his hands. "You are special to me. So much so that you've turned my life upside down. You've changed the direction I thought I was going. That's all I can promise right now, Sunni."

"Make love to me, Mark. I want you to be the first."

The heat in her body melted reason and logic away. She wanted to be touched and she wanted to touch. Dreams of making love were not enough anymore, she wanted to experience it. As he began to unbutton her summer dress, her sister's face appeared in her mind. Like cold water, her reality overwhelmed her emotions.

She stilled his hands. "I can't, Mark. As much as I want you, I can't do it. My sister has trivialized making love and I promised myself that I'd never do that."

Tears welled up in her eyes and she tried to hide her face in his shirt. "Will you wait for me, Mark? Will you wait until I know that what I'm feeling is for real?"

As his hands moved away from her, she knew she had made the only decision she could make. She was not going to repeat her mother and sister's patterns.

She lifted her face and looked at him with tenderness. "I want my body to make you happy. I want to see my reflection in your eyes and know you appreciate what I'm offering."

Waves of sensation more intense than she could have imagined overwhelmed her as he pulled her to him and buried his face in her hair.

"I'll wait as long as it takes, Sunni. When you're ready, you'll know it."

"Hold me, Mark. Hold me until all my fears disappear."

She felt more alive, more aware, more in touch with life than she had ever felt before. He held her until his breathing slowed and his body relaxed. She felt like she was cocooned by him. There was no outside world, no problems, no hurt or anxiety.

It no longer mattered that her mother couldn't love her or that distance always seemed to separate her from her father. It didn't matter that her sister was acting more and more like their mother. At this moment, she felt protected. This man, with his arms holding her, was giving her the safety she had longed for all her life. No one had ever done that for her before.

He dried her tears and his gentle touch made her feel loved. Why had she said no to him when all she wanted was to stay where she no longer felt separate?

She leaned forward and kissed his eyelids, his nose, his mouth.

"Are you angry with me, Mark? I'm sorry that I couldn't say yes. Please help me get to the place where I can say yes."

There was no reason for him to respond as her lips pressed against his and the motion of her body left no doubt that someday she would be ready for more.

Chapter Forty-four

Margo

"Mrs. Anderson, the tests give us information about what we can see with the scan. They can't predict your future. Surgery is the only way we will know for sure the extent of the cancer. Try not to worry. I promise I'll do everything I can to save your voice. But, you have some big choices to make if you want to be healthy."

She wasn't comforted by Dr. Mellon's words. He had already told her to give up the idea of returning to the stage and she had reconciled herself to the fact that this year's tour wouldn't happen. But, there was no way she was going to be defeated by this disease. Every morning she reaffirmed her vow to live differently: No drugs, alcohol or cigarettes. One year off tour wouldn't kill her career. She would rest her voice, take care of her health, and come back stronger than ever.

"Dr. Mellon, I'm trusting you to take care of this little problem. You do your part and I'll do mine." She smiled at the man and prayed that their conversation wasn't going to be in vain.

"I'll see you in the operating room tomorrow morning at seven. Try to get some rest."

He left the room and she sighed. "Michael, you know I can do this." She wanted him to agree with her. "I plan to be back on tour next year if you'll help me."

"If you're telling me things will be different, then you know I'll help. I'm tired of the self-destructive way you've lived for the last few years, so this would be a good time for me to move on if you aren't committed to change."

The tenderness was gone from his voice and something in his manner told her he meant what he was saying.

“I’m surprised you stayed this long, Michael. But, I’m glad you did.”

She wanted the tenderness to return. She wanted him to...what? What did she want from the man who had been a part of her life for twenty-six years? Did she love him? Was she ready to let go of the freedom she had left him for ten years ago? The freedom that had cost her so much–her voice, her self-respect, her family. She turned her head until she could see his face–the face that was always there, the face of the one man who had never let her down. Tears welled up and she closed her eyes to keep them from spilling onto her cheeks.

“Can you forgive me?” she whispered. “Will you let me show you that I can change?”

He crossed the room and sat on the edge of her bed. “Margo, I want nothing more than to believe you. I want you healthy for your sake and for mine. We are partners and I want it to stay that way, but I’ve made a decision to get healthy, too. I won’t stand by and watch you go back to the old ways.”

“Then we have a deal. I’ll stay sober and you’ll stay with me.”

“Are you asking me to marry you?” he asked quietly.

“Why not, Michael?” She watched as the tenderness returned to his eyes

“One step at a time, sweetheart. One step at a time. I have something to tell you that may change your mind. I wasn’t planning to discuss this with you until after your surgery, but this seems like as good a time as any.”

“What in the world are you talking about? Is there another woman?” She pulled herself up on her elbows and she didn’t hide the hurt.

“Yeah, there’s another woman,” he teased. “Well, really she’s still a girl.”

"Are you crazy?"

"You will probably think that when you hear the rest of it."

"Stop dragging this out. It won't change whether I get angry or not. Just tell me!"

"I've been thinking of letting Alli go on what's left of the tour, with some conditions and reservations, of course."

"This is no time for jokes, Michael."

"I'm not joking. She's good, Margo. Not as good as you were at that age, but she's a natural. Four of the venues have agreed to give her a chance."

"I'd rather you had another woman." She sank back on the pillow and looked at him in disbelief. "Absolutely not, Michael! I don't want her on my tour."

"I thought you'd feel that way, but think about it. She fills in for you until you're ready to return. We'll introduce her as Margo's daughter. That keeps your name out there and she gets some experience. It's a win-win." He had switched to his businessman's voice.

"I don't want her in the business at all. It will destroy her just like it destroyed me."

"No, Margo. The business didn't destroy you and you know it. You made some bad choices and maybe, just maybe, you can use your experience to help our daughter make better choices for herself."

"God help us, Michael. You know she's more like me than either of us would want her to be."

"In some ways that's painfully true."

"Michael, I promised myself that I would never tell you this. But things have changed and you need to know." She hesitated. "Alli was having an affair with Paolo. I caught them, Michael. I watched my daughter betray me. She's out of control and going on tour, getting in our crazy show business world, will put her over the edge. Can't you see that?"

The color drained out of his face. "Dear God in heaven. Please tell me you're making this up." He shook his head. "Sam tried to tell me, but I didn't believe him."

"I couldn't make this up and you know it. Part of my recovery was being able to tell Lulu about it. I've talked it through and I'm working to let it go. Someday I'll be able to do that, but right now it hurts too much. After I told Lulu she asked me to think about telling you. She reminded me that you were Alli's parent, also."

"I knew there was a problem between the two of you, but I never imagined what it was. I told her the only way she could go on tour was to make things right between the two of you and to get your approval. I didn't know, Margo. I'm so sorry."

"Do you think she'll ask me?"

"I don't have an answer for that. Part of me hopes that she will. I just know she's not leaving on tour if she doesn't." His voice cracked and he swallowed.

Feeling almost hysterical, she fought to control her laughter. "If I can get through all of this trash without drugs or alcohol, I think I might be cured. Don't you agree?"

Her laughter gave way to sobbing.

Michael held her as they cried together.

*****

She didn't remember falling asleep, but when she opened her eyes, he was still there. Sitting on the side of her bed, he looked sadder than she had ever seen him look. Her eyes felt swollen from crying and looking closely, she saw that his eyes were puffy, too.

"Michael? How long have I been asleep?" The raspy sound reminded her that she was now a singer without a voice.

"Not long," he replied and turned to look her way. "I've thought it through and you're right. Alli won't be going on tour."

"I'm calmer now and I've also thought about it. Let's see what she does before we make a final decision. If she's big enough to ask my forgiveness, then maybe she's grown-up enough to go."

"You'd be willing to let her take your place? Is that what you're saying?"

"She's not taking my place! Don't think for one minute that I'm not going back on stage."

The old pangs returned for a minute, then she sighed. "I'll let her have her chance if she tries to make amends. Four venues, right? She can have four venues for this one tour. Then if she makes it, she's on her own. Will you agree to that, Michael? I don't want you to manage her, and you've got to make her promise that she will never wear red on stage. That's my signature, not hers." She was adamant. "But, first she has some work to do. And, then she has to beg." She chuckled. "I won't make this easy for her. She'll have to beg."

"You are something else. But, then, that's why I've always loved you."

*****

Sunni stuck her head in the door and smiled at the sight of her parents holding hands. Her mom was propped up in the hospital bed and even in a hospital gown she looked beautiful. The last few hours with Mark gave her a new appreciation for the simple, yet intimate, gesture between her parents and she saw how deep their connection really was.

"You look great, Mom! Fighting the bad guys must agree with you!" Sunni gushed.

"You look great yourself. What have you been up to this afternoon?" Michael said.

She knew she was probably flushed and wondered if all the kissing she'd been doing was showing.

"Nothing much. Mark and I walked on the beach earlier. Why?" As she stumbled over her words, she caught a question in her father's eyes.

"No reason. You just look happy."

"You and Mark who?" Margo asked.

"Mark Sanders. We've sort of been dating this summer."

"Good choice, Sunni. Mark is a really nice guy." Margo liked the young man who had been her lead guitarist for the past five years. "But don't get too attached. You know he lives a crazy life and in a few weeks he'll be back on the road."

Her mother sounded genuinely interested. "I'll enjoy the next few weeks and we'll see what happens after that. How are you feeling?"

"Let's see. For someone who has cancer, is about to lose her voice, and was almost killed by a lunatic, I think I'm doing better than expected."

Chapter Forty-five

Brazil
Eduardo DaSilva

He felt dead inside and older than he should at eighty-four years old. He still had a lot of years left ahead of him, but what were they worth?

Neither his son nor his daughter had ever been interested in the business and now he had lost his two grandsons. Some days, like today, his grief for Paolo and his anger with Tomas overwhelmed him. Their loss meant he had no heirs, no one to sit behind the desk and manage the diverse businesses forged out of his back-breaking days in the oil fields.

He looked out over the lights of Rio, the city he loved, and he wanted to be young again. He wanted to be back at the starting point with his wife, Marcía, by his side–the two of them working and dreaming of how it would be 'someday.'

Grateful that she had lived long enough to share in some of the rewards of their hard work, tonight he missed her more than he wanted to admit. Her death three years ago had taken some of the fire out of him, but he'd had his grandsons to work hard for. So–he poured all of his heartbreak into growing his business into an empire that would continue to profit for years to come. Oh, how Marcía would have loved all that he had created. Lovingly, he stared at her portrait on the wall. She had the most beautiful smile, and the artist had captured it along with her playful spirit.

He remembered the first day he had seen her. He was eighteen and had been working in the oil fields as a roughneck since he was fifteen. That day he had finally been promoted to a driller and had gone into town with his friends to celebrate.

As he walked around the small square, he saw her enter the church and her beauty captured him. For weeks he returned to the square, hoping to catch a glimpse of her. When he finally met her there was no looking back. He courted her, asked her father for her hand, married her and they lived happily until her death three years ago. She had been a loving wife, a good mother to their two children, and a doting grandmother.

He had regrets, but not many. He regretted not implementing a heavier hand with his grandsons. They had been spoiled and pampered by their parents, he had been generous with money, and he had not interfered with their lifestyles. He had covered for them, protected them, and indulged them.

And, now, he had even ordered a man's death for them. With Dario Vincetti's death, it should have been over. Even though Tomas believed Paolo's death had been an accident, Eduardo knew better and his heart was heavy. Eventually, he and Tomas would have made amends. But, it was no longer a family matter. His grandson's stupidity had brought them public disgrace. Tomas was sitting in a jail cell in Miami and most likely would spend the rest of his life in a prison somewhere. How stupid!

He should have known when Paolo was murdered that the Empress had done this to him. She was making him suffer. His long-ago affair with the woman the world now called La Emperatriz de cocaina had come full circle. It had happened so long ago, he had almost forgotten her last words. He had told her he would not leave Marcía and she had vowed revenge. Never had he expected that she would hurt him where it mattered most. He had no heir. She had taken both his grandsons. And, his lack of vigilance had allowed it to happen. He had let down his guard and he could almost see her sitting in her penthouse in Miami laughing at him.

All the pieces of the puzzle had fallen in place and he knew she was the mastermind behind it all. Tomas had been a pawn on her chess board and she had used all of his weaknesses. She had controlled him with sex and drugs and driven him to evil. Yes, she had chosen the right grandson to manipulate-Tomas had always been weak. Once she had Tomas, it was easy for her to move against Paolo.

The Empress had won, at least for this moment. He stiffened his back and lifted his chin. Perhaps I'm not too old to still be in the game.

He didn't want his biggest regret of all to be that he didn't live long enough to see the Empress destroyed.

Chapter Forty-six

Alli

She paced from one side of the house to the other. She knew what she had to do, but she wanted to get it just right before she walked into Margo's hospital room. She was annoyed that she still let her mother intimidate her. And, she was angry that Sunni had let her down.

"Alli, you're going to wear out that rug. Come on to the kitchen and I'll fix you some lunch," Mrs. Davis offered.

"I'm not very hungry, but maybe something light will help settle my stomach."

Mrs. Davis's interruption reminded her that she hadn't eaten breakfast so she followed her into the kitchen.

"What's making you so antsy this afternoon? You've about walked the color off that rug with your pacing."

"I've got a lot on my mind, that's all. And I probably do need something to eat."

"Some protein might help you get a new perspective," Mrs. Davis teased.

"Mrs. Dee, I've got to go to the hospital to see Margo and hospitals always make me nervous."

"Or, could it be that you've got some explaining to do and you don't know where to start?"

"I don't know what you're talking about." Alli looked at the fruit and yogurt that had been placed in front of her. I know Mrs. Dee knows all about me and Paolo. But I'm not going to give her the satisfaction of lecturing me.

"Alli, you can stop playing games with me. I know what I know and if I were you I'd be begging for my mother's forgiveness. That's all I've got to say. But you think about it." Mrs. Davis walked out of the room before Alli could come up with a response.

*****

Walking down the hospital corridor, she mentally rehearsed the few words she thought might do the least amount of damage.

Her mother was ill, her defenses were down, and there was a chance she might not remember that horrible night in June. The shadows cast by the lingering afternoon sun danced playfully across the halls of the hospital and reminded her of games she and Sunni had played as children. Sometimes they gave silly names to the shadows and made up stories to go with the names–other times they tried to mimic the shapes the shadows created. But, she was no longer a child and the shadows were no longer entertaining. Today, they looked sinister and she could feel them closing in around her, crushing her.

As she stood in the doorway and steeled herself for what was about to unfold, she saw her mother lying in the bed with her father on one side and her sister on the other. Shadows on the wall created a perfect family picture for anyone who didn't know the truth, and she almost laughed. Margo surrounded by the shadow of a loving family.

"Hi, Alli. Come on in. I was hoping you would come." Her father walked over and put his arm around her. "We were just talking about you."

His greeting threw her off-balance. It wasn't the greeting she expected and she wiggled out from under his arm. As she walked toward her mother, she felt unsure and queasy. Where was the anger she had expected?

"Alli, I'm glad you're here. I understand there are some things we need to talk about." Margo spoke first and Alli was leery because she didn't hear any kind of threat in her mother's voice.

"You don't look sick. You must be feeling better," Alli blurted. It sounded inane, but that was all she could think to say.

"Hopefully that's a compliment," her mother said with a slight smile. Margo seemed to be looking through her and it disarmed her.

"Hi, sis. I'm glad you're here, too." Sunni started toward her to give her a hug, but something in Alli's stance made her stop. "Are you all right?"

"I'm fine. I didn't expect a family reunion, that's all."

Sensing Alli's tension, Michael looked at Sunni. "Let's go to the cafeteria and get something to drink. Margo, Alli, can we bring you back something?" Shaking heads indicated their reply, then Michael herded Sunni out of the room.

"Okay. Let's hear your spiel. I understand your father gave you a mandate and I'm guessing that's the reason you're here."

Alli sensed the undercurrent in Margo's voice and she still felt surprised that her mother showed no outward signs of anger.

"You cut to the chase, don't you?"

"Alli, there are years of misunderstanding and distance between us, but now is not the time or place to start unloading on each other. I'll listen to what you have to say and we'll go from there."

"You know about the tour?"

Margo affirmed with a nod.

"Dad said four venues will give me a chance and I want to go. I'm good enough to do this."

"That's all you've got to say? You're good and you want to go? That's all you can say that should convince me to turn my tour over to you?" Margo looked at her daughter with disbelief.

"What more can I say? My voice is good, I can learn the music and the choreography, and I deserve the chance." Alli stood tall and glared at her mother.

"If that's all you've got to say, Alli, then you've just blown your chance." Margo's raspy voice hardened.

Silence, distrust, years of neglect and misunderstanding stood between them, but Alli knew that only one incident mattered. One moment in time threatened to keep her from what she wanted more than anything. Margo was still in control. She owned it all and wasn't going to give it away easily.

Alli tasted rage and bitterness. Her whole body stiffened with memories of loneliness and loss. Years of longing for her mother's love, or even a touch, swirled in her head and she became dizzy. She grabbed on to the bed rail and tried to steady herself.

"Nothing in the world matters to you except you! You left me! All these years you've tried to deny that I exist and you didn't care what happened to me as long as I stayed out of your way. Sunni and I were the ones everyone at school pitied because no one came on our birthday, no one was there to cheer us on or celebrate our victories. And, God forbid that anyone was ever there when we were sick or disappointed or hurt. Do you know what that feels like?" She was shouting and the anger kept bubbling up from deep inside her.

"Do you know what it feels like to be afraid in the middle of the night and there is no one there to tell you things will be okay? Do you know how many times Sunni and I held on to each other because we knew there was no one else who cared or gave a damn about us?"

She let go of the bed and walked closer to her mother. "You don't know the half of what I've done to get even with you!" Hatred filled her eyes as she looked at her mother's ashen face. "I have slept with just about every man you've ever slept with. Right under your nose. In your house, when you were there and when you weren't. You think Paolo was the one and only? Well think again, Mother dear. I've marked my territory every chance I've gotten."

Alli sneered at her mother's look of disbelief. "I've been singing in clubs for the past three years and I'm good. In fact, there are people who've told me that I'm as good as you--on the stage and in bed."

She backed away so her mother would be able to see her. "I'm a better version of you than you are of yourself! You've thrown it all away–your husband, your children, and now your career. And, for what? A line of cocaine and sex? Who are you to tell me whether I can go on this tour or not? Right now, you're a sick has-been. That's all, Margo. That's all." She turned and started for the door.

"Stop right there, Alli. Don't think for one minute that you're going to unload on me and then just walk away!" Margo commanded with her raspy voice. "Now it's my turn and you're going to listen to me."

She waited until Alli had turned around to face her. "You have most of the picture right. But there are a few things you can't even begin to understand. Things beyond your maturity and experience level. And, one day, we'll talk about those things. Today isn't the day for that." Margo's shoulders slumped and she drew in a deep breath.

"I can't take back all those years. I can't give you today what I denied you for years and I won't even try. But I can and have made some decisions for my life that I hope will change me and my life for the better. I forgive you for all your foolishness and I'm struggling to forgive you for Paolo, because I thought I loved him. But that's another story." She paused in the hope that she would get the next words right.

"I want a second chance, Alli. I'm not good mother material, but I want the chance to know you. We have hurt each other deeply, but I've learned that even the deepest hurts can be healed." She closed her eyes and lay as still as possible. "I see myself in you. Even though you think you aren't like me, you're making the same kinds of mistakes and some of the same bad choices. Wake up, Alli, before it's too late." She wanted her daughter to hear her, but knew she would have to learn for herself. "I've said all I can say. My throat hurts and I need to rest."

Alli was immobile– it felt like all the energy had been sucked out of the room. Had she heard correctly? Was that really Margo talking? Confused and spent, she sat down in the chair beside her mother's bed. Closing her eyes, she hoped to find a clue that would show her what to do next.

"Are you still here?" A soft whisper floated to Alli's ears and she raised her eyes to look in her mother's direction. "Please forgive me."

She saw the tears in Margo's eyes and knew she had won her first real victory against her mother. She stood beside the bed and took her mother's hand. The words she had thought would be so hard to say rolled off her tongue with no effort.

"I'm so sorry that I hurt you. You're right. I was foolish." She wanted to add that she wasn't like her at all, but what was the use.

There was a long silence before she heard the words she had come to hear. "Go, Alli. Go and enjoy the tour."

Quietly, without saying another word, she turned and walked away from the shadows.

*****

The next day her excitement and enthusiasm were squelched when she encountered the rebellious faces of the band members. She sensed immediately that they were not happy she was there.

"Hi guys. Thanks for coming to the rehearsal. Let's get to work." Her confidence was shaken but there was no way she was going to let them see it. "Ed, what's the opening number for the show? I think we need to start at the beginning and work straight through."

She was shocked when they didn't respond or move. "What are you waiting for?"

Ed, the senior member of the band was the first to speak. “This isn’t what we’re paid to do, Miss Anderson. We’re not prepared to put our careers on the line. Sorry.”

“I think, if you’ll give me a chance, you’ll be surprised at what I can do.” She sat down on the stool that had been placed in front of the band. “I know you think I’m the spoiled, untalented daughter of your boss. You may be right–but then you might be wrong. I know what I’m doing and we’ve got a show to rehearse. Don’t you want to save what we can?”

Alli forced herself to breath calmly as she waited for their decision. After what seemed like an eternity, Ed turned to the guys and nodded.

“Okay, let’s see what she’s got.”

Chapter Forty-seven

November 1980
Sam

The tour was scheduled to leave in two days and for the first time in ten years it was leaving without him. He had relinquished his duties to Todd Madison and wished the young man good luck. Being a personal body guard and head of security for a troupe of over one hundred was not an easy job. Sam knew there would be days when he would miss it, but he had made the right decision. It would never work for Alli Anderson to be his boss.

Financially, he could afford to take a break and when he was ready, a new job would open up. He had no doubt of that. For now, he was content to focus on the event that was about to take place. He stood in Michael's living room and watched as Margo's nurse wheeled her into the room. Even in a wheelchair, she was the center of the energy and every eye was on her. She looked radiant and happier than he could ever remember seeing her.

"You don't look bad for a man who's about to be married." She touched his arm and smiled at him. "I know I've told you a hundred times. But I'll say it once more. I'm so happy for you and Lara."

"Thanks, boss lady. I'm pretty happy myself. We had a good go of it, didn't we, Margo? But, truthfully, I'm glad we're not leaving on that bus." He held her hand. "After the ceremony, let's drink a ..." Sam hesitated. "Let's drink a ginger ale to the next chapter in our lives."

Margo laughed. "Ginger ale is good, Sam. I'm all right with that."

Then she looked around the room at the people who were there to celebrate with Sam and Lara. Band members, dancers, and crew had all come to wish the couple well and to say good-bye. Today she was not going to think about the good-byes. There would be plenty of time for that in the weeks ahead. No, today was about the happiness of two people who meant so much to her.

The minister walked to the front of the room and motioned to Sam that it was time to begin. Michael pushed Margo's chair to the place where the minister stood and then he walked over to stand beside Sam.

He smiled at his ex-wife, the beautiful bridesmaid, and whispered to Sam, "She looks more beautiful today than she did on our wedding day."

When the music began, all eyes in the room turned to watch Lara Finley walk down the aisle.

Chapter Forty-eight

Randall, Martinez and Cannon

Elena looked at her husband as he poured over the papers he'd been working on for court. She still loved to watch him. The way his brow creased when he got so involved. The way he chewed the end of the pencil when he was pouring over evidence looking for anything that would keep his client out of jail. He was so intense when he was preparing for trial that he sometimes forgot to eat. Walking up behind him, she placed her hands on his shoulders and whispered in his ear.

"Hey, good looking. Your son and I would love to have you join us for dinner."

"Can't stop right now, Elena. Leave me something on the stove." He didn't look up, but moved his shoulders in a way that would dislodge her hands.

"Will you at least stop long enough to tell Jason good-night?" She asked softly. His rebuff had hurt.

"Yeah, yeah. Call me when you start to put him to bed."

Ever since the charges had been dropped against Alli Anderson, he had been withdrawing from her. When he was home he stayed in his study. He seldom came to the dinner table, played less and less with Jason, and more often than not, he ignored her playful advances. He worked late at the office several nights a week and had started going in on Sunday mornings. If she complained, he either brushed her off or became angry and sullen and wouldn't talk to her for days. She knew marriages went through dry spells, but they had never hit one before and she didn't know how to react.

Quietly, she closed the door to the study and walked into the dining room where she was greeted by the smiling face of her son.

*****

After Eric kissed Jason good night, he told Elena he'd forgotten something at the office and he'd be home in a couple of hours. "Don't wait up for me."

*****

Eric saw her standing in the parking lot of his building and his heartbeat quickened. Without acknowledging her presence, he walked through the door and waited for her to join him in the elevator.

He didn't look at her and she didn't say a word to him. But once his office door was locked behind them, he knew she'd belong to him. For weeks they'd been meeting--one or two hours of passion and laughter and more passion. Her fire never dimmed and his desire for her never seemed to lessen. She'd become his obsession and the only way he could deal with it at home was to push Elena as far away as possible.

Standing with his back to the door, he watched her undress. He didn't move toward her or try to touch her. But he took in every movement and his body reacted to every piece of clothing she removed. She stepped out of her panties, tossed them on his desk, and walked boldly to the place where he was standing. Hungrily, she began unbuttoning his shirt and loosening his belt buckle.

"Maddie, you are so good to me."

Chapter Forty-nine

Michael

Standing in the wings of the theater in Philadelphia, he watched his daughter give her all to the audience. It was Margo's music, but the presentation was all Alli. She made it her own and she did it well. He heard the appreciation in the applause and his father's heart swelled with pride. But his loyalty was to Margo, even if she never stepped on stage again, and he knew in that moment he couldn't represent his daughter. He would make inquiries among his friends in the business and he'd find the person who could promote and market Alli with the enthusiasm and loyalty she deserved.

Tonight he was tired, but that wasn't clouding his judgment. Alli was a new breed of songstress. Her style was more forceful than Margo's had ever been–her energy was wilder and untamed and she needed a manager who could match her and keep up with her.

Margo was content to stand center stage with the musicians and dancers moving left and right in the background. Not Alli. She commanded the entire stage, moving along with everyone else, yet never letting them overshadow her. Margo stood apart from the audience and let them adore her–Alli brought the audience up on the stage with her as she moved. She flirted, cajoled, interacted, and played with the people she entertained. She befriended every single one of them and for two hours she made each one of them imagine she was singing only to them.

Amazement, astonishment, and wonder filled him as he watched. How could one so young and inexperienced know how to capture an audience the way she did? He hadn't made a mistake by giving her this chance, but he hoped he hadn't unleashed a power that would too quickly crash and burn.

Watching her in rehearsal hadn't given him a clue about the way she would perform in front of hundreds of people. Even the band members hadn't prepared him for her raw magnetism and charisma. For weeks they'd told him she was good–they thought she could carry the show, they liked her style, they were willing to work with her. Perhaps her performance was taking them by surprise, also.

The nightmare of making the tour work had worn him out. Presenting Alli to the vendors had been a challenge. But changing schedules, refunding and discounting tickets, and designing and printing new promotional billboards, flyers, and programs in such a short time frame had unnerved his staff. Lara had worked night and day to help him pull it all together and on top of that she had worked with Alli to get her ready.

It had been Lara who'd convinced the makeup artists, hairstylists, costume designers and the rest of the backstage crew to give Alli a chance. And, tonight it all came together in a performance that none of them could have predicted.

Alli Anderson had launched herself and there would be no turning back.

*****

Back in the hotel, he could finally pour himself a drink and relax for a few minutes. Even at two o'clock in the morning, he knew Margo waited for his call, but he didn't know how she would handle what he had to tell her.

"Did I wake you?" he asked. He listened as she explained that she hadn't been able to close her eyes waiting to hear from him.

"She did it, Margo. She brought the house down. Your songs, her style. Our daughter is a natural." He waited for her response.

"No, she won't take your place. But she'll make her own." He softened his voice and wished he was holding her in his arms as he tried to find words to describe Alli without diminishing Margo.

"She didn't try to imitate you or your way of doing things. You bring the audience to you, she more or less takes herself to the audience. It was a different way of doing things. Not better or worse, just different."

"Yes, someday you'll have to see her for yourself. But, enough about Alli. How are you feeling? I'll be home in two days to take you to your next chemo treatment."

"I want to do it." He closed his eyes and tried to pretend that she wasn't sick. But she began to tell him that she was losing her hair and he couldn't pretend any more.

"Never! I'll never think you're ugly. With or without hair, sweetheart. How could the most beautiful woman in the world ever look ugly?"

"Sweet dreams. But before you go to sleep remember how much I love you."

He hung up the phone and closed his eyes. She was safe. She'd be well in time. And he meant what he'd said about her beauty.

The important thing was the new intimacy and love that was growing between them. After she'd been released from the hospital, she and Mrs. Davis had moved into his condo and she'd put MarGrove up for sale.

It had happened effortlessly–and for him it was like they'd never been apart.

Chapter Fifty

Sunni

She listened as Mark went on and on about the show. He had described everything--what Alli wore, how she captured the audience, how the band loved her interpretation of Margo's music. She smiled at the phone, delighted for Alli's success. "I know she's got a good voice, but I never thought she was in Mom's league. How did she do it?"

"You've told me she's in a league of her own. But, is she a threat to Margo?"

"You sound convinced that my sister is a threat to every rock star out there. I'd love to see her for myself."

"Are you asking me to come to Philly tomorrow for the show? Is my dad there?"

"My last class is over at two this afternoon, so I can be there by show time. I'm pretty sure there's a train that leaves at five-thirty that will get me to Philly about seven. I'll take a cab to the theater and I'll meet you at the Morris House after the show. And, Mark, no extra room, I'll sleep on the couch. I've missed you."

*****

Hanging up the phone, she curled up with her pillow and let her imagination go wild. It had been weeks since she'd seen him and the thought of spending the night near him made her knees weak but she knew she still wasn't ready for more.

1980 had been the strangest year she'd ever lived. Sarah Lawrence was challenging and exciting. She loved her classes and the people she met. Every day she gave herself permission to speak up and even take a few risks.

For the first time she felt like she had a support system–her mother and father, Lara, Mark–and that gave her courage. She could call them for advice, even complain if she needed to, and they listened. There were times she missed Alli, but living alone was wonderful. No more stepping all over her twin's discarded clothes and covering for her when she was breaking every rule. No more lying awake at night wondering where she was, who she was with, or whether she was falling down drunk somewhere.

Yet, there were times when she wanted to hear her sister's voice so much it hurt. They had been a team all their lives–supporting each other, wiping each other's tears, loving each other when it seemed that no one else loved them. And now, there hadn't even been a phone call. She and Alli lived in two different worlds and some nights she cried because it would never be the same again.

When she thought about the summer, she knew someday she'd use it as material for a book. It would make a good story because it had all the right elements–danger, intrigue, passion. But wonderful things had happened, too. She had a new closeness with her parents, and a man named Mark who was reshaping everything about her life.

*****

A ticket was waiting for her at the box office and she slipped into her seat unnoticed. The music of the warm-up act started her toes tapping and put her in the mood to enjoy the rest of the show. Her parents always found great talent to open the shows and set the mood for Margo. And, tonight was no exception. Then the lights went down, the theater got dark, and there was silence.

Her eyes were adjusting to the darkness when a voice of great depth and emotion splintered the air and mesmerized her. She knew the song, had heard her mother sing it many times, but never like what she heard now.

In the darkness, the voice escalated to a crescendo and as her sister hit the high note the stage lights burst on. There was electricity in the theater as the audience got their first look at Alli Anderson. She moved across the stage in a short, gold lame dress that was the sexiest thing Sunni had ever seen. Her sister's beautiful chestnut hair whipped wildly with every move. Awe filled Sunni as she watched her twin dance across the stage beckoning the audience to dance with her. It was like standing on the edge of the ocean watching a storm approach. The voice was thunder, the movements were lightning, and the impact was breath-taking.

Two hours without an intermission. One song after another, Alli's dynamic renditions kept getting better and better. Sunni had hoped to feast her eyes on Mark, but instead she couldn't keep her eyes off her twin.

The audience was on their feet for most of the show and a frenzied energy engulfed the theater. They clapped, whistled, shouted for more. And the more they asked for, the more she gave them. Her energy was endless and she seemed to ride the wave of ebullience generated by the people in the seats.

Then it was over. The house lights came on, the curtain came down, and Sunni felt glued to her seat. What had she just witnessed? Who was that person she'd been introduced to tonight? Hopes and fears collided as her mind tried to assimilate what this meant to her sister, to her mother, to her.

There was no way she was going to figure it out sitting in the theater. She let go of her thoughts, pushed her way through the crowd, and flagged down a taxi to take her to Mark's hotel.

*****

Warm in his arms, she curled around his body and began to relax. "Except for being here with you, I've never experienced anything like her performance tonight. I've lived with her my entire life and never known what lives inside her."

"That's why I wanted you to see her for yourself. I knew I couldn't explain or describe it to you."

"She's better than good and it scares me." She moved out of his embrace and her tone grew serious. "My mother can't touch that kind of performance, can she?"

"Sunni, they play to different strengths. Margo can sing a love song like nobody else. Sunni makes love to her audience while she sings. There's appeal in both." He lightly kissed her lips. "If Margo is ever able to return to the stage, her audience will still be there."

Her eyes filled with tears and she reached for Mark's hand. "I feel like I lost my sister tonight and my stomach is doing flips. I'm sad and I should be happy for her."

"I hope she never leaves you, Sunni. But for awhile, she's going to be riding a wave that looks like it's pulling her away. Give her some time to get her feet back on the ground."

He gently placed his finger on her lips. "No more sadness. You've got an early train to catch and my tour bus leaves at noon."

*****

Sitting in her apartment at Sarah Lawrence two days later, she wondered if her mother knew the impact Alli was having on the music scene. As sick as her mother was, she couldn't imagine her without some kind of reaction. She picked up the phone and dialed the number in Miami.

"Hi, Mom. How're you feeling?" Knowing her mom had just finished with a chemo treatment, she was almost hesitant to ask.

"Really? I'm glad it wasn't too bad. Yeah, I know you hate losing your hair, but Dad told me you found some really hot turbans to wear. He thinks you look sexy."

The next question didn't surprise her–she had been waiting for her mother to bring it up. "Yes, I saw the review in Variety. Looks like she's a hit." Sunni listened, then felt tears begin to build. "I'm sorry

Mom, I've got to go. I just wanted to check on you. I have a big test tomorrow and I've got to study. I'll call you in a couple of days."

*****

Two weeks later, he knocked on her door. "I need a place to crash for a couple of days."

"Mark, what are you doing in Bronxville? You're supposed to be on tour."

"Can I come in, Sunni?"

"I'm sorry. Yes, come in. I'm just surprised to see you."

"Your sister fired me and I need to find a job."

"She fired you? Why? You're good and she knows it."

"I wouldn't play her games and that made her mad."

"What are you talking about? What kind of games?"

"I wouldn't sleep with her, Sunni. She knows I'm in a relationship with you and I became her target. Last night I lost my cool and told her to leave me alone. She told me to get out and there was a new guitarist before I packed my bags."

"My God, is this for real?" She sank down on the sofa and fought back tears. "It's only going to get worse, Mark. Her power is like a sickness and there's nothing I can do to stop it."

She looked at him with love and concern. "What are you going to do?"

"I've decided to try my luck with some of my songs. I've done a lot of writing and arranging for your mother but I've got some work that doesn't belong to her. I'll show it to some people I know in New York and see what they think."

He put his duffle down and sat beside her. "Then I'll head for Miami and wait for you to come home for the holidays." He pulled her in his arms and nuzzled her hair.

Chapter Fifty-one

Miami, December 1980

Jocelyn had checked and double-checked every list she could find. The apartment was beautifully decorated, the caterers were finished with all their preparations, the guests would be arriving within the hour, and copies of Lawrence's books were arranged neatly on the table where he could reach them with ease. Her job was done and she had a few minutes to relax. Still, her nerves were on edge and all she could do was fidget.

It had been months since she'd seen Mark. Even though she'd been the one to break off their relationship, the thought of seeing him with Sunni Anderson created some anxiety for her. She knew they were coming to the party together but being forewarned didn't make it any easier.

The party was to celebrate the movie deals Lawrence had signed on two of his books. For weeks she'd been working with his publicist and the event planner to make the evening a gala that would be long-remembered.

As she looked around the room, she tried to remember the first time, long ago, that she had walked in here. She was a scared, college freshman who'd been asked by Lawrence to help him edit some manuscripts. Little did she know that his invitation would help frame her life.

Lawrence Fitz, retired FBI agent, became her boss, her mentor, the grandfather she'd never known. In five years, she'd helped him prepare four books for publication. She'd read, edited, suggested, argued her points, and talked him through the creation of a fictional character who'd become a favorite of readers across the country.

Lawrence, using his years of experience in the Bureau and his storytelling ability, had written bestselling crime dramas and she'd been an integral part of it. She loved the man and wanted the party to be perfect for him.

Tonight was a celebration of their hard work and she was going to do her best to forget Mark Sanders. Tonight, she wanted to just enjoy the moment. Her date, Ben Jordan, would arrive in a few minutes and his presence would take her mind off Mark. She'd met Ben years ago when he did a summer internship at the Miami Herald. Since then, he'd graduated from law school and had joined one of Miami's most prestigious firms. He was good looking, had a great sense of humor, and knew how to show her a good time. Most of the time, she enjoyed his company. The rest of the time, she wished he was Mark.

"My goodness, young lady! You look like a million dollars."

Lawrence walked in the room and looked with genuine appreciation at his young protégé who was wearing a long, black pencil skirt, white silk camisole, and black shawl. Her hair was pulled up in a fancy top knot that she'd accented with jeweled combs.

"Jocelyn, my dear, you look lovely. And, the house is fit for royalty. You've done a wonderful job, as usual." He surveyed the room once more and turned to her, "When do our guests begin to arrive?"

"Around eight o'clock. The musicians are here and the caterers are ready. I must say, that tuxedo makes you look like a model for Esquire." She'd always thought he was a distinguished-looking man but tonight he really fit that image. "You look like a very successful author waiting to overwhelm an adoring public."

Surprised by the sound of the doorbell, she laughed. "Somebody couldn't wait to be the first to arrive. I'll see who it is."

Opening the door, she was greeted by her father and step-mother. "Wow, Dad. Who'd have thought you'd look so good in a tux!" She hugged Carter McDeal, and laughed at his blush.

"I mean it," she whispered in his ear.

Turning to her stepmother, Sharon, Jocelyn was not surprised that this woman she'd come to love was stunning in a red, flowing gown that flattered her figure and her blond hair. "You two look like you're ready for a night on the town."

"Jocelyn, I promised Sharon I'd wear this get-up for two hours, not a minute more. So start the clock," Carter teased. "Whoever invented this cummerbund thing had to be a sadist."

More guests arrived behind her parents so she ushered them in the door and turned to greet the others.

*****

The room was crowded. Many faces she knew, some she recognized, and others were members of the publishing and film-making world that were here to be seen.

All these new elements were about to rearrange Lawrence's world and she wondered what her role would be in the new scenario. She loved working for him, but she also liked being a part of the journalistic world of the Miami Herald. She didn't know if she was ready to give that job up if her work with Lawrence expanded. As she thought about her aging boss, she wondered how much longer he would be able to keep up the pace of producing a new novel every year. He had the stories–she was afraid he might not have the stamina.

Glancing up from the wine glass she held, her eyes met Mark's. He was standing with a small group that included Sam Baxter and Sam's new wife, Lara Finley, Elena Martinez, and Sunni Anderson. She was surprised that Elena's husband, Eric Randall, was not part of the group, but she had spotted him earlier talking to the tall, stunning redhead, Maddie Sonnett, who she knew was a special friend of Lawrence's.

Sunni looked gorgeous in an emerald green gown and she was envious of the young woman's height. Sunni was almost as tall as Mark and they made a striking couple. As Mark continued to look at her, she knew that it was time to walk across the room and greet him. She tried to find Ben in the crowd--this awkward moment would be so much easier if he was holding her hand-- but he wasn't where she could see him. She took a deep breath and began making her way to where Mark stood.

"Hello. I'm glad you could make it tonight." She directed her words to the group and tried not to look at Mark. "Sunni, it's nice to see you again. How's your mother?"

"Her chemotherapy is almost finished and most days I think she feels pretty good. Losing her hair has been a little traumatic but she's handling it much better than I thought she would. The doctors are still not sure about her voice. She's working with therapists every day. So we're all hopeful she'll have a full recovery."

"I know you're pleased that she's making progress. The world would really miss her voice. I look forward to her return to the stage." She smiled as she thought about Margo's music and the comfort she found in listening to her songs. She tried to ignore the little murmur in her heart that reminded her of the nights when Mark had been on the road and she had listened to Margo's music so she wouldn't miss him so much.

"I imagine you're glad to be back in Florida for the holidays. It must be very cold in New York right now." Making small talk didn't come easy for her and she hoped she sounded sincere.

"Jocelyn, it was freezing in New York when I left there last week. Thank goodness the Miami sunshine has thawed me out." Sunni smiled at Jocelyn. "I understand you are the genius behind this fantastic party. Mr. Fitz is lucky to have your help."

"Sunni's right, Jocey. This is a great party." She turned at the sound of Mark's voice and the familiar endearment. "You look beautiful."

His eyes were still the eyes of the man she loved. The man she'd loved so long and so desperately. Still, there couldn't be a future for them. For her sake and his, she'd let him go. She just hadn't thought the hurt would never go away. Too brightly, she thanked everyone for the compliments on the party and tried to keep her attention on the others in the group.

"Mr. and Mrs. Baxter, that has a nice sound to it, doesn't it? Congratulations on your marriage. I understand you just returned from your honeymoon."

"We've been back for a few weeks and I think we almost feel settled in our new house. We were able to spend almost two weeks in Hawaii, but there's no place like home." Sam winked at Lara.

"Ms. Martinez, it's nice to see you again. Hopefully you'll have a chance to speak to my father and step-mother. I know they'd enjoy talking with you." She looked around the room to find Lawrence.

"If you'll excuse me, I have to check with Lawrence about starting the book signing. You all enjoy the party."

*****

Why is it so hard? Why can't I be happy that Mark has found someone else? Fighting hard not to cry, she walked over and put her arm on Ben's shoulder. "Are you having fun?" she whispered. "I'm so glad you're here."

Chapter Fifty-two

Margo

The third week of December, Miami's palm trees were decked out in colorful lights and tinsel. It was her kind of Christmas, the Christmas of her childhood–balmy breezes, people parading around in summer clothes, and Santa arriving by speedboat.

Turning to Lulu, she smiled. "Are you ready for the holidays, Lulu? I haven't thought about gifts or decorations or anything."

"I'd say you've had a bit on your mind these last months. They'll understand."

Lulu had been driving to Miami once a week since Margo's surgery to continue her counseling, to give her support, and to help her with the struggles of chemotherapy. "You know you're doing quite well with all that's going on in your life. Tell me what it's like to be living at Michael's. Are you okay with that arrangement?"

"More than okay. Did I tell you that I asked him to marry me?" She smiled.

"Yes, you've told me at least ten times. Has he changed his mind yet? Have the two of you set a date?"

"No change. When he's ready he'll let me know."

"Does that make you happy, Margo? When you think about going back into a marriage you once left, how does it feel?"

"I know I love him. I don't think I knew it before. I took him for granted and I think I really misunderstood everything he was trying to do for me." She still had to whisper most of the time, but she raised her voice as much as she could in the hope that Lulu would believe her.

"I think I've grown into marriage. I'm ready and I know I want to spend the rest of my life with him."

"And, how about the girls? Where do they fit in?"

"Sunni and I are doing fine. We talk on the phone every week and she's started telling me important things. That's a good sign, isn't it? But, I doubt that Alli and I will ever have a relationship. She wrote me off years ago and she's not the forgiving type."

"How does that feel?"

"I'll live with it, I guess. In some ways I really understand it–but I'm terrified for her and what she can do to herself." With a sweep of her hand, she gestured at herself.

"She has her own life and from what I understand she is on her way to rock and roll stardom. She's picked up eight new venues for the tour and that says a lot. I wish her well and pray every day that she's smarter than I was. I hope she gets where she wants to go without making the kinds of mistakes I made."

"One more question and I'll let you go back to fretting about Christmas. What does the doctor say about your voice?"

"He thinks I'm getting stronger, but he still holds on to his original diagnosis that I'll never sing again. He doesn't know me very well. I have plans. Someday the spotlight will shine on me again. Just wait and see."

Epilogue

Miami, March 1981

He held her hand as they waited for the show to begin. When she'd found out that her daughter would be headlining at the Jackie Gleason Theater on Miami Beach, she'd begged her doctors to allow her to attend. But being a spectator made her feel unsure and nervous.

"Being on this side of the stage is not my thing. It feels foreign."

She was glad it was dark in the theater and no one could see her. Michael had insisted on purchasing box seats and sneaking her in after everyone was seated and the warm-up band had already started playing. He didn't want her to have to deal with the press and the millions of questions she'd be asked about how it felt to have her daughter take her place. As always, Michael was right. It would have been a strain for her to come up with an answer.

Suddenly a voice of great depth and emotion shattered the silence and captured the attention of the audience. It was her song, a song she had sung many times, but never like it was being sung tonight.

That voice, her daughter's voice, was beyond anything she'd imagined and it startled her. She'd prepared herself for something slightly better than a school-girl's attempt to recreate her music, but she wasn't prepared for what she heard. The music soared and as Alli hit the high note, the lights illuminated the stage with brilliant colors. There she was. Beautiful, dynamic, sexy, in total command of the music, the stage, and the audience.

Envy, awe, and reality filled her as she watched a performance she knew she could never match.

She squeezed Michael's hand and whispered, "Someone once said that envy is a kind of praise." She smiled at the love she saw reflected in his eyes. "Let's go home."

There was no reason to stay.

Acknowledgements

Writing is a solitary experience, but bringing a book to life takes "a village" and I am blessed that my village consists of so many talented, inspirational, gifted, and loving individuals.

Beverly Haskins and Diane Mullen, my friends and business partners, continue to make me a better writer. This special team reads, rereads, edits, suggests, and keeps me focused on the relevancy of every word and every page. Their red pens are the first to correct my grammar and word usage, and often it is their questions that prompt me to rethink and rewrite in order to make the story more interesting or more cohesive. I value their effort and constancy, but even more, I am blessed by their friendship.

My Book Club "sisters" are my Beta readers and my cheerleaders. For thirteen years we have read, laughed, shared, and eaten at some really great restaurants. They continue to encourage me to "write us a good book."

Family is a big part of the team that makes my writing possible. Whenever I share a story idea with them, they start searching for information, facts, and points of interest that spice up the plot. They love to advocate for their favorite characters and we have spent hours in debate when they feel their character isn't receiving the attention he or she deserves. My sons, brother, and sister-in-law, enrich my writing and life!

A special thank you to my son, Dr. Troy Moon, for correcting the errors in the Portuguese and for helping me keep Margo's medical issues factual.

My story editor, Nancy Quatrano, is amazing. Her insights and suggestions tightened the story and showed me ways to cut out unnecessary words--even paragraphs--in order to keep the momentum of the plot moving forward.

Rik Feeney, my publishing coach, continues to help me understand the ever changing publishing business. His knowledge and ability to communicate what he knows always goes beyond remarkable. He also helps me laugh at myself when I begin to take it all too seriously.

Special thanks and hugs to my husband and my mother. Their love, understanding, and encouragement are my anchor.

About the Author

Proud to be a native Floridian, Jeanne Moon Farmer loves to set her stories in the diverse cities of her beautiful home state. Like her characters, her life has been lived against a background of sandy beaches, palm trees, and unbelievable humidity. And she sees a story behind every hibiscus.

As a wife, mother, daughter, teacher, writer, and friend, she is curious about the threads that bind us to other human beings and searches for significance in the life-dramas that teach us who we are. Her writing reflects the journey of people who have been tried and tested by their own choices --some are defeated by those choices, while others learn they can rise above the consequences of those choices through forgiveness and love.

Her debut novel, ***Family Shadows***, published in April 2013, is the first book in the ***Family Shadows*** series. Although each book stands alone, the characters in the story thread their way through all of the books in the trilogy.

After years as a teacher, she left the classroom to follow her passion for writing. Her writing career includes more than twenty years of technical writing in the field of education and one published work of poetry entitled Everything Makes A Difference (co-authored with Dr. Burt Bertram). Her award winning short story, Wheels of Honor, was published in the Florida Writer's Association 2012 Anthology.

She is a member of the Florida Writer's Association and two critique groups. She holds a degree in English from Florida State University where she studied creative writing with two writers who were profoundly influential, James T. Cox (O'Henry award winner) and Michael Shaara (The Killer Angels). Over the years she has led workshops on technical/grant writing and has honed her skills by attending various conferences and symposiums led by experts in the field of writing.

Joy comes from sharing life with her family--her husband, four grown sons, two daughters-in-law--and having beach sand between her toes.

Read an Excerpt from
Book Three of the Shadow Series
Coming in December 2013

City Shadows

By Jeanne Moon Farmer

Prologue

Miami 1983

Postcard perfect - blue sky, fluffy white clouds, hot, balmy, and salty. It was the kind of day the Chamber of Commerce could use to lure thousands of tourists to Miami. Except the tourists were leery of coming near a city where drug wars and violence blocked out the beauty this kind of day offered. Miami was no longer safe and the national media had begun referring to it as "Paradise Lost." Fear-filled publicity was destroying the tourist industry and overshadowing the beaches, the sunshine, the allure of the tropical Eden. Paradise had sold out to the devil called cocaine. It had lost its soul to the drug traffickers who were creating a city that was out of control. Drug money was building a concrete and glass skyline to rival any city in the world, but people lived in fear, and corruption was the norm rather than the exception. Yet, the sky was still blue, the breeze continued to whirl across the sand, and the sun warmed the skin of the innocent and the lawless without discrimination.

Jocelyn McDeal leaned over the balcony and wondered at the paradox of Miami, the place she had called home since her birth twenty-seven years ago. Good and evil; beauty and ugliness; tranquility and travesty. It was all there and it was unnerving. She heard the traffic flow past on Biscayne Boulevard and watched in the distance as a speed boat pulled a skier across the bay. Could the beauty she looked at this morning really mask the horrors she had been told existed? The horrors she read about every day in the news?

She closed her eyes and struggled to change her thoughts. She needed a diversion this morning. Her eyes were tired from working long hours on the latest manuscript by her boss, Lawrence Fitz, and her nerves were jangled by the anticipation of a chiming doorbell. She took a breath of the salty air and tried to relax.

The trap had been set and she had agreed to be the decoy. It had seemed like a good idea at the time, but as reality hit, her bravado was fading. Any minute now the doorbell would ring and she would be face-to-face with the evil, the ugliness, the travesty. She would no longer be able to pretend it didn't exist.

She knew the FBI, the DEA, and the Miami Dade police had her covered. She wasn't alone and she wasn't the one responsible for capturing the person who rang the bell. All she had to do was answer the door and invite a major player for one of the biggest drug cartels in this hemisphere to come inside. How hard could that be?

The ugly side of the paradox had to be stopped. Drugs were being openly shipped through the port, corrupt customs agents and police were turning a blind eye, and the rival cartels were staging unbridled warfare on the streets. Miami was a nightmare and she might be playing a small role in stopping it. All she had to do was open the door.

Her boss, a former FBI agent, had helped orchestrate the plans that she was part of and she believed with all her heart that he had made her safety a priority. If she knew who was going to be on the other side of the door, it would make it so much easier.

The sudden unwelcome chime of the doorbell broke the quiet and, startled in spite of her thoughts, she turned toward the door.

"What a surprise," she gasped. "I wasn't expecting to see you."

www.ingramcontent.com/pod-product-compliance
Lightning Source LLC
Chambersburg PA
CBHW031417240626
47154CB00001B/84

9781938643040